SHORT PATHWAYS IN A ROOM OF IMAGINATION

BY

JOHN NEEDHAM

*COVER ART BY

JOHN NEEDHAM

INDEX Page 3

INTRODUCTION

You are cordially invited to open a door in my mind. It is an entryway to a room that contains my imagination. Once inside, you will find that I have cleared short pathways that lead to different parts of the room. The reason for this is because it is rather crowded. I truly apologize for the mess, as well as a considerable amount of disturbing items. If you can look past the clutter, I would be honored to have you wander down each pathway to my assorted brick-a-brac of ideas. By all means, examine any thing you want closely. It is my hope that during your visit to explore my room, you will be inspired to imagine for yourself a while, but be warned to keep a proper perspective. Leave every one of my knick knacks and curios inside the room. Shut the door behind you when you go. Above all, take heed that the seeds of *might bes* not consume you, as the *could happens* have threatened to consume me. It is a good to use your imagination, but I have found through personal experience that excesses, as with all excesses, lead to compulsions. The first litmus test for that extreme, is when the lines between the real and unreal get blurred.

INDEX

FRIDAY NIGHT ON 8TH STREET	6
THE OLD LADY	20
CITY PARK	34
OUT OF CONTEXT	50
COLLINWOOD INTERSTATE TRAVELSTARS	60
WARNING-KEEP OUT	84
NEW GLASSES	98
THE TREE	134
A KNOCK ON THE DOOR	140
10-4 CANINE ONE NINERS	194
IS IT RAINING WHERE YOU ARE?	236
CRABBY PEOPLE	252
KIDS TODAY	264
VOICES	320
CHURCH OF THE MODERN APOSTLES	348

FRIDAY NIGHT ON 8TH STREET

FRIDAY NIGHT ON 8TH STREET

The walk home from work was an empty gesture. Since Gloria left, my apartment felt like a fancy place to keep my belongings and some food. It was just a place to crash. It had transformed to such a happy place while she was with me. Gloria and I never really got to the stage of discussing marriage, but I certainly thought we were headed in that direction. It became apparent to her after she moved in with me that she really did love me, but it wasn't going to work out; two completely different people, with different ideas on life, she explained. I am a self made man, started my own law firm, associated and partnered with some of the best talent money can buy. With offices all over the western coastline, the need to leave the home office was minimal at best, and I am guilty of settling into a rut I suppose.

She wanted goals, career, travel, more than one lover, and a home that was a starting point only. A place to keep personal mementos and belongings, but simply point A, as opposed to many point B's that take a person to many interesting places. Gloria was very capable of getting all of that and more, and deserved to do so. She climbed up a corporate ladder beginning as a model. Now, still beautiful, she had her own agency, was sought by many people all over the world for her expertise, talent, and a wide assortment of girls to pick and choose from to fit any advertising need. The settling down thing was definitely not for her. Her agency was a point A type of operation, but much, if not all business more than able of being conducted on the road. Truthfully, I really didn't want to change her or weigh her down. I wanted Gloria to be Gloria, but I wanted her to be with me too. I just didn't know how to make it all happen without cutting her off at the knees, and I knew it. She wanted to keep in touch because she enjoyed our time together, but in no way wanted to find herself in a trap.

So her business trip to Honk Kong was important and pressing, yes, but also semi-permanent, and I was without a steady person that could I point to and say I was in a relationship with. It was this bit of self analysis that took me on a walk after I left the office. Listless and sad, I walked without enthusiasm and not much thought as to where the wandering would end up. If I had a choice, I was looking for a comfortable bar, the kind of bar you see on television. But If I'm to be completely honest, I would not know one from the other. Frequenting bars is out of my element and not something I generally do. Clubs yes, bars no. There was also the fact that on the trajectory I was on, classy places weren't in abundance. It boiled down to a decision of choosing one and going with it. I found myself on 8th Street, not exactly an area a lawyer dressed in a business suit would be expected, but feeling sorry for oneself explains much. Best of the lot was a place called 8th Street Gentleman's Club.

The club was a single story square building with non-functional windows that blocked light form coming in or out, a big heavy oak door with over sized wooden handles for an entrance, weathered red cedar shakes exterior painted red and peeling. It may have been nice once, but deteriorated with the rest of the neighborhood. The neon sign on the edge of the roof was enough to say what was inside. Three X's next to 8th Street Gentleman's Club. As long as they had Jameson, I didn't much care. As soon as I opened the door and went inside I had second thoughts. My suit alone would need dry cleaning from the smoke. I almost turned around to leave, but a drop dead gorgeous woman that was dancing provocatively on stage drew my attention, but gorgeous isn't what stopped me in my tracks. She didn't have an audience, pretty as she was. A fair number of men were huddled at the bar, the din of conversation and laughing was all unrelated to the woman dancing. For all intents and purposes, the woman was invisible. She was dancing Vaudevillian strip tease, suggestive but not explicit, more expressionistic. Old fashioned to the point of absurdity in an average run of the mill strip joint. Very cool in a place like Las Vegas. She was leggy like a Rockette, a beautiful veteran performer, skillful as a dancer. I was drawn in to watch, even if the only one.

Sitting alone at a table in an empty room space, aside from the people at the bar, made me an easy mark for a cocktail waitress. Personalized service, you might say. I ordered up some Jameson on the rocks while I continued to mentally decrypt the reason behind the classy dancer in the strip dive. She flashed a smile at me during one of her moves. I felt cheap sitting there enjoying the show, contributing nothing, especially because girls in a place like this make money from tips.

So when the Jameson came, I paid with a large bill, told the waitress to keep a five, and bring a bunch more fives for change. But after my drink and change came, I tried to give the girl one of the of the fives, she motioned me away with a negative shake of her head, making me feel more out of place than I already was. The show continued. It was skillful, artful, but what was striking is that with the exception of me, there was no one else to take it in. No one even wanted to. She seemed not to care one way or the other, as though she was attending a one person Zumba class, except that it was exotic dancing in an erotic place. About twenty minutes more of performance, she suddenly stopped, didn't bow, say anything, or give me another one of those patented half smiles. She up and left the stage, disappeared though a curtain soon to be replaced by another girl who was introduced as a performer that was more of what would be expected in a place like that.

The cocktail waitress gave me a second round of Jameson. Men began carrying drinks over from the bar area and more filed in the front door getting set to join a growing crowd. I was still sitting up front, suddenly feeling self conscious, so I moved to the back of the room to finish my second drink. Suddenly the woman that finished dancing towered over me, coming up to me from behind. "Hello sailor! What brings a man like you into a place like this anyhow?"

"I needed a drink, or two, or three. I wasn't going to stay, but I saw your exquisite dancing, so I decided to watch. If you don't mind me saying so, you kind of look out of place here yourself."

"I don't dance here anymore, kind sir, I used to. The place has changed so much over the years. The current owner has been kind enough to allow me to warm up the stage before the main attractions come in. I don't get paid or anything. I just sort of do it for free while it's quiet. Now, can I sit for a while so I can get to the bottom of just why you are here? I know for a fact that you don't belong here at all!"

"Please do. Have a seat. Would you like a drink?"

"No no, I haven't drank in years, but I'm good to

talk to. Why don't you give it a try."

I don't know why, but I began pouring my heart out to this woman, telling her my problems. I didn't see why such a simplistic desire for love somehow would become a chore for intelligent, interesting people; in short, the ones that I am most attracted to. Their complaint was that they are interesting to me because they have lives; lives that if I was to interrupt, would choke it out of them. I summed it all up by saying, "Some people say that love and life can be juggled, but I'm not sure that's the case. Being a super person requires too much energy. Having the love sucks out some the life, and having the life sucks out some of the love, until neither one of them can exist in the same place at the same time, are you following me?"

"Yeah, I follow you just fine. The problem is that you are looking for it—love that is, hoping the interesting life comes with it, and I can't figure out why. You know, they say that love will come along when you least expect it. I believe that if you enjoy your own life, do what it is that you love best in this world, do it the best that you possibly can, then when love finds you while you are doing that, it will be by somebody that enjoys the same things that you do, and no sacrifices will have to be made at all. Two happy people will have met each other."

"I don't know about that. I am about as dull as a butter knife. I'm attracted to women who aren't just like me."

"Ah..well now I see. You aren't being honest with yourself then, or you would never be calling yourself dull."

"But I've come so far. I am very proud of myself. Are you saying I don't like what I do? " I asked her defensively.

"No, not at all. I'm saying you're bored. If you had the same passion for what you do, the last thing you would be calling yourself is dull. You would be talking about what you do right now. I haven't heard you say a word. I don't even know what you do yet because it hasn't come up."

If I argued with her logic, I wouldn't have made any sense. She was right. I wasn't the same idealistic brash young attorney that graduated from Harvard Law. Back then I was ready to take on the world. I wanted to attach the word justice' to attorney; defend the innocent; seek out the guilty. Now it was all about the bottom line, the almighty buck.

"Do you really think I would be dancing after all this time if I didn't love it? I've had so many good years dancing. I met my late husband while I danced. He was a casting director you know. It was a hell of a run. Now the only thing I have left is dancing. I hope that helps to put things in perspective for you." She started to rise and leave. "Wait, what is your name and when is the next time you dance?"

"If all goes well, I'll be here next Friday, no guarantees. Life has gotten a little hard for me these days."

She got up and walked to the door that she emerged from beside the bar, and disappeared through it. She was gone, but a second or two after the door closed and I realized she had not told me her name. I got the cocktail waitress's eye, so she headed my way. "I'll take one more before I hit the road. Say, before you get that, would you happen to know that last dancer's name?"

"You know, she only goes by Jen. I think that's short for Jennifer. But she ain't no regular here. Just showed up here and said she used to dance here years ago. She talked to the owner, Joe, asking if she might be able to dance before business picked up, you know, when it's still slow. She doesn't get paid or nothin'. She just comes in early some Fridays and does her thing; craziest thing. Hardly anybody pays her any mind at all."

"She's very beautiful."

"We have a lot of beautiful women in here. People pay to see flesh."

"Gotcha. I'll take that drink now." There wasn't any sense talking art in a place like that. But that wasn't the whole reason I wanted to know more about the woman. She had a head on her shoulders. She was a pleasure to talk to. I liked the way she dispensed advice.

FRIDAY NIGHT ON 8TH STREET

It was an interesting start to the week. A client came into my office at the head firm on Monday afternoon, not one of our satellite offices. That was a rarity in of itself, but it was an old close friend of mine who had found himself in a great deal of trouble. There was a charge of embezzlement leveled against the man, one he insisted he was not guilty of. Bail had already been met, but Kenny Wetzold, my friend, was scheduled for arraignment by the end of Wednesday. Due to some very angry clients, patrons of the financial advisement and investment firm he worked for, it looked bleak that he was going to come out of it with a whole skin. His clients wanted his head. Even if cleared, his good name would probably be tarnished. He claimed no knowledge, complete innocence. Every one of the funds he had supposedly placed the money in were healthy and fine. The problem: every dime and cent that filtered through his hands, never made it to the correct destinations. A goodly amount had, however, shown up in Kenny's personal account. But the lion share had simply vanished, temporarily. Kenny was panicking, almost hysterical.

"Calm down Kenny," I soothed, "if you are indeed innocent, then the account numbers of transfers would uncover themselves before very long. I believe you, okay man? How much showed up in your account?"

"Five hundred thousand."

"And how much is missing?"

"Two million, five hundred thou'." he answered.

"Whew, nice payday! So two and a half million is missing?"

"Yes Bill, but that's just it. In the big picture, it's just a drop in the bucket. Five hundred thousand dollars showed up in my bank account, and implicates me pretty nicely, but even with all of it, it's certainly not enough to leave the country and start over. But you're right, the rest of the transfers, and where the money really went should reveal itself pretty quickly. The question is why divert attention toward me, dragging my good name down the tubes? It has to be something bigger, something we aren't seeing yet. I'm not allowed anywhere close to my desk, and I feel so helpless."

"I see, but it's counter productive to get involved

in any way. You came to the right place Kenny. Provided you are telling me the whole truth."

"Meaning?" he said sharply.

"Meaning, you're right, there is more to the story than what you came into my office with. Nobody would implicate you just to divert attention away from a real purpose without good reason. I think you did something to tick somebody off, and I want you to tell me what it is. How can you expect for somebody to help you if you don't give them all the facts? I am your friend Kenny. If you can't tell me everything, who can you tell?"

"Alright, alright, stop! But if I did anything at all, it's unrelated to anything that happened here. I've always done the right thing at work."

"Let me be the judge of that."

It took a little time for him to trust me enough to let his guard down, but I waited patiently. Finally relenting, he told me a story about a love affair; his. He had been carrying on with the wife of the owner of **Jeremy Financial Planning** for some time. They had met at numerous company functions and flirted harmlessly for a while. But then the flirtatious verbal jabs and innuendos turned to talking and kissing, which turned into arranged meetings and lovemaking. Pretty pompous to think that his sordid affair had nothing to do with the bind he found himself in. My blood began to quicken, not because of the seamy, all too common silly story, but because of the situation. I had found myself in the middle of why I went to law school in the first place. My conversation with the dancer on 8th Street came to mind. It was because of that conversation that I didn't delegate defense strategy to any of the marvelously qualified attorneys under my aegis.

As soon as my friend and new client left my office, I hit the ground running. First up was giving a call to a very special friend who worked with me early in my career. I was making a name for myself back then, and actually doing the job hands on.

"Is Daniel Bradley in?" I asked my friend's secretary after I found his number in my Rolodex and called.

"Yes he is. Who can I say is calling?"

"If he still talks to me, I'm Bill Trapper."

FRIDAY NIGHT ON 8TH STREET

"Give him just a minute, okay?"

It took less than twenty seconds for him to pick up. He began by taunting, "You know, this is an amazing coincidence. An old friend of mine has that same name, Bill Trapper. That name brings back such fond memories, and I like thinking about him from time to time."

"Do you mean that Daniel?"

"So what can I do for you Bill Trapper?"

"I love you too."

"It's good to hear your voice, man! Don't be a stranger. Call again now!"

"Crossing the line, dude. I need you buddy, I can't work with anybody else."

"I like a groveler. Can you say hello before you tell me what you want?"

"Hello. The answer is yes, I missed you, and yes, I am working my own case, and yes, I think I am going to do it more often. Would you consider doing something with me?"

"Only if you stay my friend, yes. If this is a one time deal, then forget it."

"Always, forever and forever. Look, here's the story...."

A small amount of digging by Danny uncovered a ridiculously simple plot, and certainly not well thought through. None the money ever made it to the funds entered in for each of Kenny's five clients. The money simply stayed in the company's bank account. Two weeks worth of deposits from Kenny's office simply wallowed in the account, never making the transfer stage into the chosen growth vehicles. The only bank account numbers on record were a deposit transfer to Kenny's personal checking account. That was found out pretty quickly. The five hundred G's was in the form of a direct deposit drawn on **Jeremy Financial Planning** company account that Kenny only had limited access to. After the deposit, the boss, Jeremy Chaffer claimed to have coincidentally found a packed suitcase in his wife Rose's closet with the check stuck in a side pocket side. Of course, he called the authorities to do his civic duty a full day after the five hundred thou' was found in Kenny's account. The police, who were tipped at the time had frozen all the accounts in the course of the investigation. The District Attorney's office was hungry for a scintillating high profile case, but wasn't so stupid to be suckered swallowing a setup ruse. It was just as easy for the police as it was for me to find out about the absurd love triangle, and also just as easy to find out who initiated the deposit and wrote the check. Kenny would have been exposed no matter what, his reputation still destined to suffer, but not irreparably. The police and the District Attorney's office were still trying to sort out what it wanted to do about the situation, but all monies were due to be returned to the rightful owners in time. The real crime was done by Jeremy Chaffer, leaving the prosecution in a bit of a quandary. Two million dollars had never left company possession and five hundred thousand never spent. The prosecution had jumped to conclusions, pointing total blame before the office had all of it's facts. The means still justified the ends, however because Kenny was still out of a job, something he really did deserve.

The case was quickly resolved, and far too easily. But it still managed to have an upside. It brought two old friends with a perfectly good symbiotic working partnership together again. It also painted a very clear picture which direction I wanted my life to go. Later that week, I approached the partners in my firm about coming up with a number to buy out my holdings. It was obvious to them already that I wanted a change just from the handling of Kenny's case on my own, an instant red flag. I let myself in for heavy duty arm twisting and lecturing, all for naught. All in all, the week was a fruitful one, and it made me excited for my future.

I could think only of one person that I could share news that on the face of it, had the appearance of shooting myself in the foot. The dancer on 8th Street. I suppose too that I was looking for her approval for some strange and inexplicable reason. On Friday, at about the same time as last, I took the same walk, going directly to the 8th Street once again. I might have counted on seeing the dancer too much, but when I entered the

'Gentleman's Club', I wasn't disappointed because the dancer was hard at work at her creative passion. As I moved through the club, the cocktail waitress recognized me as I passed by the bar. “Hello sweetie, same as last week?”

Impressed that she remembered, I said, “Sure. Sounds like a plan to me. Say, you wouldn't happen to have some nuts or something, I haven't really eaten?”

“We have a kitchen and grill out back. Would you like a burger or something?”

“I would love a burger and fries, thanks.”

“I'll get right on it.” She said, knowing there was a buck to be made.

I meandered over to where the dancer was doing her thing. She was on fire that night, and was dancing like it might be the last time she danced ever. She spotted me, and gave me a little half smile and a wink in acknowledgment, but continued to get it all out of her system. What she was doing was beautiful and creative, telling a story with dance. The thing was, it wasn't done to impress anybody, only to heal herself in some way, it seemed. There was desperation in her moves but at the same time spectacularly fluid. Believe it or not, I was the sole person watching. The dancer finished her session just moments before the first of the main attractions was introduced, but she was clearly winded, very drained and tired. I felt the need to run up and help her off, but there was a compliment of bouncers that were close by when the new act was introduced, so I thought better of it. My burger and the first of my drinks showed up, dragging me back to a saner job, like pulling money out of my wallet, and changing seats to a less conspicuous spot now that yahoos were taking over the room. This Jen person came out of the side entrance door by the bar area fairly quickly, making her way over to me like she was in a hurry.

“Hello sailor! I can't stay long tonight, I really don't have that much time left. It was all I could do to remember to come by tonight. I did it because I knew that you would be here waiting for me, and I wanted to perform one last time. As far as you are concerned, it seems I should know you from somewhere, but I can't really remember why. I have had a challenging time enough as it is. But I do remember our conversation last week, and I wanted to find out if you were alright, and how you made out this week. I promised I would do the best I could to show up."

I told her of my personal milestone, and that I had taken a giant leap backwards, to a time when I was happier with myself and what I was doing. I told her of the case I accepted, the first one like it in years. Even if it didn't amount to much of an accomplishment, it felt like one to me, due mostly to our conversation last week. I told her that she made me realize what was missing, and even though I had no woman in my life yet, I was confident love would find me if I was happier with myself.

She smiled so sweetly at me, and then told me how grateful she was to her husband to teach her that same thing years ago. "My husband, God bless his soul, used to say to me; Jen, don't ever let anybody stop you from dancing. You come alive on that stage. So that is what I have been doing; keeping myself alive. But my husband gave me life too. We loved each other so much, we kept each other alive. He loved what he did too, discovering so much talent and keeping that talent inspired enough to produce so much beauty. But I can't do this anymore. I need to be with my husband. It has been an honor to meet you young man, and I am so glad you are happy, but I have to go now. I can't hold on much longer." She got up and ran to the side door by the bar to leave. I called behind her before she left, "Wait, I never got your full name."

She turned around one last time before she disappeared though the door, and said, *"Jennifer Trapper."*

"Wait," I said to myself, "I didn't just hear that!" I got up, pulled a fifty dollar bill out of my wallet, and handed it to my cocktail waitress on the way out of the club. I wanted to head this Jennifer Trapper off before she disappeared. I was out the door, desperate not to lose any advantage to catch up to her, but all I saw was a white van. The back doors were open, the lights on, two men attending to a person inside. There was no urgency to what they were doing. It was the only thing going on out there on the street, so I moved closer to the truck to see what was going on, or if they could help me with my search for Jennifer. Closer to the truck, it became clear that the two men were respectfully securing an old lady in the back. “Do you guys need any help?”

“Not any more, thanks. It's so sad, why didn't anybody offer to help before when she was wandering around out here by herself?”

“I would have, but I never did see her. Is she alive?”

“No, she was face down on the sidewalk dead. At least we had an idea where she went this time. We haven't been able to stop her from coming to this part of the city. Always going on and on how she needed to dance.”

“What?”

One of the men said,“Dementia. Came on her pretty late in life. She's ninety four now, you know. Still a sweetheart all the way to the end. She could talk, just didn't know who you were most of the time. For the last couple months, she had this fixation that she needed to dance; said her husband told her it makes her come alive. She has been pretty sneaky, I gotta tell you. She's managed to get out and downtown quite a few times in the last couple months. We've found her a couple times over this side, so this time we came directly here, or she might still be face down until morning, poor thing.”

“I'm an attorney, maybe I can help. Does she have any family?”

“Well no, not that ever shows up. Her estate is what has kept her at the home.”

“Where's the home at?”

“Harrison Nursing Home down on Gomes.”

“Got it. She have a name?”

“Sure, name's *Jennifer Trapper*.”

THE OLD LADY

THE OLD LADY

Bus 31 was late, and I was worried it wouldn't come at all. Every vehicle that came into view at the far end of the road looked like it had an illuminated route number on top, but as they got closer turned out to be a pickup truck or even worse, a Toyota or Volkswagon. It only goes to show how the mind can play tricks. When the real thing finally came around the corner, I breathed a sigh of relief. It was dark, and I was the only one at the stop until seconds before the bus pulled up. Now the bus was late, so the lady that showed up was late too, but she still showed up at the same time to beat me into the bus. Just how did that happen? She moved fast for an old lady. There was one of two reasons that she was first at the door of the bus seconds before it pulled up to the stop. Reason one, rude, reason two, assumed I was a gentleman, and she was a lady. Either way, I didn't really care, just wondered that's all. I forgot about her as soon as she boarded. I paid my fare, and picked a seat in the predominantly empty bus. Riding along, my face was at the window watching the sights of the city as we rolled by. I was so engrossed that I didn't notice the old lady slide into the seat beside me. She was small. I didn't even feel the body heat from the woman. I literally had to notice her reflection in the window glass to find out she was there, and it damned well made me jump out of my skin. “Aaaa.” I sounded.

“What's the matter hot stuff, scared of old ladies?”

“Sorry, no, not of you. You just scared the crap out of me. Can I help you?”

“I'm only sitting here riding the bus hot stuff. But if you really want to do something for me, you could pucker up darlin'.”

“Excuse me?” I said with a slight chuckle. “I thought you wanted to ask me a question or something. You were sitting somewhere else, so you changed seats just to sit here, I figured....”

“No. No.” She said sort of disappointed that I was spoiling the mood. “I just thought since we were the only two people on the bus, we could share some of this city at night ambiance. I'll give you one more chance though cutie pie, because you're worth it—I think.”

“I was a very beautiful woman once, I can assure

you of that. Look, I can prove it..." She said, fishing through her purse that had, no doubt, enough in there to cover just about anything that could be thrown her way. I believe I spotted a small pharmacy in there. She is generally the woman who holds up the line at the supermarket checkout while the entire contents of her purse needs to be emptied to find twenty five cents at the bottom to complete a sale. I always keep change in my pocket for such things, because it is easier to pay the twenty five cents to move the line along. "Here. It's right here, see?" She said flashing a picture that looked to be forty years old. She really was quite gorgeous back then. I took it from her hand because she handed it to me, giving it a detailed look-over. Even better looking, on closer examination. "There, you see, beautiful. Keep it handsome. Remember me."

"I can't accept this. It's a personal memento, handing it back. Besides, I'm always on this bus. I am sure I will see you again. Just say hello if I don't."

"My goodness! That's very sweet of you. Where have you been all my life?"

"Oh, I'm just your average Joe. I'm not anything special."

She toned her cavalier come on rhetoric down altogether, "Yes you are. You are very special, don't you ever forget it." She reached over me pulling the rope to stop the bus, but before she got off at her stop, she kissed me on the cheek. She got up, moving to the door to get off. She gave me one final gaze just before she got off, and once on the sidewalk, sadly gave me a small wave of her hand at hip level before the bus continued on down the road. It was hard to forget her that night when I finally shut the door to my condo. She haunted my thoughts, this old lady.

My eyelids fluttered open on a new day, bright, sunny, fresh. But the memory of the old lady on the bus woke up with me.

Going into my normal routine, and finally at work, she was never far from reentering my mind, and the people around me saw it. Coworkers expecting a level of efficiency that I usually provide, never expecting less than my best, got mediocre instead. This was a vital news agency. Accuracy was of the utmost importance. I am a copywriter and more than one person depended my not causing them to look stupid on camera. When it became clear into the day that I wasn't focusing, I was confronted, so I told them the story. They proceeded to laugh their self silly, both at me and the old lady. "So you let an old hag come on to you? Talk about cougar hunting! Is she mounted on your wall yet?"

"I give up. I quit. You win. I should not have given this any more thought than it was due. She was just an old fool, and I should have ignored her. Or I should forget about her now. I'm sorry, I'll go back to work now." I said. I hope I made their jesting a lot less fun. The truth was, I wondered if I would see her on the bus again. For some strange reason, she seemed an enigma for me to solve. From my perspective, there was something vulnerable and sensitive about her.

I didn't completely lie, I did go back to work. It was a particularly hard day on top of everything else. Another slumping day for the economy, the average working stiff taking blow after blow. It needed an upbeat twist for a touchy public. There is a responsibility to it, taken very seriously by those of us behind the scenes. I worked later than I generally do, and got a ride from a coworker when the night was finally done. This time with the turn of the lock, a quick strip and shower, slumber land hit me hard. The alarm went off much too soon for my taste.

My entire work day was a boring one. There was not one thing of interest from the time I arrived in the morning until I waited at the bus stop at the end of the day. I thought to myself how nice it would be to have somebody to talk to. The old lady crossed my mind, and I kept looking in every direction wondering if she would appear out of nowhere as she did before. She did not. The only company I had on the bus were a young couple taking verbal swipes at each other, and a dirty man with a cigarette behind his ear with a look in his eye that said he was trouble. It was a disappointing day start to finish. Not one thing picked up my spirits.

THE OLD LADY

By the end of the week, the old lady, I thought, was gone for good. But she did show up, much like she did before. Before the bus door swung open, she had played the part of defeatist. "Hi again handsome. Whoops, forgot me already didn't you?"

"Hello. No, actually I've been here, and you haven't. I remember you just fine."

"I was here Tuesday."

"The only day I wasn't here. I worked that night late and got a ride home. Don't put yourself down like that." I said as I followed her onto the bus. "I don't have to put my self down, I'm already there."

"Look, let's start with names, shall we? I don't like being called honey or sweetie until something blossoms. I was married once, and I still love her very much, even though she has been taken away from me almost eight years now. She didn't call me any of those things until she had a ring around her finger. The only other people who can call me that are my mom, grandmother, my aunt, or somebody who has grown to feel like my aunt; got that? Now, my name is Arthur Danbury, what's yours?"

She was cut down at the knees a bit. She didn't expect that from me, but said after a second or two, "Pardon me, my name is Theresa Collins. I am pleased to meet your acquaintance. I am sorry about your wife, by the way. What is it that you do that causes you to come home well after the foot traffic headed home from the five to six o'clock rush?"

"I am a copy writer for Channel 7 news. That is why I had such a lengthy night on Tuesday last. That was the day the stock market took that 400 point plunge. The ten o'clock news wanted me to paste a happy meal face on it. What is it that you do, or did?"

"I own Collins Fashion Plate down on 10th avenue. I felt that plunge the other day, although indirectly. We have stores, designers, and all sorts of industries coming at us to show them ways to market their fashions, designs, and fabrics. I just call the shots these days when I started to lose my looks. I have assistants do my talking for me. If I didn't have all the money, my chairwoman would walk all over me. Now I just hide out behind the scenes pulling the strings."

THE OLD LADY

I didn't press her for details, though I was totally impressed with her accomplishments. "You see? I knew there was something more to you. But that attitude of yours put me off a bit. I'm glad I met you Theresa Collins." She made a move toward pulling the rope, I pulled it for her. "See you Monday night?" I asked.

"God, I hope so handso--ah--Arthur." She said. I smiled at her near slip, but I would have reprimanded her again, and she knew it. She got up from her seat, and made her way off the bus, eyeballing me one last time when she was out. The look on her face was that of shock, but there was also a noticeable softening to her hard exterior.

I usually spend time at my parents house on the weekends, especially on Sunday when I can collect a home cooked meal off my mom. It's a good day for sports on TV, and my parents and I get caught up on the week. My dad still works, and he has as much to relate as I do. My mom too, works as a cashier in a local supermarket, has a story or two to tell that crosses her path. My passion for news and current events come from these two. We openly discussed everything since I was a boy, and my sister and I were encouraged to formulate our own opinions, backing them up with facts so that we believed in an intelligent way. My sister lives on the other coast now, but we talk every week end too. We are all very close. Cat, my nephew Tim, and her husband John are very special to me, and I could never have gotten over the loss of my wife Janet if they hadn't given me the support needed to pull through that sort of thing.

The conversation touched all the regular inputs that Sunday, but I added the topic of the old lady on the bus to the mix. "You know mom," I said, "I knew there was something about this lady as soon as we first met. She is the kind of person that would be overlooked as crazy. At the same time, there was something snappy and quick about her that led me to think she was intelligent. She was also lonely to share herself with anybody who would come along and at least listen to her for a bit. I brought it up at work, and they made nasty comments that made me back off in a hurry. It turns out hat she owns her own business, but hides behind the scenes pulling the strings, hiring others to present her ideas because she is too self conscious about her appearance. I don't think she knows that her crude personality goes a long way to making her more unattractive than she is."

"What kind of business is it Arthur?" My mom asked because she was curious.

"She told me she owns Collins Fashion Plate down on 10th."

"Big place. I seem to remember a writeup up it about ten years ago, one of our own here in the city, hobnobbing with giants in the industry. She went into obscurity after a while, something medical I think; interesting."

"I thought so too, but that's just me I guess."

"You know son, you have a hell of a heart." My dad said.

"Learned from the best in the business dad."

Monday came soon enough, and I was off to inject my personality to a pretty face you see on a camera. I've never gotten close to our news girl. I'm guessing her hair is harder than a rock. The end of the day had me craving Chinese food. It had me following the trip on the bus in my head trying to picture the various plazas on the way home; couldn't think of a one of them containing a Woo Gung Foo or a China 1, or anything at all. I would have eaten in the downtown area, but I did not want to miss my bus. I walked briskly to the stop, having only minutes to spare before the bus came. This time around had Theresa standing at the stop already. She broke into a very attractive smile I did not know she possessed. "Hello Arthur, it's nice to see you today."

"Well, aren't you the happy one today Theresa? Look, You know more about this neighborhood than I do, are there any Chinese food places on the way home?"

"Fancy, or hole in the wall?"

"Hole in the wall is fine by me."

"There's a Wang's over at Grant Crossings. I eat there sometimes."

THE OLD LADY

"You eat there?"

"Yes I do."

"Feel like Chinese?"

"Me?" She asked flustered. For me, it was a spur of the moment thing.

"Nobody else at this stop."

She paused and hesitated, obviously thrown off-guard.

"Come on, my treat. I hate eating alone."

She still didn't say anything as the bus rolled up to the stop.

"Come on, it's my treat. I won't take, 'no', for an answer.

"I really am hungry, so that's nice, but why?"

"No reason. None at all. Well yeah there is, I like egg rolls and fried rice."

She smiled that attractive smile again.

"You are going to have to point Grant Crossings out to me because I don't know where that is or I would have remembered a place to eat when I was trying to think of one."

"Oh, well then you are in good hands then." She said smiling that smile again.

"There is nothing like Chinese in Styrofoam. It makes it all so very homey, don't you think?" I asked Theresa when we finally sat down in Wangs.

"I, for one, have always wanted to know why Wang, it was Wang wasn't it that came up with the idea of Pu Pu platter? I always got the feeling it was all his leftover Chinese crap thrown in a to go container." Theresa said.

I laughed at that but changed the subject. "So tell me Theresa, why are you so down on yourself? You do have personality."

"Yeah, around you. You're bringing out the best in me. When I got this disease, I just sort of wanted to climb into a hole and pull dirt over me."

"Wait a minute, what disease?"

I have this rare thing that happened to me about eight years ago. I was about two years after getting into business. I decided that if I couldn't find Mr. Right, I would submerse my self in one thing I know the best, fashion. But then I had something happen to me. I have a very rare affliction that the Doctors I have gone to, can't even put a name to. I was getting old. It's funny too because I don't feel old at all. It got worse and worse

until I had to hide in the background because I couldn't do the job anymore—well I can, but I can't bring in the business."

"So you're telling me that you aren't that old?"

"No, I'm about your age actually."

"I knew I sensed something strange."

"You want to go now?"

"No, not at all. I told you, I don't like eating alone. It's nice to have company. Eating alone is something I've avoided since my wife Janet died about eight years ago."

"So your wife died at about the same time I felt like it."

"Don't talk like that Theresa."

"It's hard not to."

"Beauty isn't everything."'

"Said by a man that is so drop dead handsome I would cut off a tit for just one night."

"Look, let's get out of here and go home for the night. I'll see you tomorrow, and we can eat burgers or something, alright?"

"Do we have to, this was a dream for me?"

"Then you'll have another one tomorrow then. And don't cut off any tits, okay?"

We went back out to the bus stop to finish the ride home. She thanked me for a wonderful evening when her stop came, she asked, "So tomorrow then?"

"Absolutely." I told her. She got up and left with a little extra pep in her step.

Tuesday went slowly for me. Of course, I did what I had to do, but my heart wasn't in it. The truth of it was if anybody pressed me for an explanation, was that I was really looking forward to grabbing a burger with Theresa. What can I say? I liked the company. She was good to talk to, that simple. After the end of the day, I was at the bus stop in no time flat. Nobody was there, yet. Five minutes went by, and I thought she might have changed her mind—chickened out or something. But from the corner, came Theresa.

"Theresa did you go and get your hair fixed? Lookin' good there kiddo."

"No, I really didn't. I got up this way. Gives a whole new meaning to 'good hair day', doesn't it? Just dollar store shampoo, too."

"You kidding? Gorgeous, just gorgeous. That shade of pure white with the natural wave thing going on is astounding!"

She wasn't accustomed to compliments. "Come on!! You're putting me on, right?"

"No ma'am, sure not. I would not put you on, that would be cruel. Cruel is something I do not do."

"No, I don't suppose that you do." She said with a frown.

"Say, do you hold true to the belief that broiling beats frying?"

She laughed at that., a pretty laugh, not a cackle. It was my turn to frown.

We had a great talk over burgers and fries. Theresa questioned me at length about my late wife, how she died, that kind of thing. She told me that it was wonderful soaking up some of the positive energy I had left over even after all that time, from what was obviously a loving relationship. She thanked me from the bottom of her heart as she said it, for allowing her to do that. "How about doing that salad place downtown before we get on the bus tomorrow?" Theresa asked. "I often eat there."

"Sounds like a plan to me. Do I meet you in the place or out?"

"There are benches outside by the front door. I'll meet you there."

"Your on. I guess we'd better go before the final bus comes, huh?"

"Yes, that would be smart. There's tomorrow." She said, trying to sound upbeat.

I barely got out in time the next day. Some Jim Dandy decided he was way more deserving than the rest of the depositors at Smith Savings and Loan. Jim Dandy took all the money in the establishment at once, proving once and for all he should be rewarded with the 'Most Inconsiderate Award', and that he use some of that money to have the ugly hairy mole on his face sized so that he didn't have to cover it up with a bandanna. I didn't write that, but it would have improved ratings I think. I just wrote standard copy, but it did come in at the last second, needing to be on the ten o'clock, done of course at eight I broke into a run as soon as I left the building, sprinting two blocks to Magic Salad. I pulled up to the door, not seeing Theresa yet. I went back outdoors, and found the bench she spoke of, and sat. I only had to wait about a minute. Theresa came into view, strutting down the street towards me wearing a long dress and heels, hips swaying with every step, pure wavy white hair flowing in the wind. I saw, but could not compute what I was seeing. Her face looked like Theresa, but not. She looked fifty-ish.

I stood to greet her as she got closer. "What is happening Theresa? You're looking downright hot."

"I don't know Arthur. I got up feeling better than I have in years. I actually felt like getting dressed up today. I couldn't wait to see your face when I walked up. I couldn't wait to see you. I know you don't like me to talk that way, but I swear, all I wanted was to see you."

"Well I swear too, damn it, I can't believe my eyes! I'm sorta glad we're eating salad tonight, we shouldn't be spoiling a figure like that! Hey, maybe that's what it is. You did say you come here often. Maybe it's paying off. Anyway, that's beside the point. I could not wait all day for this myself."

She smiled from ear to ear with that one. "Come on charmer, let's get inside."

That night's subject was her life, such that it was. "Believe it or not, I was a nerd growing up. I never even went to the prom. I never found anybody who would love me, even when I got out of college and started to blossom. Then the disease took hold, and that was the end of that. So I poured even more energy into my business."

"What about family?"

"Orphaned. I don't have any family that I know

of. Wouldn't mind having a family, just don't know what it's like."

"You want to share mine? I go to my parents house every Sunday. I know they would love to meet you."

"I'll give it some thought, okay? I promise. I don't know how bringing an old lady home to meet the parents would go over."

We had some good conversation about nonsense, but finally figured it was time to go home for the night, getting to that final bus before we had to walk or take a taxi. "I enjoyed it here tonight. Can we come back here tomorrow?"

"You don't have to twist my arm. I'll be here if you are." She told me.

"I wouldn't miss it."

Thursday was a calm news day, average by any standard. If anything, it made the day drag on. That kind of thing happens in the news world from time to time.

"What's the matter Arthur, you look as if you want to crawl out of your skin" Asked the same man who poked fun at me for wondering about the old lady in the first place.

"Nothing, nothing at all. I just can't wait to leave tonight is all."

At seven sharp, I left for Magic Salad. Theresa had beaten me this time, but I didn't know it. A woman was looking up the street away from me. She turned when she heard my approach. I blinked. Standing before me was a raven haired beauty with arresting hazel eyes. The same smile came to her face that she flashed at me three days ago, only this lady made me feel guilty to look at her. This lady provoked lewd thoughts. Stunning would be an apt word. And the smile she had was for me. "Theresa, could you please explain to me why you get more smoking hot every time I see you?"

"I think it's the hydrating skin cream I bought at the dollar store the same day I bought the shampoo. The truth is, I think, is because I've met my prince. When I kissed you on the cheek that first night on the bus, I have felt better and better."

Well to tell the truth, me too. When you come to your bus stop later tonight, and have to say goodnight, do you think you might give me another one?”

What do you think would happen if I kissed you on the lips?” She asked me with a hopeful smile.

“I think I would enjoy that very much, Theresa—very, very much.”

CITY PARK

CITY PARK

Todd Farris is a slight man, not overly handsome, but not too shabby either. Physically, he does the best he can with what he's got. He's smart too. People come to Todd all the time when they need an idea for something, or to supply some obscure fact to solve an argument that came up when playing Jeopardy over the weekend. When Todd says it, it must be true. Todd thought to himself one day that he should take the bull by the horns as the saying goes. Instead of being the whipping post, and not the participant, he would start spending time at places where he could absorb happy vibes. From that day on, Todd went to see a movie twice a week. He bought a ball to go bowling on Saturday mornings, practicing to get good enough to join a Friday night league. But his favorite thing of all to do was spend time after work at the City Park. There are some dirt hiking paths that cut through the middle of a green expanse in a park on the outskirts of town. It is by far his favorite place in that park that offers other amazing things like a playground area, an extremely pleasant horticultural greenhouse complex, a zoo, and a meandering pond with paddle boats. The playground alone is a mecca for kids. There's a carousel and a train for goodness sakes, kids laughing and screaming, it's certainly quite pleasant. But the wooded section, is an immense magnificent area left to it's natural devices that still is a part of the city. Of course, there is a cola can or two, people are people after all, but on the whole, it's a forest in the city.

One of the paths leads to a stairway dubbed, appropriately enough, 'The Stairway'. It was left there from a time when the city was a just woods, and no city. The stairway has been the subject of many debates as to it's original use. Some say there was a giant mansion from a plantation that was long gone, but there are too many stairs for that, and the stonework is much too natural and earthy. Todd even heard a theory that the Incas wandered this far north, exploring. It goes on to say that, smitten with the area, they started to build a pyramid for remote worship. That is totally ridiculous. It bears no resemblance at all to those kinds of structures. For one thing, the stairway is far too primitive, solid, but sloppily built for artisans of that stature to pin their name on it. If anything, it's more of a Stonehenge type structure, ancient and mysterious. Little by little, Todd got wooed by the solitary section of the park, shying away from the choked up sections with all the screaming and hollering. Some things are unavoidable no matter how hard you try. That is because what Todd adores most of all about the path is that his imagination runs wild when left alone. He hears springtime birds in the middle of the summer. He sees flowers just like he used to pick for his mother by the side of the road when he was a boy; multi-colored wild irises and purple violets, flowers he hasn't seen growing in the wild in years and years. Then there are the cool breezes he feels on a ninety eight degree day, He can smell the perfume that the only girl he ever took parking, had on that night. He hears young girls singing songs while playing jump rope at recess; a pastime that is long gone. Not one of those things are actually there, only conjured up in Todd's head each time he ventures down the path to the stairway by himself.

Todd has always drawn the line at climbing the stairs to the top, he's sat on them, worked out issues that come into everybody's life from time to time, enjoyed the almost medicinal soothing effects that wash over him there, but always avoided going to the top for two main reasons. The stairs just stop at the top of a huge rock anyway, so Todd can't imagine what he'd do when he got there, for one. Rock climbers scale the back face of the cliff, which is roughly three hundred feet high. Generally, that is how the area is utilized, the stairs are not used at all. The reason being is that average people won't climb them without a railing. That was Todd's reason number two—no railing. Parents avoid taking children out there too because it's too hazardous, not to mention that the playground draws their interest much more. Consequently, the stairway had been relegated as a sight to see for a handful of curiosity seekers and adventurers—and by word of mouth at that. For Todd, it provides hours of enjoyment from the hiking experience, fresh air, and stimulating flashbacks that inspire his imagination. Sadly, in a greedy way, Todd appreciates the fact that the hiking trails aren't as popular as the rest of the park.

CITY PARK

There was this one particular day, after work, when Todd bought himself a Beefy Beefer Footlong from Dick's Manwich Shop on the way home, managing to push the whole thing down his throat in one sitting at one of their round plastic outdoor tables. Just him, the salt and pepper shakers, and a tall cardboard cup of homemade sweetened iced tea. It left him almost too full to move, exactly like the sign on the wall tried to warn, so Todd decided to walk some of it off. It was a stifling hot evening, so he drove directly to the park. As soon as the city forest swallowed him up on his favorite path, Todd's imaginary visions tended toward happy memories. There was the company picnic the summer before, when sexy Lolita from accounting got drunk. There was the wedding reception for his sister Lucy. That was followed by the memory of eating too much at the Wok and Roll Chinese buffet. Before he knew it, he was at the base of the stairway, but shocked to see a young couple just finishing descending the stairway. “Oh my God, you just came from the top? What's up there, what can you do up there?”

“Look, dude. Use your imagination!” That was all the young man said to Todd as he smiled lasciviously, walking hand in hand with his girl away from him.

Todd blinked in surprise. “So imagination is the key after all. I knew it.” Snapping his fingers. He watched as the two disappeared in the brush, then turned toward the stairway. *Should I climb it today? Well no, not today, not until I'm finished digesting this Beefy Beefer, that's for sure*, he continued thinking. *Ooooh!!! Wait a minute, I get it! Use my imagination! God, what a buffoon I am*! *In a moment of realization, what the couple meant came back to slap him on the back of his head. But if having a significant other is a requisite, I'm sunk. I can certainly imagine me up a perfect woman like no tomorrow, the trouble is thinking her up for real. Furthermore, it'd be about impossible to dream up somebody about my age to climb all those stairs without a railing, that's for sure*.

Janet Traynor spent another evening at the top of the stairs. She spent every minute she could spare since March, trying to break some kind of enigmatic code of the portal she had stumbled upon. When she braved climbing up the stairs for the first time, she knew her curiosity would kill her, or add adventure to her life. She got an adventure alright, but inherited a mystery as well. Here she was again, pleasant as it is, alone, always alone. That first day proved the top was everything she imagined, the meadow, the panoramic views, the fact that there were no bugs. These were things she imagined a perfect world would be like. But there were no flowers. That's the first thing she noticed. From there, the list grew; no birds, no animals, no people. Tonight, she had to wait while two idiots made it like rabbits on a rock ledge, at the very entrance to her portal. With a little imagination, they could have humped on the grass she was standing on now. They didn't even hear her slide behind a bush to wait out the painful experience of listening to them make whoopee on a rock; totally absurd.

The whole adventure has left her feeling quite fit, due in part to the particularly long walks she has made looking for—well anything really. She has also been discouraged. This night though, has her wondering why the young couple could not enter the threshold of the portal as she dubbed it. It became clear to her back in March that imagination was the key to entering, ergo, the young couple didn't have enough of it, or didn't have any at all. This could also mean that she didn't possess enough imagination to cause whatever this place needed to become more than it was. It would get dark soon anyway, time to go home and think it through yet again—come up with another angle. A little beaten down, Janet descended the stairs, watching her step because she knew her mind was preoccupied. She made her way out of the city forest and to her car in the in the lot. Just after she opened the driver side door to go
home, she just happened to glance at somebody just driving out of the same lot, just a glimpse. In that brief second, she imagined he was looking back at her.

Todd drove off, but he wondered to himself who the woman was. *All I remember seeing was the couple, I didn't see or hear her at all. Pretty lady though. Nope, don't remember seeing her on the path, or by the stairs. Very strange, how could I have missed her*? For the balance of the drive home, Todd devoted considerable thought to what he would be imagining as he climbed the stairs to the top for the first time. Maybe it was the young couple, maybe it was seeing someone at the park he would have enjoyed meeting, but the inspiration evoked romance. The big advantage, as Todd locked the door of his car when it sat in the apartment complex parking spot for the night, was that it was a Friday night. Except for bowling in the morning, Saturday afternoon was totally free to tackle a new adventure, no abbreviation, no time constraints. The only important issue was a little R&R, a shower, and a good night's sleep. The conclusion Todd came to, was the better the mood, the better the flow of imagination.

Janet woke up to one of the best Saturday mornings the summer produced so far. The temperature was that of late Spring, or early Fall. The afternoon was sure to warm up, but the thick humidity that choked the air so that it was almost unbreathable took a little vacation. Cool air from the north had pushed it's way southward enough to cut the region some slack. Janet put some coffee to brewing, and headed for a morning shower, singing like a nightingale in the echo of the stall. By the time she was done with her morning hygiene, one would have thought she was going someplace to be seen, instead of going to her usual spot at the park. She glowed, but if asked, could not tell why.

Toward the end of the morning, almost noon, Janet was ready to make her pilgrimage to the top of the stairway. Already on the path, she had mental flashbacks of things she hadn't thought of in years. There was that time when she was a senior in high school, she went parking after a movie, smooching out by the beach with that adorable little boy, what was his name?...Claude, Ward, something like that. There was the day her niece was born, popping out in the world just as pretty as a button, her sister Aggie just glad it was over with, twenty hours of labor leaving her with a beautiful baby, but less than impressed with pregnancy. There was a concert night with three of her girlfriends to see New Kids On The Block, screaming like they had thumb screws attached and tightened quarter turns at a time—good times. She was at the base of the stairs, but without missing a beat, pleasant thoughts and all, she began her ascension. The problem was, that at the top, and through the portal, she entered pretty much the same place as she left the previous evening. Sighing, she went for a walk heading east. She was an hour away, leaving markers so she wouldn't get lost. Looking down into a stream of crystal clear water with absolutely no sign of life in it, Janet got stung by a bee. *Son of a....* She swatted the back of her neck with her right hand desperately, because of the pain and shock. But then the reality set in. "Who's here?" She yelled. Janet was an hour away. Nobody was going to hear her this far out, so with a big ugly red welt on her neck that throbbed when she moved, she started running back to the portal. Talk about mixed emotions, mad she got stung, happy she got stung. She stopped running suddenly, voicing a question to herself, "Who the hell imagines bees?" She continued on, but this time walking, the slower pace allowing her to notice even more—birds. A small flock of them, too far off to tell what kind they were exactly, but definitely birds. "Hmmm, birds and bees." She voiced out loud, incredulously. She picked up her pace again, slightly. When she finally came over the rise to her portal, Janet noticed no movement, save a rabbit hopping through the grass. "So now we have the birds and the bees, and of course, rabbits. Next, I'll find a bottle of fertility pills. I don't know who's here, but this person has a hell of a lot better imagination than I do, any day of the week." Janet muttered. "HELLLOOO." She yelled at the top of her lungs. "HELLLOOO." She yelled again. She got no response back at all as she closed the gap between where she was and the entrance to the land at the top of the stairs. It appeared as though the grass had been walked through, a brand newly made pathway pointed due north. Janet weighed whether she should follow it, or just stay put. The self debate over, Janet headed the same direction as the trampled grass. Her neck ached, but not quite as badly as it did, evidently not allergic to bee stings.

CITY PARK

Todd bowled up a storm that morning, all by himself, but not unnoticed. When he paid up for the four strings, he was extended an invitation to join the Friday Night league in the fall by the manager behind the counter. Todd wasn't even aware it was the manager. "Look, I've been watching you week after week practicing your tail off. I mentioned you to a team that has always placed high in the final standings on Friday night. The team had one of its members die suddenly. I won't get into it, but he will be sorely missed, great guy. His team has a giant spot to be filled. If you come by next Friday, that team will be here if you want to meet up with them. They really want to meet you too.

"Oh my God! What an honor, I would love to. I will be here. What time?"

"They will be here at seven sharp, league business and all that. Just come by and I will introduce you to them."

"Thank you, thank you, so much. I'm sorry they lost a great guy."

"It happens, you know? You just never know when your time is up. One more thing though. They have seen all your score sheets for the last three months, so they know what you can do. Just come and be yourself; because at this point, it's all about chemistry, okay?"

"Well thank you very much. Good advise, I'll do my best." Todd left the alleys a happy man. Being invited rather than applying and hoping for the best was very gratifying. It also left him in a fantastic mood. It was that mood he carried with him to the City Park. So good was this mood of his, that he decided to walk around the pond first. It was a terrific morning, not quite afternoon, so he bought himself a hot dog from a vendor, dressed it up with a ton of mustard, relish, and ketchup, and sat in a gazebo. He watched couples laughing, trying desperately to peddle the paddle boats in sync enough to get from point A to point B. The more experienced couples made it look easy. These are the same folks who dance like Fred and Ginger at weddings because they are ying and yang. Todd finished his hot dog, sighed, but smiled to himself, and moved to hike back to the woods. He left his car where it was, it was just fine. Besides, it would be pleasant to leave the park from this area anyway. Entering the forest, he had a whole different frame of mind. His head wasn't filled with musings of memories. It was filled with desires. Romantic desires and simple things, like peddling the paddle boats with a significant other, feeding each other with ice cream cones bought from the snack shop because it was too hard to choose one flavor. Pushing kids on the merry go round, or watching them ride on the train, waving every time they passed by. Scraping peeling paint off of a white picket fence, so that a fresh coat could make it pretty as ever. Todd got so into imagining what his life could be like if he found someone to share it with, he didn't realize he'd reached the stairs, and was half way up them. Continuing this line of thought. *What would it actually be like to bring a new life into the world? Would I be a good dad? What kind of woman is out there that would put up with the likes of me*? All very good questions, and highly revealing, considering he wasn't close to finding answers to any of them. It was because of those questions rolling in his mind that he reached the top of the stairs without facing his fear of heights at all. But it was with those sobering questions rolling through his mind that he faced the portal for the first time. Todd went into shock the moment he walked into it, shaken to the core, abandoning all the self questioning, substituting a giant, *WHAT THE...*? Scanning the area, taking it all in, took quite a while. It rooted him to one spot. But when Todd turned around, he could clearly see the stairs leading him back down to the woods below. If the couple he saw descending the stairs had seen this place, they would not have been able to keep their mouths shut, he determined. All of a sudden an overwhelming sense of freedom and joy came over Todd. He began yelling and whooping, “Wahooooo!!”, running across the field with reckless abandon, somehow believing that it was a place rather than a world. With the entrance back down the stairs in plain sight at the edge of the field, it didn't occur to him that this imaginary spot just kept going on and on. It did, and Todd got lost. About all he had barely paid attention to was the direction the sun was at when he left, which would mean he was headed north; generally. Turning around pointed him back south; generally. But it generally put him in a whole different area, some of it woods with a stream running through it—well more like a brook, but it had polliwogs in it. They interested him somehow, squatting by the side, watching them swimming aimlessly. Todd moved on, not wanting to stay lost. Having the security of knowing where the entrance was would embolden him to explore later, so he doggedly hiked due south. An hour or so later he came to clear tracks, footprints here and there, and grass trampling. This was a person's tracks! He followed them like a hunter, which he was not. Although Todd did not know it, he had wandered southeast.

Janet glanced at her watch. It was almost two thirty. Whoever was here must have already left, probably frightened their first time visiting this strange place, just as she had been. But he or she would be back, just as she had. It was too hard to resist. While standing and waiting, she saw all kinds of new signs of life sprouting in different ways. Clumps of red clover seemed to bloom without her noticing it at all. With that, brought more bees. A deer made an appearance in the other corner of the meadow but ducked away into brush, timidly. As suspected, she saw several more rabbits. And what would any garden of Eden be without a snake? The only thing missing is an apple tree. She devoted another fifteen or so minutes to waiting, just in case she was wrong on her assumption that the visitor got frightened, but ultimately decided that she was correct. Strategy became the new plan. She would wait out in the parking lot in the morning, and hope to spot the culprit. If she caught whoever was entering the portal, it would be fun to enter, meet, and compare notes and thoughts as to what was actually going on here at the top of the stairs.

Todd finally found his way back to the meadow. It seemed like forever. He got genuinely scared; more like petrified. The tracked down grass led right back to the entrance to the stairway, but nobody was around.

CITY PARK

Thinking to himself, *I wish I knew how I missed that trampled grass when I came up here. Thank goodness I found it to come back. Next time I'll be more careful. I could have been wandering around out there until it got dark on me*. Todd left the place at the top of the stairs, eased his way back down to the path to get himself home. He wanted to mull over the events of the day because there was a lot to compute. Being invited to possibly joining the Friday night bowling league was exciting enough. Finding this...this...what was this anyway? Why was it here?

Janet woke up on Sunday morning, got herself cleaned up and dressed for the day. She put on a pair of jeans, a tank top, yes, but a long sleeved blouse over it, unbuttoned. She now had bugs to think about.

She drove to the corner gas station, topped off her tank for the week, then went inside for a large vanilla cappuccino and a pastry. Then she pointed her car toward the park. While driving she considered what somebody imagined differently than her that caused so much change in a day. *Probably some man thinking about the same thing the couple wanted*...She thought. After a second or two she amended herself, *If that was right, the couple would have entered the portal too. It must be something more specific, like love, or romance. I would love something like that too, but it's been since high school that anybody has taken an interest in me at all*. Janet pulled into the lot outside the city hiking trails, choosing a place to station herself, so as not to spook the likely person who was there the day before. Sitting with the window down, sipping on her coffee, eating her cheese danish, the day was shaping up to be another fabulous one. There wasn't a cloud in the sky.

It wasn't that Janet didn't want romance, it was more that the men she attracted, just didn't spark any her interest at all. Oh she'd been on dates alright, just none that had set off any fireworks. There'd been men who had a lot going for them, smart, successful. But work isn't everything. She couldn't picture a one of them inclined to hike in the city forest, let alone climbing the stairs or having enough imagination to enter the portal.

CITY PARK

Forget all that. She didn't picture a one of them not having accomplishments be the central most important parts of their lives. *Speaking of a man*, she thought, *here comes one now*. She watched as someone who looked like somebody she should pay attention to, drive into the parking lot and park his car.

Todd was looking forward to this all night. This time he was here early, and dressed properly. He'd gotten pretty scratched up in his hurry to find his way back to the entrance the day before, so he had on jeans, a shirt he could roll down the sleeves if he got in a jam. He put on some high top athletic shoes with some tread on the soles. He got out of the car, locked the door, took a deep breath, and headed for the path. His head was filled with ideas of what it would be like to live in that space at the top of the stairs. How cool would it be to just start over, find somebody to love, and live off the fat of the land? It was the subject of this day's thoughts as he climbed the stairs, praying the entrance was still at the top.

Todd didn't see Janet when he attacked the path, and it wasn't long when she was right on his tail. All she could see was his back, but that was good enough. He was fast, but she was just as fast. She wasn't going to lose him today. Janet was half way to the top when she lost sight of Todd over the edge at the top. She ran the rest of the way, was getting out of breath, but when she was almost out of wind, she burst through the portal. “Hey you!” She yelled at Todd who was already half way across the meadow. Todd stopped in his tracks, turned around, astonished. Looking straight at her, he said, “You're the lady I saw in the parking lot!”

“Yes, I am, and you are?”

“Why, do you own this place?” Todd asked cockily.

“Well no, but I thought it would be a good idea to introduce ourselves, don't you?”

“Sounds like a plan. My name is Todd Farris, and yours?”

CITY PARK

"Todd?"

"That would be correct."

"Todd, it's me, Janet Traynor, Remember?"

"Janet, that you? Oh my God!" Todd said, moving toward Janet, losing the cocky instantly. He grabbed the woman, giving her a hell of a hug. "It's crazy, but I've thought quite a bit about you lately. I was hiking down below in the forest, and you've crept into my head more than once. At times, I could smell the perfume you had on the night of the prom."

Janet had an embarrassed smile, but said, "Best date I ever had, Todd."

"What is this place Janet, do you know yet?"

"I know it takes imagination to enter, Todd. I have been coming here since March when I figured that out. In your first visit, you made more progress in a day than I did in all that time. What have I been doing wrong?"

"Nothing Janet, nothing at all. You just need me, that's all."

"Excuse me?"

"Well, what is it that you couldn't do, Janet?"

"I couldn't imagine a land that could reproduce. There were no bugs, animals, flowers, anything."

"Exactly."

"Exactly what?"

"Biology, Janet, biology. It takes a man and a woman to reproduce. It takes a male and female of everything to reproduce; or it takes a carrier to help, like birds and bees."

"Jeez, you're right. But why you?"

"That, I do not know. I mean to find out though because this is a hell of a coincidence, isn't it? Something else I......."

"Something else what, Todd?"

"Never mind about that now. Look behind you."

Janet turned around only to see that there was nothing to see. "Oh-My-God, the portal is gone!" She ran up to where it always was pushing her hands into empty space. Then she stood quietly, Todd knew right away what she was trying to attempt. Janet was trying to imagine the portal back. Todd joined her, maybe reinforcing would help. Nothing helped. All was the same as it was.

Essentially, they were both stuck. The world they knew was out there, the one with bowling leagues, the cars that matched the keys in their pockets, apartments, closets full of clothes, supermarkets with food, money, jobs, all of it was somewhere at the base of stairs they had no access to anymore; or right now anyway. Todd's living off the fat of the land fantasy, was now reality, and though he did not want to reveal the truth to Janet, he was petrified, in a state of pure panic. Janet, on the other hand, made no effort to put on a strong face, she broke down and cried.

Todd made a valiant effort to paint a different picture on the face of the situation, "We both asked for this in a way, playing with fire, so to speak. We both imagined our way into this world. I even got to wondering how it would be to start over and live off the fat of the land."

"You have to be kidding me, Todd. Do you have any survival skills—anything at all? I've got nothing, myself. What do we eat tonight, raw rabbit? I left my favorite comforter at home. I never leave my wallet in my purse when I leave the car, so I have about a hundred fifty dollars on me. I'll treat, let's go have us some Italian, what do you say?" She asked, caustically. "If we are actually stranded here, we can't give up, either. Or is that what you're suggesting?"

"No, you're right. But we did both ask for it. So what should we do?"

"Well, let's not leave the area for a while until we are sure the portal doesn't open up again. Aren't you hungry Todd?"

"I'm sorry Janet, but I can't think about that now. If there was a smörgåsbord right here, right now, I couldn't eat, okay? I am worried about food yes, but I want to concentrate on that portal if you don't mind because I'm more worried about the portal than the food problem. Let's not dismiss the power of imagination just yet. I think it's so critical."

"Alright, you're right again. How do we begin?"

"Numero uno, let's make ourselves comfortable because we might be spending the night. Numero dos, we sit, relax, totally let the stress float away. I want to tell you the things I imagined to get me here in the first place because you told me my way produced different results. Maybe you can get on the same page, I hope so. Come on, let's pick some grass."

After Todd explained what he had in mind, Janet went to work like a drone. They built a large haystack to be used to stay off the ground for the night. When they finally finished, the two sat down on the haystack and began talking. They talked, and talked, and talked some more. Come to find out, they were on the same page for a lot of things, not just the strategy to imagine the portal reopening. By morning, Todd woke up to Janet quite at home using him as a pillow. He felt very much at home with her there. It was so easy to imagine having her in that position. In a first for him in years, he lifted his head and kissed her on the head. Janet woke up to that.

Lazily, not really ready to rouse yet, she said, "Mmm, what was that for?"

"Because I like you there."

"I could live with it." She told him back.

"How about some breakfast."

"Could you make me an omelet?"

"No, but I know a place that makes an excellent omelet."

Janet jumped up with a start, finally dawning on her what Todd was saying.

Todd got up out of the hay, stood, and offered a hand to Janet. "Shall we go?"

It was Todd's turn to get up to feed the crabby little gal in the nursery. There's an element to Janet and Todd's relationship that puts them miles ahead of everybody else, the least of which is figuring who's turn it is to feed little Imogene without complaint. No, it is a certainty that they belong together and that they chose each other over all the other people in the world when they could have eliminated everybody by staying where they were at the top of the stairs. There was only one question left to ask. Was it better to imagine a brand new world or face the old one together with all it's imperfections? That is what Janet and Todd decided to do. Who knows who set up the blank slate in the city park at the top of the stairs? Could it have been perhaps an advanced society, leaving a lifeboat for people with enough imagination to use it? Or was it an entrance to a world, destroyed by its inhabitants, wiped clean so that a worthy 'Adam and Eve' with enough savvy to make good choices could rebuild it? Fodder for discussion between a total of two people in this world, because Janet and Todd would never share the experience with anybody else—ever. For them, it was simply a tool to bring two people together, and unite them with love. Mr. and Mrs. Farris figured there might be others to go there and figure it out for themselves if they have enough imagination, that is.

OUT OF CONTEXT

OUT OF CONTEXT

Clarissa and I had the grandkids for the weekend. We don't get them as often these days. It's not that Thomas and Debra don't want to send them, it's more that their offspring has reached an age that it is more important to spend time with their friends rather than the old fuddy duddies. Oh, they would never say that to our faces, of course, they love us too much for that. But the days of taking them to the park to play on the swings and slides are behind us now. My wife and I have worked hard to eat and exercise correctly so that we could hold on to our health and vitality. We hoped to gain some time to brave this new world, to savor it with our kids and grandkids. The idea was a miscalculation on our part because we both have the strength and energy to do almost anything while this new generation around us has less interest in things active. It is a world where the entertainment is in a category unfamiliar to my wife and I. We want baseball, they give us Wii. We suggest paint ball, they suggest World of Warcraft. This particular weekend the itinerary was going to the beach; maybe do some body surfing. What we ultimately got instead was sitting on beach chairs watching our two grandchildren text. The way they both went about it had me thinking, what with all that thumb exercise, thumbs might evolve into forearms someday.

Conversations with Gabriel and Jason are short, very much to the point. Clarisa and I both sense that it is an effort for them to talk to us and that we should break down and buy one of those pad thingies from the telephone company so that we can have an entire conversation with the two.

Clarissa and I spent almost the entire beach day bored out of our minds watching the two thumbing out messages to who knows who. I just could not stand it anymore. I finally broke the monotony. I stood, breaking the silence with a sound, “Aaahhh.” came the sound I made as I stretched. I'm starving. I could use a big old burger and some fries, what do you guys say?”

“Coo, KK, Bio, BRB.” and they got up and left.

I exploded on my poor wife Clarissa. “My God! Are these two actually related to us? This is totally unbearable. I can't wait to go home!”

OUT OF CONTEXT

"Now John, take it easy. We never get to see them anymore. Be patient."

"Patient?" I asked incredulously. "Maybe on the way home, we can drive up to that scrap metal place over on 4th, get out of the car, and if we're lucky that big magnet will assume it's more steel for the compactor."

"John!!! You don't mean that?"

"What!! They didn't have the least bit of consideration for our lives. They spent all day trying to bore us to death. My life energy is down to minimum, completely sucked out. I could die any second."

Gabriela and Jason didn't spare us any more torture, They came back, Jason with less than a mouthful of words, said to us, "C? GTG!! UOK?"

"Huh?" I asked.

"OMG, U 2 GZ R CRZY!! LOL. LMBO" Jason said cryptically.

"ME 2," said Gabriel.

"Come on, let's pack up and get some food. I wish we could have actually gone into the water today. I got too hot, I'm parched."

"SRY." said Gabriel. " IZ HNGRY & THRS-T 2"

I met my wife's eyes. It was hard to tell if these two were putting us on, or just ignorant, products of this modern school system.

"SRSLY, WE R TOTES BAD. BEN TLK N ALL DA. WE 8 UP UR TYM. SO SRY" Jason said to us. We almost understood most of that. But instead of being mad with talking this way, I was fast becoming concerned.

"It's alright, but if you wanted to be with your friends, why didn't you ask us if they could come along?"

"DNT NED UM HER. CN PLA ALL D-A CRS TWN" Gabriela showed us a happy face emoticon on her telephone.

I nudged beyond concerned, into a whole different kind of scared zone. Even Clarissa showed signs that we had entered a crazy place. There are people that are illiterate, and no one would be able to tell unless pressed for a signature, or to share something by reading it. What if this was the kind of problem that is obvious to those of us that can talk normally. Can my grandkids talk normally? Should Clarissa and I dare to ask?

"How's school?" I asked the two as we made our way back to the car.

"GTG. All A's" Gabriela said.

"ME2." Said Jason.

"Wow!!" I said. Okay, so the teachers haven't noticed that there's a problem in River City, but what about my kids? What's the excuse there?

Clarissa whispered to me on the sly, "We have to talk." But for the remainder of the afternoon, we acted as if there was nothing wrong at all.

"Does anybody feel like popcorn?" My wife asked when we got back to the house.

"I DO."

"I DO 2." Said Jason holding up two fingers

"Well go get cleaned up and we'll have a look at the pay for view movies." Clarissa told them.

Upstairs, and out of earshot, Clarissa took me aside. "No wonder our grandkids don't talk to us, they can't. They have to spell half of what they say. To punctuate, they need to point at an emoticon on the telephone. This is worse than learning math with a calculator." My wife said.

"It is worse than that. How could they be getting all A's in school? How can Thomas and Debra not tell us there has a problem? What do we do about it? I can't think of a blessed thing we can do to fix this."

Gabriela came downstairs first, and Jason a few seconds later. Both grandchildren bubbled over with joy that they were spending time with us. Two fresh made bowls of popcorn sat on the coffee table, the TV on showing one station's choice of movie order. "Why don't you thumb through the TV Guide to see what would be suitable to order." Clarissa said.

"OK GRNDMA." Every word uttered, or half spelled, my heart broke.

"WAT ABOUT THS 1 GRNDMA?" Gabriel asked, showing us a questioning face on the phone, then pointing to her choice in the Guide.

"Fine, that's a fine choice. Push the accept button and get this party rolling." I said.

Well...we laughed, we got upset, we got opinionated, all in the right places. We all equally enjoyed the movie, proving that these were just ordinary kids enjoying time with their grandparents. The only exception was that having a regular conversation was tedious.

Gabriela and Jason had to go back home the next evening already, so going to sleep that night after the movie was bittersweet. Clarissa talked to me while we lay in bed, “I don't know about you, but I'm going to miss those two. I could have used a bit more life in the house, but I got all the love I wanted and more. They're sweet kids. I can't imagine how the way they talk has gotten so out of hand.”

“I don't either. I can't get over the fact that they are both considered good students. I mean, I wonder what the two of them will be when they grow up? Could either of them be a doctor, a lawyer, or a pharmacist? I can't help wondering how widespread this thing is. I'm starting to see a major advantage to being old and at the end part of our lives than beginning them.”

“I know, right?” She agreed. “Come Monday morning, I think I'm going to investigate this further. We have completely normal conversations with Thomas and Debra all the time. They haven't ever indicated there was a problem with the kids. I do find that shocking.”

“I hope tomorrow is a better day. Today ended better than when we started it. The more time they spent with us, the easier it got to be around them. They weren't talking to us at all on Friday, or this morning.”

“Goodnight Grandpa John.” she said kissing me, turning the light off, then molding her back to my front so I could hold on to her. That's the only way we can fall asleep.”

“Goodnight baby. I love you with all my heart.” I said as I drifted off.

Clarissa and I woke together as we always do. We emptied our bladders, and padded down to the kitchen to put more liquid into them. We are always up at the crack of dawn. The kids weren't close to waking up yet. While Clarissa made a fresh pot of coffee, I got our box of Oaty O's from the cabinet, a bottle of milk from the fridge, and eating utensils. On the way, I clicked on the television mounted under the cabinet so we could watch the weather and morning news. “...as a new service to our listeners." The news team was in the middle of an announcement. "Be sure to get your free mobile app at www.newscenter3online.org. We're going to preview this exciting change to our morning news segment to show you how much more content can be fit into one place on this week's edition of Sunday Morning News Weekender. Regular changes to our format will begin tomorrow on News Center 3, so stay tuned."

"Uh-oh, I wonder what's changing. I hope it isn't the blond weather girl."

"You really like how she walks back and forth in front of the screen with those heels of hers, don't you?"

"Yeah, I can't say that I hate it. Oh, oh, it's coming on."

After the commercial, the screen changed to the familiar introductory weather screen, The rise in excitement lasting all of one second. There on the screen was a condensed synopsis of the coming day's weather. Instead of the weather girl pointing to this and that, explaining cause and effect of fronts and the like, the map had a bevy of information that took a resurrected Egyptian from the days of the pharaohs to explain.

There were abbreviated representations spanning two counties starting offshore with TID TME LW=5: HI=11:10 ///WTR TEMP=75, depicted five places on the water map. On the top of the map was info: SNRZ=6: AM SNST=8:30 PM///POLN CNT=HI///UMDTY=70%///CHNS RAN 30%.///TEMP @ 8: AM=70', 10: AM=75',12: PM=78',2: PM=80',4: PM=82',6: PM=82',8: PM=80',10: PM=75', 12: AM=75'. The land mass had indications for BAR PRSR= 29.92///STRM %G of CHNS=10%///DO PNT=55'///WND DIR=18'NW. After two minutes the screen faded, to a notification, BAC N 60 SECS, then it went to a commercial.

"Okay, what the hell was that?" I asked. "Everything is backwards. I'm sleeping with sweet dreams, and waking up to nightmares." Clarissa said absolutely nothing. Having this on top of the revelation that Gabriela and Jason can only talk in text, was almost too much for her, and damned well too much for me.

"And, welcome back. We here at Sunday Morning News Weekender hope you have a wonderful Sunday and a great week. Jenny?"

OUT OF CONTEXT

"Yes, well as you saw from the weather clip, we are in store for one terrific day, we see...."

"As I saw from the weather clip? The reason we have meteorologists on TV is to explain it to us dummies for God sake! I didn't understand a thing." I complained.

"That's because it was all in text speak." Clarissa explained to me.

"...and that's the way I see it. Over to you Ted." The camera shifted to two men and a woman on a couched circle, the one ready to speak was presumably Ted.

"We have a lot to cover this morning, so let's just get to it, shall we? In politics, well, let's go ahead and run the highlights of the president's speech last night." The screen shifted to a picture of the president talking at his podium, but mouth moving only. It was stock footage of the speech. The

reduced version of what he said was at the bottom of the screen. MY FELO AMRICNS IM SPKN 2NITE BOUT..."

"Shut it off John, I can't take one more minute of this." I got up, shut the thing off, and pulled the plug out of the wall.

"It's us, isn't it John? I mean, the world has passed us by. We haven't kept up. They're the ones who are fast, and we are the ones who are slow. But I don't want to be that way, do you?" My wife asked me as frightened as a little kitten chased by a pit bull.

When the kids woke up and came downstairs, Clarissa, and I were sitting at the kitchen table in shock. We weren't talking, moving, or eating. We actually frightened the kids. "WUT S RONG?" Jason asked.

"Y S. PLS DNT FLAK OUT N S NOW, WE LUV DA WA U GZ R SO RELAXD. TOK N SLO HELPS US THNK STR8. WE LUV U MUCH." said Gabriella who showed us an unhappy face on her phone. My wife and I had to shake ourselves out of the funk we sunk into.

"We'll be okay sweetie, and we love you too. It's just that we didn't know you two were really talking to us until yesterday. We understand now, but we didn't. But we haven't any idea how to talk like you do, and we don't know if we can keep up."

"DO NT HAV 2. STA LIK U R. UR JUS FIN." Said

Gabriela.

"Y S, WE HAV TA THNK 2 KEP UP 5 DIFRNT WA's ALL DA TYM. NO TYM 2 RELAX. (unhappy face).

"So tell us," I gave them both a hypothesis to ponder since they were so fast and my wife and I are so slow, "How do we fit in with the rest of the world now? We turned on the news and weather this morning, and they were whizzing by us with text speak, which I have to tell you, is a lot slower than us out loud than in your cyberworld. You tell us that you are enjoying being here with us because it is easier and slower, but I suggest to you that you are enjoying the pleasure of somebody else's voice. What if the movie we watched last night was only in text talk? Somebody has to be the slow ones to keep the dreaming and fantasies alive like love, romance, and adventure. When we retired, it felt like we were no longer needed, but if text talk takes over completely, we'll be obsolete. I just gave you a few thoughts to ponder in less than a minute. What would you rather hear: I will love you and keep the both of you in my heart forever, or, I CUMPLTLY LUV U 2, happy face?"

"WE CN NT CHNG WUT WE R NOW. BUT WE WIL THNK OF IDEAS 2 HELP U. WE LUV U 2, & WNT U 2 B (happy face). WIL TOK 2 MOM & DAD 2 HELP." Jason said, and the both of them, tears in their eyes, came over to give us hugs. My wife and I reciprocated,

We took the kids to the mall since their idea of a good time is congregating with like minds, the food court with abbreviated food, and the fun zone. Clarissa and I sat on a bench by the fountain in the middle, a man made oasis in the middle of dressed mannequins, fragrances, and ten different ways to sit in an easy chair. I think one of the chairs had a woman built into the back to massage you when you sit with a brewski enjoying 5000 watts of hip hop coming at you from ten directions at once. Just before we sat, Clarissa and I looked over the wares displayed around one of those mini kiosks in the concourse. A man was demonstrating how fascinating a big foam plane was when he pitched it certain ways. There was an aquarium with furry things bouncing perpetually against the glass, never having to feed them or pick up do-do with a pooper scooper. Oh no, everything is just fine. People like us would never be able to tell that life is gradually changing, forcing us into a different direction, bull crap.

The end of the day came slow, the kids had no clue that we did not have a good time, assuming that we did what all grandparents do, sit and stare at people, and pull out more money for tokens or food in a box. But we finally came to the time we could sit and have a chat with the love of our loins, the parents of our loving grand modern messes. The kids burst through their own front door to the arms of Thomas and Debra, rapid firing text talk to the two who seemed not to notice at all. It became serious, and looks of concern were flashed our way. In what seemed like an eternity at the time, our son and daughter in law finally addressed us in a way we could understand.

"The kids tell us that the both of you have trouble adopting modern technology the way we have adapted to it. Debra and I have been wondering what has been wrong with the both of you. Gabriella and Jason told us they couldn't have had a better time with you. But the only good time you had with them is when they slowed down to a mental crawl. We see that we are going to have to instruct you how to keep up with the rest of us."

"OH NO!!!" Clarissa told them. That is not going to happen. My husband and I are NOT going to fit into this...this crazy world where everything is de-emotionalized. If you want to help us, then help us find a spot where we can live out our lives at our pace. A pace I might add that is a good deal faster than yours in some ways. John and I still like hiking, swimming, and a dozen other things that aren't popular anymore. We're fast, where you are our slow. We're slow where you are fast. This is not going to work for John and I. We want to be with others like us."

"What are you saying?" Debra asked.

"Let me spell it out for you." I said. "My wife and I are going to find a place where we fit in exactly."

"But that would be somewhere off-line, no cell coverage." Our daughter in-law countered.

"Precisely, and so be it. Now we know why old folks buy travel RV's. It never made sense before, but we

get it now. It's time to hit the road jack. We'll come back here and there, but when we get too old to do it anymore, we'll land in a spot that allows us to fade away into oblivion our way. Our GPS will be a cell phone.
When the bars are gone, we'll stay for the night. It will take a while to sell the house and prepare, so I suggest you share us while the gettin's good. If Gariella and Jason want to come over next weekend, we would love to have them. Sweet kids, both of them. We would adore having you too while we can. Why not come to lunch?"

"But how will we be able to stay in touch when you go?"

"We will never disappear from your lives. We love you all too much for that. When we manage to find a land line we'll connect, don't you worry. You can bet that Grandma and I will be using the snail mail as much as we can until it stops working."

COLLINWOOD INTERSTATE TRAVELSTARS

COLLINWOOD INTERSTATE TRAVELSTARS

Back in the spring of 1967, Wally Jr, the oldest of two Thornton kids, asked his dad what his thoughts were about getting a car in the fall. He had just turned 17, his sister Melony was 16 at the time. The thought had become close to an obsession for the both of them. Brother and sister, who were particularly close, discussed it often, dreaming about what the freedom and added mobility meant to them as their junior and senior years of high school was just around the corner. When Little Wally and Melony went over the ways to bring up the subject to their parents, the best the two could come up with was to ask the question in front of the family at dinner, safety in numbers, that kind of thing. After Little Wally had asked his question, they hung on their dad's every word. Roberta, their mom, eyed her husband warily, waiting for what Wally Sr was going to say next too. The instant pressure was worse than the time when Little Wally asked him how to make a baby. Not where do babies come from, but how they were made. Anyway, he stalled as long as possible before he answered because he knew full well that anything to come out of his mouth would become instant law. He didn't pass it off to his wife to make the decision. It just wasn't done that way back in '67, but Wally Sr already knew how Roberta felt about it from the look in her eyes. If anything happened that struck her as his fault down the line, Wally Sr knew he would be held accountable and cast into his own private hell. That's also how it was done in '67. There are always two sides.

"Well you know son, your mom, and I have always told you kids that along with adult privileges come adult responsibilities." He put a forkful of food in his mouth thinking he scored a diplomatic and decisive victory. There was a small smug smirk on his face behind his chewing.

Melony quickly raised the stakes on the man though. "What does that mean, dad?" She asked, trumping his one second of triumph.

Pressed now, he had to go a little further with his explanation, "Well sweetie that just means that neither Wally or you can get anything that big unless you can pay for it yourself. That includes the cost of owning and maintaining it. I'll tell you this much right now, you have no idea how much, and how severe that will be." He didn't elaborate on any of the concerns mom and dad had about the dangers of driving, which was the real red flag for them. Wally Sr preferred to scare them both straight.

"Oh." said Melony who had been raised and called for the time being, so she folded.

For Little Wally, the statement was interpreted as a yes. Melony decided to watch what her big brother would do, somebody she loved and trusted.

A few days later, Little Wally set out to fill his dad's criteria for first car ownership. He hit the pavement after school in search of a job. It took two weeks for anybody to hear him out for all but one of the jobs he had applied. The time that lapsed worked to his favor. When he came home with the news that he had found a job, his parents had forgotten or didn't think to make the connection to the real reason he went looking. Both parents were just so proud of Little Wally, they about burst. Little Wally worked his parents pretty well by not bringing up cars, driver's ed, or anything connected. He saved all of those battles for the fall of the next school year. He figured to save every last dime he earned through the summer anyway, so it was better not thinking about it. Melony would have done the same thing, but she wasn't quite old enough to do something other than babysit, but she used the option without complaint.

Little Wally's first job beyond delivering newspapers, was in a hardware store, capitalizing on all the time his dad spent teaching him how to use tools. Thanks to his father, Little Wally convinced the owner that he knew quite a bit. It turned out to be a giant advantage knowing screw types, thread sizes, nail penny sizes, wire gauges, what every tool in the store was for, and how to use them correctly. It was all thanks to Wally Sr. Sometimes things are lost on you when you are just a kid. At a real young age, Little Wally loved using tools and building things. But hanging out with his father who insisted he do everything properly took some of the pleasure out of it at the time. Fun, for Little Wally, was like the time he found a baby carriage in somebody's trash and tried to make a hot rod out of it. His father turned that particular adventure into something else entirely. The carriage was thrown out as the trash it was, and a professional soap box racer built instead. Every time Little Wally veered off on his own to use his imagination to build something out of nothing, Little Wally would get in trouble for not listening, not asking, leaving his father's tools outside to rust in the rain, and generally showing no respect for the property of others. Truth be told that even after Little Wally discovered that he owed his dad a debt of gratitude, he still would have preferred to use his imagination in his own way. The contentious nature of the arguments with his father led his dad to protect himself and his personal things. He got Little Wally his own toolbox, and every tool in that box is clean, shiny, and rust free, even to this day, forty plus years later.

A benefit from all the head butting by father and son, is when Little Wally got that first job in Harvey's Hardware, the invaluable things he learned, both pleasantly and unpleasantly, came in mighty handy. He built a reputation with the customers as someone to ask for the best way to a job, and what to buy to do it. This impressed and pleased old man Harvey to the maximum. Little Wally quickly became his go-to guy. Harvey gave him more and more hours after school ended for the summer. Every day at 7:00 AM Little Wally showed up on time to start the day after peddling five miles on a bicycle he built from other people's trash.

Melony built up quite a clientèle of people calling her for relief from their kids so they could go out for the night. Her reputation grew as much as her brother's. Brother and sister both saved with a singular mission, neither yielding to the temptations made at summer's end when the annual back to school sales blitzes pounded the daily newspaper and mailbox. Even back in 1967, this was mandatory commercial policy. Melony stayed the course, but Little Wally was ready to strike. It was too early to drop the bomb on the parents that he wanted a car yet. The first hurdle was to get permission to take a driver education course at school. These things required patience and tact. Melony and Little Wally were averagely good kids, that is to say normal, not perfect. Both had grades that were in the

A and B range, with a C or two. The course he wanted to sign up for would draw an argument, but certainly couldn't be denied. When all was said and done, Little Wally was blazing a trail for his sister to follow when her time arrived. Until that time, she looked forward to riding to school, dances, and other interests her brother, and she shared. It was no trouble at all to throw her support to her older brother, even if she wasn't going to travel down the same avenue just yet. In a year, she would.

There was a lot of underlying concern in Little Wally's senior high school class amongst the boys. There was constant talk about Viet Nam. It seemed like there was no escaping getting involved with Nam after graduation. Still, it was their senior year, and with it came the determination to enjoy all the best of being on top of the heap. Little Wally completed his driver education course at the end October, and was due at the time to go take the test to get his drivers license. From that point forward, Little Wally's parents realized that blocking efforts by their son to get his own car, meant sacrificing theirs. The reality was pounded into them further when Wally Sr needed to take his son in the family car to the registry for testing. Wally passed the exam that day handily, but the battles Wally Sr and his son had once over tools suddenly seemed like the day before yesterday.

There was the initial celebration of having his name printed on the face of a genuine state document that identified Little Wally as Walter J. Thornton Jr, full grown man with rights and privileges for everything except imbibing booze, owning property without a parent's signature on it, or voting. A discussion developed on the way home about getting his own vehicle. That is when Wally Sr was surprised to learn that his son saved $288.00. It was enough to pick up a used car and put it on the road with a tank of gas in it.

The fact that Wally Sr had to sign his name so that little Wally could get a car, automatically gave him rights. Dad Thornton got excited with the process. Similar to the soap box racer incident, making sure the best was had for the money, suddenly became his responsibility. Wally Sr told his son, who was driving at the time, to take a quick left turn from the route they were taking home. It was his dad's intention to have a chat with the owner of his favorite dealership. Wally Sr bought all of his cars there, so in his mind it was only fair to expect Larry Urskin, owner of Urskin Motors, to take care of his son. For Little Wally, it was alright to go and talk, but he had no intention of overspending, not even for his father.

There was an arm around the shoulder in the middle of all the phony smiling from Larry Urskin that made Little Wally uncomfortable. The words 'car payment' were thrown out for consideration too. Finally, Little Wally had had enough. “Don't you have any trade ins that I could look at? I really don't want to get in over my head. Pretty cars are nice, but I really want something I can put some work into, as long as it runs good that is.”

Larry looked disappointed, as did his dad, but said, “Yeah we have a few that we took in as trade allowances, but nothing I can give a warranty with.”

“Well, if I shopped around and bought from a private party, I still wouldn't have a warranty. What do you have that has potential?” Little Wally began to take the lead.

“We park the trade ins like you're talking about out back. Why don't you take a walk around to see if there is something you like? Come in if you think it suits you, and we can come up with keys. You can walk out that back door there, and it will take you into a fenced in area on the back of the building. Hopefully you can find something that runs.” The man sounded less than positive, probably on purpose. The man was a business man, not truly Wally Sr's good buddy, that was for sure. There was a remarkably good chance that he didn't even remember his dad or any of the cars he bought from him. Having Wally Sr tie up money from the credit union, in order to create car payments, wasn't exactly a favor in Little Wally's book.

So Little Wally made his way out the door to a collection of unwantables. An assortment of nine cars that had seen their better days, all of them. The cars looked so seriously sad. One of the aging beasts was a cute, solid little car. At least it was the impression the car gave off—that it was small. Little Wally went over to it, opened the doors, sat in the driver's seat, then popped the hood to see if there was an engine. There was an engine, also cute. He closed the car back up to make his way back inside, going no further than the entrance because his dad was heading out.

"Find anything son?" He asked the question, but it was obvious that he thought it was a lesson in futility that the time he spent out in the yard would push him toward the better cars out front. He was wrong.

"Only one. It's that cute little Rambler over there. She needs love, but she's solid all over, not a bit of rust on her. I'd like to see if she runs at all. Too much engine work will scare me away, but barring that, she's still a good little car dad."

"Oh...okay then, let's go see if they have the keys then." He said, somewhat impressed with his son's conviction. He'd seen that tenacious conviction before in his son, and although he wasn't quite like that himself, he had a powerful respect for the kid. He loved this boy very much, and right then he wanted to stand by both of his kids no matter what. It was so easy to see both his wife and himself folded into their personal makeups. How could any parent not help but be proud?

Inside, Little Wally took the lead, heading Larry Urskin off before he went back into his plush office. "Yes young man?" Larry tried to make eye contact with Wally Sr to gauge if the two were still on the same wavelength. Dad stood firm behind his son, avoiding direct eye contact until his son needed him.

"Do you have keys for that Rambler out back?"

"The '59 American? Yes, of course. We took it in trade for a brand new Buick. The guy had it since new. There's a ton of miles on it. That's the reason he bought new."

"I saw, and you're right; there is a lot of mileage on her. I take that as a good thing if she starts and still runs after all that use. Can I start her up please?" Little Wally wasn't deterred for some reason or other. He seemed to know what he was getting into.

Ten minutes later, Little Wally sat behind the wheel of the Rambler American, pumped the gas furiously, and turned the key for the first time. The old girl started right up for him, like she was putting on a front so she would be adopted by a new owner. No smoke came out of the exhaust, at least not the old car blues kind anyway. She damned near purred. Little Wally disengaged the clutch and shifted it into first. Letting the clutch out slow so he could get a sense of how much wear there was. It eased into gear just fine. Reverse, too, was just fine. Back in neutral, he let it sit for a while to warm up to see how the heater was, checking knobs, wipers, radio, and anything else he could think of. He engaged the emergency brake, which seemed to have meat to it. Then he finally turned on the heater to find that it blew just fine. He turned the car off, got out, opened the hood to check for coolant leaks, saw none, so he checked the oil. It was full and clean. Then he pushed down on both bumpers to check the responsiveness of the shocks and springs. All in all, it wasn't a bad little car in Little Wally's estimation.

"How much?" He asked Larry.

"Well, let's see..." the owner pondered. I gave the man a hundred and fifty in trade. I want to get my money back."

"I see that it needs four new tires...I'll give you a hundred dollars cash." said Little Wally.

"Done" the owner declared. Wally Sr only had to put a binder on the car for his son. He said very little in the whole conversation.

"I'll be here before I go to work after school tomorrow to pay it off. I haven't figured out a plan for getting tags yet, I'm sorry."

A nicer, more even sided Larry Urskin answered Little Wally. "Don't worry about the tags right now, son, the car will be here for you when you are ready." he said with a wink to his father.

It wasn't until Saturday morning that Little Wally found out that Larry Urskin had gone ahead and picked up the tags for the car. Wally Sr had used the time during the day to call his insurance company, adding his son to the policy. Wally Sr drove the paperwork over to the dealership so that tags could be picked up. Not a word was said about it. All his dad said afterward was that the insurance company needed a couple hundred for the year more. Dad Thornton told his son not to worry about it just yet. The hardware store was closed on Saturdays, so it was a total surprise to find out that he was to go pick up his car that day.

On Saturday afternoon, a two tone, 1959 Rambler American Deluxe with a white roof and black body, sat in the Thornton driveway. She had lost her luster years ago, and it was doubtful that any heads would turn to notice the new addition to the household. Melony's aim was to change all that, offering to help her brother wash her down to see if there was anything good underneath a ton of crud, baked on tree pollen, and grease from dirty hands that serviced her. The interior looked as though it hadn't been vacuumed or cleaned in years. Still, there was nothing torn or broken that was visible. The car just needed lots and lots of tender loving care...and new tires.

For all the work sister and brother put into the car that afternoon, it didn't help much. The black paint still looked oxidized, the white stained. The car needed compounding badly. The interior too, after extensive cleaning, remained unimpressive. Upholstery had the appearance of sitting in the sun too long. To be fair, it wasn't bad, just not good enough to project how cute the car really was. But it was good enough to take to work at the hardware store on Sunday. Harvey was Jewish, his hardware store was open every Sunday morning. Not once did Little Wally's mom say to him from the time he started working on Sunday, *I wish you would go to church with us*. It was a match made in heaven.

It was coming back home that afternoon that took some of the shine off car ownership because Little Wally had his first flat tire. When he got in the door at home, the parents and Melony just got home from church services themselves. They did a double take at Little Wally's dirty clothes.

"What happened sweetheart?" asked his mom.

"I knew those tires were bad. I had a flat when I got out of work. It was lucky for me that the spare was good. I never did check to see that it had air in it, sure glad it did. It doesn't look good to take it to school tomorrow Melony, I'm sorry sis. I don't see how I can get tires after school, and get to work too. I don't know when I can get new tires. I'll probably have to wait for next Saturday again."

"Well if you're going to do that, son, you are going to have to put your car in front of mine. I have to get out in the morning to get to work."

After school on Monday, Little Wally peddled directly to McDaniel Tire. He wanted to get an idea how much four tires would set him back and to make an appointment for Saturday because he didn't have to work at the hardware store. When he talked to the service agent, the man was particularly nice and helpful.

"The problem with that car, Mr. Thornton, is that tires that fit on that 15 inch rim of yours are discontinued. I can order them or move up a size. That will cost you more. But I do have a set of tires back there that we stocked about a year ago. They never did sell. I hear the company went out of business. I can let you have those tires pretty cheap. I'll balance those babies, rotate them for the life of the car, and even repair any flats you might get for say-50,000 miles. They're all I have in that size anymore. Companies are moving toward radial tires now."

"How much?"

"I'll let you have those tires for $86.00 installed"

"Wow! Good deal! Can I get them on my car Saturday morning? I work all week after school."

"Is there some way you get the car to us in the morning and leave the keys in the drop box? We can work on it during the day, and it will be ready for you to pick it up in the afternoon."

"Swell!" Little Wally replied excitedly.

"Well then, let me write the order up, and you can leave the car in the morning. Just put the key through the mail slot in the door over there, and we'll fix you right up."

Little Wally couldn't wait for the school day to end. He was out the door and on his bike before most of the kids left the building. McDaniel Tire was about a mile and a half from the High School, so he pumped that bicycle of his for all he was worth so he wouldn't be late for work. When he came around the corner onto the street that McDaniel's was on, there she sat in the parking lot, pretty as can be! Little Wally skidded to a stop by his car and admired her for a bit. New tires did wonders. Thin strips of white walls faced out, making the tires modern looking. He propped his kickstand, knelt down to have a closer look, his eyebrows knitted a little. *Collinwood Interstate Travelstars*? He thought to himself, *I never heard of them*. The name was embossed in white just above the thin white wall. They were pretty tires, at any rate. He went inside to pay for the work done and get his keys.

Little Wally put his bike in the trunk, tied it down, and headed for home to leave off his manual transportation. Nobody was home, and Little Wally had accomplished all that he needed to do so quickly that he still had time to go into the eight minute car wash before continuing to the hardware store that was right on the way. He wanted to show old man Harvey his car with new tires in the best possible light.

Little Wally put in the quarters, pressed the button for high pressure soap, and spread it all over his car. Careful to balance his time to have enough of it for rinsing, he pushed the high pressure rinse half way into the time allotment. For each stroke of the wand, years of wear washed away down into the drain. What was left was a car that didn't look a day over a year old, but pride clouded Little Wally's judgment, to be fair. He shook his head in amazement, climbed into his car, and went to work before he was late.

"Is that the same car Wally?" Harvey Schwartz had never met Wally Sr. He never thought of his employee as Little Wally. He comported himself to be a young man to be respected. This afternoon, Harvey had been watching and waiting for Wally to get to work. Harvey was used to Wally being early, and, although not technically late, was late for the likes of Wally. He knew the young man had trouble with his car, he had seen it the afternoon of the flat tire, so he had grown concerned that tires wouldn't be all that went wrong with a car that age. But here he was driving up in a car that looked pretty near new.

COLLINWOOD INTERSTATE TRAVELSTARS

"Yes sir. After I had picked my car up from McDaniel Tire, I had enough time to run it through the car wash. She cleaned up pretty sweet, wouldn't you say? It must be that soap in the machine at the car wash —way better than the stuff my sister and I used on it, that's for sure!"

"Holy cow! All you did was wash it? Very nice looking tires, by the way."

"Thank you sir. So what's going on today..."

At home, later that evening, Little Wally parked the Rambler in the driveway, going indoors to get a bite to eat, if his mom was true to form to save leftovers from the dinner meal. On the way to the kitchen, he said, "Car's fixed, sis. I can give you a ride to school tomorrow because I plan to take her."

"Seriously?"

"Yeah, and I washed it again at the car wash. You wouldn't believe the difference. Any dinner left, mom?"

"Tsk." is all she said.

Little Wally was devouring the food left out by his mom, when Wally Sr walked into the kitchen. "Those are some great looking tires, son! I wouldn't mind a set of those on my beast. Did you pay for detailing or something at McDaniel's?"

"Nope, just the car wash on Tirrell Street on the way into work. Crazy, huh?"

"I would say so! What a transformation! My goodness son, what a nice little car!"

1967 eased into 1968 so quietly and quickly that about all that made the transition memorable for Little Wally and his sister Melony was the New Years celebration. Brother and sister's time together at school seemed like a blur. Both had worked jobs to best of their ability, and held onto what grade averages were normal for them both. Melony went out with a senior classmate of Little Wally, named Thomas Dandy. Wally went out with a pretty and hot junior named Elizabeth Saran. Betty Saran, as she was called by most, was asked out by many, but rejected all but Wally Thornton, who she clearly had an eye for. Melony and Little Wally double dated on several occasions, the opportunity to share fun activities with her brother, were cherished times in Wally's final year.

This was a year when Little Wally was destined to become Mr. Walter Thornton. The eighteen year old marker was bearing down fast, and troubling news, both nationally and internationally, was presenting life decisions that were discussed by anyone and everyone. The end of January began the Tet offensive in Viet Nam. Viet Nam was already a hotbed of controversy, and by February, much of the confusing news, along with heavy life tolls, bred discussions among Wally's senior class that ran a wild gamut. All would have to register for the draft, some had already made plans to circumvent being utilized. Wally kept himself busy, and had been told flat out by old man Harvey that he could not wait to have him full time at the hardware store after graduation.

For the last the last three months before the graduation ceremony, Wally enjoyed all the last of his youth, finally attending the prom with Betty Saran. Melony even got to share that pleasure with her brother, as she was asked to the prom herself by her boyfriend Thomas. The four of them went in the cute little Rambler American, that looked as pretty as the four of them dressed up that night. After the prom, though, Wally made it clear to everybody that when he got his diploma that he was going to enlist in the Army, and avoid all the drama of waiting for the ax to fall in his direction. A terrible foreboding came over Melony that night.

As it happened, Wally was sworn into the Army just one month after he received his High school diploma. He was resigned to go, and made all the preparations, so that when he returned home, he could resume his life. Old man Harvey assured him that his job was safe when he returned. Harvey insisted that he keep in touch during every phase of the journey, from the training as Wally headed off to Fort Dix, all the way to where it finally took him.

The Rambler was treated like royalty. It was driven up on two boards on each side to get it off the ground it, cables disconnected, servicing completed so that damage to the car would be minimized. Then it was covered over with a canvas tarpaulin weighed down by bricks. The last thing that Wally saw when he secured the cover over the entire car, was his Collinwood Interstate Travelstars. The tires were as new as the first day he bought them, and the car just as shiny as it was the day he came out of the car wash that first day.

Obligations being what they were at the time, there wasn't much fear or thought put into leaving for the Army, other than leaving his job, family, and his girlfriend behind. Wally got a send off from all the people just mentioned, but did not feel any impact from it all until he sat in coach on his first plane ride ever. The last thing he saw were the faces of his family and Betty Saran, pressed against the glass of the terminal as the plane got pushed out into the runway. That kind of hit him hard, squeezing out sobs that he had no idea were ready to come out.

It turned out that Wally should have been concerned after all about his latest venture. Basic training was long, and arduous, lasting a couple of months. That process alone caused more than a few young men, boys really, to want their mommies. Wally hated it as much as the next guy, but weathered what needed to be done as well as anyone there, showing himself to be valuable. As a result, even though Wally had the impression that he would go home to visit before he was introduced to yet something else, he was moved to another base to join an infantry division. From there, he was deployed to a province in Vietnam during the Pacification under General Abrams to fight alongside some very tough, brave soldiers. While Wally comported himself well beside these men, he found himself wounded and dragged to safety by one of those same brave soldiers.

Patched up in a medical treatment facility, Wally was forwarded to hospitals to award him with excellent care. The soldier that pulled him to safety was killed in action before Wally could even thank him. The army awarded men such as these, their highest commendations, but America was less forthcoming with pats on the backs.

After all was said and done, Wally was sent home still in uniform, thanked by his country. He was to

resume his life, strong, tall, brave, and minus one leg. Scared, but optimistic, Wally hadn't settled into any kind of depression at all until he saw when he returned, that among the faces of the people he loved most, Betty Saran wasn't one of them. A tiny downward spiral started from that point. Everybody is different, but for Wally, he had less of a problem coping with the life and death dramas of war, than he had suddenly facing civilian life, and rejection with one leg. Up until then, he hadn't felt like any less of a person. Wally was realistic enough to accept there would be no hero's welcome, was encouraged that Harvey Schwartz was side by side with his parents and sister, but less than prepared
that he would be avoided by his girl.

In the weeks to come, he went through the motions. Wally was no different from thousands of other men. Care was excellent for the wounded. As soon as military medical establishment had put all the Humpty Dumpty's back together again they sent them home. Wally went through therapy, and ultimately fitted with a permanent prosthesis from the knee down on his right leg. Still, his dad left him at the hardware store in the morning and picked him up at the end of the day. Wally Sr had a job of his own, but made the sacrifice because he loved his son. Harvey was happy to have his hardware protégé back in house, but missed Wally's innate enthusiasm.

Melony somehow lost the brother she had before he left. It wasn't that she pushed Wally away, as much as the other way around.

Roberta Thornton watched her boy's spirit wain daily, and privately, it broke her heart.

After two months back at home, Betty Saran was neither heard or seen, even though Wally lowered himself to call. He did not try again.

At just twenty years old, Wally acted like an old man. One day on the way home from work on a Friday night, Wally Sr had had enough of the walking on egg shells and confronted his son man to man. “You know son, I don't understand. I wish I had your looks, and I damned well wish I was twenty again. You have your whole life ahead of you. You need to get back in the saddle again, son.”

"What would you have me do?" he said sharply. "Nobody will want me like this!"

"Are you kidding me. Except for a limp, nobody can even tell you have a handicap! You are as capable as I am, for God's sake. You have a car sitting by the side of the garage, and you haven't even looked at it. Here, I am carting you around. I do it because I love you, but your mother, sister, and I can't stand seeing you act like some kind of invalid when you know, and I know that you could kick my ass everyday and Sunday included!"

"Maybe tomorrow." Was all he said.

Saturday morning, the Thornton household sat at the kitchen table for breakfast...well, all but Wally at any rate. Wally languished in bed. He was awake but avoiding being cornered by his father again.

"...and you talked to him about it, right?" Melony asked her dad. Melony was going to college these days. It was rare to have both the Thornton kids at home at the same time, but really, Melony made the effort to be home that morning. The whole thing was part of an ongoing family discussion to bring Wally back to the world of the living. To bring back that fire and independence that he had before going into the Army. Melony needed to have him be the loving older brother that he was, too, not this self pitying man that he settled into being the moment he stepped off the plane. Mother, father, and sister all knew that losing Betty Saran was a significant part of it, could see it the minute he realized his girlfriend wasn't there when he returned home. That was when he felt less about himself. "NO... I am not going to allow this anymore." Melony declared. She pushed herself away from the table and marched toward her brother's bedroom.

"HEY...YOU! Up and at 'em buddy."

"Awww, go away." Wally pulled his pillow over his head.

"Uh-uh, not a chance. I came home this weekend to be with you. It was because I was excited that dad was going to talk you into taking the cover off your car. I was looking forward to helping you get the car running again. I thought this was a go, and I am very disappointed in you for dodging us the way you are. I want my brother back, now! So get your lazy ass out of bed before I get tough on you. You have one minute." She stormed out.

She could hear him stirring in the bedroom as she walked back to the kitchen.

A minute later to the dot, Wally walked into the kitchen. "Look you guys...I just want to say that I appreciate that you are all here for me, but taking the cover off my car will just remind me of the life I had before..."

"That's the point, dummy."

"More than that son, it's not doing a car that old any good at all just sitting there." Added his dad.

"Wally, did you ever think that it's Betty's loss that she left you like that and that she would have anyway?" Inquired Wally and Melony's mom.

"I agree." said Melony. "She sure acted like she was with you forever before you left. She turned into a little girl pretty fast. She went to another prom in our senior year you know."

Shocked at that last bit of info, Wally asked, "Why didn't you tell me that?"

"You didn't need to have that kind of news where you were. I love you. I wanted you to come home safe."

Wally threw up his hands in surrender. "Okay, okay. I give up. Is there any breakfast left before we go uncover the old girl?"

"What do you think, I changed overnight? Does anybody want more coffee?"

Wally Sr stood off to one side as Melony helped her brother as he began to take the tarp off the Rambler. Weather had taken its toll on the material. The canvas was rotted, and ripped as soon as it was touched. Something that was whole a minute earlier was reduced to strips of material that made a mess. Wally Sr brought a trash can from behind the garage to make it easier to dispose of the useless, wasted tarp material. The car underneath was filthy but okay. It was the Collinwood Interstate Travelstars that drew attention away from the car. They were brand new. Fresh from the store new. Whitewalls were as white as the day they were covered, a little over two years before. The next job was to charge up the battery, almost certainly dead after over two years of sitting. Then a couple gas cans needed to be filled to get some fresh gas in the tank. The car was left almost dry on purpose, a suggestion from Wally Sr at the time. After that, it was a matter of starting her up to do what she was designed for, run. Any car that sits, leave alone one as old as the Rambler runs the risk of rubber and seals drying out and leaking.

Wally got a battery charger in the garage while Melony retrieved two five gallon gas cans from the garden shed. Waly Sr poked around under the hood, checking the oil, still fresh and clean. Just idly playing around, he connected the battery cables, not even thinking about what he was doing, when sparks jumped when the positive lead hit the post. “Hey!” he exclaimed, surprised.

“Son, there is power in the battery still.” Wally Sr said when Wally and Melony returned. Is there any gas left in one of those cans, Melony?”

“Yeah, one is maybe half full.”

“That's impossible. The battery can't have enough charge in it to start the car after all this time. It was you, wasn't it? You had the battery all charged for me so you can get me behind the wheel again, didn't you dad?” Wally accused.

“I admit, we all want you to get in the swing of things again, but...no...no I didn't touch it. You saw the tarp fall apart. Nobody could have moved it without disturbing all that rot. No, I didn't do a thing. It's weird, that all. Look watch.” he disconnected and touched the positive terminal cable. It sparked. “Worst come the worst, I can run jumper cables from my car. Why don't you pour that gas in the tank and try her?”

Wally drew in a big breath and let it out as a sigh. “Okay, you guys all win. I have to tell you though, I'm kind of afraid to drive like...this.” he gestured toward his leg.

“You'll be fine. I have more faith in you than you do yourself.”

“Ditto that.” Seconded Melony.

Wally poured the gasoline in the tank, opened the driver side door, and sat behind the wheel. It felt good to him. "I have to admit, it feels pretty good to sit in her again."

"Pump it." Wally Sr said.

As soon as he tried though, it took some getting used to. He had no foot control, and instead he had to push on the accelerator much like with a stick, but pushed down with pressure from his knee. It was a strange sensation, a disconcerting one. Regardless, he pumped the gas as best he could manage. At least he had total control of his left leg for the brake and clutch, but his father, mother, and sister underestimated how hard it actually was.

"Try starting her up." urged Melony.

Oddly enough, the Rambler American that sat undisturbed for twenty six months started like it was only yesterday. She idled fast for about ten seconds and settled down to a purr. The old girl purred as nicely as a sewing machine stitching a continuous straight line.

"I wish my Ford would start like that!"

"Yeah! I'll trade you even up for my Chevy II right now." added Melony. "It gave me all kinds of trouble starting last winter."

"Climb in Melony. We'll drive to the gas station and then to the car wash. If I have a problem, you can take over. I really am scared, sis. I need you with me."

"What are little sisters for? Anything for my big brother. You know that."

When Wally drove off the boards the old car sat on for so long, she moved just fine. But when on the street, that is when it became evident the world had past the old girl by. It was a time of muscle cars. First up was the beeping. It wasn't just Wally's bad reaction time, it was a car that couldn't get out of the way fast enough. It was yet something else to get used to beside driving with an artificial prosthesis. The world was not going to suddenly be patient because Wally was struggling behind the wheel. If anything it would be even less so.

After getting gas, Melony turned out to be the patient one with her brother. "I think we need to take the car out on a long drive so that you can get familiar with driving her. I now see the trouble you are having, so I think it might be best to get out in the country and away from all the people in town. Why don't we take a ride up to my school? The road is quieter, and I can show you where I live these days. You haven't seen it at all, and it would make me so happy to show it to you. Why don't you take a left on Granite Road? It will take you to the Old State Road all the way to Kramden. When you reach Kramden, my dorm is just off of that, about, oh...maybe twenty miles or so."

"Are you sure? Now you know why I avoided this so long."

"I never gave a thought to how much trouble it is to drive a clutch with your leg. You are doing better already...yeah, I'm sure. The sooner you get used to driving, the better you will feel. You'll see."

The Old State Road was a perfect choice for Wally to get his artificial sea legs, so to speak. Driving with a clutch was quite a challenge, but the better he got at it, the better he felt. He had to physically pull his leg off the gas with his right hand and place it on the brake, pushing down on it to stop the car. In a way, not having a powerful car, was probably the best thing for Wally. Wally and car were meant for each other. By the time the day was finished, and Wally set the emergency brake back at home, he had become a lot more proficient, natural even. When going inside to see and report all that went on that day to their parents, Wally produced the biggest, warmest smile. He flashed it at his sister and drew her into a heartfelt embrace. "Thank you sis. I appreciate all that you just did for me."

"You would have done the same for me, I know that for a fact. I expect you to come up to see me anytime you have a chance. Now you know where I'm at. I could use the support. School isn't easy."

On Sunday morning, Wally was up early. In one day, he became very excited, plus he planned
to go to the car wash before heading to the hardware store. He was up before his parents, grabbed something quick to eat, and hit the road. When at the car wash, he got a shock. The car only needed one cycle to get it as clean, and new looking as the day he first washed it after buying the tires way back when. Every speck of grime washed away, leaving the car to look like he spent an entire day detailing it, complete with a wax job. He stood back, looking at the car with a look of shock on his face.

Oh, she wasn't perfect...nothing ever is...but she was as close as you could get. He touched one his Collinwood Interstate Travelstars, the driver side rear. It wasn't only that they looked brand new, but rubber spikes still protruded from the tread, remnants of the original molding process at the factory.

The reception that he got from old man Harvey was of pride. This was the boy he originally hired, the one that opened his heart to feel like he had a son. This was the boy that he wanted to leave his store to one day.

About two weeks after Wally started driving again, a blood curdling scream came from Wally's bedroom one morning. Roberta Thornton thought she was well beyond one of her kids having nightmares, but here she was, racing to her son's room. He was still screaming.

"Mom!" he screamed, almost to the point of hyperventilating. "Look! What's happening to me?"

Protruding from to end of his amputated leg from the knee down was ugly red bulbous growth. It was about six inches long.

"Oh my God, Wally. Does it hurt?"

"Very much. I can't strap on my leg. I don't know what to do, mom."

"I'll call Harvey and tell him I have to get you to the VA hospital. I'm gonna have to drive your car. Is that alright? Your father can go on to work. "

"Mom! I have a pair of crutches in the closet. Can you get them for me?" Wally winced. A sharp pain came from the afflicted area. It happened again. "Aaah, damned that hurts.!"

"We have to get you to the VA. I'll have your dad call Harvey. I'll help you get dressed so we can get out of here." Mom Thornton ordered.

Wally Sr wanted to help his son, but on crutches, Wally was in plenty of control, in spite of his pain. He was in the Rambler, waiting on his mom while she made sure Wally Sr called Harvey. In a few minutes, they were on their way. Wally cradled his head in his right hand. The pain increased.

"Are you going to make it to the hospital?"

COLLINWOOD INTERSTATE TRAVELSTARS

"I think so, but the pain is getting worse, and the infection is growing; it's much bigger."

"I'll hurry."

In thirty minutes, Mrs. Thornton pulled up to the VA admitting door. The people there sent them to the emergency entrance. All that time, the pain got even worse yet, and the infection had grown too. They got around back of the hospital at emergency. It was time for bureaucratic information taking. Mrs. Thornton handled that end while Wally sat. By then the pain was excruciating. When Roberta Thornton finished with the information takers, she returned to a son that had passed out. Wally succumbed to the pain.

Wally eventually was admitted. There wasn't anything that could be done for him in the emergency room. He was kept sleeping, under sedation. Wally had what was called, a metamorphosis on his leg, not an infection. By the time he was rolled on a gurney to a room, the growth on his leg was a red, translucent, almost embryonic protrusion that was determined to be a leg in the middle of regeneration.

Two days later, Wally walked out of the VA under his own power. Every test that could be performed on Wally could not solve the mystery, so he was allowed to leave because he couldn't be kept.

The years flew by. The Thorntons are still a close knit family. Melony owns a masters in business administration and owns her own company. She married a man named Walter, believe it or not, and has a daughter of her own. Tabitha is thirty six and is due to make Melony a grandmother two times over.

Mr. and Mrs, Thornton are in their eighties, retired, still living in the same house, doing very well, thank you very much.

Wally married a girl he met at the VA back when he had the strange episode with his leg. It was never determined how his leg grew back. In all the years since, nothing else unusual has happened to him, but his leg is fine. They have two boys, thirty seven and forty. Harvey and Walter are both the spitting image of their dad, though his wife Rhonda is about as attractive as it gets, even in her sixties. Between the two boys, five grandchildren were produced, Fred, Daniel, Christopher, Janette, and Walter.

Wally inherited Harvey's Hardware after he died, and although it grew, it still remains an old time hardware experience. Wally and his wife Rhonda live in what is now the suburbs of a city that in the seventies was the suburb itself. In his garage is parked his pride and joy, a vintage 1959 Rambler American, not looking a day older than it did in 1969. The engine was rebuilt once. It isn't his everyday driver these days but taken out often enough. She still sits on Collinwood Interstate Travelstars, the originals. They still have the little rubber knobbies sticking out from the molding process from the factory in which they were made—wherever that was. There is no reference to this factory anywhere. In all the searches ever done on the tires, nobody can tell Wally a thing about Collinwood. He hoped the company found their way back into business under another name so he could buy more of their tires. Over the years Wally searched several times. Nobody was ever able to find the company that made them, or the name, for that matter.

WARNING-KEEP OUT

WARNING-KEEP OUT

Because of budget constraints, vacation this year is going to equal day trips. Freida and I went ahead and scheduled time off from our jobs. The primary reason being, it was the only time we could manage to get time off together. There was only for a week, but if we didn't use it, we would have lost the vacation time.

The weather has been terrific, the forecast that it will continue. But it is still a week before Spring. Three weekends ago we had a stretch of unusually warm weather. Our friends, Freida, and I got together in the backyard, but money turned out to be the big drawback to do anything since. Oh well, such is life. But living on the gulf coast, gives us a significant advantage. There are a lot of opportunities for entertainment beyond calling yard work entertainment, which most certainly is not. So with less than a day to go, Freida and I spent time plotting where we would go, and what we would do with time off spent together.

"Come on Frank, what on earth could be better than the first day of vacation spent on a beach, coolers filled with food and drink, and your wife jammed into a bikini?" Freida tried her best to entice me that sometimes the simplest things are best.

"I think I can do you one better. How about this? We could try to find one of those side street motels near the beach to stay for the week, so we don't have to go back and forth from the house. The gas savings would make it worthwhile. It's early in the season, and we might be able to score a good rate. Come on, we could raise hell, you and I, don't you think?" I tried to sound upbeat.

"Can we afford it, Frank?" This was her way to get me to use common sense.

"Heck, I don't know. But we could spend time the first day going in and out of those places there along the beach that have vacancy signs on them and ask, what do you say?"

"Okay." she sighed skeptically. She would have been happier with the day trips.

"You worry too much. If you stopped worrying, you would relax."

"Frank, we don't really have any throw away money. Come on, don't shoot me for pointing out the obvious." Freida was feeling as though she was being roped into the idea. She really felt that this is how her and her husband got into the jams they continually stepped into in the first place. She felt Frank couldn't be happy with what he had. She never argued too much though, not being the argumentative type. As much as she loved Frank, she felt that his constant impetuousness was tiresome, with predictable results.

"Who knows when we might get time off together again, we should make the most of it while we can." I told my wife, noticing her reluctance, opting for verbal arm twisting.

"Alright, alright already, but no expensive eating out, and we are going to have to be happy whatever entertainment that we can find that's free."

"Now your talking!" I clapped my hands once.

The first day of vacation. I was as excited as a cockroach trapped in a box of Rice Krispies. I was up and about, putting things in the car already. Freida was beginning to stir from her first night to be able to sleep in. Letting her sleep as long as possible was in my best interest. I wanted her to get through the day without any complaints. I was planning to be on my best behavior, not that Freida ever would explode, but I know her. I know when she doesn't approve of something, she attacks by wordlessly extracting guilt. I had three cases of beer and five-five for ten dollar cases of pop in the trunk that my wife had no idea I bought yet. I found where we stashed the boogie and body boards, plus the cooler we had in the garage. Then I got the idea to make coffee so that I could nudge my wife due north of a good mood.

She smelled the coffee, got up and poured herself a cup, but before she drank, a suspicious Freida said, "What is it that you want, Frank?"

"Nothing. I just want you to have a good time so I can have a good time, that's all. I promise I'll be real good—you'll see. I just want to find a place cheap enough to stay there. Just so long as it doesn't have bed bugs and mattresses that we have to climb out of with rope and tackle.

WARNING-KEEP OUT

Freida chuckled. “Yup that would be just our luck. I suppose we should get going, cause what you're asking won't be easy. I see you were out in the garage. Did you happen to see the aluminum chairs and umbrella?”

“Oopsie, I didn't think of that, shoot. I'll be right back.”

“I'll start packing I guess.” she said, backed into a corner.

The actual real drive to the beach area from where we lived was only about a forty five minutes. It was a daunting task to find a place to stay so we could access the long powder sand beach strip. It was carefully guarded by building after building, it was even hard to see the water. Even if we were to find a suitable motel or cottage, we would still be faced with walking to the nearest beach access, again, guarded like Fort Knox with private properties. Some areas were affluent, others choked with resorts. One area was chock a block full with the kind of places that we sought, but we were still two hours into the search without a place. It seemed perfect, a much more residential in feel to it, with stores and supermarkets. So Freida and I parked in a beach access parking lot, put enough money in the meter to prevent incurring a parking fine, and began hiking.

No place had everything because if it did, it cost too much. But one place that we found was more like apartments than a motel. There were a string of small homes, at least that is what they seemed. The sign above the office door read; 'I Sea U efficiencies'. Freida and I went in to investigate, and for the seven nights we wanted to stay was three hundred fifty. I promptly booked before he changed his mind.

I made small talk with the owner while he completed booking us. “Catchy name, 'I Sea U'.” I pointed out.

The owner came back with, “I needed a name like that because we have three kinds of clientèle. Customers like you I notice as soon as 'I Sea U' walking down the street. In your case, I just knew you were looking for someplace nice that you could afford. Last week we had some of the Spring break crowd. Rooms went for a premium, but the best place for some of those college kids was right here at 'I Sea U'. Before the weather gets hotter and hotter, and we go into the high season, the older crowd book heavy while it is still a little cooler looking for a deal. I mean real old people, and the perfect place for them is the "I Sea U'."

"Funny." said Freida, nonplussed, expecting to see scary for the kind of price. She wasn't about to flash the pearlies before she found out if she was being bamboozled to stay in a hive dive.

Freida's room inspection was both painstaking and meticulous because our rental seemed too good to be true. Just before entering the front door was a step up porch to sit out on at night, even though the view didn't include the panoramic views of the gulf, it would still be a nice spot to sit out at night to absorb the festive vibrations of vacationers walking up and down the main drag that housed live entertainment, places to eat, and gift shops. Inside was indeed an efficiency, and though it had no stove, did sport a decent sized microwave, and a small fridge. The package provided an opportunity for enjoyment with some of the conveniences of home. We promptly hiked back to the area that we parked so we could bring in and unpack our gear. So far, my end of the promising was holding up.

For the better part of an hour, we unpacked our stuff. "Where did all this beer and pop come from?" My wife asked, seeing it all for the first time.

"I bought it before I came home from work yesterday. I figured we would save a fortune buying it for less back home rather than at the resort area here." I said trying my best to make good common sense.

"Yeah, well..."

"What's that supposed to mean?"

"It's a lot of drinking."

"I'm not driving, and I'm on vacation."

"I just thought that if we were going to do this, we would have some romantic alone time together."

"We will, baby, we will, I promise."

"Yeah, well..."

"Okay, I won't drink tonight. Is that what you want to hear?"

"YES!.... YES!.... That's what I want to hear, alright? "

"I'm sorry baby. Alright, it will just be you and

me." I said, backing away from the edge in my tone. I was shocked to hear my wife get so vocal all of a sudden because the woman never gets vocal. I wish I could make her understand that I'm just not capable of hanging out without a few beers under my belt. The way this was going to work is to put a six pack at a time in the fridge during the day.

"Do you want to go for a walk, and check this beach out or what?"

Freida paused for a second, then replied, "Yeah, that would be nice, why not?"

The entrance to the beach closest to us was at the end of the same side street our cottage was on. There was a little alley where the cottages almost closed off the gap that lead to a wooden walkway bridge to the beach. The aqua color of water on the gulf when we got on that bridge nearly took Freida's breath away. Freida and I went straight to the waterfront. The wet surface was easier to walk on. There wasn't much of a lounge beach area at the end of the walkway, but plenty of selection within easy hoofing, but up ahead in the distance is what interested me. There was an expanse of green up against the beach instead of buildings, a place to slip away and explore, and we were headed that way. Freida was looking down, searching for shells, and I was looking up, inching closer and closer to the green expanse. With every footstep, my curiosity peaked further.

When we were even with the green expanse, it became even more attractive. It was one of those coastal hammocks that was jammed with scrub palms, sea oats, and an assortment of yellow flowers, but the middle had a stand of oak and live oak trees that had privacy written all over them. Unfortunately, the cedar log fence surrounding the nearly square mile enclave was written all over it too. That writing said, "Warning-Keep out, Unsafe Areas, Please Stay Out For Your Own Safety, and Fragile Dunes And Sea Oats-Stay Out." Every warning known to man was posted somewhere on the expanse facing the beach. I couldn't see through it because about a half square mile of the middle was thick with foliage.

WARNING-KEEP OUT

What I could see was an abandoned shed on a low foundation almost hidden from view behind the trees and brush, no tracks leading up to it at all. I had this urge to be nosy more than I ever have in my life. Being forbidden made it even more attractive, and I thirsted for a drink.

Freida and I kept on walking, long past the green area. The shells Freida was collecting adding up so much, I had to take off my shirt to make a makeshift sack to carry them all. I wish the contented look on Freida's face would stay plastered on forever, much preferable to the wary expression she wears most of the time these days. From time to time she would stand in the water, looking out to the horizon, her gaze suddenly drawn by the appearance of a dolphin breaking the surface. Standing almost knee deep, she was so very attractive hiking up the sexy cover up she wore over her swim wear, hair blowing in the ocean breeze. For now, this was acceptable time spent, and I found myself easily devoting the time to it without any other thought.

It got to be well into the afternoon, and we were both getting hungry, but Freida didn't want to head back. She wanted to continue on, stopping for fast food so we could keep on going. I was becoming antsy about it. My nerves began crawling on my epidermis, causing me to scratch.

"We can't go to eat right now." I had to point out.

"Why not?"

"Because I don't have a shirt on."

"Easy fix, not to worry." she said unyielding. "Wait here."

My wife trash picked in a refuse receptacle on the beach for a discarded plastic bag, finding two. She placed one bag in the other, re-purposing them to carry the shells. She shook out the tee shirt and handed it back to me, saying, "Voilà."

"It's a little wet." My skin crawled even more.

"It'll dry, it's only water."

This far down on the jetty was a clump of eating establishments. We entered one of the burger joints there and chose out a booth. Freida sat down and told me what she wanted so that I could order. I stood in line, hand over my mouth, holding my face, frown on the part you could see. It was clear to me I had a real a problem here. I needed to find a solution, or this was going to be a hell of long a week if I could get through it at all.

A couple cheap burgers made me feel a little better. But the smug satisfied triumphant look that spread across Freida's face irritated me somewhat. I am sure she would say that the look was only contentment, and I did not want to get into it with her.

After eating, we resumed our trek on the beach, passing resort after resort. Some had live music going on at poolside bars, an instant attraction for me. I was too afraid of an argument to point them out, so we kept on the steady slow pace until we found ourselves clear at the end of the long jetty, at least in that direction. It emptied us in a spot with a few upscale gift shops, classy restaurants, yacht clubs, and, to my relief, a shuttle stop that would return us back to where we came from. We stood with a group of people waiting for the same shuttle.

Freida asked me full out, "Are you okay? You don't look so good." Very perceptive of her.

"I'll be alright." I lied.

The shuttle pulled up, so we climbed aboard and found out the price of the fare. I slid dollar bills into the change counter to cover my wife and I, and sat down. There were people smiling in my direction, and I just knew they were going to try and engage me in conversation. They weren't my kind of people, and I didn't feel like talking, but Freida came to the rescue. I didn't really hear what was said, but glad not to participate. I kept myself busy looking out the windows at the sights we passed by, occasionally stopping to let a passenger out. Then we passed the green area from the street side. There was a chain link on the street side of the green expanse, but was posted just as much as I had seen on the beach. I sat up straighter, composing a plan while trying to tame an edgy nervous system. An idea to create an escape area to deal with a problem that was going to have to be dealt with one way or the other. Tonight was a separate issue, and should be able to be gotten through, but tomorrow...

"We need to get off now Frank." My wife said, breaking my concentration." We got off the bus and made our way to the efficiency, but I stopped at the trunk of my car, opened it, broke open the first case of beer, and took out a six pack to bring into the room. I saw the expression on Freida's face, but ignored it as embracing my personal right. Moderation, right? What would there be to criticize? I went all day. I held them up for inspection and asked, "It's okay, right?" Not that she had a choice.

"Oh sure, that's fine, just fine."

I could tell by the tone...'fine,just fine.' Those were code words right there. I cracked open a warm beer on the way to the room, downing the barley and hops nectar, barely tasting the first half of the can. I was going to need two more beers just to make a difference. Then I would slow down. There's no sense pushing all my wife's buttons the first night, or the rest of the week for that matter. The green area...

It is the second day of vacation, and my wife is gone, the bed is empty. Maybe I slept like a log because I didn't feel her get out of bed...Huh? Where is she?... Oh my God!...Get your lazy ass out of bed and find your wife! I jumped out of bed as soon as realization hit me full in the face that she must have been turned off the night before. I scrambled to find clothes to pull on quick so I could hunt her.

She wasn't on the porch, the car was still in the lot. That left the beach and the office. In a panic, I broke into a run to cover the two spots. Not in the office—the beach, must be the beach. I ran over the wooden walkway leading to the beach...Where? Where? Oh my God, there! Freida was walking the beach—Wheeew! What a relief! I left her alone to go for coffee and donuts, or danish, or something for when she came back to the room. I have to show her I love her so that she doesn't stop loving me back.

It wasn't that far away down the street to get what I needed. Two large coffees, cream, extra sugar, and cinnamon buns, and I was headed back in no time flat. Freida was on the porch, and when I came into view with a paper mache carrier containing two cups and a bag, it was plain to see where I had gone. She broke into a smile, lifting some of my apprehension. She bought the consideration angle. The green area...

"I want to get a little sunbathing in today, Frank. Nothing fancy, a walk later, but I'll be damned if I go back to work after a week off tireder than when I left. I don't want to party or any of that other stuff. I know you—you'll be wanting to draw a crowd, and I want to left out of it. I don't know if you even want to join me?"

"It sounds pretty boring to me." I conceded. "I brought the boogie and the body surfing boards. Do you mind if I play with them a little later?"

"No, but the water is still pretty cold this time of year. That sounds like torture. The most I want to do is wade. Look, I'm happy relaxing if you don't mind. Go ahead and play if that is what you want. Don't let me stop you."

So Freida and prepared to find a spot in the sun. I carried the cooler packed with pop, a six pack of beer on ice, sandwiches and fruit, and a blanket on top. Freida carried the folding chairs and an umbrella. The spot she staked was about half way from the wooden walkway and the green area. My mind instantly scrambled to imagine ways to get into the area to explore. This was starting to work out better than I'd hoped. I helped her spread the blanket out, the cooler on one corner. Both chairs faced away from the water, or the sun would be at our backs. But I faced the green area which began to taunt me and call my name.

Little by little, the beach took on more and more visitors on this sun soaked beautiful day. The wind was gentle, the waves making a constant splooosh, splooosh sound in the absence of any real swells. Listening to happy children sitting at the edge of the water building imaginary cities in the wet sand, feet soaking in the shallow pools, creating by digging close to the water. It was more than enough excitement for Freida.

I sat patiently at first, staring, imagining, plotting a way to get into the green area. About two hundred feet away from us stood an elevated lifeguard chair, a pretty but muscular babe in orange sat like a queen, intently taking in any prospects leading to danger. After an hour, while Freida's eyes began to flutter, I got up, fished out a beer from the cooler, and made my move to explore. One eye opened a little, and Freida asked, "Leaving?"

WARNING-KEEP OUT

"I'm just going to check out that area over there. I'll be right back." I slowly strode over to the green, figuring to climb over this end of the triple slatted split log fencing facing the beach. From there, I could slip into the woodsy section in the middle and conceal myself. I moved into position, and took a quick look around to see if I was watched or not. I took a breath, and with my unopened can of beer in hand, swung one leg over the fence. I did not even touch a foot to the other side before shrill whistling came from the girl sitting in the lifeguard chair, who dismounted very quickly, and ran in my direction, whistle still trilling loudly drawing the attention of just about everybody on the beach, including Freida. Freida thought I might have hurt myself, and came running at me. Within earshot of the whistling, the entire beach was gaping at me. The fence was high enough that my torso prevented the foot over the fence from touching the ground.

"Sir, I have to ask you to get your leg out of the restricted area, or I will have to radio dispatch, to have you forcibly removed from the beach, and you will not be allowed to come back or arrested, whichever is deemed appropriate" stated the lifeguard to me.

Freida had a mortified expression on her face. I could tell that romantic interludes planned for the night were irrevocably canceled. All I could do now to salvage my day was to give her something to be mad about for real. But on the off chance that she might not condemn me, I took my leg out of the area and moved toward my wife. As soon as I did, the occupants of the beach went about their business. But Freida turned on the ball of her right foot, and began marching back to the blanket. I only noticed a barely discernible negative head shake. I caught up with her in about twenty odd steps or so.

"Freida, I'm so sorry. I got a little bored, and I was curious what was in that wooded area in the middle there."

"Frank, it's alright, okay? I understand bored. I just wish you would avoid embarrassing yourself. I'll just stay over here and mind my own business and stick to my original plan. Why don't you drink that beer in your hand? You know you want to."

The truth of it was that now I wanted something

much much stronger. The beer, for me, was only a party drink, a cover up, a diversion. I wanted to use the beer to enjoy myself socially, but she didn't want any part of it. I pulled the tab on the beer and moved away from the wife. I love her, she's a good woman, and a great looking package. But the woman can't allow herself to have a good time, and what's even worse, doesn't want me to either.

What I did after that seamy episode, was go back to the room to get some clothes on with shoes so I could case the green area for another way to get in. I left my wife to turn barbecue red in the sun if that is what she wanted. I guess she never learned about the dangers of UV index. It will give me ammunition later when I need excuses.

I hit the street area scoping out the stores in the vicinity because I intended to buy myself a bottle. But for now, my main priority was finding a way to get into the green area so I could get away from the guilt trip that Freida was inflicting on me.

The chain link out in front of the green area ran building to building. The side facing the beach was corralled by the triple rail split log fence for aesthetic reasons, the chain link in front for security. Why would they be watching this natural area so closely? Closely or not, the way in was from the beach side at the corner closest to the street, and at the furthest end away from the lifeguard. From that vantage point, I could easily slip into the woods from the street side, unnoticed by the pit bull standing guard on the beach. I smiled to myself. The only thing left was to buy me a bottle, slip in, enjoy it when I wanted, and keep Freida happy at the same time. She'll never know the difference. Heck, she thinks the beer is my drink of choice. One or two beers here and there, my breath will smell like beer and not vodka. It will be just like I am home. I will survive this week.

I kept my bottle in a brown bag, and with it in hand, I slipped onto the beach from an access on the other side of the green area. With a little luck, maybe nobody will notice me coming from the other side, duck into the corner about four or five hundred feet from the lifeguard. Then it will be a simple matter to hop the fence and into the woods. My hope was that the shack, or whatever it is can hide my bottle of vodka so it will be there when I want it. That's all I want it for.

“Good, I made it to the corner unseen, quick glance around—do this—now! I made it over the fence, excellent, and I'm completely shielded from sight from either the street side, or the beach. Let's
see now, where would the building be? There aren't any paths. Straight, just walk straight ahead, I'm bound to run into it.” I reasoned to myself.

I walked two to three hundred feet into the woods. Thick it was, it seemed like nobody else ever thought to come in here, ever. Somebody must have once, or there would not be a structure in here, where ever it is.

“Ow.” something had bit my ankle. “Oww.” I yelped again. “What the...” I reached down to have a peek at what bit me, pulling up my pant legs. My ankles were crawling with red ants, so many of them, my feet looked like a bee keeper covered in bees. They were creeping up my pants, very quickly, biting all the way. Before I could think of what to do next because I was too busy screaming, a whole family of possums came out of nowhere and attacked me too. I got bit so hard, in addition to the ant bites that I fell to my knees, now on all fours. The ants crawled up my hands and onto my arms, I had nasty chunks taken out of my face, neck and back by the possums joining forces. Then some birds came. I don't know what kind they were, but they were efficient peckers. I was screaming for all I was worth. Pain on pain, all of it was too much to handle, and I could not scream...anymore....

A police car was parked in front of unit A. Freida was on the porch explaining to the officer that her husband had not returned back to the room the night before. “The car is still here, but my husband is nowhere to be seen.” She said.

“Did you have any arguments that would trip him off ma'am?” the officer asked.

“Well, no, but he did cause some trouble yesterday on the beach when he tried to enter the restricted green area on the beach. That's pretty much the last time I heard from him. He embarrassed himself fairly badly, and I went back to sun bathing."

"The green area down the street here?" Asked one of them.

"Yes, that one, why?"

The two officer's eyes met for a second, then one of them said, "He probably ran off. You will have to wait a full twenty four hours before you file a missing persons report. For now, we suggest that you try to relax."

"Freida! You look wonderful! You look so rested." said Regina, Freida's boss when she returned to work fresh on Monday morning. "How did you manage to look so awesome in a week?"

"Oh I don't know. I got a load off my mind I guess. I read three books and got some sunbathing in, thanks."

NEW GLASSES

NEW GLASSES

"E....F.....P........T.........O..........D?"

"That's enough, Mr. Snow. Please put your hand over the other eye now. Can you read the chart?"

"E.....P.....D........Z........Q??"

"I've got the idea, Mr. Snow. Why don't you have a seat in the chair? We're going to have Kay here have a quick look at some things, I'll be back in a few. Okay?"

"When was the last time you had an examination, Mr. Snow?" Kay asked curiously.

"I have never had an exam that I can remember, why?"

"Well it depends if you've taking the bus, or driving. If the answer is driving, I want to move to another town."

"Oh come on, Kay, it's not that bad, is it? You can call me Barry, by the way, I'm not really the mister type there, beautiful."

"You're going to have a whole new outlook by the time you leave here, Barry. There's going to be a bunch of people besides me you won't be calling beautiful anymore. You are almost legally blind you know."

"Why Kay, don't you think you are beautiful?"

"Well, no, I'm no looker, but I'm beautiful on the inside. That's what people say, anyhow."

"I think that's an awful thing to say, and if somebody actually said that to you, then they aren't beautiful on the inside, and I don't think they could recognize real beauty if they stubbed their toe on it." She smiled at Barry's efforts to charm. Privately, she wondered if getting new glasses would change his charming outlook? By the time she had finished with the preliminary exam, she had grown to enjoy Barry's engaging personality. "Barry, have you got a ride home after the visit? The doctor is going to put some drops in your eyes that might make you see worse than you do now."

"No, but I'm walking anyway. I live in those apartments over there across the Boulevard. Besides, I don't have anyone to do that sort of thing for me today, my friends are all working, or busy, and I don't drive or have a car."

The doctor entered the examination room for

the lengthy exam. When the doctor finally finished, Barry joined Kay out in front to choose suitable frames. The problem with that was he could not really see himself good enough in the frames to make any choices. Women are better at that sort of thing anyway. He allowed Kay the honor of making him look bad or good. Kay tried on several pair, none of them seemed to satisfy what it was she was looking to achieve. "You know Barry, there were some new frames that just came in from a different provider other day. I need something that doesn't cover your whole face, but not so small that they hide those blue eyes of yours. I think that I saw something in there that might work. Why don't you have a seat at this table, and I'll just get that box from in back, okay?"

A minute or so later she had the box of frames, and a pair of frames from it in hand when she returned to the patient man. "Okay Barry, I was right. I think I have just what you need." She said while sliding into a rolling chair across the table from Barry. Kay slid them on, ever so gently, as though she thought she might poke an eye out or something. Whatever the reason, it seemed he was in safe hands because she exclaimed, "Ahh!! Perfect. These are just what you need. She poked and prodded, felt behind his ears, made sure the nose piece didn't pinch, then took measurements as to where the different parts of the lens were aligned to his eyes. "I can adjust them further if they are pinching. How do they feel?"

"Good. Just fine. I probably look like a nerd. Oh wait a minute, I am a nerd!"

"Stop it Barry! You look very handsome as a matter of fact. You know, a lot of people wear non-prescriptions just because it's fashionable. I just want to give you some of that. Now you have to leave because you have an hour wait." After a small pause she said, "I'm kidding. You can wait here if you want, or you can go get something to eat and come back later. It's up to you. I'd rather you sit over there so I can look at you because I think you're cute." Kay must have slipped up by saying something she was thinking out loud because she blushed as red as a beet. Barry decided to stay put, so that when he ventured out from the vision center it would be with something new, the gift of sight. It wasn't as though he wasn't used to the way he was, but when it came down to it, just reading the magazines in the waiting area gave him with a headache. As far as Kay's flattery was concerned, Barry couldn't see that even with new glasses.

“Mr. Snow?... Mr. Snow?... Mr. Snow?” It took three times to break Barry's trance. His mind somewhere else, he heard nothing for a few seconds, nor did he notice Kay's smiling, floating by several times during the hour wait, trying to get his attention. Snapping out of it, his face cleared, acknowledging the hail from the technician that his glasses were ready to be fitted. He jumped up and was ushered to one of the tables with mirrors on them. Kay sat down across from him, took the new prescription from a plastic tray, and gently put them on Barry's face. Kay pointed to the mirror and said, “What do you think?” It took him the same amount of seconds to break him from his trance as it did when he was in the waiting area. He gazed across the table at Kay; indeed, he seemed stunned. “Barry, what do you think?” Kay prodded him again for his opinion.

“Hmm? Oh, beautiful, just beautiful. Pretty face, hazel eyes. You're stunning, really. Now that I can really see you...”

“Ah...no, Barry. I mean, what do you think of the glasses on you? The mirror's there.”

“Umph, what a doofus, I'm sorry. The glasses look fine. I can see, I can't believe it!”

“Can you read the card on the table there?”

“Uh-huh; E, FP, TOZ, LPED, PECFD, FELOPZD, DEFPOTEC, LEFODPCT, FDPLTCEO, FEZOLCPTD.”

“You can read all that, and you think I'm stunning?”

“Prettiest girl I've ever seen in my life.”

“I don't think so. Now, Felice over there, is the definition of pretty.”

“Huh?” Barry leaned in closer to whisper, “Kay, she might be very nice, but that is not an attractive woman—at all.”

This made Kay frown. Barry had just read the chart on the table to the littlest letters on the page. But Felice was definitely one of the hottest people on two feet, and Kay no spring chicken. Okay looking as average middle age goes, but nothing unique. Barry paid for the glasses in full, and had to say goodbye, as pleasant as his office visit was. When he left, chances were high that he would put the experience, and the lovely Kay, behind him, but he was still very much taken with how beautiful she was. Now on foot, Barry figured to take his time going home, walking across the lot to the bank to replenish his pocket money. Then he planned to go to the food market for some basic necessities, and something good to eat when he finally got home. Barry's new glasses made him feel like a new man. He walked taller and straighter than he did going into the Optical House. The first thing he noticed was how gorgeous the vivid blue sky was. The second thing he noticed were the people, ugly people and beautiful people. There was no in between, and no average folks. As he traversed the parking lot to the bank, he noticed trucks, all kinds of trucks. Trucks with powerful roaring engines, chrome, dual cabs, and tinted windows. Then there were the cars in competition with the trucks, cars with expensive exhausts, fancy wheels with skinny tires, loud—loud on loud sound systems, pumping out distorted sound like mini parades. All of them, in and out of the parking lot calling attention to themselves. The faceless owners behind tinted windows all seemed to need validation that they were the most bad ass of them all, or just deaf. Barry shook his head at the materialistic display.

When Barry came to the bank, four or five of those same cars were waiting their turn at the outside ATM machines. Barry went to the inside tellers, but there were lines inside too. He stood in one of them. There was a man in the second line, a very, very, ugly man. Barry knew from looking at him that he was up to no good, so he watched. Something tangibly wrong was about to happen, he could see it. The man inched ahead of Barry because the line was a bit faster, probably because of the kinds of transactions at that window. Barry's eyes never left the man, who was next in line to go to the window. The man walked up to the window, said something to the teller, and something clicked in Barry. It was the teller's face, a very pretty face that told it all. He saw fear in that pretty face. Barry broke out of line before another second went by, rushed the man, who at the very same time started to turn around with a gun in his hand to say something, Barry hit him like a defensive corner back, ramming him into the marble counter, dislodging the gun. Barry picked it up off the floor before he could react, trained it directly at him. A guard appeared, apparently witnessed the whole escapade. The guard took over from there, Barry handing him the gun. Before long the police came, and Barry lauded as a hero when the story unfolded. One of the officers asked Barry full out, what it was that tipped him off like that.

"I saw the man, knew he was trouble the first time I saw him. Then I saw a robbery about to happen in slow motion, so slow that I could react faster than the robber. I just knew I could stop it by surprising the man." The officer who asked the question was a squared off masculine type, a very good looking man. Whereas, the officer who handcuffed the robber, and aimed the robber into the backseat of the cruiser, was ugly. The whole good looking, ugly thing was grating on Barry's nerves, except, that's exactly how it was. Everybody he saw fit into one of two categories, ugly, or beautiful. Obligatory thank you-s were exchanged at the bank. There was picture taking for the local newspaper too. After all the torture, Barry was allowed to leave for the supermarket, and the rest of his day. As Barry retraced his steps across the parking lot to the market, he walked in front of the Optical House. Kay was out the door, concern creasing her absolutely gorgeous face. Quite obviously, she had watched him because she knew he went to the bank and that something bad had happened there.

"We heard there was a robbery over at the bank. I saw you go in, but not come out. I worried something happened to you. Are you alright?"

"I'm fine, just fine. Some slug thought he would rob the bank while I was in line. I had tackled him before anybody got hurt though."

"Say what...you tackled him? You could have been killed, Barry!"

"No, that's just it. I can see things a heck of a lot better since you put these glasses on my face."

"Well, thank you for the compliment, but you still could have been killed." She scolded.

She did not understand, and Barry knew it, so he

changed tact a bit. “If I had not of tackled him, he was turning to face innocent people when I made him drop his gun. He could have hurt us all.”

“So now you're my hero too.”

“I wasn't trying to be anybody's hero. I saw something nobody else saw, that's all. These glasses take a bit of getting used to, I'll tell you.”

“Just take it easy Barry, alright? I have to get back inside, it is close to closing, but I don't want you to be a stranger, okay?”

Barry left, turning twice to look back at Kay still standing there, arms folded across her chest, staring after him a moment longer as he was walking toward the supermarket. He grabbed a loose carriage left by the door, and entered to see a whole bunch more he couldn't explain and didn't want to. He was seeing things that were just plain crazy. There wasn't much produce in the produce department that Barry wanted to buy. The fresh spices were pretty nice, but most everything else had the appearance that was close to rotting. This was Barry's regular store, but it was horrible. Needing to get out of the disgusting department, he moved to where the condiments and salad dressings were, but where it should have been okay to open his eyes, instead were bottles and jars of chemicals, the kind you might see on a polluted stagnant stream, except all different sugary colors. The visuals weren't screaming 'buy me'. Moving along, Barry rolled his cart into the deli meat area, in his mind, a safe zone. He wanted to pick up something good to eat out of the department, but changed his mind when he saw what was offered. Behind glass were rows of meats with strange ingredients covered with salt and modified food starch. It is probably best not describing the chaffing pans of assorted cooked foods, or even the pre-made sandwiches. There was an ugly man stacking meats in the meat cooler sections off an aluminum rack. The beef that was presented for sale was dark green but worse than that was the thought of the ugly man touching the same meat that he might otherwise have bought. The experience sent Barry ducking into another aisle to escape the science fiction visuals, only to be plunked into the packaged food section. In that aisle, he got to see the real contents in the pictures on the fronts of the bagged and boxed products without looking at the ingredient list on the back. He slowed down at the end of the row of packaged foods for a little breather, then he resumed shopping in canned goods. This was rewarded with neatly stacked cans with pictures of dead food on them. It was even worse in the dairy section. Sickened, he lost his appetite altogether, and moved to the entrance of the store to escape the menagerie of goods. Barry burst out the store front entrance into the fresh air, gulping it to level off the overwhelming sensation to retch. He was hunched over, grabbing his knees, when a familiar voice called his name from the inside of a car passing by him. It was Kay. “Barry! Get in the car, I will take care of you.”

Barry would have taken any help at the point, but vertigo was added to the nauseousness he had been experiencing, and he was too helpless to move. It was at that lowest point so far that he accepted the life ring tossed in his direction from Kay. She got out of the car, opened the door for Barry, then had to help him into the car. All of this was to the consternation of the inconvenienced drivers behind her, who to her credit, she utterly ignored when the beeping and swearing began.

“The things I'm seeing...” Barry uttered as she had an arm around him to keep him from falling over.

“Get out of the way, bitch. Like, what the f....” Yelled the guy directly behind her, who could have gone around her at any time he chose. Barry glancing up on the way to the car from the curbside noticing an almost evil malevolence in the face of the driver. As soon as Barry was seated in the car, Kay shut the door, and ran around to the driver's side to pull away quickly. Kay didn't want to incite a riot, so she pulled into to closest open spot she could find so that she could assess Barry's problem. Barry finally caught a breath. In the car with Kay, there was an absence of the continual assaults on his sight. Kay was beautiful, her car, just a car.

“Oh my God, what a relief, thank you Kay.”

“What the heck is wrong, Barry? Do you need to go to a hospital or something? You really don't look too spiffy, I have to say.”

“I feel a little better, now that I'm in the car with

you. It's these glasses. I'm seeing things. The food in that the store was making me sick. Every thing was horrible, Kay."

"What do you mean seeing things? Seeing better, you mean? Sometimes when people get new glasses, there is an adjustment period. People actually get dizzy."

"No Kay, I mean seeing things. Horrible things. People are not just people. They are either ugly or beautiful like you. The food in the store, well I tried to tell you before. It was horrible looking. The people stocking the shelves weren't anybody I want to touch my food. I don't know what else to say."

"Where do you live? Can I take you home?"

"Sure, I'd like that. How did you happen to come by and see me?"

"I finished and locked up for the day. I was headed home myself and saw you out front of the store. I'm very concerned about you. Explain to me what you are seeing."

Barry pointed at a man unlocking his car door. "Do you see that man over there? What do you see?"

"I see a man unlocking his car door"

"I know that, but tell me exactly what he looks like."

"What? Do you mean about six feet, about one ninety, black hair, fairly good looking?"

"Ugly as sin, Kay. I can hardly keep my eyes on him. Hideous, actually. Same size as you see, but a dark foreboding face, his eyes are big, bulgy, wet, and cruel. Mouth with a permanent scowl. Big nose, pointed, long. He must get it stuck in places it shouldn't be. His ears are shaped like a little bit like mouse ears, but big. He has dirty hands like the meat guy in the supermarket. The man is not your typical man next door, and that is what I am complaining about. It's not that people are homely, but cartoon caricature ugly. How about that woman pushing the carriage there?"

"She's about five foot six, brown hair, plain, about like me."

"Gorgeous, almost as pretty as you, but nobody could compare to you. I can't see how anybody could take their eyes off you, or her either."

Kay stayed where she was in the parking lot, only just starting to get a grasp of Barry's problem, but not really believing the scope of it. "What made you sick and want to leave the supermarket?" She asked.

Barry described in detail his ordeal to the woman. He went on and on, right up to the point where he could not take it any longer, and she found him out front.

"So you never got anything for you to eat for tonight then?"

"No, and I really don't want to go back in there. So far, the bank went horribly wrong for me. The supermarket was off the hook. Even the walk across the parking lot was too much to handle."

"Could I take you someplace to eat before I take you home?"

The thought of going into a restaurant and seeing more of the same was an instant turn off. "I don't think I could handle seeing the same kinds of things I saw in the supermarket."

She looked over at the passenger sitting in her car, a look of extreme concern on her pretty face. Kay was trying to determine if he was a whack job. He might not have deserved the scrutiny since Barry had not asked for help. He was a gentleman, not pushing for anything out of turn with her, his real priority was an all out effort to control whatever the affliction was that was attacking him with such ferocity. When it came down to it, how did he see a robbery about to happen before the robber himself made a move? Kay made up her mind to not to deposit him to be helped by others as opposed to trying to help him herself. "Would you do me a favor?"

"Sure, what is it?"

"Take off your glasses, and look at me."

"Okay, I can do that." He took off his glasses, the familiar way he saw the world, a refreshing breather. Slowly, he turned his gaze to Kay, but when he did, she was just as stunning without the glasses as with them on. "Kay, you're still as gorgeous as the first time I saw you.

"What about out there?" She asked, pointing through the windshield toward people on the sidewalk.

NEW GLASSES

"All back to normal. People are people again."

"But you still think I'm a looker?"

"Yes. You actually had me scared to look at you."

"Proof that you're crazy. Leave the glasses off for a little while. Let's go into 'Lettuce Eat Hearty Buffet' so you can enjoy a meal without distractions. I think we should experiment after dinner, okay by you?"

Dinner went really well, even avoiding the subject for just a little while getting to know one another. Kay was further blown away when she got wind of the fact that Barry was a Registered Nurse from St. Vince Hospital. It certainly cast Barry in a different light from what she first thought of him, but it begged the question, how did he function at work when he barely read. His answer was that he was used to using reading glasses bought at the drug store if he needed to write reports and such. The conversation only prolonged the inevitable, the subject unavoidable, so it was tackled half way through the meal.

Kay began, "You know, I have a theory about all of this, but it's going to sound dumb."

"I'll be the judge. Tell me what you've got."

"I think the glasses are allowing you to see the truth about the way things really are, except for me of course. I don't have an explanation for that craziness at all. But we need to put those glasses to the test. Before I take you home, we need to try something."

"Yeah, try what? Personally, right now, I would rather see the world through rose-colored glasses, than glasses that let me see the world the way it really is any day. I don't think I could have eaten if I put those glasses back on, do you?"

"Let's put it to the test. After we leave here, let's take a ride to Organic World to finish your shopping. Let's see if there is any good in the world. What do you say? I haven't done any shopping for the week, and it's one of my favorite places to get food. We can shop together. What do you say?"

"What if the glasses just give me choices of good against bad? What if there's no good food? Not to change the subject, but I'm a nurse. Can I give the same care to somebody who is bad, over somebody who is good? Maybe those choices shouldn't really have to be made by any man or woman."

"I see your point. Have you thought of the fact that you might have an excellent opportunity?"

"Not really, I'm not over being disgusted."

"Organic world, or home, it's your choice." The truth was Barry did not want to be alone yet.

"Okay, okay, Organic World it is. Do you have somebody to get back to? I mean, do you have to call someone to tell them where you are?" He asked as she drove toward the market. "Barry!! Is that your way of trying to find out if I'm married or not?"

"NO!!....no, Kay. I'm trying to be considerate, is all. By the way, I never did think to ask... are you?...Married, that is?"

"Nope, I'm a widow, but I have been avoiding complications since my husband died. Forgive me for saying so out loud, but my late husband, God rest his soul, was tedious. I would still be with him if he hadn't been struck down by a fool drunk driver. There was no need for Joe to die that young. It was such a stupid thing to happen. But he did die, and life got so much easier for me. That isn't something I've ever told anybody. Most of my friends and relatives have been wondering, pushing me to get out of the house and form new relationships. I just haven't had the urge to be somebody's mother, you know what I mean?"

"I know exactly what you mean, although I have never been married myself. I've had two really long relationships in my lifetime, but never wanted to seal the deal with either one. It always seemed to me I am a professional caretaker. I can't have my current lady friend move in with me. Julie is hard enough to take care of across town. I have always thought it was my own fault though, to be honest. What's even worse is that Julie is becoming impatient with me dragging my feet. She wants to take the next step, but I can't see myself being happy doing everything, when all I want is a partner, a friend, somebody to share."

"Amen."

"Is that what happened to you?"

"Absolutely. All I ever wanted to be was a good wife, and I would still be that wife right now if nothing had happened to Joe. But it did happen, and my life untangled. When I am home, I am the queen. I no longer feel I am going to offend anybody. I have time to feel good about myself, and I do. Maybe, like you say, part of it of it was my fault too, I don't know."

"Well, for me, Kay, all I see, with or without glasses, is a good and beautiful person."

There was a small lull just then, when Kay and Barry sat and appraised each other individually. The conversation itself was deeply personal. From Kay's point of view, there was a truth to how Barry saw her, because of how he saw things through the glasses. Maybe how he saw her with the glasses on, left the suggestion in his mind when he took them off.

From Barry's point of view, when Kay put the glasses on him for the first time, he opened his eyes to see the most beautiful person he had ever seen in his life, and she was so humble about it. Then she saw him as a hero, when it was her that came to his rescue, and thank goodness for that. He was more confused than he had ever been in his life, and she was there to help him through it. Here he was now, pouring his heart out. He always remained guarded with Julie.

Breaking the lull, Barry asked, "So, do you want to get this over with because I'm still scared out of my wits? I'm glad you will be with me, that's for double sure!"

Smiling, Kay said, "Well, I appreciate that, Barry. If nothing else comes out of this, and I hope now that it will, at least you can tell me what is good to buy and what isn't." Barry laughed at that, Kay made it easy.

"Don't you dare put on those glasses until we walk in the door. I want to know everything as it happens, what you see, exactly when you see it."

"I don't think you're going to get an argument from me. I don't want to put them back on at all. Call me chicken."

"Okay, Chicken, don't forget, I'll be holding your hand."

"I have a question."

"Shoot, Chicken."

"Can you make me a new pair of glasses on Monday? I'm still getting headaches with the ones you made me. I think you said they were guaranteed, right?"

NEW GLASSES

"Relax, big guy, I'll take care of you, but if you can afford it, I think you should hold onto them. This is all too weird to not to get to the bottom of, don't you think?" Barry was still unnerved by the whole situation. It was disconcerting that the world is not quite what it appears to be on the surface. Partnering up with Kay made exploring the mystical glasses somewhat bearable. Kay pulled into the parking lot of Organic World, and it was a typical Friday. Tons of people, all wanting whole organic fruits, veggies, and hormone free meats.

"Wow," said Barry, "it appears there are as many people that shop in places like this as there are where I usually go."

"Oh, I wouldn't say that. On the weekends, it's the place to go, but during the week it's pretty empty. If more people shopped here, the prices would go down because organic farmers would be making more money. Growing food this way is more expensive." As Kay and Barry made their way to the front entrance, Kay said, "Okay, it's time to put the specs on. Are you ready?"

"Remember, you asked for it." He said, pulling the glasses out and putting them on. Vision acuity increased immeasurably, instantly, and the difference in people was like night and day. There were ugly people, and beautiful people, but this time around, Barry was able to notice degrees in both sets, however minute the differences were.

"Hello, welcome to Organic World." Kay and Barry were met just inside by a greeter, Barry winced, turning away.

"What is it, what did you see?"

"She looked like a bag lady. She smiled at us with the yellowest teeth I've ever seen, bloodshot eyes, she's a human skeleton, really."

"Go get a carriage, take off the glasses, and have another look."

He took the advice, coming back with a different perspective. This time around he saw a people person, nice looking, in a deal with the public kind of way. After he made his report to Kay, he said, "I don't see what these glasses will ever bring to the table that will help me or anybody else, except changing my profession to be a cop. I can't wait until Monday when you remake these damned specs. Do you want to see what the food looks like now?" They began perusing the aisles, starting with produce, which is almost always first in every supermarket. "To be honest with you Kay. Not everything looks good in here. Why would that be?"

"I don't know. Show me something that doesn't look too good, I may be guilty of buying some of it myself. I didn't think you'd find anything in here bad."

"Well, there's not an incredible amount of things real bad, but these cantaloupes don't look too healthy. I'm not really feeling some of these oranges, based on what I see, anyway. Some of these apples over here look like an artist could paint a picture with them, but these..." he pointed right next to the fancy ones, "I can't approve for human consumption. Now over here in this vegetable bin, this turnip, I could completely do without. The purple ones look pretty nice though. The rest of this looks good. Yeah, looks real good."

"But there is stuff here that still turns you off, does that about sum it up?"

"You saw my reaction to the last place I was shopping in. I think this place is a vast improvement, don't you?"

"...But not an endorsement."

"Hey, you had me put these damned glasses on again. I'm beginning to think that the way things really are, is like a package of hot dogs. It's best not knowing what's in them or you won't eat them. Look at that girl at the door. With glasses, she's having a real bad day, but without them, she's doing her job and doing it well. It could have been a lot of things causing a crappy day like that."

"Okay, so answer me this, Barry. If you didn't have the glasses on in the bank, would you have noticed that man about to rob the bank?"

"Let me answer that question this way. I think that you are just as gorgeous with or without the specs. I believe it's a perception thing. Maybe it's something I felt, as well as saw. I guess what I'm saying is, it wasn't enough to see an ugly guy in line, there was something more. There are ugly people behind you right now, it doesn't mean they are going to rob the store. But I might not trust them to babysit somebody's kids. I said I might make a good cop, but I changed my mind. Half of us has some ugly in us, and I haven't really looked at myself in the mirror real good yet, except to see how I looked in the glasses. But I was looking at the glasses, not me"

"Okay, point made. Let's get some shopping done, but leave the glasses on, because I'm gonna cheat right now. If we go on to have a relationship, I think I might carry those glasses in my purse for you to use in an emergency, or for educational purposes."

"Huh? Are you saying I have a chance with you? Did I hear that right?"

"Why, what'd you hear?"

"I don't know, but I think I heard re-la-tion-ship? It's funny too because I didn't see it coming. I had the glasses on and everything."

It was Monday. Barry had to go to Optical House after his scheduled shift at the hospital. All day Saturday and Sunday morning as well, was wonderful time spent with Kay. Some parts of that story omitted because of the fact that half the world is pretty ugly, and their time together should not be seen through those kinds of eyes. The only wrinkle that ironed out all by itself was a call from Barry's girlfriend Julie, who seemed to have her own sixth sense. That situation was indeed really ugly, but fortunately, short and sweet, and overall, a blessing that it was faced sooner than later.

When Barry walked in the door of Optical house, he was met by Kay who was expecting him. "Mr Snow, it's nice to see you again. Have a seat at the table. Your second pair of glasses is ready f or you. It was such a good idea for you to make that second pair to your new prescription." Kay sounded professional for the benefit of her boss and fellow technicians. The reality was that she looked up Barry's prescription, and scrambled to find frames as close in size as the original pair so she could duplicate them. She put the order in for her new boyfriend, making it all seem like a perfectly regular sale. It was luck that a second pair of lens were in house, or Barry would have had to wait several days. Kay directed Barry to sit down, and continued with the semi-charade, fitting the second pair, which was really now the primary pair. The mystery surrounding the glasses still begged to be solved, and would be. Kay found the original shipping carton that the frames came from, the contents already put on the display racks and priced in the showroom. This threw her into something of a panic mode that Barry's experience might happen to more customers. She ripped the company name and information from the discarded box saving it to review with Barry at the end of her work day. “So, how do they feel Mr. Snow?”

“Not bad, not bad at all! I can still see you are beautiful, just more in focus.”

Kay smiled, and said, Well we will see about that. Can you still read the card?” Barry read every letter the plastic covered card on the table top to the littlest characters.

“Okay, so you're not blind, you just have odd taste.” She said.

Barry's regular shift at work is an early one, starting at six in the morning. That led Kay to come to the apartment bearing Chinese food in cartons, truthfully, nothing in the world more romantic. As soon as they sat to eat, she pulled the side of the frames box out of her purse to hand to Barry. She let him decide what, if anything, to do about it. When he read it over a bite of spring roll, his heart skipped a beat, both from the information, and the MSG in the Chinese food. The Sight Eye Wear Frames Co. LTD. E-mail: thesight@webcore.net. *Warning: Perceptive individuals may experience visual enhancements. Please email us immediately so we can help acclimate the owner to the frames.*

“I guess it would be a smart thing to email them up, huh? That way we could find out what in the world possessed them to engineer frames that provide *visual enhancements* in the first place. I'm very curious now, and I know you are. I'll email now, rather than wait. It certainly seems to sound like the company is fully aware that this kind of thing might have happened. I wonder why they risked it. Anyway, do you have to go home?”

“Are you kidding? Spring rolls are both phallic and suggestive to me, and the sweet and sticky chicken has sesame seeds that are a proven aphrodisiac.”

NEW GLASSES

"The Sight Eye Wear Frames Company, Betty speaking. How may I direct your call?"

"I don't know, you'll have to tell me. I emailed yesterday, and when I got home from work today, your company left this number for me to call."

"You're Barry Snow?"

"Yes, I am, for goodness sakes!"

"I'm sorry, it's just that you created some excitement around here today."

"How could I possibly be a Celeb? There has to be hundreds of people emailing you every day."

"Yes sir, tons. But none in regard to the developer's pet project."

"What's the project about, may I ask?"

"I would rather not rain on Mr. Tressard's parade. His parade, is really his vision, so to speak—his dream."

"Can I talk to him then?"

"Oh, I definitely think so, yes Mr. Snow. Just give him a moment."

Barry waited on his end of the telephone, eventually whistling to the hold music. Just at the very edge of his patience, one ear sweating and itching, the line went active.

"I am sorry you were kept waiting Mr. Snow. My name is Richard Tressard. I am so glad you emailed us, Mr. Snow."

"Please call me Barry sir. The Mister nomenclature demands respect, I haven't done anything to deserve it yet."

"To the contrary, Barry, you most certainly have. In an experimental program spanning nearly fifteen months, you are the only one to indicate the program has had any impact at all. It would take an extraordinarily perceptive individual to notice anything. Could you please describe the enhancements that you indicated you experienced in your email?"

"I would be absolutely very pleased to do that, especially since I suspect now that I am fit for a loony bin, unless I can blame it all on you."

"Why, how bad were these enhancements anyway? We were only shooting for perfect vision, a cure, eventually leading to not needing the glasses, or any kind of corrective lenses."

"That isn't exactly what happened. The enhancements were overshadowed by side effects involving seeing the world way the it really is, and people the way they really are. The whole package is presented as extreme abstract. My glasses show people as either ugly or beautiful, as though I can see their souls. I get to view the world in ways that show objects as good or bad, materialistic, or functional. I view most food as uneatable, rotten, chemical ridden, or even worse, poisonous. It makes for a pretty bad experience, nauseating, and frightening. I thought your reference to helping already took this into account. Now you're telling me that it wasn't what you intended."

"No, Barry, it wasn't, I'm shocked and very sorry. I was shooting for full natural restoration of eyesight."

"I already discontinued the use of the glasses. I had a second pair made that corrects my vision the way I expected in the beginning. But my experience with the first pair is something I still find disturbing. The only thing good that came out of this so far is that the first person I saw through the glasses was the technician who helped pick out the frames, fitting them after the prescription was filled. I am spending a good deal of time with her now, and thank goodness, because she has been helping me adjust from going bonkers."

"Again, I can't apologize enough, Barry. I will do my best to make everything right."

Four rings seemed an eternity. As soon as Kay picked up, Barry asked, "Kay, are you free to talk? I have some news about that frame company I called today."

"Of course. I've been home for twenty minutes already. What happened?"

"They don't know what happened. They have no clue. Their intention, they said, is that they wanted to cure a perceptive guy like me. Isn't that special? I'm a one in a million perceptive guy! They want me and my glasses to fly all the way to the west coast so they can pinch me and poke me to see if I'm real. Then they want to make it all better, you know, for screwing up so badly and all. The whole trip there and back is on them so it will be like a free vacation, especially since I don't have anything else to do right now. These people must think they are the only ones with a job for goodness sake."

"Are you going to able to get time off?"

"I think so, but short notice is going to rub the head nurse the wrong way. I don't ever ask for time off though, I don't see how she can refuse. Why, do you want to come with me?"

"Yes and no. Yes, I would love to come with you, but no, I can't."

"Too bad, you could have prevented me from exploding on these people. Now I'm afraid there's nothing that can be done about it."

"You're not going to explode, Barry, I know you already, you're a pussycat."

"Just venting. I do wish you could come with me though. If it weren't for you, I would have had a meltdown. Thank you for all of that, by the way."

"My pleasure. Did they give you an idea of how they did it?"

"No, but I believe they are going to do their level best to explain the merits of the decision making process at The Sight Eye Wear Frames Company. Maybe it was some kind of over sight, pun intended." Kay laughed at that, weak as his joke was.

"I just wanted to know how you felt about me flying out to meet with these folks. For myself, I feel they have done enough damage, and I can only wonder what they would have in store next. They have no idea how much they frightened me. It's all pretty supernatural."

"Honestly, Barry, I don't know how I feel about it either. I wasn't going to see you tonight, to give you some space, but I miss you already. If you were gone for a while, I would have to deal with it like I always have, but I wouldn't like it too much. I miss you, and you haven't even gone anywhere."

"Well, I miss you too. Why don't you come on over so we can spend the time we do have together. If I give the people at The Sight the thumbs up, they will arrange for me to pick up tickets at the airport tomorrow. I haven't done that yet. I kind of wanted your opinion on it first, plus I might be gone until the weekend. This man sounded confident he could fix my vision permanently, no glasses. It's because I responded to the frames, where nobody else has, at least so far. If others respond, then they move into the vision cure business. That's what they're saying. Look, come on over so I can spend some time with you. Should I call the guy or not?"

"Yeah, You probably should give them a call." She said with a sigh. At least you might investigate whether or not to litigate against this company. I'll be there soon."

Barry recalled Mr. Tressard at The Sight Eye Wear, to accept his invitation, to go ahead and make travel arrangements. "Richard," he said when he had him on the line, "you've got yourself a deal.

"Okay, excellent. I'll have my secretary make all the reservations. She will call you back with the travel itinerary. I am really looking forward to meeting you, Barry."

"Good night, Richard." Said Barry abruptly.

"Good night."

Barry was met like a dignitary at the airport. A well dressed woman in heels held a cardboard sign with 'Barry Snow' written on it stood at the foot of the escalator to baggage claim. "I'm Barry Snow. Are you going to take me to my hotel?"

"No no, Mr. Snow. I am Ms. Withers. I hope you remember me, I am the woman you talked to when you first called. Mr. Tressard instructed me to bring you straight to the office. Richard will take you to the hotel himself. He is anxious to meet and talk to you. We will take care of you well, Mr. Snow, good eats, nice place to sleep at night, plus time to check out the city."

"I just want to get this over with, Ms. Withers." Barry didn't exactly sound like a willing subject.

"This is not a death sentence, Mr. Snow."

"Look, I know it's your job to talk nicey nicey, but you weren't there to experience what I did. I think if you did, you would feel precisely as I do. So let's just go visit this Richard Tressard guy so we can find out what he tried to do to me, shall we?

It was about a forty five minute quiet ride to the office from the airport, another fifteen minutes from the car to Tressard's office. Richard popped up from his desk chair like a jack in the box when his secretary ushered in Barry, who pretty much gave an instant impression that he wanted heads to roll.

"Barry, what's the matter? You look pissed."

"You think? I have had a few days to rehearse what I wanted to say to you, and it has me wound up like a coiled spring. I just want to get out what I have to say to you face to face, man to man. I have no idea how your frames do it, drugs, or whatever. But what gives you the right....?"

"Hold on Barry, just wait right there. The frames were fully documented with brochures spelling out what they were designed to do and how. Here, this is the documentation that was included along with the packing slip." He pulled one off of his desk, handing it to Barry. He continued, "Further, it was a box of samples that were supplied free of charge, with the hope of successful debut usage. We are a glass frame company, yes, but they were experimental homeopathic frames. I am a certified homeopathic physician, and it was my intention to cure you. I still might be able to achieve that goal, if you would relax. Please sit down and listen to what I have to say. Barry grudgingly sat facing Richard Tressard.

"The kind of hallucinations you experienced were not intentional, nor can I immediately explain how they happened. Homeopathy is a tried and true system of medicine, and I have never heard of such an experience. But I can assure you, I will get to the bottom of it, and send you home better off than when you came." This pulled the rug from underneath Barry's feet, and he became a little more reticent.

When nothing more came from the man, Richard said to him, "I need you to answer some questions so I can pinpoint everything about you from the top of your head, to the bottom of your feet. This is what homeopathy is and how I practice it. I will then explain how I intended to use a homeopathic remedy to try and cure. I will disclose of how the frames were made, and how the remedy was administered. I admit to possibly making a mistake here. The frames might work on you alone, and I should have known that. So let me begin...."

NEW GLASSES

With pad and pen, taking notes, the questioning proceeded, none of it making a whole lot of sense to a Registered Nurse, but they were harmless on the surface of it. Hair type, difficulties with dry scalp, mind influences, phobias and the like, a thorough examination that continued as promised, head to foot. "Richard, are you trying to diagnose me for something?" Barry asked when he was done documenting.

"No, not at all. That's not what this is about. Homeopathy uses agents, remedies if you will that in large doses would duplicate the symptoms a patient is experiencing. In minuscule doses, diluted and broken down so small it is rendered harmless, it triggers the body to cure itself. Symptoms, patient type, and temperaments are matched to remedies as completely and closely as can be had if it were delivered in the large dose. I believe this remedy matches your modalities so closely, it is trying to cure several things at once. Perception is indicated, but perhaps I didn't take into account how the remedy would perceive that you perceive. Please tell me; if your eye sight is as bad as you said without corrective lenses, how did you manage to get though school and become a nurse? How on earth do you function as a nurse day to day?"

"I never really thought about it, but I guess I am just sensitive to certain things. I can make up for what I can't see very well with my other senses, figuring out what I need to know intuitively."

"And just how many people out there do you think view the world in this way Barry? This is a remarkable attribute, very uncommon, very wonderful."

"So what do you think will get cured if I wear the frames you developed?"

"I don't know for sure, but I suspect that your eyesight will settle down to perceive with clarity, what you have been sensing with the remainder of your senses all along. I am a traditional Hahnemann purist type of homeopath. The original application of this practice of medicine insisted that only one remedy be used at any time, so that when some of the symptoms went away, a new remedy would have to be administered to match the new sets of symptoms more precisely. Nowadays homeopaths mix remedies, muddling the confused list of symptoms. That is counterproductive. I believe that the remedy I chose for my experiment was a personal polychrest to you only, matching every symptom down to the minute degree. You are sensitive to them all. Tell me Barry, do you drink a lot of stimulating drinks, coffee, tea, liquor, wine; that sort of thing?"

"No, not really."

"That is probably why you react so fast to the cure."

"Can you tell me what I will see when my vision is cured as you say?"

"Your case is very peculiar, Barry, but I think that your vision will be heightened without glasses, aided by the rest of your senses just the way it has been all along."

"But these frightening images I get from objects and people, what about that?"

"I think you will more than likely be cured of this disease. I think it was starting to do the job before you interrupted the process."

"Yeah, because I was scared crapless!"

"Well, I have you with me now, and I can stay with you until that process is complete. You will go home cured. I am sure of it."

"Explain to me how the frames have anything to do with it."

"Ahh, here is where it gets interesting. I used the frames as a delivery system. They were crafted from bioplastics. I have a contingent of really talented biochemists and bioplastic engineers working here with me.

"The frames are biodegradable?"

"In a sense. They still have to be disposed of properly, and we have a facility here at 'The Sight" that have the special micro organisms that break them down when the frames are no longer needed. The frames have been designed to touch all areas of the face as close to the optic nerves as can be had externally. Can I see your glasses?" Barry took them from a case in his shirt pocket, handing them to Richard, who opened them to present them for closer examination. "Do you see these little holes, here, here, and here?"

NEW GLASSES

"Yes sir, I do."

"Well that is a hollowed out area in the frames that I filled with the remedy, Aconitinum, which is an alkaloid derivative of Aconitum Napellus, Latin for Monkshood, or Wolfbane. The remedy was installed and plugged with the same bioplastic, essentially fused inside the frame. My hope was to deliver the remedy minutely, but directly, to the area that I wanted to cure. But I did not know for sure that it would work. Now that I do, I would like to finish the job before you go home."

"But I bought this other pair of glasses to replace yours when I got so frightened."

"Not to worry, I will reimburse you for them, but if I am right, you will never need the glasses again, and I won't either. I will go back to traditional homeopathy, and just produce bioplastic frames. I have learned that everyone is an individual, and can not be generalized into groups having the same needs or symptoms. The same gripe I have about modern homeopathy, I am now guilty of myself. For that, I am truly sorry. But you can come out of this a winner."

"I'm here, I may as well get on with it. Where do we start?"

"Put the glasses on, and we can go get something to eat." He pressed a button on an intercom,

"Betty, we can all go to eat now, why don't you get ready, and we can close up for the night?" Looking up to Barry, he said, "Betty is my fiancée. There is indeed hanky panky going on here, but it's all legal beagle."

"I have one other question. Are you prepared to have me put on my glasses and see what I see?"

"What do you mean?"

"For a smart guy, you didn't think of that one, did you? I mean that I see people as bad or good, ugly or beautiful. Until I am cured as you say, I see people displayed very literally."

"I am not afraid, and I trust Betty with my life. So, yes, I am ready. I think that particular modality will level out though in a short time, too."

"Well, here goes then. Do I have to keep them on all the time?" He asked, picking the glasses off the desk, readying them toward his face."

NEW GLASSES

"All the time you're awake, yes"

Just before Barry put them on, he added, "I hope you are planning to eat in a good place then because I could never eat anything that isn't pure with the specs on."

He finished the aim toward his face, settling them on his nose and ears, focusing in on Richard front and center. Barry was pleasantly surprised to find a handsome man sitting across from him. Pulling up beside him, smiling, with a hand on Richard's back, was Betty. They were a stunningly gorgeous couple relieving Barry of a considerable amount of pent up dreaded tension.

"Come on, let's go get something to eat so that you can get to the hotel for some sleep. It's late where you came from, and it is going to catch up to you. Betty and I are taking you to a real nice place. The food is amazing. You'll love it." The ride in Richard's car though the city should have been impressive. The fact was that no one could put themselves in Barry's shoes. No one could picture in their head what it was that he saw this way. Betty and Richard were in the front seat, assuming that Barry was wild eyed with wonder at their beautiful city, but the real fact was that ugly was edging out beautiful by a mile. It left Barry in a bad spot because he didn't want to be rude, or even to reveal that what they thought was mind blowing, was not. The waterfront was a perfect example. Opulence was another, as was every fifth or sixth person walking on the sidewalks. The depressing reality of it was like a graphic picture book. Thankfully, the car rolled up to a valet station at the restaurant so that the misery of it all would be postponed for a while, or would it? Inside the opulent edifice were the marble tiled floors, ornate crystal chandeliers, and a starchily dressed maitre d ready to greet to seat them. The truth....ugly in a tux. The tables were decorated with white lace table cloths, place mats to keep them clean for the night's servicing, and a floating candle in a clear glass vase. Salads were being served at a neighboring table, and that is when Barry just knew.

"I am so embarrassed to ask this, and I don't want to in the worst way, but can I take the glasses off to eat?"

Man and fiancée sat across from Barry, trying

their absolute sincere best to dazzle and impress, were figuratively punched in their faces. Thinking that this was the best they could offer the man, it took them by surprise that it wasn't the case.

"No, you can't, but we are about to leave. I will not have you uncomfortable. But as soon as we are out of here, you are going to have to explain to us what it is that you see. Come on, let's get out of here."

Barry could not have been more relieved. He was more than glad to have to explain himself if he did not to see one more thing. The valet already tucked Richard's car into an automobile sandwich, and it had only been twenty minutes. The restaurant was one of the most popular in the city. But, to his credit, the valet attendant was very professional, jockeying the car back out of the limited space lot, returning with a smile. He would have turned ugly only if he had not been properly tipped, a little change in perception that Barry was noticing.

"What have you been able to eat Barry, with the glasses on that is?" Asked Richard, trying to get a feel of where they might try next.

"Nothing. I was rescued by the lady who sold me the glasses in the first place. She found me retching outside the supermarket next door to the Optical House. I could not bear staying inside shopping one second longer. She spent time calming me down, and eventually took me to a place named 'Lettuce Eat Hearty', but I did not want to chance it any more then than I do now sir. I ate with my glasses off like I always have. Kay and I have been spending time together since. I have been eating stuff bought from 'Organic World', and even then, there are things in that store that turn my stomach. We ate Chinese food the other night, but these glasses were not involved in any way. The leftover thought of what I saw in the supermarket is still stuck in my head."

Betty looked over the table at Barry, sympathy in her eyes, the couple beginning to understand why Barry was so upset in the first place. Betty said, "There's an organic and vegan restaurant downtown that might work to our advantage here."

"Where is it honey?"

"Oh you know, Richard, it's that old fire house building down on Harper Street."

NEW GLASSES

"Oh yeah, yeah, yeah—I remember now. That might do very nicely. I don't want Barry to take the glasses off until he's cured, and I don't have any idea how long it will be. It could be four hours, or a couple days. But I do think that if he has reactions as soon as he puts them on, then I should think, sooner than later."

Barry was chauffeured by the couple to the alternative place to eat, and they made their way in. In a way, it was an upscale place too, but in a different good way, classy but not decadent. Most of the clientèle had ugly superiority faces on them. Several were handsome couples, but the bulk were what creeps were like in Barry's viewers.

"Is this place any better for you?" Asked Betty.

"It's like Kay, and I found out about 'Organic World', better, but not perfect. But nothing ever is, is it? It will be just fine I think."

Richard made some remarks after the meals came. "I can see why you flew out here to visit us so upset. But I feel confident that there will be changes in the way you see before long. Tell me, how do you function on a day to day basis? How do you fill meds at the hospital, for instance?"

"I can function very well. Nobody even notices I have bad eyesight, not even me. When I read, I anticipate what comes next, or use reading glasses I buy at the drug store. There are some things I won't attempt, like driving. But I don't see how anybody can drive out there on the streets. I think it should be left to professionals. But the rest is something I have grown up with. When it comes down to it, I assumed everybody else perceives the same way I do. I don't know what to tell you. I renewed my state ID card recently, and was given a cursory eye exam to put into my profile for the card. They told me I was legally blind that I would not be able to drive unless I could prove I met the minimal vision parameters with corrective lenses. I told them I had no interest in driving. But I decided to have my eyes done by an eye doctor. I thought that I might be missing out on something. So far, it appears I should continue missing out."

Both Betty and Richard laughed, but Betty said, "You may be dead right about that."

NEW GLASSES

Betty chose well, because the food was able to be eaten. Barry felt safe enough ordering organic chicken on a salad of baby spinach, alfalfa sprouts, cherry tomatoes, cucumber, pecans, and dried cranberries. It was preceded with a bowl of vegetarian house soup. Betty and Richard ordered something different, but similarly, hoping to squash any more of his discomfort. Conversation revolved around becoming friends, growing more and more apparent that the trio had much in common. It also drew attention away from what and who else was in the dining area, a fast non issue.

"I would like to turn in if you wouldn't mind. I'm sorry because you both are great hosts and terrific company. I am super tired. Thank you for keeping my mind off the glasses. My new girlfriend did that for me also, at a time that I needed it most. You would like her, although she might have been the one who overlooked the homeopathic information in with the shipping receipts. But then again, I did not know diddly squat about homeopathy before I came here, other than the natural cough drops in the drug store I always see when I get a cold. I really don't read the fine print for that matter. You two have kept me so busy, I haven't had a chance to call her. It's late, but I would like to do that at the hotel before I crash."

"Okay!" Richard said, clapping his hands once decisively.

"I want those glasses back on you as soon as you wake up, and when you wake up during the night to go to the bathroom. I think having them off while you sleep will be a good thing, it works like traditional therapy, but resuming remedy treatment in the morning is imperative. Let me give you my number so you a can program it into your phone. I want you to call me first thing in the morning. This is a challenge to me, making all this right. I know you're the man that will make it work. In fact, there won't be any other after this. But if we succeeded with you, it would have made it all worthwhile. It's just that I'll have to back up ten yards to punt, that's all. I was trying to come up with a plan to market my help to people. If I advertised that I could cure poor vision, it would be false advertisement because just like this case, it might work, but might not. My thought was to have a percentage of people wearing the frames, come to me for help to finish the process. I made a fundamental error, and for that I am truly sorry."

"There's no sense beating yourself up for trying, Richard. What would it take to help every patient?" Barry asked as he was driven to his hotel for the night.

"It would require one on one interaction with every patient, being as exact as possible with remedies to that individual until symptoms reduced enough to be handled by a final knockout remedy. At that point, the patient would be declared, cured."

"I see your problem, no way to mass market your help on a grand scale. I'm sorry, that is quite a blow to your plans."

"I still have the glass frame business. If I were to create an exchange program, the frames would be completely biodegradable. That's something at least. My calling as a homeopath would have to be scaled back. Perhaps teaching would be a better option."

Before Barry went to bed, he called Kay, hoping she would be up waiting for his call. She was, and worried to boot. "Thank God you called. I was so worried something happened. I thought you would call when you got off the plane."

"I know, I know, I apologize. I was snaked off as soon as I got off the plane." He fully went into what had transpired from the time he exited the jet way.

"So you're telling me that the paperwork in the box of frames would have cleared this whole thing up and that it was primarily my fault?" Kay summarized, sobered at her inattention.

"Don't forget that Mr. Tessard said that out of all the frames sent out, I was the only one to come back with any reaction so far. This all could work out for the best. At the very least, I will be reimbursed, and I got a little vacation in the deal. I'll let you go to sleep so I can get some too. Richard wants to spend the day with me tomorrow. I don't know what he expects. It has been a learning process for him too. He didn't quite comprehend when I told him that I see the world the way it really is.

He does now."

Morning came and with it, bright sunshine. Barry reached toward the bed side table for his glasses to put on as he promised. He only took them off to get showered and dressed so he could go in search of coffee, but immediately put them back on when he finished. Before he left the room, he called Richard, telling him he was in the hunt for organic coffee, but would be handy when he wanted him.

"I'm getting motivated myself. I'll pick you up at the hotel in about, oooh, forty five minutes or so. Any changes in your vision that you notice?"

"I have noticed little things, even last night. People get uglier if you irritate them, or cross them in some way. But that's it; that I can tell."

"But it's a change, that's good, not that I really know what to expect until you are cured. Be there soon, my new friend."

Good, he seemed confident about one thing at least, a cure. Barry thought to himself. He made his way out of the hotel to explore the area for a cup of Joe. Outside, a good looking couple were walking hand in hand, romantically or so it appeared. There was animated conversation between the two, and Barry would not have given them a second thought, except that in the middle of talking to one another, the lady turned a shade of red, her eyes had a deceitful look to them just as he passed them by going the other direction. He gave backward glance to watch them continue on, shocked that what he viewed was not the ugly versus beautiful pattern that he'd been experiencing. Then he began to see that all the people walking past him had some kind of issue. Two teen boys with backpacks were ashen-faced, with dull drugged eyes, high. Two babbling young girls were motor mouthing at each other that should have been cute, but had empty, stupid eyes. Barry could tell that nothing interesting would come out of the two without a crowbar. A mother hustled her young ones along so they would not be late for school. Mom had a look of preoccupation. Barry could tell she was already into the next plans for the day, pushing the kids to go to school simply a necessary nuisance. The kids, on the other hand, all three boys were bullies, mean beady eyes, cruel mouths, and probably a handful when they got to school, not that mom would notice.

All these people were average, not outstanding at all. There is a saying that went through Barry's head as he saw one person after another display the contents of their character in plain sight for him to see. *I can tell you are lying because it is written all over your face*. Except that every flaw passing by him was detectable. But then the worst thing of all happened since he first put the spectacles on. He had moved back to the front of the hotel, cardboard coffee cup in hand, waiting for his new friend and physician, Richard, to drive by to pick him up. His eyes blurred, became unfocused. Barry couldn't see a thing clearly, pushing him to be more frightened than he'd ever been. Barry, placed all his faith in Richard, wavering at the moment, but too scared to stop believing in the cure. He sat down on the closest curb he could find, too afraid to move, and praying to God that he wasn't going blind.

Later, a hand was on Barry's shoulder. “Barry, I've been calling you, didn't you hear me?”

No answer. Barry was unresponsive, even with the touch. He sat on the curb like he was in another world, or comatose.

“Barry, can you hear me? BARRY!” It was as though all his senses shut down. Richard panicked, kneeling down in front of him, tears welling up in his eyes. “God, what have I done to you? Barry...Barry, come back man. I'm sorry. Oh God!” There was only one thing Richard could think of to do before calling for emergency services. Check to see if Barry's pupils were fixed and dilated. He gently eased off the glasses to have a better look. As soon as he did, however, Barry came alive.

Richard was looking straight into Barry's eyes when Barry asked, “What?”

“Are you kidding me? You just gave me the fright

of my life! Where were you just now?"

"Beats me. The last thing I remember was siting down here on the curb. These glasses were out of focus all of a sudden, and I was praying that I wasn't going to go blind." He said, but then he noticed the glasses were in Richard's hand. "Hold on here, what's going on?"

"It seems like you are cured, but the pivotal word is—seems. After what just happened I can't be sure of anything. Can you get up?"

"Sure I can, I've never felt better." Barry jumped to his feet be means of demonstration.

"Nah, I won't believe it now until you prove it. Let's go to breakfast and find out how cool you really are."

"That brings up something. Just before I went out of focus and winked out, I started seeing people a whole different way."

"How did you see them?"

"Like this...right now your heart is beating much too fast, and I want to calm you down a bit. That's why I am acting so cavalier about winking out. It's because now I am more worried about you than me. You have high blood pressure, hypertensive actually. I estimate 220 over 130 right now. I think you are in danger of a stroke if that is a regular reading for you. It is elevating a little more right now that I point it out. Your face says to me that if I spill the beans about this to Betty, you'll strangle me with your bare hands. This is something you have been hiding from her. Oop, there you go. Now you're getting ready to deny it and lie to me so you can smooth it over. Don't. I can read you like a book. You need to cure yourself, doctor. No, wait a minute, I wonder if I can help." Barry took Richard's left wrist in his left hand, and placed his right hand on Richard's temple, closed his eyes in concentration. This kept up for nearly a minute.

"My goodness Richard. That was really bad." Barry said when he opened his eyes again. You need to start eating like we did last night, consistently. Cut out the fried foods and junk. Please, please promise me! You make a great friend, and I think you'll make a hell of a husband. But we will both lose you if you keep up those bad habits of yours. You had renal artery stenosis with an imminent blockage from the thinning of your arteries, a thick, gooey cholesterol sticking to the sides. I pushed some of the worst of it along, so your kidneys don't do the funky. Holding onto the stuff that causes the high blood pressure. The arteries themselves seem pretty flexible, or I would have stressed them pretty good with what I just did. It's not me that's going to make you die Richard, it's you. Your pressure has dropped quite a bit right now, but you need to exercise with that pretty wife of yours and eat organic for goodness sake. I only helped you. You have to be the one to get yourself better. You are a homeopath for goodness sakes. You know better."

If it were a minute earlier, Richard would have had a full stroke. The implications of what had just happened were obvious, and even if Richard didn't believe that what had transpired, didn't happen at all, the undeniable fact was that he felt pretty good.

"I can see that you don't really believe that I just helped you, but that's alright, as long as you follow my advice, you should be okay. Don't, and you won't, that simple. How about some organic coffee?"

"Where do we get that?"

"Any quality coffee shop will have it. I'll be able to tell if the breads or muffins are good, too."

"Are you seeing everything as ugly and beautiful?"

"No, all of that's very much under control. Instead of perceiving with only my eyes, now I perceive like I have been seeing all my life. I am using all my senses in harmony. I don't need to see things like they really are to know what they really are. I can smell, touch, taste, and hear, to go along with my sight. None of my senses are overpowered."

"Good Lord, I hope you are not a monster!"

Barry laughed. "I hope not too! If I am, it's your fault! I can't wait to go home and help people by being the perfect nurse. Just by giving good care, I might be able to help without anybody knowing that it was me. If your heart was bad, I would not have been able to help you. But fundamental fixes certainly can be fixed. The rest, just like with you, is up to the patient. I may be able to steer some patients toward correct therapies when I notice errors made. In a way, it is better than being a doctor. Interventions would be picked up on if I was the doctor. I guarantee that the only one who will know I sense things differently, are you, your wife to be, and Kay, my new significant other. Are you are going to dismantle the homeopathic glasses idea then?"

"Yes, unless somebody else is affected by the samples I distributed. But for now, you have been the only one. What do you think I should do?"

"You know the Hippocratic Oath as well as I do. You know more about homeopathy than I do. If you think you will do any harm, recall them and offer just the bioplastic frames as you said you would do. You are going to have to contact the people you sent out the frames samples anyway, to set up a disposal program. Or you can leave the samples you sent out where they are, and deal with the fallout if and when it happens."

"Thanks a lot, but no thanks. I am going to ask for my frames back, and replace them with plain, designer frames, to try and get business. The only thing that is bad about it is that we don't have an exotic enough name. But the frames are high quality, and green tech."

"There you go. Problem solved."

After getting coffee, Richard and Barry went to The Sight Eye Wear. Barry got a tour of the facility, but Barry had Betty arrange a return trip home. The trip wasn't about the glasses anymore. Barry reached the point where the trip would be very much more appreciated if it were shared with someone else, Kay to be more exact.

"I want you to keep in touch, please. The next time we get together, I would like to have my girl with me. Kay and I are new to each other, so trips like that are down the road I should think, but I have a good feeling about her. I miss her very much. Oh, hell we will see each other again if I have to invite you out to my side of the world, or fake a relapse that only you can cure."

Barry stepped out of the plane, comforted to be home, and so so happy he would be seeing Kay. Proud too, because he was without glasses, contacts, or anything corrective, seeing better than he ever did in his whole life. The symphony of extra senses was to be a non issue to start the reunion, information to be filled in later. But this is where is got funky. The symphony of senses were an issue, and they came alive the moment he got close. The first perception to hit him is what he saw, a face put on to hide the truth. The rest of the senses kicked in during the welcome home hug. Within thirty seconds of taking hold of her, touching her face with his hand while he kissed her, he knew the reason she stayed behind on the trip—what was wrong, and it made him start to cry. It wasn't out sympathy, although that was part of it. It was because he could see, but was impotent to do anything about it. After feeling so powerful, his first case was someone special, and she did not need a fundamental fix. She had acute leukemia. It only goes to show that God alone has to make the ultimate choices. Sometimes those choices can be tough ones, and probably not that at all acceptable, even to God. The plan all along was to have the best of these creations fold into the eternal realm where he has a bit more control over such things. That job would be too much of a burden on any other being, even with extraordinary abilities, and totally impossible in this less than perfect universe full of imperfect things like people, bodies, weather, and the earth itself. Even in the eternal realm where God has complete control, there was a little problem, or Satan surely would not have come to be. But that's just it, he came to be. God was always there, and is there still, waiting for the best of his best to come and join him.

THE TREE

THE TREE

It was early spring. The first mockingbirds had arrived north. I truly love listening to mockingbirds, songs never the same, wondering how the next string of notes will change. My wife and I sat on our front porch in the first sixty five degree morning of the new season. The air was refreshing, washed clean by an unusually harsh winter that kept my wife and I housebound and indoors. We took our coffee outdoors just because we were able to, not because sitting in sixty five degree weather was our perfect choice. But the yard—well the yard was the product of only two years of living in this house that we decided to purchase after so many years living in an apartment. Nothing at all was done to the yard; not by us.

"What do you say we take a spin this morning to the home improvement nursery to look at some plants for the yard Harry?" My wife asked me in a hopeful manner. She wasn't giving me a choice exactly. It was more along the lines of not giving her too much of an argument if she asked nicely. She knew how much I hated being dragged along up and down aisles. But the nursery was closer to a tool department than women's shoes, so there was no argument. That's not saying I said something, but remaining quiet meant yes. She reached over to give my hand a squeeze and a bright beautiful smile that I could not have said anything negative to her regardless.

"Can I drink my coffee?" I asked.

Her right hand flipped back and forth, a gesture that said without words, "Don't be silly Harry."

And so we sat, listening to the children file out of the house next door to enjoy the Saturday morning. No school today, you could hear the happiness in their chattering, as compared with how they usually sound on a week day. Julia and I didn't have children, not for lack of trying. It simply just was not in the cards, that's all. The strange thing was that all systems were a go, but our systems did not know when, why, or where. A garage door opened with a creak, and a groan, Three bicycles, mounted by determined boys, pumped out the entrance as if they were going a hundred. They emptied out into the driveway, made a hard right, and disappeared down the sidewalk. The sound was almost as pleasant as the mockingbirds.

I wasn't able to pretend I was still drinking my coffee any longer, it was cold as ice, so I rose from my seat. Julia rose in tandem, like the other end of set of bookends. We made our way to the kitchen, placing the cups in the sink to 'soak' as they say. Heading to the car wasn't as painful as I'd expected, I was even a little anxious to go to the garden center. The Buick fired up easily as she always does, and the ride on that spring Saturday morning was as nice as everything else we had done until then. I don't know, I was just happy I guess.

The parking lot was fuller than I would have desired, a nice way of saying there were way too many people for my taste. I found one of those flat carts for heavy shopping items close by. I staked a claim to it before it was lost, and Julia and I worked our way into the entrance of chain linked outdoor garden area. Even before entering, the place was ablaze with colors and scents. We went inside first, and walked the interior offerings, some of which were lovingly placed on the flat cart by my wife. I have to admit, I would have picked up what she did, no gripes. We discussed putting window boxes on the rails of the porch, and just a few plants around the steps leading up to the front door. After a while, we figured there was just about as much as we needed for our project except for bagged soil for the long window boxes we picked out. We stood in line for what seemed like hours until we came even up with a skid of dejected looking plants, marked down because they seemed either ill, or not that pretty. One that caught my eye was a little scrawny tree, about ten inches, maybe a foot tall. It was still green, but not by much. It was in a two gallon bucket, with a tag on it that said, **Northern Cultivators. Hardy in all zones. Easy care, and festive seasonally. $2.00. Festive seasonally?** *Festive seasonally*, I wondered what that meant. I picked up the bucket, and a frown came to my wife's otherwise smooth face.

"You interested in that?" My wife asked surprised.

"Kinda, yeah. It just seems to need love, you know? It's only two bucks. I think I'll get it and see if it comes back. For that price, what's the harm?"

THE TREE

"Okay..." She said. He tone suggested that we might be stopping by the vitamin and supplement store on the way home for something that supports healthy brain function.

Regardless, I bought the tree, I can't really say why. It sorta said hello to me from the first glance.

We spent the rest of the afternoon planting our plants in just the right way. All that was left was my tree, and my Julia was not too interested in having it planted in front of the house. I got a little headstrong about it. I don't really know why I made such a big deal of it, but I decided to argue in defense of my tree. I took it to the middle of the front yard, just to the left of the front door, looking at the house. I dug a fair sized hole, put some water in the hole, and planted my sickly looking baby. I then made a ring around it to protect it from my crazy mowing frenzies. The bricks that were stored in the backyard by the previous owners of the house, finally found a use. I got fairly artistic if I do say so myself, sticking them in the ground the long way, one up, one down until it made a complete circle around the tree. Then I talked to it. "Come on baby, show Julia how gorgeous you can be," I said, and pet it as if it was a cat."

Julia watched me and smiled the whole time, treating the tree as something precious. When I finished, she gave me a hug and a kiss. "What was that for?" I asked.

"I just love you that's all."

Sunday brought another nice day. After such a bad winter, having a complete turnaround like this was most welcome. I had coffee made before my wife came into the kitchen. I even had both our cups poured, ready for another pleasant wake up sitting on the porch. As soon as we opened the door, a waft of bacon smell came toward us from one of the neighbors that smelled wonderful. We no sooner sat down on the glider when, "Harry, look at the tree!"

"What in God's green earth?" The tree had filled out, laid down it's branches to soak up the morning sun with a hundred times more needles If that wasn't enough, it was about four or five inches taller.

"Harry, what did you put on that tree to make it

grow like that?" Julia asked.

"Not one blessed thing, honey. I only gave it water and love." I said over my shoulder as I set my cup down on the porch to walk down into the front yard for a better gander.

Well I have to say, that though the course of the spring, the yard filled out nicely. So did my tree. It became a ritual to visit all the plants in the morning, as well as the tree. We watered, touched, talked to, and did whatever it took to make our babies happy and healthy. By summer's end, the tree was a perfectly formed six foot Christmas tree beauty. By fall, the only thing that wasn't growing sadder daily as the days shortened was the tree. It was just as beautiful as ever, now almost ten feet tall.

One morning, early in October, A rather large bird came to visit us one morning. It landed on the tree. Big thing it was, with a huge bill on its head. "Honey," I asked, "what kind of bird do you think that is?" I was alarmed. I thought it might break some branches on my tree.

Julia pulled a curtain back in the front room and proclaimed, "You know, we don't have pelicans in these parts, and it is too big to be a crane. I am no expert or anything, but I think that might be a stork!"

It picked up a flew away, majestically I might add. For every flap, it lifted a good four feet into the air, and before long had disappeared from view, and out of our lives ever to be seen again.

At the beginning of December, my wife had some news for me. She had been vomiting and feeling under the weather. She had made an appointment with her doctor in case what she had might be dangerous. It turned out to be a simple case of pregnancy. I nearly fainted, but Julia and I were so happy, but confused that we were rewarded after so many years of hoping. At that point, no thought at all was given to the tree, and even if we did, we might not have believed it had anything to do with anything.

The third week of December, just before Christmas, we looked out the window, and the tree was decorated. We had no idea where it all came from. Ornaments, tinsel, angels, garland, the works. Best we could figure was that an anonymous neighbor came in the middle of the night, to decorate a tree that just begged to be decorated. We had nothing else that could explain it. As we left for work, we nodded toward our neighbors, and again when we returned home to some of the others. None of the neighbors smiled with any clue they held some mysterious secret.

On Christmas morning, we found presents under the tree. We went out to the yard and carried them all into the house, all were labeled with our names on them, from Santa. When we opened them, there were baby supplies, furniture for the nursery, bassinet, newborn pampers, just everything baby. It was the most slack jawed experience of our lives. We got up off the floor, sat on the couch, and held each other because the love in our house had simmered, boiled, and finally boiled over.

The day after Christmas, the decorations went away, but the tree was as gorgeous as ever.

Years have gone by, and our tree is just as much a part of our family as Kris, our son. Every year just before Christmas, the decorations come back. We don't really wish for anything else because we feel we have everything we want in this life, except for love, which comes in abundance more and more every year that passes. Long live the Kringle family.

A KNOCK ON THE DOOR

A KNOCK ON THE DOOR

I'd been looking at the clock for well over an hour. Watching it made the the last hour even longer if that was possible. As five o'clock neared, I pushed all the paperwork I was working on into a neat pile on my desk. My desk is always neat, and always getting me ton of ribbing. I get a lot of: “How do you find anything in all that neat, Rich? If you spill coffee, does it land in a nice little puddle? Oh I forgot, you don't spill coffee. Why is the 'in' pile so much smaller than the 'out' pile, Rich? Are you some kind of brown noser? Do you have you a spare bottle of lemon oil, Rich?” All so very funny, I forgot to laugh. But then it goes the other way of the spectrum: “I just love a man who's organized. I'll bet your so easy to live with; neat, and handsome too!” And the ever popular; “I'll bet a week's pay you are good in bed.” I have never made the connection with that one.

I didn't feel like working anymore, and didn't know the reason. At five o'clock straight up, I grabbed my briefcase and left my office for the weekend. It is technically not my office, it belongs to United Certified Accounting. Just a spoke in a wheel, I truly believe that being organized is the key to efficiency, and for me it is a constant battle to stay that way, especially in that office building. My coworkers annoy me as much as I annoy them.

Spontaneity is not my strong suit, but on this particular day I deviated from my usual bus ride home. I opted to walk, hunting a place to eat.

The smells at that time of the night coming from this establishment, and that establishment, made my stomach boil, anticipation for something delectable. I passed by the Rib House advertising the best ribs in town, yeah right, they can't all be the best ribs; liar liar pants on fire. Ribs are messy to eat. Another window had a sign boasting a sixteen ounce rib eye steak, potato, and vegetable for fourteen ninety five—close, no cigar. As I turned the corner of 20th at the First Baptist Church, I thought, *how can they make that claim*? *That's one for the historians to sort out, I suppose*. Another half block and Charlie's Family Restaurant caught my eye. Without a reason, I picked it to be the place for me to eat.

A KNOCK ON THE DOOR

I entered through the heavy double oak doors. The etched glass in them were frosted and lined with mirrored silver. Very classy for a family restaurant.

"One to dine tonight?' asked a pretty young thing standing at a podium just inside.

"Yes please."

She ushered me into a solarium type addition off the main floor that needed to be stepped down into, and had a number of tables for two to four people. "Your server will be along shortly, can I offer you something to drink before you get started?"

"Thank you, ginger brandy—neat." I told her, smiling at the terminology that had been the theme of my thoughts from before I left the office going forward. My preoccupation at being neat went back as far as I can remember, the reasons for it elude me completely, but I think my mom was partially to blame. She died about ten years back, but I can still recall the life lessons she worked so hard to instill in me. I can take care of myself very well thanks to her. It was her way, as a single parent, to ingrain what she termed, "essential survival skills." I don't specifically recall her having me line up my shoes in a straight row though.

"I will get right on it." The hostess said, turning on her heel to head to the bar area instead of the podium.

I watched until she spoke to a server at the bar area, but my vision was drawn to a woman sitting alone, looking back at me. I swear there was something familiar but unusual about her. More than just unusual, it was as though my eyes had teared up, and had blurred. Her face had a slight glow on and around it that I could not blink or rub out with my fingers. I did try a couple of times. I barely made out that she seemed to be smiling at me. The server walked in front of her blocking my vision momentarily, but when she passed by, the woman behind her had completely disappeared.

The server walked directly to my table, round tray in her hand with the drink I had ordered. I took a sip as soon as she set it down on a napkin in front of me.

"So, have you decided what you would like to eat?"

"Actually, no. Could you give me a couple of

minutes to look over the menu?...You know what? I've changed my mind, what would you suggest is good—any specials?"

"Sir, this being Friday and all, our special is fried haddock and steak fries; comes with homemade cole slaw that is to die. There are two pieces of fish that are yay big." She said, gesturing with her left hand and the writing tablet she carried in her right. You won't go away hungry."

"You know, that sounds just fine. Do you have any fresh coffee made?"

"Well, no, but it is probably worth your while to have me make a fresh pot now isn't it?" She said smiling. "Do you always eat alone, or are you fending for yourself tonight?" She asked, phishing.

"I am single, miss. I always eat alone." I told her. She may have been making conversation, but I thought I had just sparked some interest. Just then I caught another glimpse of the elusive woman I saw earlier standing at the furthest corner of the room. I was only able to make a knowing smile from that distance. "Excuse me, does that lady standing over there work here or something? She keeps looking at me as though she knows me." I inquired.

"What lady sir?" She asked, but when I looked again, she was gone.

"Never mind, she seems to have left." I said apologetically. My server's expression turned from interested to quizzical. "I guess I'll take that coffee as soon as it's ready. I must be getting tired." I tried my best to recover from projecting insanity.

"Certainly sir." she said more professionally this time, interest suddenly leaked out because I punched a hole in her emotional bucket. I was neat alright. I did a real neat job of making me less attractive.

As promised, she came back with excellent fish and chips with cole slaw. It was followed up with my first cup of coffee to accompany my meal. Other than that, she left me to eat without bothering me much at all. I was alone, yet, I felt watched. Scanning the restaurant, I only saw a few other couples eating together. It was early after all, and the supper crowd hadn't kicked into gear yet. The elusive lady was gone, as far as I knew. I finished up, was asked if I wanted desert. I declined, but had a final cup of coffee before hoofing home. I tipped my server well, and received the proper thanks, but I left wanting something I never got. The problem was, I really didn't know what I wanted.

Forty five minutes later, I hooked the inside chain on the door, locking myself in an empty apartment. I kicked off my shoes on the appropriate carpet and slumped into my cushy easy chair. I sat silently contemplating the merits of changing my brand of cologne, mouthwash., and a possible personality transplant.

About ready to turn on television, with few other choices for entertainment other than resuming my jigsaw puzzle or changing the linens on my bed, there was a knock at the door.

Speaking of puzzles, here was one made to order. “Who on earth...” I muttered, got up, walked to the door and peeped out the little magnifying spy hole. Beyond, stood an older gentleman, clean cut, handsome, well dressed. “Who is it?” I asked with a raised voice. No answer came, making it necessary to open up and face the speechless visitor eyeball to eyeball.

“Hello.” I said, obvious miff in my voice when I yanked the door open.

“I am Richard Jenkins Sr., your father.” He said as he inched his way into the apartment, and very much before I knew it, he shut the door behind him since he was all the way in.

Incredulously I asked, “What?...I don't even know my father. You could be anybody. If you were my father, why come out of the woodwork now?” I was shaking while addressing the pushy visitor, and frightened at his audacity.

“Because your mother strongly suggested that I should make the effort. She says that I need to spend a little time talking to you, helping you to come to grips with things you should have come to grips with a long time ago.”

“Well, it's a little late too late to be following her wishes, don't you think? She's dead.” I informed the boob standing in front of me.

“It's never too late son. I'm sorry I wasn't around,

but your mom just could not take any more of what I was dishing. Get over it. Your mom feels that if I am right in front of you, you might find yourself learning a thing or two."

"You talk like she told you to do this yesterday." I pointed out.

"Look. Let's not waste time with nonsense, alright? Every second of this is valuable, and I'm not going to be here long. Do you like girls, Rich? Wait a minute, don't answer that yet. Have a seat in that cushy chair of yours. You're gonna want to sit down for some of this, and I have to say my feet hurt following you around, so I'll take the couch here to take a load off." He said, guiding me to my own chair. He continued, "So do you...like girls? I'm just asking."

"Yes, but..."

"...Then this is what you have to do. It's time to share Rich. Spend a little less time worrying about the creases of your pants," He said wiggling his own perfect creases with his right hand, "and a little more time complimenting them, because Rich, they actually respond to that kind of thing. Women have a better quality of love than we do Rich, and that fact doesn't make us the least bit superior. Have you ever noticed how easily most women break into a smile Rich? And the way they laugh; have you noticed how much more melodic they laugh as compared to us men? It's like music, Rich. It's one of the ways they let us know they love us. But you have to keep an ear tuned to it Rich, or you'll miss it altogether. Here's something you might not know, Rich. All the time you worry about having your clothes lined up in the closet? Newsflash, most women do it naturally. They press their own clothes for the most part, and take care of them because they enjoy being pretty. They can find any of their favorite things instantly. They don't even have to be trained, they are born that way, Rich. Even if you are neater, straighter, more organized, women will always be prettier than you, Rich. I've been looking in on you, and you have been aggravating the snot out of me, Rich. There's so much of me in you, I can't stomach watching you. Your mom dumped my butt years ago, didn't ask for a thing because she was the one escorting me out. But she didn't do it to you because she was your mom. That's how much she loved you. Now it's come high time for you to learn to love the same way. You need to give something of yourself, give up that attitude of yours, so you can enjoy the company of others. If you do that, you will learn to love, Rich." He paused to come up for air.

"How do I know you're my dad?"

"There you go again! Drop it, will you? You know damned well I'm your dad. You can look into my face and see yourself there, You can look at my clothes, the way I'm dressed, and it's plain as the nose on your face. Unless you are so used to lying to yourself, you can convince yourself white is black, and black is white. Your problem is that you think that your way is the highway, and everybody else is on a side street. That attitude will get you alone. I know you aren't listening to a damned thing I'm saying because you're preoccupied with the shock of having a man in your living room you can't really come to grips is your father. All this good material is probably going to waste."

"No..."

"No, what do you mean no? You believe I'm your dad then, and every thing is going to be fine because you hear me loud and clear?"

"No!"

"Well I won't give a bunch of facts and figures to prove I am whom I say I am because I really don't have the time. For once in my miserable life, I have a much better place to go, and I only have a short time left here, so I'll love you and leave you son. Consider this though, before I go. Do you see that nice neat stack of magazines on the table beside you? I won't wait for an answer, but if you stagger every other binding away from each other, they will stack better instead of leaning to one side like that. Plus the space between them will allow you to read what's on the binding because they aren't so close to each other. The point here is that there is always somebody better than you, and in this case, more anal than you. The best scenario is read them, clip out a recipe if it is exciting, and throw the rest away. Better yet, recycle it, so there is enough paper to send you a new magazine next month. Do you see how stupid all of that was? My bet is that you don't."

A KNOCK ON THE DOOR

"I have some parting thoughts I have to say." The strange man reached into his shirt pocket to pull out a business card. "This is the address of a man who will make all your earthly dreams come true. Look him up, it will be time well spent. But remember that you heard this from me. Even if you have everything, none of it is bloody good without somebody to share it with. Put everything you've got to good use because I'm here to tell you that you can't take it with you." He rose, came over to me and said with his arms held out, "get up and bring it in son. I won't be seeing you like this ever again. This was my one, and only opportunity to try to fix the biggest thing in my life that I regret."

I tentatively got up from my chair, because he had such a commanding presence, I could not quite refuse. He gave me a hug that pretty near broke my ribs, kissed me between my ear and my neck and said, "Your mom and I will always love and be with you. You are the only good thing that came out of us. You were produced from sheer love." He walked straight out of my apartment, leaving me still holding the business card in my hand, and a bewildered look on my face.

I went over to the window that looks down over the street, but he was nowhere in sight. He must have gotten into a waiting car or something because there wasn't anybody or anything down there.

I examined the card still between my fingers. It was the name, address, and phone number of a lawyer, because there was the title attorney at law printed after his name, but not much else. I put the card next to my phone to give me time to think through what I wanted to do with it, and went back to my cushy chair to mull over what had just happened.

I guess it just wasn't my night because no sooner I sat down, there was another knock at the door.

This time around made me a little leery of what was next, but I went to the door and opened it right away this time. "See here..." I stopped mid sentence, my facial expression replaced with that of shock. It was the server from the restaurant earlier. The server had my briefcase in her hand that I must have left at the restaurant without thinking.

"Excuse me," she said, "You left this under your

table. Your address is on the back written in magic marker. Since I live really close by, I volunteered to return it to you. Charlie's is closed for the night, and the earliest you could get it is tomorrow."

"Oh my God, thank you! Come in, come in. Sit a spell, you must be tired."

"No, I can't, I have to pick up my son at my sitter's house. She needs to be relieved. She has a family of her own to take care of, so I can't dawdle."

"Alright then, I'll let you go with my thanks, but I did not know there was anybody left in the world that excellent." She laughed, light and melodious, very pleasant on the ears. I was instantly reminded of my so-called dad's words on the subject.

"You know where I work. Come to dinner. Your a good tipper, by the way." She said, turning to go downstairs to go home.

"Wait. What's your name?." I asked when she'd reached the first level.

"Carolyn." She answered over her shoulder, and bolted out the door before I could ask any more questions.

I developed a headache thinking about everything that had happened since I got home. There wasn't much I could do about this Carolyn woman with a son and a possible husband, so I refocused my curiosity. I made the call to the number on the card the man gave me, leaving my name, number, and address on voice mail, then had a long hot shower to unwind.

Finally, finally, I could relax and enjoy my weekend. Too much excitement, far too much. I had chores to do, but that's a Saturday morning thing. I had a date with a bag of microwave popcorn and a movie, but less than four minutes later it got off to a rocky start. The bag I put in the mike burned, setting off the smoke alarm and stinking up the place pretty good. It took opening the windows to get fresh air in to get the smoke and smell under control. With the windows open and Spring Rain aerosol choking me up as badly as the burnt popcorn, my phone chimed a ring tone. Ready to scream, I just went ahead and did. Then I opened the link to the caller, and said calmly, "Hello there."

It was the voice of the man calling himself dad.

"Rich...your old man again." He launched himself faster than I could react. "Look, I can't talk long, I have a date with your mom, and this time I'm not letting her down. I only have a few seconds, son. Your mom and I were talking, and she thought that before I joined her, I should tell you how much we like this Carolyn woman. If you think you could find it in your heart to give her a chance, she's good people, Rich. I can only tell you not to screw it up. I'm sorry son, I have to go, we love you..." The phone line died. I lowered the phone from my ear and stared at it. A second or two later, I maneuvered through the menu to calls received. My backbone steeled up enough to ring him back and give him a piece of my mind. There was no call received in the last three days.

"Aww." I growled, frustrated. So this is Friday night at the Jenkins's place? Well, if I ever do get all my earthly dreams, I'll pack them 'em in a big old bag, and move to a Caribbean tropical island serviced by the post office. All I need is one hut on a secluded end of it. It needs to be furnished with my cushy easy chair, a solar powered DVD player, a Netflix subscription, and enough stamps for movie returns. Oh, and a maid who wears short skirts with a Ph.D who can make real popcorn. Contrary to what my supposed dad thinks, I would be happy with a couple pair of permanent pressed shorts, and seven tee shirts with one through seven printed on them. I smiled as I thought that I easily could survive with only four pairs of undershorts marked week one through week four.

Filling my brain with these happy fantasies were working toward forgetting being irritated until I had another knock on my door. I reacted by pretty near pulling the doorknob off when I opened it.

"Hello!" I snapped.

"Hello sir, my name is Mike T. Handy of the law firm of Handy, Smith, Gershwitz, Moody, and Sleeponit. You can call me Mike." He said, extending his hand.

"Honest Injun? That's your for names for real? Sleeponit, that hilarious!"

"Be that as it may, sir, I happen to be your father's financial attorney for his personal affairs. We need to sit down and discuss the trusts he has set up for you, and his business as well." He explained, a little put out it seemed. I guess he did not appreciate jabbing at the firm's nomenclatures.

“For me, Richard Jenkins, are you sure?”

“Oh, yes indeed. He has been my client for many years, and I know about all of his wishes as he was a close friend of mine. I hold the personal documents stating all of them. I'm curious, how did you know to call?”

“How did you know to come here?

“A question for a question, but you left an address, and I was hunting for a last known address here in the city. Well—so now answer mine, how did this coincidence come about?”

“Because he came to my apartment earlier tonight.”

“I'm afraid that would be quite impossible since he died almost day ago. He suffered a massive heart attack. I was at the hospital when he died. He was an important man, and important to me. We did not release news about it yet so as not to create a panic. The board members at R. Jenkins Corporation know about it, of course, but otherwise we have been hushed up about it until some kind plan can be set up to continue business as normal. R. Jenkins Corp is not publicly traded, that's a good thing, but having a mass exodus of good employees to another place would be catastrophic. I also think that it is quite cruel to suggest that he faked his death and talked to you.” He went on and on. It appeared he perceived me differently after that.

“I'm sorry.” I said defensively. I didn't mean to suggest that at all. A man knocked on my door, and announced himself as Richard Jenkins Sr., my father, someone I can't even remember, I was so young when he went away.”

“What did the man look like, may I ask?”

“Well, he had black hair, graying at the temples, rugged but handsome face, hazel eyes, about five ten or so, intimidating if I had to choose a word, and well dressed. He had gray dress pants, pressed sharp, matching tweed sports jacket, white shirt, and a tie that wasn't too obtuse.” I finished while observing the color draining from Mike's face.

“Do you mind?” He asked, holding up his phone

as asking permission without verbalizing it.

"Certainly." I responded.

He walked off to one side of the room, dialing as he did so. Pressing the phone to his ear, with hushed tones that I could hear perfectly well, he asked if Richard Jenkin's body had been transferred to the funeral home yet for viewing preparation. "It has?" he said in a vindicated voice. "Well, I'm at the son's house. At least I think it's the son of Richard. This guy says Richard showed up here to talk to him earlier tonight, and gave him my card to call. I don't know what to think." He waited as the caller gave him his piece of advice. He continued, "Yeah, I think so too. I think that's a good idea." He listened with a pause. "Okay, will do. I'll call back as soon as I can." He turned to me and said frankly, "I want to check this all out. There is a great deal of money involved here, as well as a responsibility to the corporation that we were seeking to protect. We were wondering if you could supply us something we could verify your relationship with Mr. Jenkins."

"Are you kidding? I really didn't think I was related. This guy sort of pushed his way into my apartment, and unloaded a bucketful of personal stuff that made me feel very uncomfortable. He gave me this card to call you, and I did because I got curious if you want to know the truth. But I am in no way inferring that I believe any of this."

"I understand, sir, but you have to understand my position in all this. If you did prove to be his direct heir, and I have instructions in his will to find that heir, it would resolve a host of issues popping up all over the place. But I also have a problem with your story. Your man sure does fit the description of Richard Jenkins to a tee, but I don't believe in ghosts. Do you have any documents that might help us verify a relationship, a birth certificate or something? Can you tell me your mom's name, maiden name, that sort of stuff?"

"I can place my hands right on it, sir. My file system is totally organized. My mom's name was Bertha. Her maiden name was Lansing." I said as I moved to my desk to open a short file cabinet alongside it. I opened the bottom drawer and found the proper folder with personal documents. I pulled a leather bound sheath with my passport, my birth certificate folded and stuffed in a pocket. I opened it. I handed it and the passport to Mr. Handy.

"I must say I see a resemblance of character. That is impressively organized, I must say." Said Mike. He examined the document, fingers trembling, evidently nervous that the preposterous story might check out somehow. Examining the certificate and the passport, it indeed proved I was Richard Jenkins. Would you happen to be free this evening? I would like to have you meet some people. Some people that are as skittish as can be right now I apologize. On top of all that, your story makes me skittish too, no offense."

"None taken, but you are in my house right now, not the other way around. I wasn't asking for anything but information on this so-called, 'lost daddy'. It is a little hard to believe that he has somehow reached out to me, alive or dead. It seems to be in my best interest to proceed. Can you arrange for me to view the body somehow?"

"Probably not until after the mortician has finished preparing him for viewing at this point, but certainly by tomorrow he should be ready I would think. We will be taking the balance of the night for you to ask and answer questions from these people. Perhaps you should pack some things so that you can spend the night. I have an extra bedroom, Or if you prefer, you can spend the night in a hotel if that makes you more comfortable."

"How did you get here? Why can't I stay in my own place?"

"I took a corporate jet from my firm to come here, Mr. Jenkins. It shouldn't take more than an hour to get to where we are going. I'm lying...plus travel time to and from airports. Come on, I'll take a chance if you will." He said, observing my reluctance."

"This isn't what I thought my weekend would be, I'll tell you that." I complained.

A little over two hours later, what would usually be the end of my night and time to pull the covers down on my bed to slip into cool, crisp sheets, I was offered a drink in what looked like a company cocktail hour in Mike Handy's living room. It was quite late, and his family were in some other part of the house, presumably ready for bed. There was a gaggle of starchy business upitties that would usually intrigue me, a kinship of sorts. They somehow turned me off after the heart to heart from my so-called dad. But these were his people, an oddity that I hoped might be explained at some point.

"Mr Jenkins, "began a titular head of the group, "What is it that you do for a living?"

"I could not imagine what a question like that would have anything to do with any business we might have, but I am a certified public accountant. I work in mortgage banking."

"Any degrees?" I was asked.

"Like an MBA or something? No sir, I do not."

"Pity." I was told, as though I was less of a person.

I was learning fast though. "Can we be formally introduced, so that I know who and what is grilling me? It would seem that I was whisked away in the middle of my Friday night because you gentlemen seem desperate about something."

"Indeed, Mr. Jenkins. My name is Gerry Frampton. I am the current vice president of R. Jenkins and it would appear that you are my new boss."

"Indeed—back to you, boss of what?" I inquired.

"We are an advanced consulting firm for the energy industry."

"Oh, is that so? Do you make anything?" I asked.

"No, we advise the oil industry where the best opportunities to drill exist, and where the best spots to consider getting at natural gas." He told me.

"So you have a staff of geologists that analyze areas to see if oil rigs, or gas fracking operations can be set up? Have I got that right?"

"Precisely, sir."

"And what is it that you do, Mr. Fancypants?" I said in the same demeaning manner, he had for me.

I coordinate our findings for an entire petroleum industry desperate for fresh places to drill that don't encroach on sensitive or protected land or sea floors protected by the government."

"Oh, and are there any such areas in existence?"

"Increasingly diminishing."

"If any. It seems to me that your geologists would be much better off working at the source, than for you."

"That is exactly what we are working to prevent." Gerry came back, looking less polished and professional as we went on.

"I see. What is it that you want from me?"

"We need a captain, or what appears to be a captain, sitting in Richard's office so that our staff don't move away stemming from a lack of confidence."

"A figurehead, somebody who has these people convinced that they will be cared for if they remain under your employ. Does that about sum it up?"

"Well, I wouldn't put it exactly that way..."

"I would. Furthermore, I don't know how I feel about the whole dirty business yet. I read the news, sir." I turned my attention, "Mike, what trusts did my father set up, and what do I have to do with them?"

"Well, beside a personal trust account set up on your behalf, he set up a further system, giving you access to the company store, so to speak. It was his hope that you would come in after his demise to run the company and continue his dream. It gives you total executive control."

"Oh, I see. Is that the reason why Gerry and the quiet gentlemen behind him are so nervous? Well sirs, we will let my father's financial lawyer here do his thing, and I will be back on Monday morning to assess the situation here. Please try not to work yourselves into a state that makes you throw up. I will be as fair as my father thought I should be, I promise."

Gerry muttered, "That's what we were afraid of."

I smiled to myself. This was a crazy, but eventful Friday night. I began to surmise why my father deemed it necessary to come out of the woodwork, as a ghost, or somebody about to run away to enjoy the rest of his life. I could not wait for Saturday to see the body. "Mike, could you show me to a suitable hotel for the night? I think I have seen and heard enough for one Friday night."

"Are you sure?...."

A KNOCK ON THE DOOR

"Absolutely. We can rendezvous tomorrow, and go view the body. Can you get a taxi for me or something?"

"I wouldn't hear of it. You are the son of a very good friend, and I will take care of this myself after we show these men out so they can go home."

"Much appreciated."

The men showed an even more phony side, by instantly wiping their faces clean of any concerns, and smiling in cordial fashion. I, on the other hand, was guarded. We all said our goodbyes in the large reception hall at the front door. When they departed, I spoke a bit more frankly with Mike Handy. "Do I have the ultimate say here, or am I the figurehead they portrayed me to be Mike?"

"Make no mistake you hold all the cards and I couldn't be more impressed how you handled yourself with these men. I would be careful though. Such people can get even more desperate as they slide into an abyss."

"I very much agree. Would you give me a call when we are able to view the body? I would like to check it out before he is unveiled for public viewing if that is okay with you."

"I would be honored sir. You seem very much my friend's son so far."

"I hope not! I think I have been a pompous fool for most of my life, and seeing those men had me looking in a mirror."

"Richard Sr. went through much the same metamorphosis. We spent hours talking about some of the choices he made in his life, regretting quite a few of them, if not all I'm afraid."

"Like father, like son?"

"It certainly looks that way. I hope you won't judge me harshly because I would like to remain your friend as was the case of your dad and I." I shook his hand.

"Let's get me to a hotel, alright? I want to fall asleep to a good movie."

I later laid in bed going over everything that had happened, now the previous night, as it was now early morning Saturday. I still had this eerie feeling that I was being watched, a sort of antsy concerned feeling that could very well be all me and my imagination, because to be honest, I could not believe what that room full of men were trying to sell me. Before I finally dozed off, I gave a great deal of thought to my dad.

Morning woke me up because I neglected to pull the drapes in the room shut. It was an excellent bright sunny morning, but rudely shining in my eyes. I rolled out of bed for my ritual morning micturition. I hopped into a most refreshing shower, letting the hot water hit my back, allowing me to think where I had left off the night before. Making myself presentable, I went in search of breakfast, finding, to my delight, a full service restaurant next door to the hotel. Revived by a couple of cups of coffee, I gave Mike a buzz to find out where we stood. “Mike?.....this is Rich. Look, I have a very awkward question if you don't mind. I need to know if my dad died of a natural heart attack?”

“All I was told was that he had a massive cardiac arrest.”

“Yes, but did they verify it to be sure, I mean so that the doctor who signed off on the death certificate, stated the reason for the cause as fact?”

“Well, I don't know. What are you suggesting?”

“I'm suggesting it might be good to have an autopsy. I want to know for sure the exact reason for his death. Do you think you can arrange that for me? And let's keep this action as quiet as you kept his death. Can you do that for me?”

“But why...”

“Because I have been creeped out from the very first moment I got involved with this. Call it a premonition, or whatever you like, but as the only next of kin, I want this.”

“Alright, I'll call as soon as I get off the phone. Would you like for me to pick you up?” Mike asked, offering.

“Call—get this action underway for me please, and then give me a call when you come to get me. I'm having breakfast at the moment, but I will wait for you in my room at the hotel. I will bounce out to meet you when you get here.”

“Okay then, if you're sure. I'll do it as soon as I

can. Goodbye for now." He hung up.

I needed to go for a walk before I went back to the hotel room, both to help digest my breakfast and to clear my head at the same time. I thought about Carolyn some. I really didn't know the woman well enough to dis her, or give her thumbs up. I haven't considered any woman seriously, really. But this one kept seeping into my head. Suddenly, it occurred to me that she might have a Ph.D and can make real popcorn. This fueled my fantasy a tad, and left me wondering what she looked like in a short skirt.

It was well over two hours later when my phone went off. Mike was ready to pick me up. Maybe some of the torture would ease up of not having enough facts to formulate a conjecture.

The first thing he said to me was, "The body is at the coroner's office, a county pathologist is working on the case now. It is one of the best facilities in the state, and even if samples need to be sent for further evaluation elsewhere, we should have a definitive answer by the afternoon, Richard." It was the very first time he called me Richard, as though it would have been sacrilege if he uttered the whole name. It didn't bother me to be called by my nickname, but from him, this was a form of letting his guard down into another world of familiar endearment.

"Yes, well, it will be a long day then, huh?" I really wanted a visual identification of the man. It would make me feel a ton better knowing the man in my apartment was somebody that was tipping me off, rather than speaking directly as my late dear old dad. I take it you're bringing me to have a look see at the company?"

"Actually, no. I'm taking you to your dad's house. It's yours now, such as it is as it is really rather unpretentious. He had the home built about four years ago, making a handsome profit from his old place. It's not anything small and crappy, mind you, it's just that it doesn't come anything close to his old digs, which was set up to entertain big wigs and CEO's. Richard felt he ran all the way to the end of that particular road he was on. He decided to make some serious life changes, much to the dismay of his staff at the office. Personally, I loved the new direction he took. It made him easier to be around, more relaxed, easier to talk to, joke with, and so forth. At the office, he had slated some changes as well, causing consternation in his staff. He wanted to make a move to develop and use green energy products. Since, as I already mentioned to you, R. Jenkins was not publicly traded, he was free to do that. But the whole company was set up for traditional energy exploration. All his geologists, everyone in the place were trained and geared to what they were already doing. This was causing panic way before his death. He had hoped that some or all of his geologists, and a lot of his staffs would come on board, embrace moving into the twenty first century and into areas that make sense for this day and age. He confided in me that the resistance was overwhelming. He threatened to pull out, start over. Since we hold the purse strings, and sole ownership of the place, the staff and employees would essentially have to start over themselves."

"Oh my God, it all becomes clear!" I said. "Did you support these moves?"

"Wholeheartedly. I was completely on board, in spite of the fierce opposition. You will find that his house is very energy efficient, to the point of being revolutionary. The direction the home faces takes advantage of whatever the sun has to offer. Insulation values are off the chart. Heat is geothermal, hot water supplied by solar, both directly, and indirectly. He cooked by newly developed electric elements that are powered by extremely efficient solar energy panels. The house is not off grid, however, the footprint is so small, it is negligible. Even his car is gas free."

"And this was the philosophy he adopted, away from R. Jenkins?"

"Indeed he did, Richard, indeed he did, and I was very proud of him. I did not see his death happening at all. This new life of his made him more animated every day." We pulled up the drive of a solid little ranch style house. As warned, it was much like any other home. The front was constructed of reflective Thermopane panels for much of the forward part of the edifice. We got out of the car, Mike handed me the keys and told me, "After you." Old habits were hard to break, I suppose, because his home was so neat and tidy, pests and rodents would run away in disgust. I fit right in. Mike explained to me, “The bulk of his estate is in trusts, and in your name I might add. His personal belongings were his, and as such, need to go through probate. But it is a matter of formality, and you can well afford jumping through the hoops.”

“I think we should have a service come in and keep the place free from dust settling from non-use, and to appear that there is still traffic through it.”

“That makes perfect sense, Richard.” Mike said, a tone of admiration in his voice.

The home had everything to maintain a regular life. It surprised me to see a laundry room with an ironing board set up in it, a rack of clean pants and shirts neatly lined up on a wire shelf in the closet. I felt my father's shirts with my hand. It was as though I would feel my father in them. Several shirts were still in the dryer. We traced back into the living area. He had no fireplace, but did have a mantel with some pictures on it, and a thirty six inch average flat screen television above it, hanging on the wall. I moved closer to the mantel, suddenly realizing a clue may reside in the frames adorning it. I picked up the assortment of pictures, one by one, all old pictures from a time long since past. A young man who looked a lot like me stood alongside a very young version of my mom. There was a picture of me at about three years old, one I had never seen, and one of my graduation picture from high school. That was about it. All of them were from a time that age made them unrecognizable. Warmed, but a little disappointed, I toured the rest of the home. A patio at the back of the home held promise of many comfortable summer evenings lounging in privacy, overlooking a spacious backyard, with a pretty little garden at the far end. I did not want to leave. It felt like home in a very short time.

“Come, we will go to my office and get this process underway. I promise to work hard to make all this as painless as I can.” Mike said, guiding me back out the way we came. On the drive to his office, Mike outlined a friendship going back some twenty years, a span that included changes in the man's interests as well as personality.

Mike was married, and had a seventeen year old

daughter who was very independent at the moment and bound for college in the coming year. But she regarded my dad as something of an uncle and addressed him as such. It seemed my dad managed to have a few people love him at least. Mike told me that he was the one who made funeral arrangements for my dad though, so the love nest might end at that dead end street.

Much time was spent at Mike's law firm hashing out details of business holdings, the transfer of control, the worth of the trust set up in my name, and procedures to weather the probate storm. But time flew in the process, and Mike was interrupted mid sentence well into our legal hoopla by the call we were expecting. We found out soon enough that a homicide case was opened up by the district attorney's office. The autopsy had revealed foul play, showing chemicals ingested over a period of time, making my father quite sick, eventually killing him was the conclusion. The investigation hoped to prove where, when, and by whom had caused it. A search warrant was taken out for R. Jenkins Corporation, in the hope that clues could be recovered there. It seemed some of my suspicions were confirmed for the time being. "Do you need help gaining access?" Asked Mike helpfully.

"Come on," Mike said after he hung up, "We have to meet the police at R. Jenkins. Just hold on one second while I get my extra key."

We took the freeway to shave some time off the trip, doggedly breaking speed laws of every place on earth, including the Autobahn. It wasn't a sightseeing trip, that's for sure. We pulled up to a circle of cars, unmarked, that transported a number of experts, each of whom had a job to do. Two well dressed detectives came our way and extended hands in greeting, but got down to business quickly as they had a job to do. We were not allowed in the building with the crew during, or after the investigation for that matter. "Ahh...sir," I asked as the detectives started to walk away, "are we allowed to know if you found something, I mean, can you call my man here who called for the autopsy of my father and keep him somewhat in the loop, or is that against company procedure?"

"Nooo...I don't think we can do that. We'll let the D.A.'s office know you were interested though. It sure ain't for us to step on toes. Oh, by the way, you will be available for questioning should we need you, right?" They stated more than questioned and turned heading for their part in the job.

"When was the last time you came here, Mike?"

"Years." Mike said.

"I guess that means we are both off the hook if there are clues in there, huh?" I concluded.

"You know what they say, everybody's a suspect."

"Even them?"

We left the same way we came in, not being of further service. Mike said to me, "Why don't you come and meet the family tonight after we are all done for the night. I won't even put my wife on the spot to cook. I'll take you all out for dinner. I know just the place."

"I think there will be plenty of time for that. Why don't we wait until I am in better spirits. I'm sure I'd make a better first impression." I told him.

"Alright, but you have made a fine impression on me."

"Thank you, I don't get that a lot. Maybe this experience will make me a better person, huh, let's hope?"

We showed up at the funeral home to see if my dad's body had returned for viewing preparation. I was anxious to identify this guy. I wanted the load off my mind, so as soon as we got indoors, I went straight for the office. "Excuse me, " I began, "I am here to see if I can see the body of Richard Jenkins Sr.. I know you haven't had time to prep him yet, but I was wondering if I might get a peek at the guy's face. If not now, when would be convenient?"

"You are absolutely right, mister...ahh??..."

"Jenkins—the son."

"Oh, I'm sorry, but still no. It should be ready for about seven o'clock this evening. We have him scheduled for the Pink Room across the hall."

"And the reason it is pink is?..."

"Oh, no reason. It's not all pink. Why don't you

have a look to see if it meets up with your approval."

"I imagine everything will be fine. I'm just a bit testy right now, I am sorry sir." I apologized. "I guess I can come back at seven. What's a few more hours?"

"I totally understand my good man. The obituary went into the paper yesterday, and the burial service will be Monday morning."

"My good man you called me, that's speculative, but I thank you." I said. I shook the man's hand to assuage his fear that he'd done something wrong, and Mike and I left.

"You know, I have to insist that you come home with me. We have to discuss if you want to go back home, or stay here in the city through the wake and funeral. I can take you back to the hotel later, and I am perfectly one hundred per cent sure that my wife will be sympathetic to your position in all this. Besides, now that you are embroiled in this sordid affair, you can't leave in the middle of it. I guarantee you have enough money not to concern yourself with finances."

"Oh, alright. But you're still not going to have your wife cook, right?"

"Not unless I decide it might be fun sleeping outside on the yard furniture."

"I see your point."

All in all, we had a wonderful late afternoon. I really haven't befriended anybody since high school, so it was virtually a new experience for me, and I must say that I liked it. Mike's daughter Karen was charming and smart. She had a genuine affection for my dad, and I could see why he liked her. Mike's wife Laura was equally gracious and warm. I can't say I am an ace judge of character, but the family was one I hoped I could call my friends from that point forward. It was a pleasant, simple sharing of time and meal, and a welcome change from the induced stress of the last thirty or so hours. During the afternoon, Carolyn crossed my mind again. Lack of social skills aside, I think I would like to try my hand at luring her into conversation when I get back home. I've enjoyed company more than I would have guessed. But, all good things must come to an end, and at around a little after five, I told them all that would like to get to the funeral home by seven, but thanked them all for taking me at face value, and I would enjoy it if I could see them all again soon. Mike and his family left me off at my hotel, with my renewed thanks. I took no more offers of rides. I told them all that I was perfectly capable of getting myself back to Oliveira's Funeral Home. I wanted some alone time with my dad, even if he was deceased. The trio understood. I called for a taxi at six fifteen, hoping to get picked up before six forty five. I got freshened up as best I could hope for under the circumstances. I was not prepared for a funeral.

"You sure are prompt." said the funeral director when I showed up exactly at seven. "Why the hurry?"

"You know, " I said, "I would really rather not get into it. Is he ready for me to see, or not?"

"Yes sir, exactly as promised." The man, I assumed was Mr. Oliviera, led me into the Pink room. But there in the coffin was a shock to all my sensibilities.. This was the man who came to my apartment on Friday. A frown was on my face, and my eyebrows quite knitted.

"Are you okay Mr. Jenkins? I have seen this kind of thing before. Perhaps you should sit down before you pass out."

"Oh—oh no. I'm alright. I wasn't prepared for him to look this way." I lied. I was flying by the seat of my pants throughout this whole thing. I was shaking like a leaf in the wind. Here, I thought that someone in my dad's employ, or a friend of his was trying to express his interests to me, and to point me at a sinister plot that made my dad pay with his life. That was my theory anyhow. Smart guy I am! I rationalized the un-rationable! I stared at my dad's countenance for quite awhile. He obviously said his piece, as clear, and concise as he possibly could. I would have to accept that and deal with it. Turn the next page. I figured a good idea would be to have a seat since I needed one, and wait to see who would show up, if anybody. The people I met last night I would count as enemies—better defined, suspects. I wondered how the working stiffs felt about him, or if he had any friends aside from Mike, Laura, and, Karen. Did he have a girlfriend? No, he would not have looked forward to seeing my mom the way he did if there was a woman in his life. Besides, I saw no evidence of a female in his home. Acquaintances maybe, significant other, certainly not. I also think the pictures on the mantle said it all.

"Dad. You there? I'm confused. I am getting to know you, and just look at you, you're toast man! It doesn't look like you had enough time to complete your atonement." I said, empowered because I was alone in a big room with just him. I sat for two hours. Not one person came in until nine o'clock. Some stragglers signed the guest book and came in to pay respects—none of them sniffed, none of them asked if I was family. The line grew heavier with the same results; sad. The procession persisted until about a little after ten, and then stopped. I tried to keep a mental picture in my head of the people who came, all of them obviously acquaintances, work or otherwise. If I came tomorrow, I could get a clue of just about everybody in my dad's life. It seemed there was a mad rush to drop the guy in a hole, and pull the dirt back over him so the grass would grow again. Mental note to self, "Self?...After all this is done, it might be time to make some friends." Maybe it didn't matter. The guy I met in my apartment seemed happy to take the next step.

I called a taxi before eleven to get back to the hotel. When I walked into the hotel lobby, I noticed a bank of computers on tables with fancy schmancy chairs to sit and look at them. "How much is it to use them things?" I asked the lobby person on duty as I pointed to the computers. "It's free sir. No charge for guests." She told me.

"Oh. Thank you very much."

Saddling up to a computer in a far corner so I could concentrate, I set out to educate myself on green energy. I wanted to investigate every avenue I could think of that my dad might have come up with lucrative enough to rock the boat at R. Jenkins the way he did. Every innovation I could remember in dad's house needed further examination. To get involved in a venture that dad got so passionate that he would scrap the direction of an already successful business, intrigued me. Deciding that he was going in the wrong direction after years of success was motivation too. In that case, he might not have come up with anything at all. He did seem to be wrestling with demons, seeking rectification for past sins. Both scenarios would make his employees pretty antsy, perhaps enough to murder. The thought that I was now the head of this business and that I had no particular love for it, would put me at odds with these people now. Somebody there has already demonstrated he or she was dangerous. I felt even stronger about that now. Taking out the boss and owner because you didn't agree with his policies was unacceptable, especially since I agree with the boss and owner.

I spent several hours going over things like, Thermopane glass, geothermal heating, cooling, solar panel technology, cooking, solar hot water, all of it. None presented pressing research and development that could revolutionize R. Jenkins. It looked more and more to me like he just didn't believe in what the company stood for anymore. Any inventions he would have liked to see developed would likely be known by his crew, and relegated to R, Jenkins exclusively. These were questions I would ask there on Monday afternoon if the police were done and allowed it. I couldn't think of anything else to explore, though I did learn a few things. Gaining insight into what was in Dad's mind to transform the R Jenkins giant was impossible. He might just have wanted to slow down at his age and build energy efficient houses, for all I could tell. Wouldn't that have been a kick in the pants to all those hifalutins? The more I pondered that thought, the attitude of the man I met on Friday night might just have had that in mind.

I finally called it quits for the night, actually, early morning again. When I woke up in the morning, I had no plans other than breakfast again at the same place. I would be going back to the funeral home that night to see what floated in, but in the meantime, I gave Mike a call. “Mike,” I said when he answered, “Would it be inconvenient for me to swing by to get the key to my dad's house? I would like to see if he might have something to wear in there that is more proper for the funeral tomorrow.”

“I'm sorry, I can't allow that because it is in the court's hands for now, but I can help you out. Let me come pick you up. You can spend the day here." The dependency on someone other than myself was disconcerting at first, but this was such a nice family, it made it much easier to grow into the unaccustomed sensation.

An hour later, I was sitting in Mike's family room, doted on by his charming wife and daughter.

"Would you mind sitting with me, and telling me a little about my dad? You have to know that, before this, I don't remember much about him at all. My mom never said much about him when I brought him up, maneuvering the conversation away every time."

"Why don't you tell us a little about yourself, and then we can compare notes." Mike's wife Laura switched up on me.

"Well you know, I really don't talk about myself much, I'm not all that exciting. What would you like to know?"

"Do you have a girlfriend?" Karen asked quickly, but innocently enough.

"You know, it's funny you should ask that, but the other night....."

The banter was give and take, questions and advice, serious and laughing—well into the afternoon. Laura made us all supper. Karen left at some point to do homework and study. I felt so at ease in a situation that generally sends me running for the hills. But when both women were tied up elsewhere, I brought up what I was trying to find out the night before.

"Mike, did my father bring up what he had in mind as far as taking R. Jenkins in a new direction?"

"Not specifically. He kept us in the loop when he built his house. He explained the reason behind every choice he made, what each appliance meant to the energy savings on the whole. He outlined why he placed the house in the location he did, and why it faced the street, the short side facing south with the front porch on it, the patio on the short side back, extreme Thermopane windows facing east and west on the private sides, and what their function entailed. The slopes of the roof facilitate snow melt in the winter. Each step drew out more passion from him , more than Laura, Karen, or I had ever seen."

"Did you get a feeling there was some innovation that he wanted to exploit some particular device to develop it further?" I asked.

"No, not really. He seemed happy using all his selections in his house. I think he was testing the efficiency of the house as a whole." He said.

"I agree. I can't find one thing that needs work on it to make it better, all of it state of the art. It seems to me he wanted to build houses. His name would be on a state of the art, energy penny pinching monsters that could save millions of kilowatt hours if there were enough of them. That would be something I could endorse, but not with the crew in R. Jenkins, that's for sure. What would you say if I took the same path as my father against the people who worked for him?"

"It goes without saying you need to take care, but I think it's a great idea. I can't see giving up the R. Jenkins name. It's your name and don't forget, the reason they wanted you as a figurehead in the first place is that they dread the best of the help going someplace else. The best of the help will get jobs, it's almost unstoppable. There's not a whole lot to keep them here in the first place."

"What do you mean by that?"

"Your father wanted to do something with his own company, but wanted to offer a better incentives to stay at the same time. His geologists make decent money, probably much better than if they all moved and they worked for the oil industry itself, but have have mediocre benefits for the long term. He wanted to change the structure of all that so that they would have something at the end of it all. The money wouldn't be flowing from the oil companies if we detached from them, but R. Jenkins and the employees would be a lot more secure."

"So these people would not be making as much money per week?"

"No, Richard. Cash flow from the oil industry is lucrative at times, but during tough times, not so good. You make it when you can get it. Your father wanted something a little more solid and steady, not to mention getting out of the crossfire of environmentalists and the like."

"Tough choices—so his geologists just might be able to negotiate themselves better packages within the oil industry itself?"

A KNOCK ON THE DOOR

"Essentially, yes." he said frankly.

"But what do these folks offer R. Jenkins in a different structure?" I asked.

"Not much. They can test for radon, water for wells..."

"So it's inevitable that it shuts down, even if we try to do the right thing. The biggest losers are in administrative positions."

"Now you're all caught up, your dad's rock and a hard place."

"Can we assemble severance packages for the lot of them?"

"Sure, but start over capital would be down quite a bit."

"Then, the way I see it, R. Jenkins has to do a transformation just the same way my father's house did. The big fancy building is mostly show anyway. Do we own it outright?"

"Leased."

"How long until it's up?"

"I'm supposed to be privy, but I haven't kept up. Expenditures are automatically dispensed these days for mandatory debt, but I can check the records tomorrow when I get back to the office, why?"

"The way I feel about it is that the current crew felt so strongly opposed to what my father wanted in his own business that it got him dead. Even if my dad owed loyalty to the folks in his employ, death paid off the debt, and that is exactly what I intend to tell the crew on Monday. I mean to carry out my father's wishes. For those who want to join us, an invitation will be extended to go along for the ride. It's up to them; otherwise, there are plenty of people who'd jump at the chance for a construction job. We could use an architect, and geologists who can perform perk testing and the like, plus it would be nice to have expertise that could tune a project to land it is built on. These days people are always talking about retraining to keep up with changing markets. It seems to me that this is the time. I'm already on board with it, and I'm a CPA. I was learning about what my father had done in that house of his, and it's fascinating, really cool stuff. It might be nice to be on top of a new emerging market like that. What do you think if we tackled a small neighborhood development like an apartment complex, something innocuous, but revolutionary, small scale enough not to be overly ambitious? That way, it slips through a side door into a community where we make sure the tenants are happy with amenities that make them happy to be there, but beyond the rent, the rest of the utilities don't drain either the tenant or the owner? The overall footprint on the area that it resides would be negligible. Power outages would be almost painless. It would be nice also to treat the sewerage from the place so that gray water maintains the grounds."

"Jeez Richard, you've only been here a day. You came up with all this in that short a time? What are you, some kind of whiz kid?"

"Not at all. I'm filled with all kinds of emotions right now. I'm angry, and appalled at the attitudes of the self righteous folks at R. Jenkins. Such a pious group that someone may even have felt the need to take a life to preserve something that didn't deserve to be preserved. They were trying to out muscle me, and they need to be shown who is in control. At the same time, I feel more inspired than I ever have been in my lifetime. I feel closer to family than I ever have before, even though they have been taken away from me. I feel blessed to have made friends, and hopeful to make more. I feel strongly that I can establish a reason and purpose for my organizational skills, besides annoying the people around me that is. I feel good about myself, Mike."

"I want to help you if you will let me."

"Let you?" I said confused. "I was trying to win your approval and endorsement."

"Well, you have it." Mike said simply.

I buried a father I didn't know in life at all, only to grow close after his death. I struggled to keep my composure after the funeral to confront his business associates. The tension got even worse when I arrived at R. Jenkins. Caution tape still quartered off my father's office. But when I called the administrative staff together and outlined my ideas, it did not go well. The quiet office people that stood behind snotty Gerry during his initial dissertation exploded on me, drawing Mike to the line of fire. After they pounded us, owning attitudes that they were the ones in charge. I kept *an above it all* demeanor but shut it all down with one broad stroke.

"I came today to give you all a chance to come along an exciting ride with me. My dad started something that kindled a powerful interest in me, but this dream is not his anymore, it is mine. I own this place now, and I hold the purse strings. You have no say at all. I figuratively extended my hand, and hoped you would take it, but instead you all tried to bite my fingers. Therefore, I regret to tell you all that your services are no longer needed. Thank you very much, but please pack your things and leave." I said leaving the office space, taking Mike in tow, heading for the office of cubicles containing the balance of the employees.

"We have contracts! The yelled at us as we left."

I turned just long enough to say, "Fine, why don't you go ahead and test them against me, but my order stands. Take your things and leave my property."

Cubicles that held the very core of R. Jenkins listened with the same apprehension that the administrative staff did, but listened to my whole spiel before saying anything. My speech was a tiny bit more lengthy for the six men in this part of the crew. I explained the steps that led me to contract this disease of passion. I outlined the very same ideas that I did only minutes before. I finished by saying, "I don't know if any of you are interested, but if you are, I would be glad to have you with me."

"We all have something to offer. We waited to be approached but never were. The water cooler talk has run wild around here. The rumors that flew about your father's plans interested all of us. Yours intrigues me even more."

"Yeah." almost all the rest of them said in unison.

One of the others said, "Each of us has geological engineering degrees, and all of this falls into our chosen fields, fields that to be honest, we would have chosen for ourselves in the first place. How did you come up with the idea of apartments?"

"That's what I asked him." Mike agreed.

A KNOCK ON THE DOOR

I answered, “Because I got to crunching numbers in my head how many kilowatt hours could be saved if you have enough dwellings in a spot. But having a neighborhood of single family dwellings sort of leaves the owner free to change all our hard work back to traditional energy guzzlers. I also got to thinking how cookie cutter the area would look when all the houses face the same direction on boxed blocks. It would lose the charm we could build into each building. The grounds could be maintained better by sharing the landscape.”

“Logical.” said one of the men.

“You got that right, but that only leaves one question. Until we find which one of us did your dad in, I am having trouble trusting anybody here right now. Personally, I'm not staying very long until this mess gets sorted out”

I reminded the man, “If you guys are all on the same page, it seems like the motive to kill my father is lacking in here, unless one of you just couldn't stand the way he looked. The people packing their bags in the big office space down the hall are the ones bucking the tide, but I'm no detective. All we can do is wait to see what the police come up with. Which leads to another question. Mike, about the lease, did you get a chance to find out when it's up?”

“About three months Richard.”

“Good, because it's high time we found ourselves a smaller, less pretentious building, that would not have as big a hoof print as this fancy dancy monstrosity. This building will not fit our new image. One that we would be working together as equals in the end, you know, no intercoms needed because what I am proposing here is a business partnership, that gives us all incentive not to slack. Everybody in here would have to pull our weight or we sink together, understood? The venture capital is what this business has already generated, but where we go from here is all new territory. My friend here will continue to manage our—and I stress—our, finances. Are we all in agreement here?”

Two detectives approached us from the side unnoticed. One asked, “could somebody tell us where we could find a Mister Gerry Frampton?” They were the detectives that Mike had let into the building the day before, but they flashed badges in case we forgot; protocol and all that.

"He should be packing his stuff in the office down the hall. I fired him." I informed the starchy men.

"Thank you." was all one of them said. The two turned with militaristic precision, and marched out the way they came, but turned for a second at the door to tell us not to disturb evidence that was quartered off in any way, or we would face tampering charges. A short time later they emerged on either side of Gerry who was handcuffed, continuing to march right out of the building to an unmarked car with a grate between the front and back seat, sliding him neatly into the rear of the vehicle.

"Is there a place we could go to lunch and talk over all of this without standing in this building? Quite honestly, it gives me the creeps." I told the people in the room.

I turned the key in the deadbolt on the outside of the door to my apartment. It was a long and stressful week, and I finally flew home to do all those things that must be done—things you can't just walk away from. But my place somehow seemed not mine anymore. I walked in without kicking off my shoes on the shoe carpet by the door. I could still smell the burnt microwave popcorn in the discarded bag in the trash, and the saw jigsaw puzzle on the card table with the border completed just where I'd left it. I threw the hastily packed bag of clothes on the bed in my bedroom, and began to get cleaned up with fresh clothes from my closet, and not the packed bag that I lived out of for the week. Except for a suit I borrowed from Mike for the funeral, I had gone Friday to Friday literally with two changes. It was another personal milestone for me, but something without wrinkles would still be really nice. Come Monday, I would have to let the office know that I would be resigning. If they wanted a two week notice, I would be glad to comply. Although I deluded myself for quite awhile, I knew the place would keep going on just fine without me. I would empty my desk, and another CPA would mount a new picture of a framed loved one on it, adjust the telephone comfortable for their taste, and attack the in pile just as I have always done. I felt sadder about the delusion than the fact. I dressed casual, and intended to go to lunch at Charlie's Family Restaurant. With no idea what I would pull off there, I knew I could count on good food.

I hefted the heavy oak door at Charlie's to yank it open, and felt a sense of foolishness wash over me that I would think Carolyn would have me in the back of her head as I had her for the last week. This would be a pretty good indicator of my social ineptitude. But I stood tall because everybody has to eat. “One to dine this afternoon.” I told the pretty little thing behind the podium. She had a big smile filled with white teeth that instantly cause you to smile back. She took me to the same area as last because it suited single persons and small parties better. I thanked her and saved her from her automatic seating repertoire, asking for a diet coke. I wanted a clear head so as not to make any of the social mishaps that I am prone to. She seemed disappointed that I didn't select a more costly drink, but she wasn't the server and there was time for that sort of thing later.

I didn't see the hostess alert a server this time around, but somebody did catch me by surprise sneaking up on me. I did not know where she came from, the bathroom maybe, or dropped in from the ceiling, but she made me jump, nerves and all that. “So you decided to come back after all.” Carolyn said. I knew so little about this woman, I didn't know her last name.

“I sort of got tied up this week. Just after you dropped off my briefcase for me, I found out that my father died. I had to fly out of town.”

“Oh....oh, I am so sorry, I had no idea.” She stumbled, a little stunned.

“Nothing to be sorry about, you could not have known. I could not stop thinking about your random act of Samaritanism the whole time I was away.” She smiled at that. I thought it best not to compliment her too much, since the way she looked, although amazing, was forced on her as a uniform for work. How could any man not look at a hot woman in a short black skirt, white top, and a too tight leather bustier type accessory? It was best to keep my big mouth shut about that one. Not enjoying the show would be silly.

“What can you suggest other than fish? I just

want to try something else. I'm not exactly bound by religious constraints. Spiritual, yes, religious, no."

"How do you feel about baked pasta with mushrooms? The folks here are religious, but not spiritual."

I laughed out loud at that. "You know, that sounds very good. I love mushrooms anyway."

"What did you tell Julie that you wanted to drink?"

"Diet coke for right now." She went off on her mission to serve. I sat contemplating what I might say next, if anything.

Carolyn came back with a twenty ounce glass of diet cola with a lemon stuck on the rim, and a straw. "Thank you very much, I am thirsty from my walk." I told her.

"Oh, do you walk too?"

"Every chance I get these days. One of the advantages to living in a city is that you have access to the bus, and walking. I really don't believe in cars much. If I lived in the suburbs, then I would understand, but we all can't be out driving at the same time. The other side of that is that by walking, I discover places like this. If I were driving right now, my eyes would be on the road trying to avoid getting hit."

"I agree, and I have to walk anyway since I can't afford a car."

"Well that's how you keep a figure like that!" I segued very nicely.

"I'll bet you say that to every girl in a leather bustier."

"Oh nooooo! I didn't even notice."

"Liar! Every time I take this thing off, I shrink two inches. Let me check on my other customers, and your food."

Twenty minutes later, she came back to bring me my food. "Thank you Carolyn."

"You remembered my name, how sweet."

"Yup, and I'm not usually good with names, but even though I came to eat hoping I could thank you again for what you did, I'm not really flirting with a married woman."

"Oh I'm not married anymore. My husband ran

off after I got pregnant with my son Joshua. We divorced after a year. Consummate deadbeat dad."

"Now I'm sorry."

"Not at all. Joshua's a great kid, good company. I love him with all my heart. He's been my life."

"How old is he now?"

"In a month, he'll be eight."

"Sounds like somebody I would like to meet someday. Any friend of yours must be a good guy."

"Nice of you to say, but if you hang around, I can walk you home. I get off my shift in under an hour at four. I pick my son just a couple of doors down from your place. You can meet him, and practically walk into your door afterwards."

"I would enjoy that very much. How fast do you walk?"

She laughed that melodious laugh again, the one my dad so aptly described in his diatribe. "Should I put on a fresh pot of coffee?" She asked, indicating that she really did remember me from last time.

"Good idea. I can stretch the time after I eat with that, and maybe desert so that I don't get the jitters." She laughed again.

I nursed the food I had in front of me wishing I had a book, so I did not look so conspicuous. But Carolyn came with my check just shortly before she had to go. I gave her the same tip as I did last time, so that I could avoid the appearance of trying to buy favors, which I certainly did not. I only wanted to see if I liked the woman, I mean, beyond the physical of course. It would be nice to find out if she liked me. Truth be told, I was working on a recommendation from my parents, who must certainly know something from their viewpoint. If the afterlife brought more of being only human, it would be disappointing. But mom and dad could very well be urging me to open my heart so that I would be capable of opening it in the future, who knows? I pondered these things waiting for an opportunity for God knows what.

"So are you ready?" Carolyn said, breaking my reverie.

"Most assuredly. If I drink any more coffee, my nerves will jump off the table like Mexican jumping beans."

"Placebo effect. I've been serving you decaf."

"Well maybe I'm just nervous about the walk then."

"Nervous about what?"

"About whether or not you find me worth walking with, I guess."

"Well, let's find out."

The walk was far too short for me to learn all I wanted to know about her, and far shorter to give any impression that I was worth having as a friend as we pulled up at the front door of where her son spent his few hours after school. He came bounding out before she had to walk up the stoop to the door. This was a boy that loved his mom enough to look forward to her picking him up.

"Who's this mom?" he asked more curious than protective.

I answered him for her, "I walked your mom home after work. I live right over there, so it was on the way. She talked you up so nice, I just had to meet you."

"Well sir, it's real nice to meet you too. Thank you for keeping my mom safe. I worry about her walking alone here in the city. She's too pretty to be out by herself."

"Boy do I ever agree with that!" I said. "My name is Richard Jenkins, what's yours?"

"Joshua Crabtree. We have to get home now for supper. Will I see you again sometime?"

"It's up to your mom Josh."

"If he comes to dinner, he can walk me home."

"You really are a heck of a server, aren't you?"

"I just want to see if you show up two days in a row." She said smiling.

"See you tomorrow Josh." I told him shaking his hand. I bounded up the street to my apartment. To look at me, you'd swear I just got my first kiss.

Mike was my eyes and ears at R Jenkins. We had run off the administration staff, and they weren't to return after Gerry's arrest. It was plain they did not want to be labeled guilty by association. Gerry found himself a defense attorney, but we were all in the dark as to the particulars. When he faced a grand jury, we would get some sense of the charges and reasons for them if he had to face a trial. The rest of us in the new alliance at R. Jenkins were not going to wait around for another shoe to drop. The crew was searching for land to purchase for our project. The group fanned out in six different directions, in pursuit of suitable spots. If and when a spot was found, we could tow temporary office space to conduct our business until the project nudged toward completion. We all knew full well obstacles would present themselves along the way, and temporary headquarters seemed a logical move to keep complications down to a roar. Getting permission from local governments, be it townships or city, on up to the state level, could prove stressful. But with the amount of expertise on our side, we at least had some of the odds stacked in our favor. Large tax payers coming to a region that don't want to destroy the environment, or be a drain on resources, would offer something very hard to refuse. On the other hand, part of the system, as people think of it, is the utility infrastructure. Eliminating most of the dependence on those utilities would be destined to stick in a few board members craw. My crew felt that it would be hard for them to protest too loudly or run the risk of raising the ire of public sentiment. The only hard thing to overcome was whether our not the folks in an area we chose trusted us to do what we were saying we would do. After all, anybody will tell you if it sounds too good to be true, it probably isn't. Mike caught me after I got in, chilling out from the natural high of Carolyn and Joshua's acceptance. "Hello," I said into the telephone receiver.

“Well! Don't we sound upbeat today.” Mike said. “Look, the men have scoured the state, and there are plenty of areas that fit the bill. There doesn't seem to be any reason to leave the region entirely, and not in our best interests. Being on bus lines provides extra convenience for future tenants. One of the men, Freddy I think his name is, found a ten acre parcel south of the city zoned for low density business. He billed the project as single story condos as we discussed. The owners of the parcel said anything goes, but down at City Hall, the answer was that they'd *look into it*. Ohio has building code requirements that mandate certain things, but on the whole the concept has been well received."

"Good news, Mike, thanks. We knew there would be hemming and hawing, but if we keep leaders in the loop, and they can take some of the credit for the model, we shouldn't have much of a problem. If we were in a Township, there would be even more crabbing, maybe even voting by the residents. I think it's better to clean up an area that needs improving, than to change a nice spot, bringing an element of uncertainty to it."

"Agreed. How did it go at the office?"

"Resigned as of today. They didn't pack a box for me, but they offered. Goodness, it's nice to feel wanted." I related.

"Don't take it personal. There's a swinging saloon door for employees nowadays. It's gotten to be the new normal."

"That is why I made my guys partners. There's got to be pride, or we don't have anything. I would love to change the name of the business, but nothing like yours. I'm still laughing about that."

"What?... That's his name, Sleeponit." Mike said defensively.

"Well what about this guy Moody? Is he the cranky guy in the firm?"

"As a matter of fact..."

"Still, R. Jenkins isn't a corporation anymore. Can we fix that? You're the expert in such things."

"Yeah, you're right though. Your father kind of figured from the beginning, that the company would go public. But he ultimately retained control, making things easier, and less answerable to shareholders, thank God. It would make sense to move toward making the company an LLC for tax purposes. It's lucky that R. Jenkins did not incur any debts, or the creditors could have come after you. It would be a smart thing to protect the men and yourself from personal liability."

"What about Gerry and the staff? Can contracts be called in on us?"

"Already paid off. Severance was spelled out very clearly. Your father did not want to be beholding to them, any more than he did shareholders. It made him antsy. He was just one man. The staff was more iron fisted than he was and at the same time, they were applying pressure to be publicly traded. It would have been in their financial interests, and they would have gotten their wishes eventually. It wasn't what he wanted anymore. He reached a point in his life where he just got tired running over people and exploiting them. He wanted to apply the brakes, but he had to buck the trend all the time. He felt if he yielded control, R. Jenkins would run amok. It was a constant battle for him at the end, and his bane, since he loved everything neat and tidy, plus one step beyond that, making the Jenkins name right. I'll work on it as soon as I can."

"I'll let you go then. Keep in touch."

Carolyn and Joshua went home. Mike hung up to get into his own routine. I was left with my cushy easy chair. How exciting! A little over a week ago, my easy chair and I were good buddies. I remember distinctly wanting to move somewhere in the Caribbean with it. All I had was about twenty two hours left until I went to dinner and got served again by Carolyn, and hoping that she would be interested in me. The walls seemed to close in on me. I went for a walk to get some air. Outside, having people around me eased up my pressure cooked nerve endings. A crowd of young teen boys took turns practicing on a slight grade with skate boards, no doubt the next extreme sports stars. A mama bleated at the top of her lungs for her son Paul to get inside this instant and do his homework. A man and a wife walked together, husband pushing a stroller with a very small child in it, wife all smiles from pride flashed at anybody who looked their way. Three teenybopper girls sat on a stoop of steps, eyes trained on some super significant message on a telephone, squealing in delight. Two twenty somethings walked hand in hand, spending quality time in the sunshine. Another man and woman stood at a strategic corner, woman singing like an angel, accompanied by the man showing amazing skill on his guitar. The box in front of them had dollar bills in it held down with a rock. I stopped and listened a while. They were as good as anybody I'd heard recently. I dropped a five spot in the box, the couple gave a slight nod of appreciation but kept on with the music. An old man read a newspaper on a bench at a bus stop. A lady watered some flowers blooming in a flower box outside one of the window sills of her apartment. Yet another woman a few doors down, brought in a pretty dress that had dried in the sun after washing and draping it over the railing on her balcony. All these things assaulting my eyes and ears had a tranquilizing effect and all of it completely preferable to searching high and low for another piece of the half finished jigsaw puzzle on the card table in my apartment. That was something best saved as a natural cure for insomnia. The balance of my time before dusk, was spent at the city park, a place crammed with the sights and sounds of life. I watched a female softball game. The pitchers hurled underhanded pitches that rivaled anything I could throw, over hand or otherwise. After the conclusion of the game, lights were on to illuminate the last three innings. It was a sign that it was safe to return to my empty apartment—until morning that is.

The following morning, I went out to a diner for breakfast, but after that, kept myself busy consolidating my personal belongings, cleaning and throwing away things that weren't useful to me anymore. The time would come soon when I would have to move, I knew that. Still, I missed being a part of going someplace to do something all day. At about two o'clock, I readied to go to dinner. My walks became more enjoyable with every trip out. I was at Charlie's before I knew it, yanking open the door and entering like a regular patron. "Hello again." said the hostess, deviating from her routine. "Yup, here I am again. How are you tonight?"

"Very good thank you. Come to see Carolyn again I take it?"

"Well yeah, I guess so. How did you know that?"

"It's a small restaurant, sir. We were talking about it today, she's moving you know?"

"What?" I asked stunned.

"Put in her notice today." This dampened my mood a bit, although I had no idea how I would handle the situation either. I got seated and offered a drink. This time around, I ordered a rum and cola, with an order of fried cheese sticks because I didn't have anything in my stomach. Soon Carolyn came with my drink. "I suppose blabbermouth over there already told you I put in my notice today?"

A KNOCK ON THE DOOR

"Yes she did, and now I am coming to grips with it. I am sorry to see you go. We were just getting to know each other. Where are you headed?"

Things have been tough for my son and I. I'm going to Cincinnati to move in with my mom for the time being. It will be a help to me, and it will give my mom something to do. I'm worried about her health too these days, she's gotten so old and frail. She lives by herself you know."

I brightened and bubbled, "I don't believe it! I'm headed there myself. As I told you, my dad just died. I'm trying to consolidate the business I inherited from him. As we speak, we're trying to launch a project that he wanted to do before he died. I'm going to make happen. I gave notice to my job yesterday! Wow, what a coincidence! I actually spent the day cleaning up my apartment, getting ready to move. I hope you don't think I'm stalking you because it's just not the case."

"You mean I already have a friend there?" She asked me.

"If you want one, I would be honored." I replied.

"My God, gee whiz, I can't even think straight now. Let me get your appetizer." she said moving off.

I ordered and ate dinner, but can't remember what I had; didn't care. Before I knew it, it was time for us both to go.

"So, do I get an address where I can look you up when I get there myself?" I asked Carolyn when we were out the door heading home.

"Hand me your telephone and I'll enter it in." She fidgeted with the contraption when I handed it to her, punching the keypad as we walked.

"Tell me, why would you even give a guy like me a chance anyway?"

"Normally I wouldn't. A man came into Charlie's for lunch. He started telling me about how anxious he was to reunite with his son after not having any contact at all since he was a boy. He said he'd been following him all over the place, trying to get a feel for where he might go or do when he got off from work. He told me he didn't have too much of a life. In fact he told me, he was a chip off the old block. The man told me that he would somehow try to suggest to his son that he go to eat at

Charlie's as a deviation from his dull routine. He told me that he might not be much for conversation but that he was generous and probably a good tipper. He described him, and told me to be on the lookout for him, to treat him well that I would get out of it what I put in. Well, you were the only person that even came close to that description, but I really could not be sure. You were a lost soul though, and I did not want to get involved, but you ended up a good tipper; weird, but it was a hell of a coincidence. You deserved to have me deliver your briefcase to you since you lived so close to where I had to pick up my son on the way home. You seemed so much less uptight the next time I saw you, I figured you must have had something pressing on your mind. I can't put my finger on it, but for some reason your personality was a lot stronger the second time I saw you. I can't carry a man. My life life is too complicated for that.

"I can certainly understand that." I told her. "I'm not in the mood to carry a woman either. I would like for somebody to come along and meet me half way. I have been doing just fine on my own, but lately I have been hungry for something more. Your son Joshua blew me away last night. You blew me away too—hell you raised him; an excellent job. By the way, what did the man look like?"

"He had black hair, graying at the temples, rugged but handsome face, hazel eyes, about five ten, very neatly dressed. He made me very uncomfortable."

I didn't say anything, though I was stunned. So my dad really did follow me around. That's why his feet were tired.

Our trip ended once again at the stoop where Josh was at. He came running out just as he did the night before. "Hello again Mr. Jenkins. Thank you for walking my mom home again, I appreciate it." He walked up to me and gave me a hug. My heart melted. I wasn't sure where to put my arms, but decided to put them around him to hug him back.

"Thank you Joshua. You can count on seeing me again. You too, Carolyn. I will call as soon as I can. Be safe, both of you." I walked the rest of the way to my empty apartment, looking back at Carolyn and Joshua walking home. They both turned to give me a final wave.

A KNOCK ON THE DOOR

I entered my apartment, going directly to the bathroom to splash cold water on my face. A lot of this was pretty hard to take in. I looked at my face in the mirror and wondered how many changes could happen to one man in so short a time.

But then there was a knock on my door. I wasn't the least bit irritated—but I was confused. I wondered if it might be Carolyn and Joshua. I went to the door and opened it. It was an older lady who I mistakenly thought knocked on the wrong door. I did not know the woman. "Can I help you?" I asked

"Yes, young man. I am Carolyn's mother. I came here to plead with you. Please to look after my baby girl. Your mother and father have contacted me, and told me to talk to you before I move on to meet with my beloved Harry, and it is too late. She is expecting to move in with me in a couple of days, but I could not hold on. This is the best thing for her anyhow, but I think she will be distraught. I have not left her in a very good spot to be in. Your mom and dad think that you are in a good position to help her through this, both emotionally and financially. Your father told me to remind you of what he spoke to you about not being able to take it with you. Your mom told me to say that you should be strong, and she means, right now. I can't talk to my daughter, that would be my wish. She is not ready for love, you are. That is what made you susceptible to hear us. You reached out with your heart, which was empty at the time, and wanted something more. That is why we are able to help you now. We believe that Carolyn and Joshua will fill that void nicely. Be there for her at the proper time, and I am sure my daughter will see the good in it. Don't force it, just be there at the right time. You know what's coming, rendezvous with it. I have to go now. It was nice to have met you. We will be with you always." She gave me a hug, and a kiss on the cheek. "Wait, what's your name?" I asked.

"Martha Westcott." She said, then left, never to be seen again.

I was quite shaken. I could not function for a while, a long while. When I almost came to my senses, I tried to call Mike. Thankfully, I could not get him, or he would have heard my voice crack, definitely an indicator that Richard had something wrong with him. He called me back when he noticed a missed call. By that time, I felt a little better. "Mike," I said, trying to sound confident. "Would you do me a favor? Remember when I told you I met a woman that I like? Well, she was planning to move to Cincinnati to be with her mom, but I got wind that something happened to the lady. Her name is Martha Westcott. Could you help me find out more about the woman, you know, has she left Carolyn with the responsibility of burial, or cremation? Has she left bills? I don't want this woman in over her head. She has already quit her job and is bound for Cincinnati. I don't know how to handle this without anybody knowing we helped though."

"I think I'm getting to know you pretty good. You like this girl more than a lot. The only thing bad about this is that you are going to have to level with her that you are helping."

"Well, maybe I can call when her back is up against the wall and help her then. She'll know by tonight or the morning the latest. I could call her when she is drowning in strawberry jam. She'll be at that point anyway. I could offer help then, what do you think?"

"I think it's a better idea than being an invisible philanthropist and have her find out the truth of it later. You won't come out on top of that one."

"You're right." I said releasing a sighing breath.

"Call a mover, Rich. We need you here, and she is going to need you here. Get somebody good. They box, ship, unpack, bingo, you're moved."

"I need to take care of my lease. I have three months left."

"Handle it. You are a big boy."

"Okay, okay. I'm on it."

"In the meantime, I'll find out everything I can on this Martha Westcott. That way you aren't flying blind, okay friend?"

"Thank you. Good night Mike."

"Good night."

I hit the ground running the next day. I called a large moving company to find out if my job could be handled by them, and how quickly. I didn't ask for the price, a rule that has always been my credo. But this needed to get done. I needed to be stable if I was able to come to Carolyn's rescue. I had information in advance that I had no idea if I could use. Carolyn's mom wouldn't squeal on me, but that didn't mean much. The sensitive issue of losing a loved one had to be dealt with genuine empathy, and I wasn't in a good position to do that. Prior knowledge would make it phony.

I've had contact directly and indirectly from two moms and a dad. An emotional bond was created by both my parents reaching out from a better place because they love me. It was an experience that can't be shared, but will always give me a perspective that nobody else could match. I can only hope that I develop a love so strong that I can give of myself as strongly, but I aim to do my best at giving out of a simple act of kindness. Who knows if Carolyn and I will ever grow to love each other, but I know that I am ready for it.

I met with my landlord, leveling with him that I was needed in Cincinnati, and needed to move as of yesterday, a problem stemming from the recent death of my father. I wanted to know if I could pay off the rest of my lease so that no repercussions would come out of the woodwork later on. He flat out told me that it was the silliest thing he had ever heard. He told me that this was the meaning of extenuating circumstances. “Go. You've been a good tenant, no troubles at all. Your rent always paid on time.” He said. He thanked me for all of that, but that I needed to get my butt to Cincinnati. I shook his hand with heartfelt thanks and left with a clear conscience.

I picked a full service moving company. I wanted to handle more important issues. Carolyn and Joshua were on my front burner. The project at the newly renamed Jenkins and Associates LLC, was on a front side burner, not the big one, but the smaller one right in front. My associates were making strong inroads to expedite a purchase of land. All six men conferred with each other and viewed a chosen parcel together. The jobs were overwhelming, stemming from licensing, getting a sense how a city council felt about us coming in with a project so different from the norm as this one presented. Talking with lawyers and agents, hoping for closing dates sooner than later. Testing the parcel to see if potential cleanups were necessary. Testing to see if issues couldn't be cleaned up. We needed to question if the water table could accept drilling a well if it was permissible. Does the city have to supply us with water instead? A project of this magnitude might mandate it. Mapping topography to accommodate drainage according to code. My associates kept themselves very busy, and I was proud of them.

As soon as I had checked in with the men, I moved on to Carolyn and Joshua. I called at the earliest possible moment. I reached her in a state of turmoil. She almost didn't want to talk to me. She did it to be nice because she told me to call, eventually telling me about her mom dying. I had inside information, so I kept prying to get her to tell me exactly what was happening. I needed to pull teeth to get straight information. I suggested that in these kinds of situations, all sorts of expenses rear their ugly heads.

This is what I asked her, “Look, Carolyn, I know that you have committed yourself to moving here, and you haven't even had a chance to unpack, leave alone look for a job. As friends, new or not, I can help with all this, and it would be my honor to do it. Truthfully, I inherited a lot of money, and I can take the pressure off. I could give you a job. My associates and I are starting up a huge construction project, and we could use some help in a thousand capacities. If secretarial work is not your forte, then running errands might be. We have no formal office yet, purchasing and receiving will be a challenge at best. But beyond that, I can't stand idly by while a friend drowns. Further, Joshua plainly doesn't deserve that kind of struggle. He needs a stable atmosphere. Please, please let me help, no sex involved or expected, I promise.” I concluded as genuine and eloquent as I could muster. “Are you set up? Do you have a place to sleep?”

“Yes we do. This happened too fast for anything to change or be shut off. I have my old bedroom, and Josh can sleep in a third bedroom my mom had. That was the plan from the start.”

“Is Joshua okay with that, or a little frightened?”

“Josh is a very strong boy. Joshua claims to have

had a visit from his Grandmother, who told him that everything would be fine that she wanted to say she loved him, and I before she went on. I think it was his firm way of putting my mind at ease."

I didn't tell her, but Joshua was reaching out with his heart just as I was. I guessed this is how these things happen. I was meant to reach out to Joshua, and he to me. Carolyn would be a bonus, only if she could open her heart.

"Would you like to stay in my spare bedrooms?" I blurted out. We could eat, talk, sort out what you want to do and whether or not I can help. I would love to talk to Joshua again. All my stuff is moved and put away, no boxes. Life made comfortable for a night. Take a chance, I promise I won't come on to you." She laughed at that, a very pleasant sound."

"I spent all my money on movers. I don't have a car." She said. I could tell that she was close to tears.

"I have one now. It was my part of my father's estate. It's a little weird though, it's electric." I warned.

She relented, but didn't seem like she really wanted to. She reluctantly gave me her address. As soon as I climbed into my my new little car, I set the GPS gadajamajiggy, and off I went.

Later I was pinned against a figurative wall when we were all seated in the little car. Carolyn did not beat around the bush. She asked straight out, "Why Richard? Why would you help us?"

"Because we have some kind of kismet thing going on. I don't have any idea where it will lead, even if it will, but I owe it to myself for the first time in my life to find out. From the minute we met, I was attracted to you. Then I grew to love your independence, your relationship with Joshua. Speaking of Joshua, I very much adore him too. I figure right now that you don't know where to start. I know I wouldn't. I just buried my dad. He left everything for me neat and tidy, and even then it was hard. I can't imagine being in your shoes. That was a pretty big house I saw."

"I know. I couldn't get my mom out of it and into something more manageable. I thought the only solution was to double up with her, and now this. I would never have left my apartment if I knew. I would have signed another year lease."

Would you feel more comfortable in a place you can handle?"

"Quite frankly, yes."

"Well, between the three of us, maybe we can figure out the best way to handle that, huh? As for me, I am going to live in my father's house. What can I say, it's perfect? I fell in love with it the first time I toured it after my dad died. My attorney just got it pushed through probate"

"Were you close to your Father?" Joshua asked intuitively.

"No, not really. He went away when I was real young. I couldn't remember him at all. It was just my mom and I. I feel closer to him now that he's gone than I ever did."

"So we are the same?" Joshua stated more than asked.

"Here we are. It wasn't that far was it?" Two sets of eyes opened until there was more whites than irises. It wasn't what they expected. It was just a typical place, nothing pretentious about it at all, save the glass wall that had an inside shutter drawn so that you couldn't see into it."

"Wow!" the duo said collectively.

"It's not what I expected at all." Carolyn stated.

"I know—right? I would have taken another apartment too if this house wasn't exactly like this. Come on, I'll help you with your bags and we can have a look inside."

"Inside, mother and son began exploring immediately. Each innovation more fascinating than the last. But then Carolyn saw the pictures on the mantel. "So this was your family?" she inquired.

"Yup. I don't remember a bit of it, except the graduation picture that is."

"So your father kept up with you, thinking about his family the whole time he was gone out of your lives."

"Yes, apparently my mom was the one who turned him loose. He was just too hard to live with it seems."

"That's so sad."

"It seems that older he got the wiser he grew. He

was making good life choices that have blown me away. I want to continue in the same direction he left off, so I came up with something that encompasses it all. Why don't you get settled in? We can get something to eat after that."

"Would you mind if I took a shower? I have been going strong for a day and a half. I feel filthy."

"No, not at all. Go right ahead."

"As soon as she left the room, I took Joshua aside. "I hear from your mom that you said you had a visit from your Grandmother? Did she have a navy blue dress on?"

"How did you know?"

"Because she came to my apartment to talk to me too. It is the second time in two weeks that this has happened to me. My dad came to visit too. But your grandmother was very concerned about you and your mom. I don't want to say much about it because I don't want to come off crazy. I had a problem believing it myself. But she wanted me to look after you and your mom right now. I hope I can help. I don't know if your mom will let me. I will do my best. What did your grandmother say to you?"

"Just that I shouldn't be scared, everything would turn out okay. Gramma said that she will be watching us and that she will always love us."

"That's what my dad said to me, too. But then he warned me to be something more than I have been. He knew, because he was just like me. Then I met you and your mom, and then you moved all the way out here just like me. Crazy, just crazy. I still don't know what to think."

"I think that we should be together." He said just before Carolyn emerged from her shower, hair still wet, matted, but sexy.

"What are you two talking about?" She demanded.

"I think we should be together." Joshua stated bluntly.

"That's very kind of you, but do I have a say in all this?"

"Yes you do, yes indeed, you do. I just want to help, and to get something to eat. I don't have very much in the house just yet"

"Let me brush this hair out, and we can go then."

As soon as she was gone, I said, "phew, that was close. Ease up guy, I don't want to scare her away, okay? Take it slow and easy, my man."

We climbed into the car. I turned the key on to the car and asked, "so what do you two feel like eating?"

"Pizza sounds good!" Josh said.

"The only real food there is. Everything else is something to swallow to keep you alive. How about it? Does that sound alright?"

"Sure, but we need to get something on the way back for tomorrow morning." Carolyn suggested. "We can't go out for all our meals.

"Sounds good to me. Keep your eyes peeled. I haven't got the foggiest idea where stuff is at yet. I was born and raised in Columbus."

"I wasn't. Take a left at the lights up there. There used to be a pizza place on the right hand side of the street if it's still there." Carolyn instructed.

Just before I burned the roof of my mouth with a scalding hot slice of pizza, I was guilty of saying something stupid. I mentioned something to the effect that I wouldn't mind if I had their company all the time. It was true, but hardly suggestive, more of a statement that having great company, conversation, and very pretty lady around the house was infinitely better than being alone all the time. I said that I would miss them intensely when they were gone. Back in Columbus I could think of nothing else but seeing them both the next day. Perhaps I went overboard because a scowl spread across Carolyn's face. "I'm sorry." I said to her, "I didn't mean to make you uncomfortable, far be it. Judging by the look on you face, I've done precisely that."

"It's not that Richard, it's that I haven't had any man in my life since I divorced Josh's father. It's hard for me to let my guard down. I'm seeing you, it's that I'm trying to ignore you. If you and Josh hadn't twisted my arm, I would be at my mom's house right now, wondering what to do."

"We can look for a small apartment tomorrow. Then you can work on doing something with your mom's house. You will be fine. I'll make sure of it."

A KNOCK ON THE DOOR

"You're the first man that..."

"What? First man that what?"

"Nothing." She retreated back into her shell.

"My mom likes you!" Joshua said, embarrassing the hell out of her.

"Are you kidding me? She's scared stiff of me. She's so scared, she's making me scared."

After we ate, we stopped to pick up a few items for morning. After shopping, I finally drove home so we could prepare for bed.

I had fallen asleep quickly, and slept for a while, succumbing to exhaustion from what I have to admit was largely sexual tension. I was awakened by a soft kiss to the lips, adding to my problem. For me, this only happened in the movies. When I opened my eyes, an angel stood over me in the darkened room, but this time she was alive. I reached up and pulled her down on me. I lavished her with kisses that spoke volumes to how I really felt. She had no chance of escaping. She could not just wander into my bedroom the way she did. She couldn't wake me up with a soft kiss, stand over me dressed in that—well that white flowing thing that made her look an angel. Not and walk out again with her virtue intact. Not in the kind of mood I was in anyhow.

I whispered to her, "I'm totally good with cuddling if you want."

Two naked and sweaty bodies later, I searched for a way to bring up the word, *why*? What I asked instead was, "How did you know I was completely miserable? I mean really, I did not even hear a knock at the door! It's okay though, only angels come through my door."

"I know you are coming to Joshua and I with an open heart. You are so primed and ready to love it shows all over your face. It has not been so easy for me to be the same way with anybody except my son. But you haven't gone unnoticed. I find you intensely attractive. I haven't felt that way about any man since Joshua's dad. But letting go of complete control is hard, you know?"

I answered that load of crap patiently, "We have already had this talk to some degree. I don't want you to lose control. I only want you to lose half of it. I'll pick up the other half. That is what we just did, by the way.

You just lost half of your control, and I controlled the other half. We could not have been that wonderful together any other way. In my mind, it is the most intimate act a man and a woman can have. It comes with an explicit responsibility, and should have a guarantee that what ever comes as a result of it, is shared by both people equally. That is what love is...and I don't believe I just said that."

"Yeah but you did say it hotshot, and now you are going to have to live with it because I agree with you and feel the same way. From now on, if the bedroom's a rockin' nobody better come a knockin'. This is when we both decided to shut the hell up. We kissed deeply and fell asleep while I held her. The last thing I thought about when I drifted off to dreamland was, "Oh my God, Joshua!"

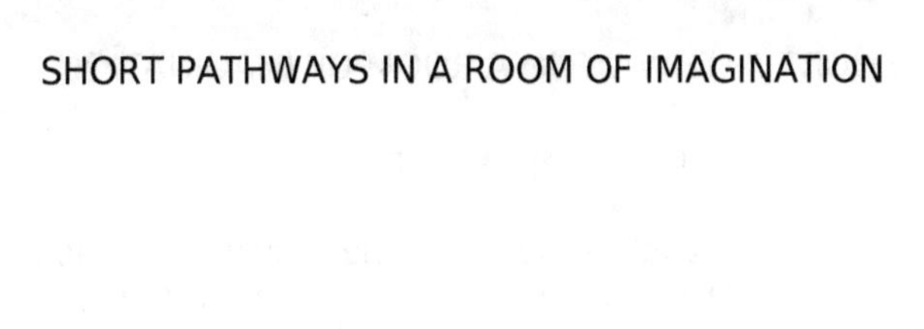

10-4 CANINE ONE NINERS

10-4 CANINE ONE NINERS

In the vast wilderness that occupies Alaska, a small, proud gray wolf was run off from his pack, solely because he was an omega, the tiniest runt of a litter. It wasn't his father and mother that had done so, it was others in the pack that did not want to bother competing with a runt for food if they didn't have to.

He was small even for an omega. He had no ranking. The reality of it is that he would never earn ranking. After being run off from his pack he continued on as a lone wolf, competing for food everywhere he went. He knew he would starve to death unless he learned the skill to survive in an intelligent way. Hunting amounted to stealing, when done in another pack's territory, and since he could not establish one of his own, that way of life was risky business indeed.

He taught himself to run long distances—very long distances. He kept at it until the power in his legs, belied his size. His jaws too, coupled with cunning developed by eating on the run, allowed him to make kills that needed to be seen to be believed. Even so, most, if not all of his diet were things consumed quickly.

It was still the coldest part of the third winter season on his own, the darkness still much longer than the light. That fact was fortuitous for the runt because most pack hunting is done during the light time, taking some, but not all of the danger away. But the cold is a dangerous thing too, temperatures dipping so that a single small wolf had a great deal of trouble trying to insulate himself against it. Finding a suitable cave that wasn't occupied by a larger predator than himself was a rarity. But the runt always, always got by, in spite of not having a pack to share heat with.

The little lone wolf lost count of the darknesses spent alone after his exile. He had finished dining on a horseshoe hare in a territory quite clearly marked by a large pack. Tracks were all around in the snow where he was, evidence that the pack had hunted and eaten in the vicinity recently. The runt knew his scent would attack the pack's noses powerfully, especially the leader. They were close by. But it seemed they had eaten their fill and had already laid down to sleep for a couple hours. The runt was one of two things; running on luck, or the pack was friendly and could be approached to come join them. If the latter was the case, the runt would have to compete to stay with them, so he ran like the same wind his scent was carried on, putting as many miles as he could put between them. He could never clear the territory completely in a short time, being much too large an area. But his defense was brilliant and could be used at any time. He outran anything or anybody who crossed his path. His defense was also his offense, for it wasn't just enemies he outran. None of his prey could get away from the runt. Furthermore, he only stopped to rest if it was safe, not because he was full.

He hunted so fast, no other wolf could have kept up to his pace. Because of the lifestyle that was forced on him, running abilities made him faster than any other wolf. Because of his small size, his jumping talents matched those of his running abilities. It wasn't uncommon to see the small wolf jump over 8 meters, often in combination with his long distance running. He would have made a wonderful addition to any pack, except that he wasn't strong. Speed was his advantage, strength was not. The runt stabbed fleeing birds right out of the air. Hare, voles, marmots, muskrat, squirrel, and even tenacious mink were no match at all. Larger game for the runt tended toward beaver, or the dangerous wolverine, both of which he managed to kill on many an occasion. Fishing skills were second to none, but not in the winter.

The runt ran about 50 kilometers or so, and could easily have run three times that distance because of his strong legs. But he caught a scent and heard a small weak whine in a rocky crevice that lay in an outcrop to the left of the flatter path he was on. Against his better judgment, he stopped to investigate. What he found was a small female omega, pathetic and sickly. She appeared not to have eaten in days. She was too weak to move, yet she growled at him anyway, feistiness her natural demeanor.

Head bowed submissively, eyes closed to small slits, the runt moved closer to the female, sniffing, and finally licking the face of the near-death female. From that very instant on, the runt was transformed and became thought of as Master, and the female considered as Mated.

Master's first priority was to hunt quickly to secure food. His plan, formulated on the spot, was to feed Mated like a pup.

The omega, something that would never change, had to use his experience. There was no time to plan, plot, stalk, or any of the other niceties. Master's style, borne out of necessity, was strike, eat, and run. This hunt to save the life of Mated was not to be the exception.

Master accomplished what he wanted. He quite gorged himself in a decidedly short time, even in the darkness, it didn't matter. He made his way back to the female omega to tend to feeding her in a way done only to pups just past the point of nursing. He caused himself to regurgitate into her mouth. Close to death, she accepted the food. It took two times to serve her, but after a while, Master got her to stand and follow him. He needed to make progress getting them as close to getting out of the territory as they could be, if not all the way. What he did, is what he always did; hunt on the run, even if he wasn't in the mood to eat just yet. As dawn came to the wilderness, Master fed Mated birds and rodents as they traveled, and she ate ravenously.

Mated got stronger as nourishment revived her exponentially. Master even located water for her to drink that wasn't frozen.

Forward motion was slower than if he was by himself. It increased the danger to them both, but Mated got faster nightly, due to her wanting to prove to Master that she was worthy to stay and travel with him. Every day, Mated made an effort to keep up. She practiced hard, matching how Master comported himself, and his lifestyle. Each day she got faster. The continuous exercise was not like patrolling territory, jogging like drones on paths reaching every corner marked by the scent of a pack. No—Master's way had no regard for anybody's area. But no deer, elk, or caribou were ever felled. Danger from other packs and lack of time were the reasons. Very little was left after Master made his kills, almost always entirely consumed. Mated was learning fast, becoming more skilled in Master's methods, and becoming faster, as well. Her development could not come fast enough. Inevitable confrontations with bigger, stronger gray wolves, even dangerous predators, was only a matter of time. Leaving enemies behind, the way Master could do with ease, had to be only a matter of time also. Either one or both of them would die if she could not match his speed. Master made the commitment to train her, and she was an excellent student. It seemed Master and Mated were meant for each other.

Two full moons worth of darknesses had passed. Here and there, examples of budding life began to appear. The heavy cold yielded to just plain cold. Darkness hours shortened, the light times got longer. Master and Mated were inseparable. Mutual respect for each other had reached a level unmatched by any other pair that were mated. Yet, they weren't truly mated. To be mated usually meant searching a defensible area to stop for a while and sire young; even settle down. Settling down would never be an option for Master.

The area that Master first found Mated instilled a crazy notion that seemed a natural at the time, even more so now that Mated starting to match Master's skill to run and jump. It gave them opportunities to utilize terrain no other wolf would consider, and game that enjoyed elusive habitats too hard for most to consider. The couple decided to prepare a den at the top of a steep rocky mountain, previously home only to goats and sheep. They would go on to become some of the biggest prey to both of them they had ever known to hunt.

The pair frolicked, enjoying freedom neither of them had ever dreamed in their omega lives. This was not to say that the lovers found a spot free from danger. One misplaced step could send either of them to certain death, plummeting thousands of feet. Even avoiding falling great distances, falling off large rocks and boulders into treacherous ravines was all but probable. But by training daily in this new territory, negotiation became second nature. They were better still than the current occupants. Due to the conditioning of their legs and their nimble abilities to run and leap tremendous distances. Huge feet from running crazy distances made paws toughened against rock surfaces. Watching the two leap about was much like watching graceful does in the forest, a thing of beauty. Landing 4 or 5 meters away from cliff, to rock, and cliff again, touching down gently on paws as though a feather floated down to the ground. It made the effortless act appear as though it was ingrained naturally in them. Lightness played an important factor. Consequently animals that generally felt safe from most predators suddenly found themselves confronted with hunters who were more like cats. Yet they were much faster than patient cats, ferocious in their own right, sure footed also, but lacked the stamina of persistent sustained speed. This consistently tipped hunting skills in Master and Mated's favor.

Mated spent time preparing a den to give birth, expecting a litter, never guessing she would produce young going into the winter; or ever. Now spring brought wondrous changes, and a chance to build a pack for the two outcasts. Mated helped Master hunt right up until the end of her pregnancy. A spot was chosen by the parents close to a small spring that only swelled when it rained. It was deep between two boulders that had an overhang. Not quite a cave, but just as protected. This is where she produced a litter of five tiny pups in the spring. The whole pregnancy deviated from the normal behavior of other packs. But this was Mated and Master's way, and they made the rules. The rules for them felt right and good.

Danger from predators of a different sort came at the two new parents. Large birds and cats that shared hunting in the very same area, needed to be warded off. Neither parent was particularly intimidated. Indeed, these predators had sampled fierce, quick, decisive battles with the pair in the past. Though hungry, for the most part these same enemies gave them a wide berth, lest they find themselves prey.

Master was more than up for the task of producing enough food for the both of them while Mated nursed, never wandering too far to get the job done. He was always available to join Mated to defend the pups, even when hunting on such hazardous terrain. Often times Master would physically drag a whole carcass back to the den to be shared by his mate. She didn't have to drop her guard for even a second.

In only a thirty darknesses time, the five pups were eating the same food as the parents. One of the pups was noticeably larger than the other four, and at the end of twelve more darknesses, began bullying his brothers and sister, allowing them to eat only after he was finished. His parents put a stop to it when they could catch him, but the battle for superiority waged as soon as backs were turned.

Mated was back at full speed actually quickly, anxious to share duties of the hunt once again. After two full moons time, the precocious pups were pushing to run with the parents, except for one, the largest pup. The biggest pup, believe it or not, in spite of his bullying tendencies, was the least sure footed pup in the litter. He would wander off and put himself in harms way when he got lost. The other pups were abnormally serious, mimicking their parents, running, jumping, getting stronger with every darkness that passed. The only real normal pup in the bunch was the big one, who was content to wander around the den. For the other four, running with the parents should not have been an interest until well past summer, but was.

All five pups were maturing quickly. But the four easy to recognize omega pups developed strangely, as opposed to the aspiring beta pup, who was a larger version of his parents in some ways.

Something happened with the design build of the omega pups though. Leg development was different from that of even their parents, who had toughened paws, from intense conditioning. The pups inherited characteristics that gave them the advantage of having parts built in at birth.

All four had abnormally shaped legs, or maybe perfectly normal for those pups at any rate. The over-sized clumps growing where the paws should have been gave them the appearance of being canine Clydesdale puppies. There was a strange growth of fur on them that disguised them so that hind feet could not be seen. The length of all the legs were long in comparison with the rest of their bodies. Massive paws thinned out clear to the carpals and hocks that remained sinewy. But forearms, shoulders, thighs, and hips were large and deadly agile. Overall, the omega pups were almost as tall as the beta pup, but the beta pup was nature's answer to a total hunting machine.

The difference between the four pups compared

to the to the one, was that the four were ready to hunt with the parents, where the beta pup and bully was nowhere near qualified to compete at that level yet, perhaps by the fall at the closest. Maybe not even then.

But there were other differences between the pups as well, all now highly recognizable by their differences, rather than as a whole essential unit of the pack. There was White, of course, charming and beautiful, and Tan, who was the biggest of the five and a protector, but also a bully. And then there was Afraid, whose whole head was light gray in comparison with the rest of his body that was the dark gray coloring of his dad. Blue eye had one brown, and one blue eye. Finally, there was Dark. Dark was dark gray all over and was stealthy in shadows.

The decision was made to take leave of the den and camp. Master's pack was nomadic, would remain so, and it was time to move on. Tan introduced the most pressing issue, and had to be dealt with one way or the other, and sooner rather than later seemed the most wise course. Tan was healthy and strong. He would make a fine addition to any other pack other than Master and Mated's.

The descent down the mountain proved to be the most challenging task of all, with Tan included that is. The first two thirds of the way took the combined effort of the entire pack to help, guide, push, and even be carried by Master in some cases, down the treacherous cliffs. A whole light time was consumed in the accomplishment. Finally, at the bottom, all of the pack was famished, and a doe happened along at an unfortunate time. The whole pack surrounded her in seconds, Tan, as well. The doe had no chance at all to escape the style of hunters that were in Master's pack, including Tan who did a surprising job of helping.

But that was the only redemption on the part of Tan as they all tore flesh to eat. Tan felt as though he deserved the fresh kill more than his brothers and sister.. Mated chased him outside the circle at that point, to eat whatever was left after the rest of the pack had eaten it's fill, the other way around.

Master and Mated, White, Dark, Blue Eye, and Afraid, were finished pretty quickly, as they could have more at any time. They moved out of the way so that Tan could eat. Tan moved in to gorge himself, but the pack made to move off and travel on. It took the greedy Tan about a minute or two to realize that he was alone, probably not for long. But his parents and siblings were long gone, running and jumping in combination, on earth, as well as the rocky deposits that lay at the base of the mountain range they were following. Tan attempted a howl but wasn't quite capable of it yet. The sound he made sounded more like a yelp. Firmly in another pack's territory, it was only a matter of time before he was discovered, and hopefully accepted into the new pack as one of their own, a place he would be much more comfortable. Yet, the ironic part of it was that he would have to compete for ranking like everybody else. The fact that he was still a pup might bode well for him and be in his favor for a time.

Unfettered, the mated pair, accompanied by their yet still pups, bounded along, looking from a distance like grasshoppers, leaping rock to rock, even preferring the difficult over the made easy flat terrain in plain sight of them. In the five hours left of light time after abandoning Tan, the group had covered over 250 kilometers, stopping only twice to eat lightly. A small, but valid question begged to be asked about the pups premature progress.

Some mountains weren't as safe because they were forested. Whenever nature could not oblige the pack, they raced in the uppermost summits. Not too much time was wasted on such places, because plenty of better options took up the slack soon enough. When something from the aviation world threatened the pups, either Master or Mated jumped up to actually snatch them out of the air with powerful jaws. But most of the time, the pups would simply jump out of the way. They were found too hard to snag.

One particularly productive light time, the pack emerged from the shadows of a forested area to be surprised. Master was doubly surprised. He was the Master, in charge of protecting the whole pack with his life if needs be. But with any pack, more so in Master's, the day had to come when bigger and stronger would move in to threaten his job. Master was nervous from the first time he saw the larger wolf because he knew he would be challenged sooner or later, but had to welcome him because it was Master's way. None of it needed to happen, but it must. It was a time to show strength. Why it was true, was because Challenger, as he was come to be known, had clearly run into trouble himself for some unknown reason. He was by himself and blood matted his fur coat that hadn't washed off the last time he hunted fish. Challenger was too weak to hunt and catch game, so resorted to fishing until he gained his strength back. After eating, Challenger slept on the bank close by. It could have been two darkness times for all he could guess. When he awoke, except for some pain that made him limp from his left hind quarter, he felt stronger and rested. He was thirsty and hungry once again. It was a coincidence that Master and his pack came from the woods to happen across Challenger, who turned and growled at the intrusion and possible threat. Master, fearless and strong came close enough to stare Challenger down into submission, to join the pack until he was well. It was then that Master cared for Challenger as though he were one of his own pups. In fact, the whole pack, following suit, adopted, and welcomed. This was a mistake, and viewed as possible weakness of the Master, and that of his Mated for that matter.

Master's pack hunted larger game while in the presence of Challenger, and as he got stronger, it was clear his power for that kind of hunt exceeded that of Master and Mated. But Challenger did fit well into the pack for a time, attending campaign after campaign in the food hunt for the greater good. The greater good, was feeding the whole pack, not just the four pups that could almost care for themselves at a mere three months old.

But Challenger couldn't; wouldn't recognize the remarkable achievement of having such a young pack participating in a major hunt. It was judged mistakenly as weaknesses. Challenger made mental notes as he watched Master lead. Another misjudgment Challenger made was that after the pack hunted together, Master always offered food to the pups, and to Mated first and foremost before he ate. Master then allowed Challenger to share what was left with him, which was more than enough, but not the natural order of things. So he watched.

Mated also watched. A feeling she sensed with a combination of female and animal intuition told her that Challenger was investing time in strategy. Challenger had no mate of his own, and chances were if he moved on in pursuit of his own, he could well be killed by another pack led by their own master. Perhaps that was got him into trouble before they all met. But Mated belonged to Master, and Challenger would find stiff opposition from all of them; Master, Mated, and the pups. This was a pack unified by Master, and by Mated herself; melded from fierce loyalty, and something else that could not be fully understood by her.

Twenty six darknesses had passed, marked by the passage of the last full moon. A river was found to drink and fish to catch much like Challenger found when they all first met. Master was an excellent fisher. He caught enough and more to feed them all to gorging. Yet Challenger showed only grudging respect toward Master. Master treated him as any in the pack.

Mated knew Challenger would be looking for any opportunity to get Master in a compromising position; sensed it. An opening would happen in the servitude of Master's family. It would be then that he would strike. Now that he was fully recovered, there was much power in his jaws, much more than Master, but not more than Mated and Master combined. Mated had not lost vigilance in the whole of almost thirty darknesses. There was no confidence in her for Challenger.

Nothing had gotten past Master's eyes, it was only the appearance that some things had. Master had not gotten what he had by strength alone. Master was the smallest in his father's pack. He was driven off as a runt. So was Mated for that matter. After they had found each other, they had come further than either one of them should have. There were many light times before the pack, when Master was a lone omega wolf, when other masters of other packs crossed his path in the forest. All of them had more size than he did. But none wanted to do battle with him because he never gave them cause, nor could they catch him. Still, he worried about Challenger. He could not allow him to do harm to his family.

It was a darkness of the second full moon of five. It was at it's brightest. The pack was on a hunt for game to feed four pups, Master and Mated; and now a hugely hungry Challenger who ate more than his share of one kill. For the large game they were hunting, the best time to hunt was going into and coming back out of darkness. But Master's pack lived and hunted as they traveled. It wasn't only how they liked it, it was also to avoid battles with mightier wolves that for the most part, owned the territories they traveled in. The mated pair felt vulnerable needlessly. If there were a reason to it all, it was that Master and Mated were reaching out to make a friend, trying to prove they could do it.

Master was on a ledge, stalking an elk with a large rack on his head. He used care not to scare him to running. Master stood quietly, ready to jump as the beast stopped his foraging, but moved closer and closer. Soon he would be close enough to lunge. Challenger decided it was then he would overpower Master by making him lose balance on the edge, jumping on him afterward to finish the kill. It would have worked, except that when Master heard Challenger's swift feet, he turned around to take Challenger's momentum and inertia in his powerful jaws and propel him over the ledge, a turnaround from what Challenger wanted to do himself. Mated, ever wary of danger to her mate since the day she sighted Challenger for the first time, jumped to Master's aid. Together they made short work of the ungrateful upstart. In less than a minute, a high squeal came from Challenger, and that was the end of his breathing forever.

However, there were howls that came from every direction from other packs that heard and smelled a serious fight. They would come to investigate in a short enough time to put Master's pack back into danger from the competition for spoils. Mated and Master became liked minded just then, herding the young, and running as fast as the pups could go to leave the area entirely. Before morning, Master's pack was well outside the range of the defending pack's territory. Just before their energy was completely depleted, smaller game was hunted to feed empty stomachs, and a defensible spot chosen to sleep.

10-4 CANINE ONE NINERS

When the sun was high in the sky, the pack woke up, one by one. The spot they had chosen, made an excellent rendezvous spot, but neither Mated nor Master wanted any part of it. As a matter of fact, after the Challenger episode, it made Mated wonder if beyond Master and the pups, the rest of the world was the enemy. Tan, her own son, had to be expelled from the pack due to his strong tendency toward hierarchy competition. Would it be possible to meet friends to trust, grow a pack that protects each other? It seemed Master read her mind though because, after rest time, the pack was driven to wander southeast, hugging the rugged mountain range that gave them security. They only paused, not actually stopping long to eat and drink here and there before darkness folded in on them once more.

A brand new dawn came to the wilderness. Another long day of light because of the season, but a beautiful one. The pups were still sleeping, except for Dark who was up. He had wandered off running around already by himself. His range to get lost was pretty far compared to other pups because of his abilities. When Mated opened her eyes for the day, she knew Dark was gone instantly. The rest of the pack got up just after she did, but Mated was searching for Dark already.

Something neither of the parents had ever done, never had to do, was howling to call back a member of their pack. In fact, neither of them ever howled in their lifetime. But seeing Mated fretting over where Dark would be, made Master try and attempt his very first howl. He couldn't. What came out was a yip-yip-wahoooooo-aaah...Wahoooooo-aaah...yip-yip-wahoooooo-aaah. White, Blue Eye, and Afraid saw great fun and mimicked their father. Soon, father and offspring were making a small racket with the same howl call. Mated turned to look at them in astonishment, but due to her worry over where Dark might be, or if he was in trouble, decided to join in, as well. Yip-yip-wahoooooo-aaah...wahoooooo-aaah...yip-yip-wahoooooo-aaah.

The call worked perfectly as Dark came running back, jumping his last 8 meters to land in a skidding cloud of dust, a slight miscalculation as he stopped just shy of the middle of the pack. Mated, delighted that her son was not really lost, was only being adventurous, nuzzled her fourth offspring with her nose. Emotion took over the whole pack like contagion. They began short jumping all around where they had slept the night, piercing the morning sounds of bird song with yip-yip sounds of their own. Yip-yip...yip-yip...yip-yip. Indeed, it seemed the first time the pups ever displayed happiness so openly, generally stoic, and serious. What usually drove their light times were training and learning to be like Master and Mated. For good measure, the group let out one last chorus of a group howl together. Yip-yip-wahoooooo-ah...yip-yip...wahooooo-ah, when out of the bushes came Tan.

He was tired, and hungry because he had spent every one of his light time hours, and the darkness hours too, following the scent of his family as they traveled. He had caught them finally. He triumphantly began jumping all about the makeshift camp. He came to the pack to nuzzle his siblings, and his parents. From that day forward, he never displayed aggression at his pack ever again. Tan was not the same as his three brothers and sister, but he was a little more like Master and Mated. Training for Tan took longer but was inevitable.

It took another thirty darknesses for Tan to match the speed of his parents, becoming faster each light time as he matured. Tan was big; bigger still than his parents by a head. He remained a sweet, important part of the pack, loving his other siblings as much as the day he came back to his family. He would never leave the pack for the uncertainty of what was out beyond the world Master and Mated created for him and the pack. He never got to witness what was learned from Challenger, but ran into his own trials and tribulations along his trip alone. It was a short lesson that was much like his dad's much longer journey as a lone wolf. Tan vowed never to repeat his mistake, choosing to stay in the loving atmosphere of his family, carrying on someday just as they had.

White, Blue Eye, Dark, and Afraid matured in that same thirty darkness period. Blue Eye, Dark, and Afraid were equal in height to Master, and White to that of her mother. But that is where the physical similarity ended. All of them had limbs with tremendous power in them, far exceeding that of Master, Mated, and Tan. They had learned to kick larger dangerous prey to death with back legs, much like a mule. Often times they would send prey larger than a cat, sailing 4 to 5 meters away, crushing a skull with one mighty kick. The quartet could easily out distance their parents and Tan during a light time travel period, but would not, content to play full strength at times when they were camped for rest periods, or after sleeping. Each one of the four could run over 135 Kilometers per hour in spurts, Tan and his parents could clock out at just under 130, remarkable by itself, however, it took considerably more effort. Tan joined the play sessions too, but only as far as his capacity allowed him to. There were never any judgmental attitudes displayed between them, or jealousy for that matter because each had talents. Tan, like his mom and dad, had power in his jaws. Tan of course, having larger body mass, had the power to compete in any pack. He was not omega but comported himself like one.

Master and his family were high on a ridge looking down on fires, some kind of community. They had all traveled a long way, and working together had produced more than enough to eat along
the way. But the controlled fires below held curiosity for them all, the smells confusing. There was some, but not a lot of movement that could be seen, none of it particularly projected hostility. Master let loose a low yip-yip-wahoooooo-aaah...yip-yip-wahoooooo-aaah, to be carried on the night wind. It was answered, but not by a wolf. It wasn't far away, this low lonely siren kind of call that answered. In fact, it seemed to be in the foothills just below them. The pack reverberated excitement that an answer would come back to them as a call meant to bring back one of their own.

A consensus emerged from the group to investigate the answer using absolutely no communication at all. But instead of running separately, they moved as a group, down into the foothills. As soon as they came to the general area that the answer came from, a scent came strongly to all of them. Out of a dark corner near a structure, one single bark emitted from the throat of a strange looking wolf. Master and Mated moved slightly ahead of the group, protectively. He was only a bit smaller than Mated. A shiny black, lean, alert, mutt. Master repeated his low soft call...wahooooo-aah. It was answered as a strange siren mimic by Black, who moved closer to the abnormally gregarious pack standing in back of Mated and Master. One of the group of five was female, smaller than the rest, with white on her breast plate, so her brothers became protective when Black chose her out to nuzzle noses with. Then Black got to sniffing her all over, getting a sense of what was what. White became curious too, taking in as much of the unfamiliar scents on him as she could take in. The pack sensed no danger at all from Black; indeed this little interlude presented them with a friend. The pack surrounded Black in an effort to find out if he was transient, or interested in joining the pack for a time. Not getting a feel for Black's intent, Master turned to climb back up the foothills to find a place to rest before they resumed their journey southeastward at the top of the ridge. The pack received an answer again when they turned for a moment, only to find Black right on their tails. It was a particularly different kind of darkness. They all laid down together to sleep near the top of the ridge for the rest of darkness.

The journey, migration, or whatever it was they were all embarked on, had to continue, but it brought brand new challenges to the mix. There needed to be a hunt before the pack traveled, the task easily handled by Master and his crew. Combined hunting skills were honed sharper with every light time period. But Black seemed put off by the hunt. He seemed to enjoy running and playing, but the serious duty of surviving seemed lost on him. It was only when a combined effort found a family of hare for a meal that Black was hit with a dose of reality. Master offered him food. Black poked his nose at it a few times, but thought better of refusal and ate.

After only one darkness with Master's pack, it became clear that Black was not finding his place to fit in. Black was perpetually animated and chipper. The pups loved him. Black loved them back. He recognized them for their differences, rather than as a whole essential unit of the pack. But he could never keep up with any one of them, and it was senseless to try. Black had a warm place to spend all of his darknesses. So with a whine to announce a change of plans, Black greeted them all one last time, turning to head back home where he belonged. Black was Black, but not much of hunter since he was a touch petrified of animals different and bigger than he was. Still, there were sad moans that came from the pack, that sounded much like mmmm-aaah....mmmm-aaah. Black disappeared from them with happy barks from a friend should they ever return.

The pack of underdogs learned something new from their encounter with Black. It is not enough to survive. Play is a critical component to a light time. Master and Mated joined in the early morning romps with their offspring. It was an integral part of exercise, each to their own capacities. Games of tag became an adventure, as well as a challenge. The game required cunning and trickery to outwit the the speedy likes of White, Dark, Afraid, and Blue Eye. Tan couldn't compete with his siblings in a test of speed, but was happy just to join in all the frivolity. On the other hand, Tan could catch Master and Mated any time he chose, but gave an impression that it was harder than it looked.

Another twenty three darknesses had gone by, the new full moon not yet at it's brightest. A whole lot of miles had been traversed in that time. Following the high mountains, they pushed further and further southward. Rules changed as they went. Weather was different. Fresh game to hunt was different. Still, it wasn't that hard to adapt, hunting and eating when the opportunity presented itself, always traveling. It was getting into the fall season, but the constant speed the pack of seven ran and jumped, ate up mile after mile. When the pack ran into a populated area, the novelty of using the runt pack's patented howl call was used, making occasional friends. But this one night brought a surprise.

It was darkness. The pack had just completed a long light time of travel, lasting from just after sunup play time, to sundown. In thirteen hours, they had gone 650 kilometers, the pack's best time yet with Tan included. But they were stopped and tired, looking down from a high rocky ridge high above a sparsely forested area far below. Wind did not carry the scent of a sizable wolf pack as far up as they were, and they could not even be seen. The pack below numbered perhaps 35 or so.

Yet, high above them, on the first of the new full moons, gave a picture book setting of a mated pair and their young on a giant cliff, silhouetted by the light. On a crazy whim, no reason for it at all except that the situation reminded Master of finding yet another village area as they had done in the past. He let out a yip-yip-wahoooooo-aaah...whahoooooo-aaah...yip-yip-wahoooooo-aaah. It was answered...exactly. A faint yip-yip-wahoooooo-aaah...wahooooo-aaah...yip-yip-wahoooooo-aaah came from far below them. Clearly stunned, the pack repeated the call, and yet again it was answered, this time the direction from where it emanated was noted. The pack began a long descent down the mountain. Half way down, the howl was repeated. This time it was obvious that it was answered by more than one wolf. This stunned them even more, signaling potential danger. But the call was answered precisely as Master's pack delivered it, so the descent was resumed. It is said that curiosity kills cats. Well, they were not cats, so if this was to be a test, so be it.

Finally, at the bottom of the high, rugged mountain, the clear scent of a pack that had been in the area of its own territory came strong. Tentatively, as has been the custom when meeting new friends, Master repeated a very low wahoooooo-aaah. Out of the dark cover of trees, came the answer, wahoooooo-aaah, just as cautious. The pack moved toward the sound. Hiding, but frightened, were three small omega wolves, freshly expelled from the sizable pack that had already moved off. The large pack had a successful hunt, but not enough to satisfy and feed the entire group. The omegas were threatened with their lives, the effort made to conserve food for members of the pack that had rankings. Going into the fall, and ultimately winter, the drain on resources had to be managed. The lowest of the scavengers among them were to be the losers. The omegas had no choice but to bolt away for their lives. They cowered in hiding when Master's pack found them. It seemed that the pack call resonated with omegas.

Three runt-sized dogs emerged that came out

into the moonlight only when coaxed, not vying for a second fight in the same night. To make matters worse for them, they turned out to be two small females, and a slightly larger male. The runts did not know it, but even though they found themselves counted among friendlies that the rigors of joining Master's pack over the potentially deadly one from which they'd been just extricated, might prove to be not all that worth it. Training began immediately. There was danger about, and Master and Mated were anxious to take the pack back up the mountain to safety. There was no time for pleasantries, getting to know each other, or noticing that the three had spots on different parts of their bodies from each other.

The ascent back up the mountain was a most challenging one. These runts were not pups, the only noteworthy positive. The ascent took a while, even with abilities Master's pack alone possessed. Still, Mated was trained in just the same fashion, and if it was revealed to be in the new runt's best interests, the hard work ahead of them would prove valuable both to the runts and to the pack.

The runts placed one leg in front of the other, slowly, carefully. Chancing to go from rock to rock was accomplished only when self motivated enough to chance a 2 meter jump. Each milestone brought the new additions higher and higher, into zones that taxed muscles and lungs as the air thinned in the climb closer and closer to the top. These were not paths with obstacles on them. These were obstacles with no paths at all. The whole trip almost consumed the entire balance of the darkness. When the summit was reached, the pack was maybe not as tired as the new recruits but tired. Patience tires as much as exertion. The bulk of the work at coaxing the runts to the top of the mountain was shouldered by the pack siblings, especially White, Afraid, and Blue Eye, who seemed to have a strong interest in coaching the exhausted runts. There was also a little doting going on by White, Afraid, and Blue Eye to find a comfortable place to rest for several hours.

The morning sun was up, warming the still sleepy dogs. Hunger was the only stimulus to make them all rise, even for play time. In the rocky terrain of the mountain summit, not much was known yet about what could be hunted to eat. It wasn't much of a concern for the pack, but for the new arrivals, they were more than hungry. The three did not have a chance to eat at all with the last pack. But rising on paws that were bruised by rock surfaces, deflated hopes of joining any hunt. The runts were not to be allowed to wallow in any self pity however, and were strongly urged to get with it.

It wasn't long when the pack felled a big horn sheep, providing more than enough to feed all the hungry mouths. The runts were not used to being invited, even encouraged to eat their fill at the same time as pack members with higher rankings. It gave new insight as to what lie ahead, and sore or not, would do their best to earn a place with the pack, no matter what it took.

So with bruised and cut pads on all three of the runts paws, they willingly joined the light time travel that the pack was used to. The only exception was that it was a slow undertaking, the whole light time worth of travel amounted to only 50 kilometers. But the hunt along the way gave the pack just enough challenge to satisfy the thirst to stay on the move, and nobody was hungry.

When finally stopped again for the darkness, attention was given to the differences in the runts. One of the two females had a white spot on her head. She went on to be viewed as Face Spot. The other female had a white spot on her back. She was Body Spot. And then there was a perky, pleasant little male, tail perpetually wagging. He was larger than the two females but smaller than Afraid, Blue Eye, and Dark. His happy attitude forgave having to pull him along that whole light time. But it was apparent that it didn't bother Master or Mated. Fifty kilometers was pretty good and deserved respect. The male had a white spot smack dab on his butt area below his tail and on both sides. He became thought of as Tail Ender. Starting the light time, paws were hurting, and at the end, hurt no worse.

With the sun setting beyond the horizon, Master pulled a surprise move. Once again he let out a yip-yip-wahoooooo-aaah...wahoooooo-aaah...yip-yip-wahoooooo-aaah. This time he was clearly calling to any omegas within earshot. Nothing was heard, so he turned to aim the call facing the other direction...yip-yip-wahoooooo-aaah...wahoooooo-aaaah...yip-yip-wahoooooo-aaah. Faintly off in the distance, an answer? It was so elevated where he was at, the pack joined him. The newcomers joined in the chorus, as well. But the answer was far off, not just back down the mountain. Master established a rendezvous camp. He made it clear that he wanted for the pack to stay where they were to protect the newcomers. Mated was to come with him to go on an adventure which might well take the whole darkness. He would go nowhere without Mated.

The pair moved away from the pack only for the second time ever, the first, when they left Tan behind. Progress was much faster without the new omegas. Going down only took a minute or two, and once closer to sea level, they repeated the howl. The mated pair moved toward the answer because it was stronger the third time around. Whoever answered was moving, just picking up and moving toward them, fast.

With the incredible speed of Master and Mated, the gap closed quickly for the distance traveled but still burned another two hours. But what was found when the reached the far end of the territory stopped both Master and Mated dead in their tracks, Nothing could have prepared them for what had congregated there. It seemed that every omega within the range of the call responded, left whatever pack they were joined to, if not three or four. There, in a clearing was a convention of omegas, each hearing, not master's pack call, but the answering howl, which answered them. The spread of the original howl call could have been limitless because there was no counting them, and a couple more arrived when they did. There may have been as many as 10 to 15 of them. All of them were ready to follow a pied piper that caused them to imagine a life based on hard work instead of tyranny.

Master herded them, and set them to following his mate and himself to whatever new adventures awaited them. Originally, Master was interested in adding to his pack, providing mates like themselves for his offspring. He got much more than that. He got believers that trusted they honestly belonged somewhere. Master would not let them down, no matter what. Training them all at the same time, would hurt for sure, but Master hoped the reward would be a pack that leans against each other to push at every struggle, instead of competing against each other, the weak left behind. No weak would be left behind if they could be made to believe in themselves.

For the second time in one light and dark period, patience would be taxed to the hilt. Not having the younger pack members with them this time around was strength, especially in the darkness. Finding the way back to the mountain with so many at once presented an awful lot of danger moving back into the outer fringes of the territory owned by the pack that Face Spot, Body Spot, and Tail Ender came from. That particular pack had just expelled the three, and quite well could be off their guards. But having so many breach their territory at once could very well fill noses with the scent of them. On top of that, to climb the mountain with the inexperienced omegas posed a real problem where fear alone could kill any one of them. But commitment was made, and commitment was accepted.

The trip back to the base of the mountain housing the rendezvous camp, was a long way back then away from, but a normal pace was maintained. The destination reached in a little more than two and a half times what it took Master and Mated to traverse it. When there, Mated made a move to begin the climb, and that was when reluctance reared it's head. Reluctant or not, there were no defectors in the whole bunch. Mated led the way, the omegas followed, Master instructed from behind. By morning, no omega was lost, no omega left behind, save the ones who may have congregated after they had left the clearing where they had first met. It took the entire darkness and into the following light time.

White, Tan, Blue Eye, and Afraid were hunting, bringing down several birds. They had already found and procured another big horn sheep. The new pack of omegas watched Masters and Mated's offspring finding and attacking small game without much effort. They were attended by Face Spot, Body Spot, and Tail Ender. The three were participating as far as they were capable, and certainly showing valiant efforts. The brand new pack got their first lesson on what was expected from them. Belonging was joining and contributing. Eating was ahead, traveling just beyond that. Many of them would be hungry unless Master's pack showed them the pack method of eating what was found along the way. Because many of them would be hungry, senses would be more and more finely tuned. This was defensive nomadic living and would be all their way of life from that point forward.

Throughout the fall, Master, Mated, Tan, Blue Eye, Afraid, Dark, and White, taught by example. No grumbling was allowed by the pack trainees, and no sympathy given. The pack did not feed the trainees, although they did share. The expectation demanded that they provide for themselves individually. Living that way would provide for them all. Methods of hunting, the advantage of which was in Master's pack favor, required intense training and constant practice at copying the original seven. All total, there were 24 members in the whole pack. No doubt there was a constant drain on resources, time spent on the smaller distances traveled in a light time, and feeding the new arrivals without skill. Some members continued to hunt well after others had stopped, but travel was always in a group.

Master's pack adhered to the routine that was comfortable for them. Play time was still part of the morning routine, exercise while hunting, each to their own ability. However, forward progress was slow—much slower through the rest of the fall months, and certainly through the winter with its short light times, and long darknesses. Still, it was noticeable that individuals got better and better, faster and faster, stronger and stronger, even if progress was quicker for some than others. All of them were toughening. By just before spring, travel distances lengthened dramatically. The stronger parts of the pack pulled the weaker along. Master and Mated did not mate for offspring that winter. The progress of the pack was more significant. Sacrifices were made for the benefit of the pack, and it's success. The time would come for mating.

By the middle of spring, the whole pack of 24, moved like grasshoppers again. Combinations of running and jumping for tremendous distances became the norm. Nobody got to see the odd looking group zipping through an area like fast moving jumping beans on four legs, and if anybody did see them, it wouldn't have been for long. If birds were plentiful, that is what they stopped to eat if other game provided enough for all of them to kill and eat, then that is where they would pause for a time. Most times the pause would be a smörgåsbord, lasting for an hour or two at most, continuing, gaining speed again as they went. Sleep and rest times were as a group again, patterns establishing. Individual affinities became obvious, only mating was strongly discouraged so as not to impede the southward migration of the pack. It was not clear to any one of them where they would come to rest the following winter, but it was plain the environment was becoming more suited to this pack every light time and darkness that passed. The mountains gave up quality cover, yet mighty rivers with good fishing and smaller game were on the rise, adding to the hunt. This was as close to what they all thought of as home as it came, with vast spaces to roam, not putting limits to a territory. Each place that was traveled to surprise game not expecting to be threatened by predators.

The weather was warmer at ground level than where they all came from originally. There wasn't anybody in the pack that were used to temperatures that soared between 22 to 25 degrees Celsius in spring. The land below the foothills bloomed with lush vegetation that drew the attention of insects, and more game. In spite of it's size, the pack did not lack for food sources. The new side of the pack seem to relish in its newfound independence, all the while being a part of what might be loosely described as family. Master, Mated, and Tan were very highly revered and respected while White, Blue Eye, Afraid, and Dark were watched, and mimicked as much as any in the pack could hope to. Face Spot, Body Spot, and Tail Ender were enamored with, for lack of better terminology, the offspring of the royal family.

Tan had this thing for a newcomer that came into the group to join them that his mother and dad found. She was sleek, with a beautiful red coat that seemed to shine in the sun after shedding extra fur from the winter.

10-4 CANINE ONE NINERS

She was Taller than his sister White, but clearly omega. It seemed Tan went for smaller females because she only came to a little more than half his height, Tan had grown to be quite large. She had not left Tan's side for more than thirty darknesses. The pack recognized her as Red Dog.

Blue Eye could not shake Body Spot if he wanted to, even though he could outrun and out distance her by 3 to 1. He may have run away from her, but she always managed to catch him when he stopped. His attitude toward her was indifferent.

It was the same for Afraid, who was consistently pursued by Face Spot as though she might lose him or something. Afraid seemed afraid to make any commitments.

There was a cute little omega wolf that came out of the out of the crowd of omegas, very much overshadowed because she was small and perfectly proportioned. She had a brown coat and a high pitched bark and growl that if wolves could laugh, would have made the whole pack do so. Brown was so loyal to Dark that it rivaled Mated to Master. Dark tolerated her presence.

Finally, there was White, who allowed Tail Ender to hang around because he was pleasant. It was known from the start how gregarious the small male omega was. His pleasant happy demeanor could not be diminished in any light time. White decided that Tail Ender was acceptable to stay around her.

Royalty or no, none of the five were of age to mate age yet, nor did they ever exhibit any desires to do so.

Spring gave way to summer. With each light time, the pack became more and more of a well oiled machine. The whole pack became just like it was in the days when Master and Mated traveled alone with the young pups. Hunting was relegated as an afterthought, completely contingent to traveling. A good analogy would be if a school of fish swimming together noticed minnows hiding in shallows, secure that they are concealed from threats. The larger fish detour temporarily, move in for a feast, then move on contentedly after they have eaten their fill. It's just business, short and sweet—fast food. On the other hand, a good day of fishing is not business, it is fun.

That is precisely what the pack was doing one light time. It was a warm day, and the pack had traveled a fair distance. The group paused on a high ridge, thirsty, warm, and were suddenly presented with a river flowing off a lake to chill off, drink, and fish. The temptation simply could not be resisted. Secondary to the cold river was the fact that there was sparsely populated village nearby. A condition Master's pack had seen plenty of times before when they had met friends in the course of travel. They all converged on the river to frolic, the anticipation that a good time was to be had all the way around.

Down in the river, 24 strange wolves canvassed the river for fish. The chance that any fish would get by the canine crowd was slim to none. The only tick in the fur was a scream heard from the lake nearby. Tan became alert, every nerve ending exposed at once. He instantly mobilized, running toward the lake, several seconds before the rest of the pack followed him to something they were less sure they were to be involved in than Tan. In less than a minute, Tan was at the shore at a full run, slightly crouched for the fateful leap clear out to where a little two legged was in the throes of a losing a battle to stay above the surface. She had hit a submerged rock while paddling a canoe, and ended up in water well over her head. She fought to gain control of something she had no skill at. In the process of a losing battle, Tan landed within a foot of the little girl with a mighty splash. A larger two legged on the shore began screaming worse than the little girl when she fell in. In reality, she thought the girl was a goner, what with a pack of wolves at the other end of the shoreline, and a hungry looking beast scoring them dinner. The fact was that Tan let the girl grab hold, and he swam ashore with her. Once there, the larger two legged scooped the little girl off Tan's back, instantly turning the tide from horrified, to relieved, to overwhelmingly grateful. She bent down, girl in one arm on her hip, the other arm around Tan in an outpouring of love to the animal. The rest of the little two legged's family flowed down to the scene, took in the spectacle of 23 other wolves crowding the shoreline, as close as they had ever been to a pack, and one big wolf. Then father and mother came out of the pack to inch slowly and cautiously to join Tan. The other 21 held back off to the side. They were not emboldened enough to move closer to meet the two leggeds. More grateful outcries came from family, and tears of joy, and a delight to meet the wolves as friends. Master nudged the hand of the two legged with the child, inferring that he understood her nearness to grief. From the mouths of the two leggeds came cheers, that though was in their native tongue, could be loosely translated to mean: “proud pack of runts...proud pack of runts”. Tan and his parents lingered a second longer, then moved off to join the rest of the pack and continue on with their light time. That was the day that Master's pack became the legendary 'pack of runts', forever enshrined in the minds of a grateful people who would pass the word from two legged to two legged.

Tan and the pack of runts continued to explore section after section of the mountains, quite at home in the thousands of miles high on the mountain tops, but even more so this far south where the mountains had turned into the Rocky Mountain chain. Word spread far and wide, and seemed to follow them almost as fast as they explored. From word of mouth descriptions, the two leggeds watched the mountains, hoping to catch a glimpse of the pack running and jumping along at high speeds. If any caught sight of the pack invariably the two leggeds pointed excitedly before the pack disappeared almost faster than the two leggeds could yell, “Look, look, it's the pack of runts!!”

On darknesses when the moon was at it's fullest, the pack of runts would howl to other omegas. There was always, always a response, even though there weren't yet darknesses riddled with desperation for the omegas they met. Darknesses would come when that would show more. But friends were made everywhere the pack of runts went. It was a good summer season for every pack.

The DNA handiwork born to Master and Mated were the best parts of them both, becoming better than either of them ever hoped to be. Already, all five of the pups were full grown. They had matured so quickly that even the desire to mate took hold of them, except for

Tan. On more than one occasion, Afraid had consummated with Brown, the two inseparable. White, Blue Eye, and Dark were so always on the move, it was a wonder the three ever made time for anything; always in a hurry. But Tan and Red Dog never mated. Tan was kind, but serious, and mysterious. His real purpose for anything seemed reserved for his knowledge only. He may have been waiting for the right time, or maybe even the right mate. At any rate, Red Dog seemed a friend to Tan, who was actually more of a mate if he opened his eyes to see it.

There seemed no reason to stop because nothing ever pressed the pack to do so. Mating amounted to nothing at all. Master and Mated were pulled along with the rest of the pack, no better or worse than the rest of the omegas; several steps gone from their pace.

Summer gave way to fall as time has a sense of humor, and it likes playing tricks. It runs slow when there are hardships, but fast when enjoyed. The travel life style of the pack became an adventure. Each season put the pack into new areas that changed both geographically and environmentally. Each kilometer became more and more to the pack's liking. The mountains were high and teeming with life.The continuous southward trek pushed on, with not one hindrance from any of the packs that made full time jobs of hunting and patrolling on claimed territories along the way.

The weather became cooler but at comfortable ranges that increased the stamina of every wolf in the pack. The pack of runts followed the soothing climate as late fall eased into winter. Along the way, they still drew looks of surprise and shock from the occasional two leggeds they ran across that spotted them along the southwesterly routes that were taken. None of them had any idea what to make of the strange pack when they invaded the areas where they lived. All any of the two leggeds knew was that a crazy looking pack of small tough wolves came into their village, and stopped. Four of the wolves moved in frighteningly close. Encounters scared all the two leggeds they came in contact with out of their wits. Time and time again, it was found out that the pack only stopped to say hello spearheaded by a small mated pair of wolves, and a large tan wolf, accompanied by a small, perfectly formed wolf with a pretty red coat of fur. The rest of the pack held back, somewhat ominously. They left scores of two leggeds perplexed when the four wolves got close enough to get pats on the head, then hopped and ran away, taking the rest of the pack with them, disappearing again. Every repeated story was either backed up, or enhanced by another, building on the legend of the pack of runts.

By the middle of winter, the pack of runts found themselves on top of an almost bald rocky mountain. Looking down on a valley floor, saw forested places, rolling grassy hills in others. For the first time since Master was pushed out of his first pack to be on his own, he needed, more than wanted, to stay put. It had nothing to do with siring young. The pack did not know about Master's dilemma, nor would they for a while, because Red Dog was expecting. Tan had taken her as a mate after all, and Tan was the only father to be.

Much of the pack was weary. The only five who had not lost running speed were White, Dark, Afraid, Blue Eye, and the strongest of all, Tan. Of the five, Tan was the strongest, and tireless, but still not the fastest. Except for Tan, play time in the morning had stopped altogether, as though the four had outgrown such nonsense. Tan used the time, taking the time to shoulder the responsibility of scouting safe spots for the pack to hunt, and to find out where likely game resided to make the hunt easier for the slower among them, which amounted to the whole pack. Master and Mated would have borne that responsibility if possible, but Tan knew that they could not. In fact, Tan was the only one who noticed all these things.

At first light time in the new area, Tan opened his eyes and nose to the sights and and smells of green. Green...still in the winter! Some snow had fallen on the mountains, but the valley floors still had enough green for game to forage. He could not detect the scent of dangerous rivals in the wind. Tan used his early light time as it had become a part of his routine anyway, to scout the valley floor. This time though, Red Dog was up for the challenge of joining her mate for the chore. Red Dog and Tan did not run and jump at breakneck speed. A normal pace was all that was necessary for the job. Even at the slower pace, enough new territory was covered quickly enough to see that small game was in more than ample abundance, and easy to fell or catch with short bursts. Tan and Red dog ate their fill, returning to the pack afterward in plenty enough time to draw them out of lethargy. With a dead hare in his mouth used to spike interest, Tan offered it to Mated, who took it thankfully, sharing it with her mate. It was clear Master and Mated were going to stay behind this light time.

Tan steered the rest of the pack to fan out into the valley. The pack hunted and marked trails as they went. The four speedsters of the siblings took parts of the pack with them individually. Tan and Red Dog were free to venture further out to explore more of the valley. It was important to the pair to locate strategic areas, water, and so forth to build a den to raise new pups. As far as Red Dog and Tan traveled in a Light time, nothing was shown to cause a significant danger that could potentially overwhelm the pair, even if they stood alone. It was well into darkness before Red Dog and Tan returned to the rendezvous camp where they had left Master and Mated in the early light. They were greeted by the rest of the pack of runts. Tan's brothers and sister were nowhere to be seen.

It turned out that Master and Mated had passed away sometime during the light time. Both of their big hearts had beat one beat too many. It could not be told what it was that killed them, but Mated's head was rested on top of Master. Vulchers had been pecking and feeding on the expired mates. Tan went into instant mourning.

Tan lost both parents and siblings in the same light time. He was overcome with all the conflicting griefs inside. Master and Mated were guarded by a family that weren't real family while their real family happily ran off with no ties at all. Tan emitted a strange moaning howl, that sounded like a sad: wa-woooooo-wa-wa-woooooo. All the rest of the omegas in the pack joined him for one reason or another. Face Spot, Body Spot, Brown, and Tail Ender didn't just lose pack leaders, they also lost potential mates. At least that was how the four rejected omegas perceived it. The rest of the omegas had lost a leader that they loved much more than tan any had realized. Every last one of them made a commitment to Tan that darkness, pledging their lives to the leader if he would have them, starting with joining him in a chorus of wa-woooooo-wa-wa-woooooo, but ending with, mmmm-aaaah, when they had to take leave Master and Mated for the last time.

The speedy siblings White, Blue Eye, Afraid, and Dark, were never seen again, nor were they followed. They were allowed to make their own way in an uncertain world. For sure, the four had talents and power to fend for themselves. But none of the legends handed down from village to village of two leggeds spoke of small wolves with Clydesdale-like, hairy, clumpy paws, meeting at the end of legs that kick like mules. It is a sad non-memorial to a mighty quartet.

Spring arrived, bringing with it scents of blooms, water runoff into streams fresh with new life, and new pups born to Red Dog. Tan was not allowed close to the pups early on, Red Dog choosing Body spot as nurse maid and source of food while the pups nursed. There were four in all, four males.

Tan used that time to work with the omegas, hunting. Securing food had to be done anyway, but beyond that, Tan was working on pack issues. It was something the omegas still wrestled with from the first darkness that Master and Mated found and brought them up the mountain to join them all. They followed, did what they were told, but not much beyond that. When greeting new omegas on darknesses of the full moon, they hung back, leaving the diplomacy to his dead parents, or Tan and Red Dog. It was the same when traveling. Tan's penchant for making new friends with two leggeds, and experiencing pleasure from their approval was not shared. They became more than timid. Also, if there was large game, and of the dangerous variety, they all displayed cowardice to participate. Therefore, his exercises when hunting with them, was to steer them toward game that none of them normally would hunt. None of them could think of themselves as part of the pack of runts if they were not proud and honored to be a part of it.

It began with stalking a fair sized elk in a small herd of them. The elk were becoming skittish, well aware of enemies moving in on them. Before the elk had the opportunity to turn and run, making the hunt more difficult, Tan had decided to attack sooner than later. He moved in, barking for his back up to follow. As soon as he made to run, the omegas hung back, content to let their large leader do the dirty work. It was the same when taking goats and sheep on the mountains. The omegas were starting to salivate from the anticipation of a hearty big meal, but Tan stopped mid stride as they had. He completely stopped his pursuit of the elk. Disappointed, the shocked omegas watched as a perfect opportunity to fell the beast get away. Group decision took hold. The omegas had speed, cunning, and collaboration of strength. The elk could not possibly outrun this particular group of omegas, so they were all off. In seconds, sixteen runts jumped into action, joined by tan a half second later. The group effort was no match for the elk, first tripping the beast by grabbing at all four legs at once. When knocked down, he was finished in seconds, twitching the last of his life while the rest of the herd continued to safety. There was no competition for parts to eat. There was plenty for all. It was a poignant moment for the omegas. They knew they were tricked. Pride gripped them all at the same time. It was that moment that truly defined them all to be the 'proud pack of runts'. Never again would they shun away from uncomfortable danger. They would claim what was theirs, both in pleasure, and the not so pleasurable. Together, they were strong.

Body spot came back to the den with more than enough meat in her jaws to feed Red Dog, still with her newborns at the den. The den was prepared in an abandoned cave, any previous inhabitants were unknown. It did not enjoy the defensive placement in high altitudes that the pack generally favored. But Tan saw an advantage in choosing to utilize both ends of the mountain. Building strength by defending where danger is always imminent. Not running to the mountains to run away but for the added range of game and travel. Tan respected his brothers and sister, even Master and Mated, though they were much smaller than himself. These particular omegas could be just as powerful, not individually, but when they depended on each other. This would be what he taught, in contrast to what Master taught. Master instructed the pack to strike at small game, take care of number one. Master taught that a member of his pack should never inflict a burden on others. It was good in theory, but bred self centered pack members that could survive on their own, but shared nothing. His pack would share everything, and through participation together, would be an engine that could not be stopped. They would travel together, protect together, hunt together, and share rewards together. As skills developed, two elk, or caribou could be felled and shared. If any would try to take it away, the Omegas could defend together. On the other hand, the main goal would still be to avoid confrontation if possible.

Light times passed with a lot of progress. The pack became more skilled every light time to work as a machine. Tan and Red Dog's new pups made progress even faster than that witnessed of Master and Mated's young. Only four light times passed before they opened their eyes to see the world for the first time. In ten light times, nursing ended, new teeth appeared, and the pups began wandering around the den and needed meat. In twenty lightnesses, all four pups took trips with the parents. Twenty five light times passed, milk teeth were replaced with viscously sharp teeth, and the pups attended their first hunts with the adults. A short time after thirty darknesses, the pups were not pups at all, but larger than Tan, and ready to hunt as well as any in the pack. They learned quickly, so quickly in fact that the mannerisms of the pack were adopted as their own. They considered themselves just as much a part of the pack as the omegas and never once noticed any differences between the omegas and themselves.

In the time it took for two full moons to appear in the darkness, the pack was ready once again to travel. Tan and Red Dog's offspring inherited Tan's strength and agility. They got his size too, but to an even greater degree. The four were tall; almost as tall as a deer, and just as fast. They were strong, though they did not laud it over the others.

From Red Dog, the four received the gift of handsomeness. Nothing at all could distinguish one from the other, like quadruplets. The luscious red coats were stunningly beautiful; shiny, red, lush, healthy looking. Only their faces had lighter fur and color around the mouth and eyes, the rest was dark crimson. It was as though the four took baths every day, or that they were endowed with natural lanolin. There was no mistaking the wolf in any of them, though the bodies set up a lie. The heads, shoulders, and faces of each had the classic wolf look. Their jaws alone were enough to intimidate any other wolf. The lie that was just spoken of is where the confusion entered. The trunk of their bodies tapered from the powerful shoulders back to some extremely muscular hindquarters; Stomachs with no ponch whatsoever, just lean trim muscle. Running style had such grace, while still yielding incredible speed. Traveling as a whole pack would scare any animal on earth.

Coming out of spring into summer caused the pack to stick to the mountain tops again. Travel was just as fast as with master's pack. Two hundred fifty kilometers in a light time would place the pack in cooler climes when the summer brought most of its heat. Retracing some of the routes that were taken before, passed some of the same villages that were visited before, scaring some even more than the first time around.

One village wasn't reached yet, a hunting party from it was out searching for game. The pack had no way of knowing that of course, but what the pack did know is that this particular party had gotten themselves in trouble. A great grizzly bear had one of a party of six, cornered. The two legged had taken a blow from one of the bears powerful paws. He was down on the ground unconscious, the other five in the party, had no chance at all to take the massive animal down before their friend was made to have no more breaths in him as the bear made a move to finish the job. It was the omegas that took the initiative this time around, attacking an animal that any other pack of wolves would have decoyed instead. Tan, reluctant for only a split second, his red sons just behind him, raced to join the omegas in a heroic maneuver that may well have been only to knock a chip off their shoulders. They jumped at the massive beast from all angles, taking good sized hunks out of his limbs and body. It was a full frontal assault, with caution thrown to the wind, no waiting for perfect timing. The beast roared, both in fury and rage. The incredible strength in his two mighty paws could not be contained, even with three omega wolves hanging off them with teeth firmly clamped down into the flesh. The giant bear flung the wolves off his arm with a back-handed swipe, sending three of the omegas sailing. They landed on the ground with a high pitched sequel, but quickly got to their feet, launching themselves back at the target they had temporarily been dislodged. The bear began to panic, running off with all the omegas biting at some portion of him at once. One of the red sons took a hunk out of his midsection that began to bleed profusely while Tan himself ate a nasty hole near his throat. Still running, the bear was overcome with blood loss that could not be stopped, falling over to succumb to his final breaths a short time later, but nearly 75 meters away from where the attack first started. A minute later, he lay lifeless, not one member of the pack seriously injured.

The four hunting members from the village revived their friend from unconsciousness, but needed to carry him back to their village to get help to care for him. The animals surrounded the party of five, ominously. Tan moved even closer to the injured man on the ground, nudging him with his muzzle. The man reached up, caressed Tan's neck because he couldn't do much else. That was when the five two leggeds realized the pack bore no ill will toward them at all. For the first time, everybody in the pack moved closer to receive their shares of reward, love expressed with hand gestures to their heads and body, the big red sons included. No one were deprived of the pleasure of the two leggeds touch this time, and at once the pack knew what Tan experienced of his visits. The two leggeds then attended to their downed companion, reaching underneath him to carry him back to the village. When the two leggeds disappeared into the woods, the pack then feasted on something that should not be tasted by any wolf. They chowed and gorged on the felled beast until no more could be eaten, sleeping right where they were at when darkness came. At first light, Tan's Red Ones and the pack of runts moved on after consuming what they could find. After the pack made for the summit of the mountain they were traveling on, they were all okay to move again, but speed was not necessary for travel that lightness. They patrolled at the top of the mountains instead, cruising at a normal pace for wolves, heads held high.

Many pictures were drawn depicting the incident by two leggeds. The encounter with the bear had caves and rock faces covered with them. It was hoped that generations born after them would remember the stories, and pass them on to others. Not exactly sacred, but certainly sacrosanct. Tan's Red Ones and the pack of runts were considered as brothers by many two leggeds, revered by their culture that valued good spirits housed in the bodies of brave animals that clearly looked out for them. Even the bear housed powerful spirits that were mighty overall, but not truly evil. The spirits in the bear that did battle were present on that light time, solely to draw out the best of Tan and his pack; or so they believed. Tan fed on affection, and after they saved the two leggeds from the bear, so did the others. It was a language that they all could understand. The same could be said about the darknesses of the fullest moon. The calls sent out to other omegas that hadn't been met was a similar language, the channel it was sent out on the wind in the darkness, was always on a common wavelength.

The pack had migrated northward enough to enjoy a cool night on one of the hottest nights in summer. They had eaten a successful hunt, and were more than satisfied. They stood close by, on a high grassy knoll, silhouetted by a full moon that had cleared the horizon, appearing huge in the dark sky. It seemed a good time to greet more omegas from a pack Tan and the others knew to exist in the area. The scent of them was strong, but they had not made sight of them. Tan's Red Ones and the pack of runts were not standing in a safe, protected area that could not be reached by the pack that owned the territory. Tan and the others had pushed the hot buttons of that pack. When the pack of runts set out the omega calling howl to carry on the wind, it was heard by the omegas of the other pack, the leader, and the other members, as well. The whole pack followed their leader to chase out invaders to their territory. When the defending pack came close enough to see Tan' Red Ones and the pack of runts standing firm in their house, so to speak, the leader made challenge. Tan stepped forward. He did not want to fight one of his own kind, so he began herding his pack to run away to high ground. Such was custom for the pack going back all the way to Master and Mated. But the leader would hear none of it, enraged and strong himself, had Tan's pack surrounded. The leader made his move to attack Tan, baring his fangs, crouching, ready to leap to a fight with Tan. Tan stood his ground, digging in for a fair fight, but Tan's Red Ones made the decision not to play fair. When the leader jumped at Tan, prepared to rip Tan's throat out, the Red Ones jumped to his aid, making such short work of the leader. It was too hard to record how many milliseconds it took. The rest of the now leaderless pack vied for superiority. Depending where they were standing at the time, the rest of the pack of runts mobilized, jumping anywhere from 4 to 7 meters to fight the rest of the defending pack. The omegas then fought so ferociously, that in an extremely small space of time, overwhelmed the pack, driving them to run away from their own territory.

Tan's Red Ones and the pack of runts did not make new friends that darkness because the whole pack had run off, omega members included. The pack of runts tried one last time with the call. Yip-yip-wahoooooo-aaah...wahoooooo-aaah...yip yip-wahoooooo-aaah, they tried again while still in range. The call was not answered. It was a sad darkness for Tan and his pack. This time they did run away to higher ground, not stopping until a summit was reached to sleep for the rest of darkness. The fight made them all tired. Confrontation was needed, but not wanted. They started out trying to make friends, and made enemies instead.

Even with the passing of fifteen darknesses, the revelation that acceptance was not guaranteed without a fight with their own kind was disheartening. A misconception had formed from the belief that respect automatically would be rewarded if strength was displayed. It could not be assumed that senseless fights like the one they had with the pack that owned the territory, would not have to be fought. The omegas in the pack had not wanted to join them after Tan and his pack clearly demonstrated they could stand up to bullies and even defeat them if they had to. Tan's pack became the bullies. For Tan, the only thing that made sense of it all is that the Red Ones, the pack of runts, and Tan himself were trespassers. They had hunted on territory that did not belong to them. Tan's pack was in violation. The higher position of being right belonged to the leader of the other pack, and the omegas in that pack totally correct in following the pack that showed principal. Strength of character is not the same as a character that is strong. Tan and the others should have learned from experience. If they had come to the rescue of that same pack by felling a bear that threatened them and shared it with them afterward, then they would earn respect. Fifteen darknesses later, tails still hung down in shame. For a while, the pack went through the motions of slow travel, hunting along the way.

But then, pride slowly came back to the pack, and fun was had again. They stopped to greet and get greeted by villagers they had seen before on the pilgrimage south. Headed north revisited the same good times, except that the addition of the Red Ones were a shock to those who had never seen them before. The Red Ones could carry a two legged on their backs. Most gave pause to come close to them, but did. But when the chance was taken, both two legged and Red Ones got rewards from the encounter. First and foremost, the lack of ill will toward each other, created bonds between them that would endure forever, in village after village.

The very next darkness, the full moon yielded somewhat different results from the last. After the omega calling howl was issued, answers came. It sounded like a small group, and not all that strong a response. The group that answered the call was close by, coming from the direction already traveled by Tan and his pack. Travel had been leisurely at best, especially after being subdued after the fighting episode for a time. Stopping at villages along the way, also impeded forward progress. None in the pack had paid much attention to what was behind them, but Tan and the others had been tracked. But scents still were not that clear, due to the wind carrying it away.

10-4 CANINE ONE NINERS

The omegas from the pack that Tan's Red One's and the pack of runts did battle with had a new leader. He and the others chased out the omegas from the pack, blaming them for the troubles they had. The poor small wolves took all the blame and punishment. Furthermore, they found themselves without the protection of their pack. They began tracking Tan and the others ever since. There were six of them altogether, very much worse for wear. Hunting was helped by the fact that it was the summer season, and small game was plentiful. But they were not as skillful as Tan's omegas, and certainly not as powerful. But it was the recently ejected omegas that found Tan and the pack, not the other way around. It was because Tan's Red Ones and the pack of runts were not on top of a mountain. They had come down out of the high altitudes to place the omega calling howl so they might be heard.

Out of the darkness, under a shining full moon, six bedraggled omegas entered the area where Tan and the others were waiting to get another answering call so that they could begin moving toward them. Tan didn't have to move a fraction of a meter. Six barely standing omegas emerged from the woods to make themselves known to Tan and the pack of runts. But the omegas were hungry and tired, having used all their energy to track the pack. The funny thing was that all four of Tan and Red Dog's offspring took an almost paternal interest in the group, stepping out of the pack to dote on the poor souls.

For the next four light times, Tan and his pack of omegas ran and jumped as a group in their customary combination and style, but just as odd were the Red Ones and their followers. The ragtag omegas followed the Red Ones like fleas in fur. The tall strange wolves ran with a graceful stride that only took one gait to four of the new omegas. Even more striking was that the Red Ones stood at least two and a half times as tall as their new friends. They all ran separately from Tan and the pack of runts. It was very unusual but just as obvious that the four red wolves were bound in a collective leadership over a new pack. The new omegas spent hours and hours of every daylight, copying the Red Ones style of running. Even their hunting styles mimicked those of the Red Ones. The Red Ones were constantly hungry because of their body mass, and larger game is about all that would satisfy them. This new group of omegas saw it as normal, and having never been included in such hunts before, looked upon it as an honor to participate. Tan and the pack of runts could survive on anything; indeed they preferred eating and running so that they didn't constantly find themselves stopping to tend to business instead of exploring. It became just as obvious that the two groups would have to part ways to be totally happy. If it was any indication from the Red Ones and that of their new pack, their behavior showed that they would go on to be a powerful pack, one that would hold their own if they established a territory. The sad part of it all was that Tan and the pack of runts and the Red Ones pack would have to go their separate ways. Tan and Red Dog didn't honestly want to separate from their offspring, but Tan, Red Dog, and the pack of runts very much had an itch to run in the high altitudes again. So after a lot of nose to nose nudging, Tan and the pack of runts took their leave, climbed the nearest mountain, and continued on in the way life pleased them most. The Red Ones and their pack were never seen again. It is unclear if they ever made a mark on the world, just survived in it, or instilled enough fear by their appearance that they were avoided.

Stories come, and stories go. Pictures drawn disappear from ravages of time and weather. Others that do remain legible, probably not understood unless a two legged explains the true meaning if they deciphered them correctly. But memories live on, even if distorted from the original facts. Was something different and special about Tan and his pack of runts from all the other thousands of wolves, and packs that followed them roaming carefully marked territories? Well of course there was!

Master and Mated only produced one litter of offspring, and could not seem to reproduce after that. Tan and Red Dog had the same problem. White, Afraid, Blue Eye, Dark, and even Tan's Red Ones could not reproduce at all. As fast as they all grew, it seemed their lifespan was considerably shortened.

But Tan prospered, and his real family were the

omegas that bonded with him. Together, they were mighty, but kind. The language they spoke that carried on the full moon darkness wind channels was a language that was universally understood only by other omegas. The language of love was universally understood by Tan and the pack of runts and two leggeds.

The two leggeds at the time of their roaming the Rocky Mountains from the coldest northerly regions all the way to the desert considered them brothers and friends. Debts of gratitude had grown into enduring friendships from the first time they met. The two legged's repaid their gratitude by working to keep the relationship thriving, telling others of their kind to watch for the pack, to pay them respect. But most of all, no matter what any other pack of wolves might do, keep the friendship of Tan and the pack of runts sacrosanct. They deserved that and more. Such was the real legend of Tan and the pack of runts

IS IT RAINING WHERE YOU ARE?

IS IT RAINING WHERE YOU ARE?

It was another hot day in the little city of Lemming. The second month of the summer season was a brutal one this year. The mercury reached the 98 degree line for pretty near 12 days straight. That sort of heat wasn't normal in the part of the country Lemming was in. Indeed the whole country, not just Lemming, was feeling detrimental effects of a really bad heat wave. Global warming? Probably...well maybe. Who cares after a while? Hot is hot, it's not something to argue about.

Lemming was a city that has enjoyed more than it's share of good times and fortune. Too small to attract big city problems, fortunate enough to pay its bills and enjoy essential creature comforts for it's residents. The city enjoyed average to good weather to support the farming community surrounding it. That's what the city was built to service; the farming community.

That said; ponds, lakes, and rivers in and around the city were drying up or at low levels since the middle of spring, even before the heat. Birds with long legs pranced around in shallow water, searching, probing for food, finding little sustenance. Also, uncommon for the region, was enforcement of water bans that saw lawns and gardens drying up. The farms, Lemming's bread and butter, were allowed to tap the ground water and kept protected, but a moderate threat was growing. As a result, an invasion of environmentalists from the east and west coasts swooped in one day. They carried printed signs in the street with men stooping before them with fancy cameras on their shoulders. They were using Lemming as an example of a city that was experiencing something far from the norm. Some were even overheard suggesting that the government deploy giant man made coolers in the Arctic powered by the sun, just a touch far fetched. Somebody had watched one too many science fiction movies. It was just one of many ideas coming from all quarters to halt the receding ice shelves. Some of these so called experts breezed into town to warn the rest of the country that the oceans would rise up enough for farmers in the central time zones to consider making career changes to shrimp fishing. What all of that had to do with an abnormal drought in Lemming was anybody's guess.

Meanwhile, in the rest of the country,

meteorologists fought with politicians. Politicians fought with meteorologists. Sunday morning political junkie shows on television were borderline fisticuffs, with childish name calling. The whole affair was a product of brand new troubling times. Finger pointing was the newest rage. The pointing finger giving the bird finger a serious run for the money. The thumb, however, emerged the true winner from it's over use to plug millions of anus areas by sitting on them. This caused an outbreak of constipation, driving up drug company stock to produce pills for remedies. All of that gave something else for people to cry about—nationally speaking that is, but an entirely different topic.

Meanwhile, when push came to shove, with drought a separate issue, it was only the twelfth day of high temperature weather in Lemming. But the odd thing about the heat wave in Lemming, as compared with the troubles of the rest of the country, was that it was humid and muggy, not a dry heat at all. The residents of Lemming felt that it really should be raining, especially since the dew point was well over 75 degrees, closer to 80. The air reeked of moisture with no rain, and it always rained in Lemming. Bones and joints were aching in just the right way, and the only real relief for symptoms like that was for the high moisture content in the air looming over the area to finally get it out of it's system. It would be when a low pressure system came in. Most felt it would be an explosive event with possible flood conditions. Every coffee klatch in every diner in Lemming concurred. Rain was imminent.

Before that happened, the environmentalist people with the signs had to leave, even if they were bringing in extra business. It just wasn't worth the aggravation to listen to them. The poor folks in the south that were dealing with devastating tornadoes could use a real hand. *Put down the signs and pick up a shovel, the Lemmingsters all said.* Instead, true to form, when the tornado barrage got even worse, off went the men and women with signs, flying out right away to herald the end of the earth as we all know it, beginning with the victims. The television was plastered with know-it-alls lending expertise and platitudes, instead of arms, hands, and wheelbarrows. It would have been refreshing to see these people with all the time in the world to torture us with rhetoric, using communities like Lemming, and tornado ravaged areas, to show up and get their clothes dirty with the back breaking jobs that needed to get done. The rest of us can only send food and money.

Left alone, quiet and peace came back to little Lemming. The stifling heat still persisted into the thirteenth day. Anything done, was done indoors, bringing the small community even closer together. Coffee klatches turned into lemonade and iced tea competitions. Signs were put up in restaurants and diners claiming drinks to be, 'voted best in town'; harmless bologna while things were slowed by the heat.

There was a new car dealership on the outskirts of Lemming, the owner of the establishment had a serious penchant for classic driving machines. A few years back, the owner, his name was Gerald, showcased a few of his rebuild projects prominently in his lot for sale. They caused quite a buzz. The classic car rebuilds got more attention than the brand new vehicles cramming the rest of the lot. Gerald's service area began earning a fine reputation that came from some of the top notch cars that were transformed there. After that, Gerald's was visited by many an owner of older muscle cars, hot rods, older pick up trucks, as well as custom fine automobiles. Gerald's shop drew accolades from all over the state, and even nationally after some magazine publications got a whiff of some of the completed jobs that were produced there. His shop grew and took on machine shop work, body work and fabrication, custom paint, and a bevy of expanding services—all in house. Over time, Saturday morning car shows became a regular social bonanza to the city, rivaling the area flea market by ten to one. Some of the shows even developed into auctions, held quarterly. The quality coming out of them was heard far and wide. Other organizations wanted to sign on to join in these auctions, because of the exploding reputation that j ust kept on gaining momentum. Once again, without benefit of major industry beyond farming, Lemming enjoyed modest prosperity.

The deepening drought accompanied by choking heat grew into deep concern when a Saturday morning auto show was canceled due to the uncomfortable weather. It was just too hard to breathe outside in hot moisture drenched air. Thus, the otherwise level headed citizens of Lemming began a rapid meltdown. Men and women with signs drawing unneeded attention was only a small blip of aggravation. Uncomfortable weather that kept people indoors drinking lemonade and iced tea, dead grass that postponed mowing caused by the drought, minuscule problems in the scheme of things. Threats to the farmer's ground water supply were perceived as a temporary problem. But...canceling the Saturday morning car show caused panic...well, at least very deep discussions in the lemonade and iced tea klatches. The news had showed up in the paper on Wednesday afternoon, creating an instant buzz. This kind of craziness would happen only one week in a row if the Lemmingsters had any say in it. It was all anybody anybody talked about all day on Thursday.

One of the klatch discussions convened by chance over at The Place Next To The Diner Barbershop, during big Bob's haircut. Randy Harper was the barber, and one of the biggest fans of the car show ever. His 1948 Ford F1 was an attention getter for sure. Randy was always hungry for attention. Randy was Gerald's first customer to do a build.

The F1 sat out in Randy's barn for years, the plan all along was to rebuild her someday. She originally belonged to Randy's dad back before his dad sold the most of his land to the Hetherton place. Randy went to barber school, and there didn't seem much sense holding the farm together. Dad Harper needed to retire as his health had been failing. Maintaining a farm was much too much at the time. But The Ford F1 and some farm machinery stayed in the barn where it had always been. After dad Harper passed away, Randy took care of his mom, and kept everything in the barn just where it belonged. The F1 was a dream of Randy's to restore one day. When Gerald revealed his first restore, Randy approached him right away, and the rest is, shall we say, history.

It wasn't really true, but it seemed as though Randy subscribed to every auto magazine ever published, the latest editions of each sat neatly stacked on a glass table in his waiting area. A haircut at Randy's took a while because most of the patrons coming in for a haircut, also wanted to get caught up on city nonsense, sports, and to browse the magazines at the same time. This day, big Bob sat in the chair taking extra time by Randy to cut his hair. Big Bob had a lot of hair. His hair had to be cut just right so it would look like a man's haircut. It involved a ponytail. Conversation between the five waiting regulars in the shop got a little more involved than usual because of it. Somebody brought up the subject of Harry Senprey.

Mr. Senprey was a very enterprising young man that lived over on Sycamore Street. Harry came up with an advertising gimmick to draw people into the three car washes he had strategically situated in the city. It started when Harry was approached by the city manager at the end of Spring in June, to make the idea of washing cars in his car washes attractive to the public. The water ban had just been issued. The city manager's thought was to discourage washing of cars in driveways at home. Harry's way to accommodate was to modify the change collectors in the wash stalls. The engine wash cycle spot on the dial was discontinued, soap for it cost too much anyway. Instead of the engine wash, more minutes were added to the regular wash. For two dollars, the standard block of ten minutes was increased to twelve. The empty slot created by eliminating engine wash was replaced with a novelty selection. It read: ***twenty five hours rain free for 25 cents***. It was only a novelty choice. What really happened when 25 cents was inserted, was that two extra minutes was added to the wash cycle, nothing more. Finally, the billboards in front of all three car washes advertised that Harry's car wash guaranteed 25 hours rain free with every wash for just 25 cents extra. Harry never thought anybody would take the claim seriously. A few of the chatterboxes at the barber shop apparently did take it seriously on that Friday afternoon. The discussion got a little heated.

IS IT RAINING WHERE YOU ARE?

There were a fair amount of classic cars and trucks belonging to residents in Lemming. Washing them to keep them pristine was a priority to preserve investments. Had a show taken place, preparation would have been worse. Even with the show canceled that Saturday, all three car washes were full, lines out into the street. Of course, not all of the cars were classic, pride was not inclusive to just one group. Besides, attending the alternative flea market wasn't exactly a viable thing to do in the heat, now into day seventeen. It is fair to say that most, if not all the folks washing cars that day, took note of the extra spot on the selector to avoid the rain. One or two of those people may even have taken it as seriously as the klatch that babbled away the afternoon at The Place Next To The Diner Barbershop. Evidence of this might explain the first crime recorded in Lemming in several years. Of course, it was only a matter of time that something bad would happen in Lemming eventually. The place wouldn't be healthy if it didn't. Still, it was a crying shame that Mr. and Mrs. Senprey came home from shopping to find several of the windows of their home broken with rocks. It was silly and childish. It was damned inconvenient, especially on a Saturday afternoon. Poor Harry had to cover his windows with cardboard to conserve air conditioning. The closest time given to them that somebody could fix them was on Monday morning. Harry and his wife had no idea at the time why anybody would vandalize their home.

It took an observation of one of the patrolmen who showed up when called to give Harry and his wife a clue as to why. The patrolman, coincidentally, was one of the patrons at the barbershop on Friday, the day before. He related the discussion that took place to Harry and his wife. It made the reason clear, but the reasoning muddled. Harry was stunned that he could be viewed as the person that caused any of the meteorological issues Lemming suffered. His wife was livid. Like his windows, there was not much he could do about it until Monday. Henry Wadsworth Longfellow wrote, “Into each life, some rain must fall.” Maybe if a little rain had fallen, Mr. and Mrs. Senprey's windows would not be broken. When Monday came around, the 'no rain' choices would be clean off the selector. Harry made a solemn oath to the officers. The officers told him sympathetically that everything possible would be done to try to find who had broken the windows, but waiting for positive results might be just as crazy as the crime itself.

On Sunday, day eighteen of the muggiest heat wave ever recorded at the national weather service, rain finally came to Lemming, but only in particular sections of the city. Relatives called each other, friends called friends. When lines on phones connected, the first thing asked was, “Hey...is it raining where you are?” That is about all that could be uttered into phone mouthpieces as the folks that got rained on faced larger problems.

It turns out that some of the people who washed cars the day before, talked a good talk, but couldn't walk the good walk. They all said no way to the extra quarter, but did it anyway on the sly. A smaller percentage did not, and by golly did they ever get rain!

Conservative estimates had the hour long deluge measured at seven inches when the worst of the hour long sheet dropped from the sky. It was a very strange rain indeed, where it rained. Not a drop of rain flowed into drains on the street. Water was directed into the yards and onto the homes of the folks who avoided putting in the extra quarter. The poor people that stuck to their guns were repaid with cataclysmic floods. Sump pumps pumped water out, but with no place to go, water came right back in. Walls of water ended at the curbs in front of the homes like Moses himself commanded it. The streets were dry as a bone. On the other hand, the folks who dropped the quarter in the box before they were seen, found themselves on Sunday evening completely untouched.

The moisture in the air was magically sucked out. With the humidity gone from the air. Cooler air moved in even before the rain stopped. The temperature, which dropped to 85 degrees, was cool and comfortable by comparison to the 95 degree heat with matching 95 degree dew point. Just a short hour plus after the heaviest of the rainfall, Lemming was provided with much needed relief. However, even though it didn't rain near as hard, it rained all the way through Sunday night. There was no way to assess how much damage there was until the rain stopped completely.

IS IT RAINING WHERE YOU ARE?

Monday morning heralded a gorgeous day. White gentle cumulus clouds decorated an intensely blue sky. The temperature started out at 70 degrees at 5:30 AM. The forecast predicted no more than a high temp of 82 without a rain cloud in sight. When eyelids fluttered open throughout the city, the reality of the freak unexplainable storm left stark reminders. Fortunately, the highly visible tornado ravaged regions of the country drew attention away from Lemming. The unbearable scrutiny of the environmentalists that invaded Lemming just a week before never even noticed the bizarre weather that happened in Lemming. Many a Lemminster attended Mass that morning. Lines to the confessional were as heavy as the lines at the car washes on Saturday.

Noteworthy was the fact that the Harry Senprey place had all broken windows replaced by 8:30 AM straight up. But schedules to repair damaged homes was close to impossible. By the end of the afternoon, every neighborhood in the city had full regiments of volunteers to help each other sort through the remnants of the disaster. The problem was, that every home that got rained on looked like an aquarium. Water ended at the edges of each affected property. A person could stand on the sidewalk and stay dry. A good twenty feet or more of water pressed against nonexistent glass. All that was visible from the street was the pitch of roofs. There was no place for the water to go but to soak into the ground, or possibly be pumped out into the street to be carried away by the city sewerage drains. Rescuing the families trapped upstairs or on the roof of their homes was very successful. Roughly half of the victims stayed with their homes guarding personal belongings, which was totally ludicrous. The other half of the affected victims left their homes when water lapped at their feet. At the time, they simply waded out to the street to find they could stand and watch the whole thing happening right before their eyes. Somebody had the unmitigated gall to make a joke. He suggested a team of scuba divers should be sent in to flush toilets. The joke was completely not funny, but might have been a defense mechanism that was triggered from fear. Many unaffected volunteers that were helping with rescues had tears flowing freely from their eyes.

IS IT RAINING WHERE YOU ARE?

Word had come that farms as far as twenty five miles out were underwater, as well. Vast acreage spread the water out but was still four to six inches deep; much deeper in ruts and valleys. Farms adjoining those properties were not touched at all.

If it was any consolation, Harry Senprey made a statement that his car washes would be closed down for as long as it took to get Lemming back to the way it was. It was an absurd statement. Lemming would never be normal again. He was temporarily forgotten in favor of much larger problems. Community spirit was up 100 per cent, but not much help overall because water surrounded one in every two or three thousand or so homes simply would not drain away. Just in case anybody thought the whole thing was a nightmare, all one had to do was drive through the city, or fly over submerged farmland.

The general consensus of the volunteers was that calling for outside help would open up the gates of hell on Lemming if they weren't already. What would the country say? No, make that what would the world say about the otherworldly phenomenon that absolutely could not be denied if it was seen? The residents felt they would be viewed as either scorned by God, or paid up in full to the Devil. Either way, there was some serious 'splaining to do. But stalling could only last so long. Not much could be done about outsiders missing the car shows. They would be calling or driving over to Gerald's to check up on them. After that, for sure, the state would be alerted, followed by the media that would be town criers to the world. There was one thing that was definitely for sure. None of this had a thing to do with global warming.

The cliques and klatches that were a part of what Lemming's lifestyle were things of the past. A new era of community was ushered in instead. Before all of the craziness, Lemming was always a good place to live, but now every resident of Lemming were family. Each and every person, man, woman, or child, were necessary parts of the whole. The opinion of a small child was considered as much as anyone else's. After all, didn't it say somewhere in the Bible; *out of the mouths of babes*...? It was one of these miniature geniuses that pointed out, "Hey, maybe we can fix the car washes to have a dry cycle!!"

Well, light bulbs went on over everybody's head at the same time because it made perfect sense, didn't it? Hope gained a foothold until Harry Senprey was approached. He was part of the very same volunteer group that stood around hand wringing at the time little Betsy Minner came up with her gem. Harry felt he had somehow done quite enough damage. Who could tell what sort of thing might happen if something like that was done? He was right of course, but something needed to be done regardless of the danger. Why if word leaked out into the world, religious zealots would pop out of the woodwork to over run Lemming. There would be no controlling them, excepting maybe to install filters in every affected yard, and adding fish. Still, the fact that water was contained without the benefit of any glass would be a dead giveaway that something was amiss. The name of the city would have to be changed also, to something like Tank World. No, the risk needed to be taken on. It was pointed out that Harry had some culpability in all of it. But the volunteers instantly backed away from that hard stance. They attempted instead to show him where it made sense. There would be no vigilantism in Lemming. It was because of that respect that Harry Senprey was easily talked into changing to selection spot from ***25 hours rain free***, to ***Air Drying***.

It took about four and a half hours to relabel the selectors at all three car washes. Care was taken to remove all traces of the old labeling and referencing to rain free. The timers were reset to give another whole minute to the regular wash if a quarter was installed. Ladders were leaned against the billboards out front. Spelled out plainly, both sides of the signs said, ***Air Drying for 25 cents***. Care was taken in the wording to avoid further complications that might arise. Word was spread to all the affected victims in an all out effort to gather them all to where it all began. This led to yet another problem. All of the cars that went though the car wash the first time were completely underwater.

A loaner car idea was floated as a remedy. "But what if somebody else's stuff is dried? Shouldn't something from the drowned properties be used?"

Somebody yelled out.

An answer came from yet another volunteer in the crowd, “Yeah! I agree. We need to get something that is underwater to bring to the car wash to use. I'll be glad to swim in to get something.”

“What if we need to use the whole car that was washed to begin with?” asked another.

Thus began a salvage mission to drag every car out of the water to get them to where it all started. It was a monumental mission. It involving pickups, tow trucks, chain, rope, keys, and most of all, people who could swim real good. Some of the cars were parked behind garage doors. The trick was to get into where the car happened to be parked before the swimmer ran out of air. Apart from the joke earlier in the day, there wasn't any scuba gear in Lemming.

The entire day was consumed with tackling all the ideas initiated up until then. But the sun set before all of it could be finished, so the displaced families were put up for the night anywhere space could be found. There wasn't a motel room left in the city. Children from some of the families could be overheard asking, “Mommy. Are we going on vacation?”

Answered with, “Yes honey. Now you'll be a good boy for me won't you?”

Tuesday morning brought even more problems. Word had gotten out overnight about Lemming's bout with supernatural misfortune. True to prediction, somebody's big mouth unleashed a plague of people. Some were just rubberneckers. Some were experts in something no expertise was to be had. Some were doom and gloomers. Worst of all, the environmentalists were back. All the extra people were a hindrance to the jobs that needed to be done. Explanations were demanded about jobs undertaken that had no rational explanation at all. All because of somebody's big fat mouth.

Be that as it may, the good folks of Lemming went about their business with devotion to their intent. As soon as a car was recovered from underwater, it was loaded up on a tow truck and whisked away along with its owner.

One by one, in a process that was far from easy, drenched automobiles were recovered from all the watery tombs and hauled away. It was when working at the fifth home that something happened at the first home that was worked on. A cloud formed over the house like a thunderhead. The cloud got darker and darker. It hovered high in the sky directly over the home. Changes in the water levels stayed exactly the same, but tiny lightning strikes connected the contained water to the cloud in the sky. Water in and around the home formed small bubbles, but nothing more. More and more of the homes that had a car taken from it and whisked away, joined a list of homes that shared the same reaction. Work was slow, but soon, all throughout the city, bystanders joined hands with Lemmingsters in the job they undertook. It was not clear why any of it was done, but evidence showed that something was happening and seemed worth doing. The constant questioning thankfully ceased. Not even the environmentalists asked where the cars went.

Word had gotten out to the Hetherton farm and eventually to the rest of the flooded farms as to what was going in town. The water on the farms was spread out—not near as deep as the house lots in the city. Though treacherous, the independent farmers managed to get vehicles off properties on their own.

When dusk came, all work had to stop for the night, concluding only half of what still needed to be done. But with the new dawn on Wednesday, all hands that called it quits the night before joined together once again. This time it was done without question or badgering. You see, when the sun peaked over the horizon, it ended a night that didn't allow any of the residents to sleep. Almost a hundred separate thunderstorms rumbled, accompanied by the tiny lightning flashes that could be seen all throughout Lemming, as well as outside of it. One flash would end, another would begin. It gave an eerie strobe light glow. Morning light showed the mini-storms still in progress, surrounded by sunrise. The effect was surreal. Frightened folks whose original intention was to pry or disrupt, drove in to town that Wednesday to witness a city under siege, with no real relief. Yards were still flooded with bubbling water, clouds overhead, tiny bolts of light sparking into the water. Sunny yards were right next door, or across the street. People there to disrupt had no answers. All they had to offer was help, and help they did; with a vengeance.

By late afternoon, the last of the cars to be extracted from underwater was on a tow truck headed for a car wash. An hour later, every flooded home was bubbling. The sound in Lemming was deafening. By dinnertime, the noise of rumbling storms increased until it was almost unbearable. Diners and restaurants opened all their doors to feed resident volunteers as well as the radically changed people that had come to town with agendas that had all but been forgotten. All were exhausted and hungry. While eating the donated meals cooked by the owners of all of the diners and restaurants in town, outsiders finally got answers to questions hanging in the air. The truth is, nobody really knew what was going on, only what had happened. What would happen next? No one could say. All that could be told were the facts, which were not held back. What had happened because of the car washes? There were no answers to that either. Everyone in Lemming were in just as much in the dark as the visitors. Before conversations could develop into speculation, the rumbling got even worse.

Suddenly an odd swirling wind picked up. Clouds closed in together, swallowing the sun. It became pitch dark outdoors, more like a total eclipse than an impending storm. The swirling wind calmed down after that, but then the sky glowed a blue-white strobe. A clap of thunder rolled so loud that it shook buildings like an earthquake. Then the ground erupted, instead of the sky. If witnesses were not there to see it first hand, there would not be a soul on earth who would believe the stories. Maybe not even with witnesses would it be believed. It rained up. It rained a deluge that would most certainly have drowned everyone in town, except that it rained up for goodness sake! For three hours straight, Lemming had an upside down rainstorm. All that could be done was watch from indoors as a freak of nature, never seen or heard of before by all the folks watching. It took water that was on the ground completely away. Darkness started dispersing. The sun peeked through, and dark clouds moved. They gathered over every pond, lake, and river around Lemming. The rain then came down, replenishing city's depleted water supplies. There was not one drop of water in all of Lemming, or the drowned farms surrounding it. People ventured outdoors to watch the last of the storm in amazement. The last of the remaining dark clouds faded, faded some more, converted to rolling white cotton puffs, and then disappeared altogether. Blue sky and bright sunshine took the place of the strange occurrence that shook the city only moments earlier.

In the calm, streets filled with people that poured out from all the places where they were trapped indoors. Lemming again had experienced something otherworldly. It was out of the realm of experience. Nobody could come forward to say, “You know? I know exactly what happened here. It was that damned global warming again!!” Nope, nobody at all could say that. The fact that this thrown together mob of people pulled together to save Lemming, however unorthodox, was a testament to what humans can accomplish with each other. Rather than fight, bicker, and criticize, these people came together. Skeptics, enemies, political grandstanding bureaucrats, and short sighted fools rose above differences. Very likely, it would never be known what happened in Lemming. But it surely didn't matter. This assortment of different cross sections of society won a battle. As such, venturing outdoors as a team, as it were, was to explore a war zone to find what was left to rebuild. Groups formed and fanned out in all directions, reconnaissance style.

So what was it that was found? Damage for sure. But the city was whole. Formerly flooded yards were strewn with children's toys, yard furniture, household items, and trash. There was not one trace of water, only the aftermath. Indoors had much of what might be expected. Destroyed pictures, books, walls, all were in horrible shape, but dry as a bone. It was inconceivable that only the damage was left, but not a drop of water. One owner picked a book up off of his floor and flipped through the pages. It was fluffy but dry. It was absolutely remarkable. Before the storm, and the drought, average life in Lemming was as much a struggle as anywhere else. A small amount of destroyed homes had no homeowners insurance at all. It was this revelation that the non residents felt they had a personal stake in Lemming and thus decided then and there that they wanted to stay and be a part of the community. About thirty five out of the hundred or so volunteers that had never stepped foot in Lemming but once before, offered to purchase the homes from the victims that weren't covered. This would give the owners cash to start over, and provide restoration projects for brand new prospective residents. These were finely built old homes, but the true reason was that they just did not want to leave. These people ran the whole gamut. They reached a level that caused them to want to call Lemming home, to be a part of this extended family. Some of the rest of the non residents had family and homes of their own, and developed a pressing need to get back to them where they belonged. Bureaucrats were still bureaucrats, but the ones who visited Lemming for two days went back to jobs with attitude shifts. There were places to the south that were leveled by tornadoes. Places that needed help, not lip service, and they meant to give them just that. Places that may or may not have been affected by the global warming, but surely did need help for sure. Putting the reason down on paper to further a government study does little to pick up piles of twisted two by fours that used to be part of a bedroom.

And so the small, not so perfect, but good City of Lemming inherited another group with human frailties. They would add different views to discussions held in the coffee klatches that could be expected to return shortly. Old habits are habits after all. Swivel stools at the diner would make room for a few former doom and gloom rubberneckers, experts that were not really experts, but opinionated just like the rest of us. Their names would be changed from the various expletives they were dubbed, to Fred, Patrick, or whatever the real names were in the first place. Discussions pending before the informal boards would include the efficiency of the current city manager, and when it would be proper to hold the next car show. Lastly, Harry Sempler had to be convinced to reinstall the engine wash selection.

CRABBY PEOPLE

CRABBY PEOPLE

I woke up one Saturday morning clearly on another planet. I must have been whisked away while I slept, and delivered back to a wrong destination. I swear if there is a race so advanced as to take us away for whatever study they might have in mind, all without our being aware I might add, the very least that race could do is keep up the good work and return us back where we belong. I hate when people borrow stuff without asking and not return it back to where they took it from.

I made myself a pot of coffee, took it and myself to the television room to find out what the weather would be. The predictions were for a windy, cloudy, unseasonably cool day, with imminent threats of rain to the tune of a 98% chance. Getting outside to do yard work so I could escape the kind of chores my wife more than likely had in store for me indoors, had me close to choking bile. Thirty minutes later, my wife Emma caught me still sitting and staring at Saturday morning fishing shows, the host on camera bleeped because he lost a big one on film. I never saw a bleep on a fishing show before. Yup...kind of a new one. But then I almost had a heart attack when Emma sneaked up on me and said some bleeping words of her own. She was chewing me out from the corner of the room for catching quiet time before I knew damned well all hell would break loose that day. The truth is with that kind of grand entrance that I was in for certain death by browbeating. Donning a poker face, I did not let on just how relieved I really was that all she needed me to do was cart her around town. I could do that. I just didn't let her know I could do that. I figured to match her ornery so she'd stop at the first round of volleys. I just had to drop the defenses a split second before a second round of volleys were launched or I'd go down in flames.

“Listen, Walt, I'm sorry for yellin' at you baby. I thought you were going to yell at me because you wanted to sit on your ass all day.”

“Nah sweetie. Do you want to go out for breakfast or something? This guy on the fishing show is swearing anyway for goodness sake. I don't want to hear that! I always thought just comedians did that kind of shit nowadays.”

“Don't say 'shit', Walt!”

CRABBY PEOPLE

"What? That ain't a swear, is it?"

"It's vulgar, Walt. It's a vulgarity."

"Yeah, well, that's exactly what came out of his God damned mouth on TV, Emma. What do you want me to call it, do do?"

"I take it all back. I'm not sorry I yelled at you, even if you are taking me out for breakfast."

"But it was okay for you to swear at me for your good morning Walt'?"

"That's different."

"Why is that so effing different?"

"Because I'm the *M..F* lady of the house!"

"Bitch, more like it! At least I use effing instead of the real thing."

"Why don't you change your underwear and pull on some pants so we can go. God, talk about baggage!"

Emma and I have a ravine out back of the house. Depending on how rainy it is, the ravine can be anything from a river, to a small brook, all the way down to what's left of a pond with lily pads in it like it was that Saturday. I have to keep it weed whacked, so we don't attract, shall we say, undesirable company. This day did attract some company, a couple small ducks. When Emma and I left for breakfast, we went out the breezeway door to get to the car. That is when I noticed the ducks. I thought they were playing happily in the water. All of a sudden one of the ducks pushed the other one under the surface with his bill, holding him there. I watched and waited. I'd never seen anything like that before, but the other duck stayed under the surface, making me uncomfortable. After a full minute, the duck under water popped to the surface, fluttering his wings, paddling his feet in a big hurry to get away from the creepy duck that was on top.

"Emma, did you see that?" She was behind me, and I hoped she had followed my gaze down to the pond and saw what stunned me."

"Yeah I saw it. What of it?"

"That duck tried to drown the other one!"

"So? We would have been eating duck l'orange for supper tonight. I was just waiting for the loser...our loss."

CRABBY PEOPLE

"Are you kid-ding me? Man, that's harsh!" I said. Emma coughed and laughed like crazy.

Five minutes later on the road, we were driving down Harrison Avenue, speed limit thirty five, I'm going forty five; man passes me giving me dirty looks with mouth jawing something not nice. I couldn't hear him through a closed window, but it wasn't nice. His hand remained on the horn from behind, alongside, and in front, only then replaced with the middle finger in the air over his shoulder.

"What was that, God damn it?"

"Well Walt, you WERE going a little slow."

"Seriously? I was going ten miles an hour over the speed limit. What should I do, get myself a ticket just to make people happy? I'm not getting it! Maybe I should act like that when I see douches on telephones."

"I would have done the same thing if I was behind you."

"For real?" I felt myself getting angry, so I dropped the subject.

Thinking about the guy who passed me by made time go by without the awareness of it. We were at the restaurant and being hungry made me forget my irritation. I trailed my wife to find that the place came up in the world from the last time we were in, which was two weeks prior. The new system is: sign in and wait....and wait....and watch people shift from one foot to the other and sigh. "Huuuhh," shift to another foot, "Huuuhh"

So I stood up to watch the pies in a glass rotiseree so I didn't have to see them anymore. Nobody has that much nervous energy, plus none of it is going to make the people inside eat faster. I wanted to grab shoulders and make them stop. Getting behind somebody that moves from one foot to the other constantly, drives me nuts. No, not nuts, mad. Just about ready to explode...."Walt and Emma Franklin?" Hoo, baby, just in time...saved from murder, and only a forty five minute wait!

Escorted to the table our hostess asked, "Coffee?"

"Yes, please, but we're kind of hungry." Emma said.

CRABBY PEOPLE

"Your waitress this morning is Cynthia, and she''ll be right with you, okaaayy...?" she said condescendingly.

"Smooth this, bitch, okaaayy?" I said under my breath.

My wife heard me and nodded at me with approval.

"Hi, I'm Cynthia. I'm your girl this morning. Whew, it's been a busy morning. I just want to tell you before you order out what you want, we don't have any more eggs."

"Not our girl, nope, not today. See ya." In unison, my wife and I stood and left the building. "What the ff...sorry effing hell is going on? Forty five minutes, a near miss homicide charge for no eggs?" I pointed my words at my wife, but spoke to God because I woke up in purgatory.

So now the morning breakfast hours were almost done, unless we choose out one of those twenty four places that have perfect scrambled eggs because they come from a container with yellow liquid, or fried eggs that are perfect but taste like vegetable oil; the bacon precooked and warmed as is the sausage. Pancakes aren't much better because they are the fat bready kind that no way anybody can eat a whole plate of them. I'm not hungry anymore, so I asked Emma, "How do you feel about donuts?"

"If I'd known you couldn't get me a simple breakfast, I would have stayed home and cooked for myself!"

Stunned that the perception was that I had failed and that the circumstances we stepped into weren't the real cause, I drove over to the place off the highway that makes twenty four hour waffles and assorted breakfast items, including eggs and chicken fried steak.

The 'Waffle Iron' was a take off of a national chain, but was housed in a larger building leftover from another national chain that had closed it's doors that still had some the leftover decor from when it remodeled after it took over from another chain that had closed it's doors. The real name should have been 'Two Strikes And A Fowl'. When I drove into the establishment's lot, a homeless guy rushed over to heap guilt on us for having money to go eat, offering to clean my windshield that was still clean from going to the car wash the day before. He didn't bother to wait for me to decline, squirting water from a plastic bottle, swiping it off with a squeegee. It left large steaks that showed up like a sore thumb in the now afternoon sun shining through it. He was at my window with a smile and a half a mouthful of teeth, holding his hand out. A revelation struck me about the real reason for the new Katana shop over at Gazebo City Shopping Mall, a mystery to me the first time I noticed it. The need for quiet weaponry is now very clear. I handed the man a dollar, who then called me an a-hole, muttering at the same time he wandered off in the direction of his next victim.

Emma and I entered 'Waffle Iron' to be seated after yet another small wait, Emma finally getting coffee, before her head did a complete three hundred sixty; spewing even more venom than usual. Even this place was busy, but our waitress came with food, servicing three tables at once to take up the slack. She blew an unruly sprig of hair out of her eyes with the corner of her mouth, choosing out our waffles and sides of home fries and sausage from an armful of food stretching all the way to a growing wet spot under her armpit. Emma and I were fresh out of criticism about food service, so even though the plates skidded to a stop exactly in front us like in a game of suffleboard, we were happy to get food. We did not say grace. Oh wait—we never say grace.

We left the house at nine thirty. It was twelve thirty before we finished breakfast. We needed to tackle food shopping so that at the rate we were going, could get it done by sundown. I realized that if I had been more open to chores, I could have whipped them out and been back to my vegetative state much quicker, which proved that easier isn't always better.

I started my car, put it into gear, and catapulted out of the parking lot before my streaky windshield got another squeegee job from Mr. Cleanjeans. The city synchronized the streetlights in an effort to impede the progress of white cars that were recently found to be moving far too fast in relation to other colors. But after a mere five light cycles, we found ourselves over at Earth

Treats supermarket.

The food store owned ten operational electric shopping carts, every one of them were in use, half of them by people who could easily kick my ass. The other half were legitimate users that could not get around very well on their own, but were equally adept at taking up the whole aisle, or when in motion, could flatten you but for quick reflexes.

Emma was circuiting each aisle systematically, but was waiting to get in the next aisle before sending me back to get what she wanted from the previous aisle. She passed it off as forgetfulness, but I suspected it was by design. I grumbled, she snapped. I backed off because she snaps better than I grumble. It was on the third such trip that I noticed another fellow poor schlep trailing his significant other riding in an electric cart.

"FRED! You know perfectly well I don't eat store brand slop! Now go back and get what I asked for, right now!" She was the type that the high end of her verbal attack vibrated tonsils, or whatever vibrated at the back of ones throat at a yell pitches. It instantly grated on my nerves.

"Gertrude, maybe if we had food you hated in the house, you wouldn't be such a fat bitch!"

So abusive—goodness. On a whim, I picked up cans of cheaper tomato sauce, five for a dollar instead of three. I caught up to Emma, readying to add it to the cart.

"Oh no! Not happening! Bring those back this instant and get what I told you to get. Can't you follow directions?" Emma declared.

I returned the sauces to where I got them, only to see yet another couple taking verbal swipes at each other. Instead of matching irritation levels to what was happening around me, this time noticed how pathetic I was because I was no better than any of these people. Picking up the correct sauces, and returning to Emma, I dismissed myself from the constant button pushing, and trailed my wife up and down the aisles taking in one sad epiphany after another, each one profoundly punching me in the face. It even took the wind out of me to see my reflection in the glass freezer section doors. The pear shape staring back at me pointed to the fact that I wasn't all that at all. A surly, out of shape nasty dude with a face that sucked one too many lemons, permanently plaster on. The sights and sounds around me all contained fighting, bickering, condescension, impatience, all seeming to be the new norm. Emma continued to poke, prod, and show disapproval of almost everything I did, minute to minute, even if I was just following orders.

When Emma and I got to the check out, it was more of the same. People jockeyed back and forth between lines that appeared to move quicker than their own. A new line opened, and the cashier announced that he would take the next person in line. It was instantly filled by people standing at the end of the existing lines. Young people tripped over older and slower people to be first in line. I became introspective at the spectacle, quiet and sad. We put the goods on the carousel, paying for them while the groceries were packed and put into the carriage. Emma hadn't noticed my reticence toward her as we unloaded groceries into the trunk. We simply loaded up for the drive home in silence.

After loading up the car, we climbed into the passenger compartment where I sat, both hands on the wheel, staring out to windshield deep in thought.

Emma finally asked, “Um...are we going home sometime today?”

“Emma, do you love me?”

“Excuse me? We've been married seventeen years, and you're asking me that now?”

“Can you answer the question for me? Do you love me?”

“Yyyyes, of course I do.” she said nervously. “What are you trying to say?”

“Then prove it.”

“Excuse me?”

“Prove it. Kiss me right here, right now, like we used to seventeen years ago when we used to go to the movies and just kiss.”

“This is total nonsense! Walt, what has gotten into you?”

“I'm tired Emma, I don't remember us and the world being this way. I'm only asking for a kiss. How about it Emma, can I have a kiss?”

You might have thought I'd asked for her to take

some bad tasting medicine or something. She gave me a peck on the cheek, short and not that sweet.

Sunday morning I got up about the same time as the day before but changed up the order of things. I pulled on some clothes and left the house to go for a walk, an extremely long walk heading for the park about five blocks away. There's some green space there, with a small pond, ducks and a couple of swans, all tranquil, no dunking. A concrete walk encircled the pond, with paths leading off it to baseball fields, a small playground for kids, and an outside amphitheater for summer concerts. It was so early that not a whole lot was going on. A couple kids were on the playground rides, a protective mother with a stroller with a baby in it close by listening to the delighted screams of two little girls pumping hard on swings to beat each other in height. Two young teens on skateboards were on a halfpipe the city had installed for the use. I paused only to marvel at the skill demonstrated, but continued on the circuitous walkway. Both the boys nodded in my direction, acknowledging my appreciation.

After walking the park, I left to add a bit more to the distance before turning around to return home. When I returned home I got into some of the yard work I had been procrastinating. Emma was at the kitchen window watching me for the longest time, finally coming outside with two cups of coffee in hand, putting them down on the patio table that we hadn't sat at since the in laws were over for a visit last Spring. Emma motioned me over, so I got up from my weeding to walk over to her, giving her a similar kiss that she graced me with the previous afternoon. She turned and gave me lips instead.

"Thank you honey." I said, but not much else. I was still a little put off, but not put out, by her attitude on Saturday.

The work week started, but I did not stop my my sudden life style change. Every day was an early one, starting out with walks at first, gradually transforming to jogs. Lunches were skipped in favor of walks and fresh air. After work, I did a little more each day on the yard. By Friday, it became clear my aim was to convert it into a lush paradise.

Emma said nothing about any of this sudden shift in character, but intuitively had meals that reflected my attitude rebirth. In fact, she didn't have much to say at all; a kiss in the morning, and again at night. Bickering ceased and desisted, but wariness replaced it.

By Saturday, Emma went off by herself in the car to shop, something that I couldn't remember the last time, if at all. I did my morning routine, and went right out into the yard, to mow this time. Something I noticed while I was out and about exercising was that it became normal to collect friendly nods from several young people. One young lady actually asked how I was that morning. The small, innocuous, but nice stroke, left me with a smile on my face.

After Saturday's yard work left me satisfied with my day, Emma had yet again made another healthy meal consisting of a salad with a vegy burger. Again, not much conversation between us.

I joined a movie club, and my first DVD arrived in the mail that day. I had to test the DVD player to see if it was still functional and found out it was. When I had settled into the couch to watch the DVD, Emma settled in beside me, cuddling up wordlessly.

Almost a month has gone by, and I have lost fifteen pounds. Emma has lost too. She managed to do it a little more slyly than I because I had no idea she was doing anything other that eating better with the food she'd been serving me. She looked wonderful. The comfortable, yet uncomfortable silence that has stayed rooted between us since that day at the supermarket; cordial, but not deep conversation only.

On the anniversary of an entire month, Emma woke up on Saturday morning with me. She came across the bedroom toward me, wrapped her arms around me, and rocked my world with a kiss that, well I can't remember back to when I was seventeen. She pulled back, handed me my clean running attire, and proceeded to pull on her own. Wide eyed, I went with the flow, hitting the city sidewalks on a humid August morning with my wife by my side. Pace for pace, we matched like bookends. I was so very proud of her.

"Walter?" she asked to get my attention while we still pounded the pavement, barely out of breath.

"Yes Emma?"

"I love you so much it hurts."

"I hoped so, I trusted so. I just wanted to give you the option to move on in case you just couldn't take a minute more of me. It seemed as though everything we did irritated each other. I became frightened that we reached the end of our line. I couldn't stand being me one minute longer either. I never stopped loving you Emma.

We kept on running without another word, finally ending up back at the house. We slowed down just up the street from home to cool down, slower still until we were walking. Up the sidewalk, into the door, my wife took me by the hand and led me to the shower in our ensuite off the bedroom. We undressed each other sensuously, ending with a deep kiss when we were both naked and sweaty. After our shower, we sat in the kitchen with our morning coffee. There was a clipped out ad from the newspaper on the table in front of me. I picked it up to read it. It was an ad for an adult nightclub that had a jazz ensemble playing that night with dinner and dancing. There was a question mark on it penned in ink.

I pointed to my wife, "You—me--tonight baby." I said.

When evening came, I asked Emma if she thought we should get ready to go..

"I thought you'd never ask. On one of my food shopping trips, I made a little side trip to the thrift store to pick up a little surprise for tonight." She said with a flirtatious smile.

We got cleaned up together but dressed separately. Emma disappeared into the bathroom with a black garment bag. She had thought of everything, sly thing. I was dressed because men have it easy. After twenty - twenty five minutes or so, out came Emma in a white, long, slim, extremely alluring evening gown. Her hair! No description. The lipstick—gonna get smudged!

"Holy mackerel!" I said, knocked out of the socks I just put on.

CRABBY PEOPLE

That night in bed after we danced all evening, my Emma reached over and grabbed my hand, intertwining our fingers. We went to sleep that way. I think we shall always go to sleep that way.

I don't know what is the matter with folks these days, or with the ducks. But I have become highly aware that the more I take care of myself, the more that people interact with me, not just my Emma, although she is the most important one of all. The fact is I can't really imagine that there is a whole lot can be done about the crabby people. But I found out if I don't join them and participate, I can sift through the chaff to find the happy ones. The rest I can influence without even knowing.

KIDS TODAY

KIDS TODAY

Garretville is a school town. Anybody can learn almost anything in Garretville. A person can learn to cut hair, cook, and even learn to pose in ads for store fliers in the big city. It has the finest Community College in the State. Many fine nurses aides have graduated from Garretville Community. There is a high school, three junior high schools, three middle schools, and three elementary schools. The biggest of the three elementary schools is Wickens Elementary.

Wickens Elementary is where I work. I was dispatched for duty by Hanklin Security. My name is Sargent Kyle Yatsworth, no partner. I work alone. The mission given to me is to steer young people away from a life of crime while they are entrusted to the Garrettville school system. When a child is sent to my school, they are mine! I carry a badge. Discipline is imperative! Why? Because Wickens Elementary is a no tolerance school.

I was summoned to the principal's office to be made aware of a serious infraction to the rules. It was a Monday morning. The school had gone through a total dress down inspection Friday evening before the cleaning staff gave Wickens a complete detailing over the weekend. Ms. Farris appeared somber before she gave me the results of the dress down, and I steeled myself for bad news instinctively.

"I brought you in here, Sargent Yatsworth, to inform you of a most grave situation. It is my sad duty to tell you that the dress down on this Friday last, found several aspirin under the radiator in room 12 of the 3rd grade section. Do you believe it? When I was their age, my biggest concern was whether or not my mom gave me jelly with my peanut butter sandwich. I can't believe kids today. The evidence has been procured and saved, Sargent Yatsworth. It is a shame the area was cleaned so thoroughly, sterilized of anything that can be used as tools for apprehension. I trust you can come up with some kind of strategy to get to the bottom of this so we can isolate the perpetrator?"

"You know that you can place all your trust in me, Ms. Farris. I will begin my investigation immediately." I sighed and stood up in one motion. I made to move out into the school so I could perform my duties. I had to outline a plan, and to get away from Ms. Farris before I slipped up and began laughing in front of her. I already suppressed a grin.

"You ARE the best, Sargent Yatsworth. I know that I leave this matter in good hands. See to it that you do your best." Ms. Farris said. She rose to usher me out all starchy-like..

As I walked down the hall toward my locker, a curious thought crossed my mind. Hadn't jelly been banned from the new school lunch program? A most curious thought indeed. Ms. Farris may have slipped a bit, revealing latent tendencies and desires for the forbidden. Perhaps she does not practice the rules she preaches? Maybe sugary contraband makes its way in from the top down, rather than the bottom up. I chuckled to myself. And where would a third grader get the money to buy aspirin anyway? Things worth considering while putting the pieces back together in the big picture puzzle. Speaking of the big picture—I mean really, Ms. Farris has to be pulling my leg, right? She has to have some kind of clue that I am a Sargent from a rent-a-cop place. Either that or we're dealing with a little more than too much sugar!

Room 12 is Miss Haigonwrather's homeroom. A petite, very soft-spoken woman, and well respected teacher. I have seen her many times, and lately she has been the embodiment of stress. Scuttlebutt has it that her mother is quite ill, speculation was all over the road map about her personal life, poor thing. Anyway...surely a stroll by her door on the way to my inspections wouldn't hurt to confirm what kind of mood she might be in just two hours into a new week?

Outside room 12, I paused to look through the heavy glass in the door of the classroom. I couldn't believe my eyes! There was Miss Haigonwrather with her head resting sideways on the big gray colored steel teachers desk. Her eyes were wide open, a number 2 yellow pencil was under her cheek, arms hanging limply by the side of the chair she was sitting in. "Holy sh..." I started to say.

KIDS TODAY

Reacting quickly, I burst through the door of the classroom and moved in to check on the teacher. I called out her name, receiving no response. When close enough, I reached out with my right hand to press a finger on her carotid artery to feel for a pulse. There was a strong one, but she wasn't coming to. "What happened here?" I questioned the emotionless class. Emotionless wasn't all they were. The class sat there offering no help, no answers, no sympathy—anything. For lack of a better word, it was spooky. I ran out of the room, back toward the office area. Our school nurse had a small office next door to the principal. Seconds later I stuck a head in her open door. "Nurse Jill! I need you ASAP! Teacher down!"

Nurse Jill snapped to attention. She needed answers that would take too long. I reached out my left hand, a gesture not really meant for her to grab my hand back, but to come with me immediately. She got the message to come on the double.

As she matched my jogging pace down the hall, I told her, "It's Ruth Haigonwrather, Jill. I found her unconscious when I walked by her room, and I can't seem to revive her. She DOES have a pulse." I filled her in while we ran to the first through third grade section. When we reached room 12, I looked like a fool with egg on my face. I almost pulled the door off the hinges, only to find Ms. Haigonwrather giving English lessons to an attentive class.

"Wwwhat's going on here?" asked the stunned teacher after I made her jump out of her skin.

"I...I just found you unconscious, Ruth!" I explained.

"Ah...no! I'm just fine as you can see." she told us, giving me the eye that I had a marble or two rolling around loose in my head. "I have another headache again today, but you couldn't know that."

I looked over at the class helplessly. "When did she come to?" I asked no one in particular. The whole class gave me the same look as the teacher. They were all shrugging, shaking their heads no, indicating they had no idea what I was talking about at all. "I...Nothing! I'm sorry I interrupted the class."

On the way back to the front offices, Nurse Jill asked, "What was that all about?"

KIDS TODAY

"I don't have an answer for you Jill. I'm just telling you what I saw. She scared the bejesus out of me."

"Are you okay? Getting enough sleep...all that?"

"I'm fine Jill. I know how all this looks, but I'm telling you—the woman was out for the count. I'm sorry I had to do that to you. I can't explain any of this. I will though. I sure...will..." my voice trailed off into a whisper as I went deep into thought. What can I do now? One thing I DO know—those kids out and out lied! Well, they didn't actually lie per say, come to think of it. They just sat there and let me look like a fool, and Miss Haigonwrather didn't seem to know or remember anything. Okay, plan two. What is plan two? There is no plan two. No way can I be so blatant as to stand around watching through the door until Ruth passes out again! And one other thing...why did the kids just sit there so calm and collected. Shouldn't the episode have scared them out of their wits? I would be frantic if my teacher winked out of consciousness in front of me for a while, that's for sure! At recess, I decided to have a chat with Ruth Haigonwrather about these headaches of hers. I would come right out and ask her if the aspirin found on Friday was hers.

"Yes, Kyle, they were mine. I opened the bottle after class that day. My head hurt again, and hands were shaking like you couldn't believe!" Ruth told me at the ten o'clock recess. "I've been chocking the headaches up to my mom being sick, you know? I have been worrying like crazy. She's been incredible, trying not to be a burden, always with a happy face. Besides my kids here at school, she's all I have. But I'm losing her. I just don't know what I'll do if something happens to her. It's selfish of me, I know, she's in such pain right now. Anyway, getting back on the subject, I haven't wanted anybody to know I have had these pounding headaches lately. I need to be there for my mother right now, not the other way around. These headaches have been so strong, I have had to sit down for spells to let the queasiness pass that goes with them. I seem to get through the day, but..."

"Have you gone in for a checkup? You really

should get yourself a physical. Maybe Nurse Jill can help out?"

"NO! No...not right now. I'll be alright. It's just stress is all."

"Well, if it's all the same to you Ruth, I think I'm gonna keep an eye on you." She smiled at that. It was nice to see. If anybody deserved some happiness, it would be Ruth.

I had my talk with Ruth Haigonwrather in the middle of a bustling school yard. Grades one through three all took a break from class, running around, teasing, laughing, playing on the rides in the gym set area. Miss Haigonwrather's class was off to one side of the playground huddled together having some kind of secret society meeting or something. I pointed this fact out to the teacher. She agreed with me by saying, "I know...huh? The kids look like they would be just as happy to be back in room 12!"

I had her attention, so I attempted to get her to talk some more before the recess session ended. "So Ruth, about your mom, what is the story anyway?"

"She smoked for years. For such a smart lady, it was such a dumb ugly habit to have. But we all do some dumb things, don't we? The first time she was diagnosed, she was in stage one. After all she went through at the time, you would think that when got herself into remission after the chemotherapy she had to suffer through that she would have quit. I thought she had. But I'm not her nurse maid, and I didn't follow her everywhere. The short of it is she didn't quit. Even just before this latest, she still didn't quit. She is at the end of stage three now and hope for her is...well...there is none."

"I'm sorry." I said truthfully. "Is she still at home?"

"No, she's beyond that now, and she is well aware of the fault of it all. I am so lucky that I have this job, with my kids to teach and all, it keeps me occupied and busy. That's why I can't afford to show I have been having some problems with these headaches, you know?"

"You mean like mother, like daughter?" I pointed out.

KIDS TODAY

"What do you mean by that?"

"I mean that I saw you unconscious, and I believe that along with the kids, you knew it too. I don't mind being made to look like a fool. God knows I do a fair job of being one all by myself. But you know, and I know that there is something seriously wrong here."

"I just sat down for a spell, that's all. What do you propose I do without upsetting my life even further?"

"Go to Nurse Jill to see if she can help you without throwing you under the bus? What do you think? Or better yet, if you want, I could give you the name of a walk in clinic I like to go to. How about it?"

"I'll think about it." she said icily.

"No...of course you can think about it. I'm not here to twist your arm. I'm just trying to help." I told the woman. "After this morning, I'm really worried about you. I hope you understand?"

"I'm okay, really."

"No, Ruth, you are not. If you won't go, I'll be watching you like a hawk. I'll talk to you later. This isn't over." After I stated my case, I walked away to get into my regular routine; duties that are part of my job. But first, I took a walk to nurse Jill's space. I thought it would be smart to let her know about some of my concerns, and maybe for an opinion on my offer to help. Maybe she could give me insight as to what the cause might really be.

"Drop it." Nurse Jill told me. "She's right. Stress is a complicated thing, Lyle. Sometimes things have to run their natural course. Let it be!"

"Okay then, do you have any bright ideas on how to juggle Ms. Farris? She's like a ferret. She's thinking she has a bead on kids smuggling aspirin into school! The woman needs a boyfriend!"

"Are you volunteering?"

"No way, not me, uh uh. The only thing I can think of to make her drop this thing is to catch her smuggling in jelly sandwiches. I have a hunch too that she is disguising high sugar soda in that refillable coffee cup of hers. If I caught her red handed, she might have to come off her high horse."

Jill laughed at that. "I see her going off property at lunch time. She might be sneaking off to get sausage pizza and high-caff cola. You need to do a sting, Lyle. Don't worry about Ruth Haigonwrather. She'll be fine." I guess I was dismissed because she turned back to a computer monitor.

When I left the room, I got to thinking it was funny; maybe Nurse Jill was on to something about Ms. Farris. My experience has always been that the person that worries most about stuff kinda has a problem with it themselves. Besides, pizza sounds pretty good. I could use me some pizza. I don't have a problem with it. That potent cola knocks me for a loop though. I checked my wallet to see how much money I had on me. There was plenty enough for pizza, chicken nuggets, or whatever it is that Ms. Farris has for lunch. At first I began planing to eat at the same place Ms. Harris ate at. But to follow Ms. Farris would be breaking the rules. I was supposed to be available at lunch when the kids were all together. I knew this very well, so I reconsidered. There was something else I thought was kinda funny. I think of the principal as Ms. Harris, and my fainting teacher friend as...Miss...Haigonwrather. I have no idea why.

I made my morning rounds, checking rest rooms for kids hiding out from class or smoking. The parking lot and school yard are a perennial problem spots in schools with older kids than mine, but the job mandates the areas to be checked. The job is easy when it comes down to it. Little kids aren't hard. They just like to test the water every once in a while to see what they can get away with. The kids at Wickens are cute as a button. The way they see the world is whittled down to truth almost all the time. Every once in a while a kid that age will resort to lying, but they tell you the truth about it later. It's very endearing. Nobody ever knows what might happen when one bad kid comes along and gets mixed in with the rest of the good ones. That's why I was hired...to be a presence and all...I got all that. Everybody needs to work at something to make money to eat, including me. But I thought to myself that I just don't believe in what I am doing anymore. I continued to ponder one more thing before the subject was dropped. Coming to work every day in make believe cop clothes doesn't exactly exude warm and fuzzies either. I scare the crap out of myself every time I go to the bathroom and wash my hands. What stares back at me in the mirror is just plain uncool. If I walked the halls in a martial arts uniform and had my own class room with mats, it would be far, far superior. The way it is, I look like an overgrown hall monitor.

Anyway, I had walked every nook and cranny, both inside and out of the school. I let enough time slip by to ease on by room 12 for another random check. This time I patrolled from the higher grade section side, rather than from the office. A quick look inside the door window gave me another start. Ruth was standing against the corner of the room by the blackboard with a stick of chalk in her hand, head lolled backwards against the wall at an inconvenient angle to breathe. Her eyes were wide open, staring at the ceiling, mouth slack jawed, and totally motionless. “Hey!” I yelled startled from outside in the corridor. In motion, I reached for the handle of the door to room 12, but before I got myself inside, Miss Haigonwrather was smack dab in the middle of a sentence of the lesson she was teaching. As she spoke, she looked in my direction, sort of stunned, and massaged her right temple with her fingers. The class and Ruth were perfect pictures of innocence once again, and I looked like a perfect pest. I walked out of the classroom with only a cursory apology, and a curse under my breath.

It was close to lunch, so I stood for a while by the locker that was given to me to store my belongings. I used it to hold my bagged lunches and an attache case. The case holds paperwork in it that has to be filled in before I head over to the Hanklin Security home office at the end of the day. The bell was about ready to ring, and I would have given my eye teeth to tail Ms. Farris to wherever it was she went to during lunch hour, I just couldn't, that's all. Two tuna fish salad sandwiches and an apple would have to suffice. Wait a minute! Home office! I spent all this effort to protect little Ruth Haigonwrather, at the same time I wanted to take the haughty Ms. Farris down a peg from her high judgmental perch where she can use her authority to enforce her values on young hungry minds. I didn't think. The home office! My goodness, what a fog I was in—thick and impenetrable. But then just the right amount of sun comes along to clear it!

I made a call to the home office over tuna fish. It was a little hard to hear in the echo filled auditorium pulling double duty as cafeteria. The high pitched voices of so many youngsters at once sent me to a place behind the serving line in a separate space. I only had to contend with the clatter of metal serving spoons and a dishwasher. “Mr Hanklin? This is Sargent Lyle Yatsworth.” I started, but thought to myself how utterly ludicrous the nomenclature prefix Sargent added to my name was. “Lyle...sir. I have a little situation over here at the Wickens Elementary.”

“Oh yes...Sargent Yatsworth. You're doing a great job over there, by the way—nothing but good things to say about you. What can I do for you?”

“Principal Farris wanted me to investigate some aspirin that was found on the last dress down on Friday. I have done some checking into the situation, and in the process have found suspicious behavior in one of the rooms. I was wondering if we have access to small video devices that could help me monitor what goes on in the room sir?”

“Do you need something close circuited?”

“No sir, nothing so invasive. These are only small children after all. Any disciplining coming out of it will involve the parents only. This is by no means, a serious problem. But I DO want to get to the bottom of it if I can.” I stretched the truth a little. I did not want to bring Ruth Haigonwrather's name into it yet.

“I understand, Lyle. When you submit your regular report tonight, I will have what I think will do the job perfectly. Nobody will even see it if you can place it correctly.”

“Perfect sir. I will see you tonight then. Goodbye sir.”

“Goodbye Lyle.”

Now I had a plan. I would be able to find out what went on in room 12. If I could catch Ruth on video passing out, she might see the problem as something she should have checked out. I had no decision on Principal Farris yet. Chances were there would never be one.

There are people that love the crack of dawn.

KIDS TODAY

These people brag, "You know, I get up at three o'clock in the morning every day. I don't even have an alarm clock. Why—if I went to bed at one in the morning, I would still get up at three o'clock. It's just the way I roll." I am not one of those people. Three o'clock in the morning was made for losers that can't figure out what to do with their time at night. Three o'clock in the morning was designed to make me cranky. The lady at the gas station where I got coffee to help open up my peepers was overly talkative and bubbly. I should have asked her personal questions back, just to shut her up. Something like, "Wow! Is that your real hair color? What nationality has orange hair anyway—Irish offshoot or what?"

I just wanted to get into the school building early to install the video device where it couldn't be detected. I was thinking maybe on top of the announcement speaker, but I couldn't know until I saw it first hand. That's the reason for three o'clock wake up call, nothing more.

The video box was small enough to be made to look part of the chart rack mounted on the wall on the side of the room. It looked like part of the rack mechanism, being small, square, and black. Mounted, I aimed the tiny red light that came on to face back to the wall. Placement location would show a fair view of the room when dialed up on my phone. When I dialed the number on my phone to test the unit, it came on perfectly. The contraption had memory to store images, but when I asked my boss how long it would record, he had no idea. It wasn't up to professional spy standards, but it would do. I left the school to re-tank with coffee and get a bite to eat. Getting up early I forgot to make a lunch, and it was going to be a long day.

About two miles from the school sat a breakfast diner, sort of a greasy spoon type of place. It was close by, and the logical choice to go. Healthy fare wasn't really on the menu, and that's okay because you always get your moneys worth at a place like that. Belly aches are free. The waitresses, Dawn and Gina, wore pink uniform smocks with name tags. Both chewed gum with their mouths open and snapped. They both knew all the regulars, so the formal pad and pencil could be forgone, and was. Customer order entries were made at a micros to save time. I was the irregular customer. I didn't know what I wanted. I know I didn't want what the customer in the next booth had. On his plate were two eggs, grr-easy over hockey pucks on a plate, sausage that could be over-sized rabbit droppings, and wimpy bacon that would stay lodged in my gall bladder all day long. The home fries did look delicious. I ordered blueberry pancakes, and was told there were no blueberry pancakes; I had the eggs. The coffee would do it's job nicely, brown and bitter. It was a six sugar blend.

I didn't believe my eyes when I happened to glance over to the other side of the diner. Sitting at the bar eating the same crap I did was Principal Farris. I said hello when I paid my bill at the register near her. She looked somewhat flustered and embarrassed.

“Gooood morning Ms. Farris!” I said cheerfully. “I never eat here, but I forgot my lunch today, and breakfast could well be my only meal all day long.” I told her truthfully. “It's nice to see you eating at a regular place like this. I didn't think you were the type!” I made the conversation sound like it was nice to share a like-interest with normal-folk. “I like it here, maybe I'll see you here again tomorrow morning?” I asked her. The woman looked positively trapped. Her image was definitely tarnished because now we have something in common. Maybe mortified is a better word.

“Hello Yatsworth.” she called me by my last name only, clutching at her last vestiges of superiority. I was more than glad she dropped the Sargent label, personally.

“Well, off I go then. The early bird gets the worm!” I told her, keeping the cheerful attitude going. I really did feel a whole lot better. I walked out before any more conversation, not that we would connect on other levels.

“Are you watching me?” Ruth Haigonwrather asked me to my face after the third time she'd seen me before recess, not including recess that made it four.

“I'm sorry Ruth. I don't mean to spook you, just worried is all. How's your mom?” I asked, changing the subject.

"Not real great, but that's beside the point. Don't be worrying about me now, I can take care of myself."

"Yeah? How's the headaches?"

"Truthfully, I feel pretty good today."

As I walked away, I realized that I was coming off like a stalker. It was cracks like, "How's the headaches?" that were Just a little pushy. No headache probably meant she'd not passed out yet that day. Pushy or not, the video device was turned on before I went on my rounds, and allowed to record continuously until lunch time.

Speaking of lunchtime, Ms. Farris noticed me in the hallway before the bell. She pointed an accusatory question at me. "I hope you aren't going to leave the property because you forgot your lunch today, Yatsworth."

"I had no intention to leave at all. I told you that this morning. I bet you are though. I never see you on property at lunch. I bet you go to the gym at lunchtime to keep up that fine physique of yours, mama." I jabbed back. She took it as a compliment.

"Well, that was kind of you, thank you Lyle!" she beamed a smile at me and walked away.

I sat alone in the lunch auditorium. It was too much to hope to be buddies with any of the kids, even though I would love that. The teachers sat together, including Miss Haigonwrather. She never even looked my way. I did notice that her class sat off to one side, not socializing any more than I. They acted a whole lot differently than the rest of the kids in the room. Happy squeals, laughing, animated conversations, all taking place at once made it a stiff competition to think. But Miss Haigonwrather's class sat as emotionless as I had seen them in room 12. I wanted so much to ask Miss Haigonwrather what kind of students these were. Were they sad, nerdy, super intelligent, or the opposite, dull and witless. I didn't dare. I know I have scared the teacher too much to ask her anything right now. She had enough going on in her life without worrying what an overgrown hall monitor with a fake badge thinks about anything. The only thing wrong with that picture was that I wasn't quitting. I know something is wrong with Miss

Haigonwrather. I knew it even if she didn't. Her class knew it too, and that made them spooky and something to get to the bottom of.

It was all of those reasons that I wanted so much to go back to recording as soon as my monitoring lunch and the recess afterward was done. Having a record of one of Miss Haigonwrather's spells would validate my behavior somewhat. But on this particular video device, activation was achieved by dialing it by phone. I could turn it back on, but not review it until it was retrieved and memory transferred to a proper monitor like a computer. I went online the night before to investigate how long I could get out of sixteen gigabytes, since my boss did not know. Estimates at low end quality were about four hours. I didn't want to push it too far, so I turned it on as soon as class resumed, but planned to turn it off after three hours of steady recording, no more. I stuck to my guns the rest of the day. Not once had I peered into room 12, and I wouldn't. If nothing showed on the video when I played it, I made up my mind to drop the matter entirely. I would pin the aspirin fiasco on her, and that would be the end of it. Surely Miss Haigonwrather should be able to deal with her life, and her mom, in her own way with no involvement from me. Reviewing three hours of video was only my way to satisfy that my bad feeling was unjustified. I even hoped it was.

There was a problem developing that far exceeded the stress of waiting to get my little black box back from room 12 after a very long day. The problem was hunger. If I had another plate of those greasy eggs I had in the morning, in front of me, I would slide those babies right down my throat and possibly not notice that they sucked. Never, and say this twice...never would I ever put on of those rabbit dropping sausages between my lips again. I use the terminology rabbit droppings facetiously because that could not be possibly so. Rabbit droppings are much too small to be analogous. No, they were definitely re-purposed scat from some larger, as yet, unidentified animal...a coyote or something. I'm no zoologist. The good that came out of keeping this unpleasant thought fresh in my mind is that it worked to stave off the constant bubbling going on in my abdomen.

KIDS TODAY

An hour into recording after lunch, I had three hours of recording. I shut the box down, then walked the halls of the school to each of my checkpoints.

When the last school bell rings, the kids file out of the building with all manner of backpacks mounted on their backs. Bunny packs, superhero packs, clear packs, pink packs, and plain old black back packs. Each fit all the different personalities according to taste. In just a few years, that kind of personal definition is refined to customized phone covers. But for this short window into a child's life, the same simple preference that will embarrass them in a few years is what defines them now. It is always my pleasure to watch these full of life, mini humans leave to enjoy what is next for the day. Happiness is contagious. When the last of them are gone, teachers and faculty linger for a while afterward, wrapping up the day, grading papers, conferencing, and other trivial chores in comparison with the job of handling young lives directly. When that was done, I could retrieve the box that I was waiting for so I could eat. After nearly twelve hours, ten since the last meal, eating was priority one. It had been a long day, and few changes that had happened along the way. Priority two was seeing if I caught Miss Haigonwrather passed out.

Honestly, after Miss Haigonwrather let me know in no uncertain terms that my concerns for her made her uncomfortable, the plan was to tread lightly. Corroboration from Nurse Jill also contributed to the shift in how much I should show concern for the teacher.

At four o'clock, the school was finally empty. I got my box, battened down the hatches, filled out my report for the day, and headed out toward Hanklin Security to leave it off. The reports are necessary for a couple of reasons. One is to document anything that I saw or witnessed, suspicions or otherwise. Two is to show that I was actually where I was assigned to be. It would be checked up on later so that I could get paid. A set of keyed checkpoint boxes also proved I was everywhere I said I would be. It all sounds more technical than it is. The bottom line is that I finally got to eat a six o'clock. At seven thirty, I checked my emails, and sports scores. Eyes half lidded and heavier by the second, I inserted the little memory chip thing into a reader in my computer. The system found the volume perfectly. I opened the file, and there was Miss Haigonwrather teaching class, but it looked like any other class. The teacher did what she was trained to do: teach. The class seemed eager and hungry to learn. I was too tired to notice that the students were still uptight and guarded. What I did see was give and take. Hands were raised to questions asked, answered by random selection from a pointed finger. There was no audio to go with it, and it was all just boring enough to have me sit in my easy chair, lean back, and let the video play out. I really didn't expect anything because it all seemed a typical enough scene.

I almost succumbed to sleep in the middle of it all when about an hour in, I mistook a hand raised to respond to another question, but Miss Haigonwrather passed out—mid sentence, sitting on a counter in a, connect to the class folksy way. Her head leaned back peacefully against a window that was behind her. Her eyes looked to the ceiling, blank. I was jolted from my lack of attention to full focus. The students got into an argument then, but one boy stood up, pointed a finger at the teacher while he spoke back at them, then aimed something at his fellow classmates. Fear entered their faces, and they shut up. Even without sound, it was clear the boy instilled fear into the rest of the class. The boy sat down, as did the class. He pulled some paper work from his pile of books and went about his own business intently. The rest of the class sat motionless—petrified might be a good word choice. The whole time this went on, Miss Haigonwrather did not move a fraction of an inch. Had she done so, she would have ended up in a heap on the floor. So far I had witnessed three episodes. The first was at her sitting at her desk with her head on it. In the second, I saw her standing against a wall in a corner with chalk in her hand, but head lolled back, supported against the wall. Now, of course, she was sitting, albeit on a counter, but her head was supported by a window. Each time, her body had frozen, but her head clearly took a breather from the rest of her body. The only good thing about this time around was that I couldn't make a fool of myself running in to her rescue. However, now I sat riveted to my computer screen to see what would happen next, smack dab in front of my computer monitor.

The boy, whoever he really was, sat with paperwork all around him. It was by no means clear what it was he was working on. The video quality was not all that sharp. I took notice of the bottom of the screen that an hour, and thirty six minutes had passed. That told me that what I was viewing was still before just before lunch. I tensed in anticipation that something would happen any minute. One hour and fifty minutes into the video, the boy, who was sitting in the front row, picked up a key chain lying on his desk. What was that he pointed at Miss Haigonwrather, a flashlight or something? The teacher came out of her trance state and continued on teaching. She slid off the counter, but was stiff from sitting in an uncomfortable spot for as long as she did. She nearly lost her balance. A hand simultaneously went to rub her temple as though she could rub pain away. She started right back into talking though, completing what it was that she wanted to get across before the lunch break. She moved to her desk, wrapped up her thoughts, and let the class start to prepare themselves for the lunch time break. Miss Haigonwrather reached down into a drawer on her desk for a purse she had stashed there, opened it, and fumbled around the contents looking for something. Her hand came out, producing a bottle of aspirin. She shook out a couple, then got up to move to the door of room 12 out into the corridor, I presumed to the wall bubbler outside.

Well there it was! It wasn't exactly what I thought there would be on the recording, that much was for sure. But it explained all of what was going on, or did it? I still had one more hour of video to view, but I paused it where it was at for a bit. I set a pot of coffee to brewing in my kitchen to drink while I watched the last hour. I needed to pass this evidence on to somebody more qualified than myself to take it and use it correctly. I reached the full limit of how much it took to look like a total fool. I damned well wasn't going to barge in the next day to accuse the young man of stopping his teacher with some sort of stun ray. Nurse Jill would have me carted away strapped to a gurney so I would not hurt myself. I gave a call instead to the Hanklin home office. It went to voice mail. I would not get a live person until morning. I hung up without leaving a message. The rest of the footage had nothing disturbing on it. I guess the boy was finished with his work for the day, and Miss Haigonwrather no longer posed a disturbance to him. What was it that he did to her, I wondered? This boy is a third grader for goodness sake. What kind of skills did he possess? How dangerous was this kid? I took a shower and went to bed. I needed the sleep. There was no need to get up at three in the morning again. No way I would eat another breakfast such as I had that morning, or spend any more time than I had to with Principal Farris in the next. Nor would I go to work and announce how right I was that something was wrong after all in room 12. No, the plan was to turn the device back over to my boss, sometime during the day. If I couldn't do it as soon as that, I would turn it over to him in the afternoon. I would tell him that I had gotten to the bottom of the aspirin debacle that I would appreciate it if he would review the recording because it was really troubling and needed his opinion on it. Satisfied with the course of action plan, I slipped into slumber.

"Mr Yatsworth, did you get to the bottom of who brought the aspirin into the school?" principal Farris asked when she saw me as she came walking into school to start her day.

"I think so, Ms. Farris. I should know for sure that it wasn't a kid who brought them into school by tomorrow. I figured you would be happy to know we have good kids here, am I right?"

"Of course, Yatsworth, of course." She said as she disappeared into her office. It was a little hard to tell how much, but the tone of her voice clearly showed she was a little annoyed. I wondered where it was aimed at, me, or at the facts? After my morning routine, I called the home office only to find that Mr. Hanklin wasn't in. I asked if he would be and if would be, when. His secretary didn't know. He was out on business she told me. Great, the day is starting off really great.

I planned to wait it out and hope for the best

that my boss would show up when he was finished with his business. I did not want to worry...Now that would have been a perfect resolution had a student from Room 13 not been excused from class to go to the boys room. The young man found Miss Haigonworth passed out in room 12 about forty minutes or so before lunch. The boy thought the teacher was dead while the class just sat there so scared they couldn't move. He was a little hero. He made an instant decision to make a beeline to Nurse Jill's space. I popped my head around the corner because I heard little Jimmy Travis, his name I later found out, frantically begging for her to come help. "Room 12?" I asked the youngster, raising my voice from just behind him.

"Yes sir, Miss Haigonwrather's class." I locked eyes with Nurse Jill for a split second, and bolted for the room. Nurse Jill was right on my tail.

"Go back to your class young man." I ordered as we ran and this Jimmy kid followed. "I promise to come tell you how it all works out later, but please go back to you room now! It would be a very big help to me, okay? I will catch you later, I promise." I didn't watch after that to see if he followed my order. I looked at Nurse Jill because I was about to expose myself with absolutely nothing I could do about it. I yanked open the door to room 12 which contained a familiar scene, except this time the class was startled we we invaded the room as witnesses, but they regained composure quickly. The boy in the front row didn't even flinch. Nurse Jill went to attend to Miss Haigonwrather, who sat at her desk, hair hanging over the back of her chair because she was staring at the ceiling. She had the same lifeless eyes I had seen the first time I caught her that way. But this time, I walked up to the desk of the boy with the key chain on it. I snatched the ring of keys away. He yelled indignantly, "HEY!" I paid no attention. Instead, I pointed the flashlight on the chain at Miss Haigonwrather and pushed the button on the barrel. The teacher resumed her lessons in the middle of a sentence, only to find she had people other than her class, or me for that matter, in her classroom. This time she had Nurse Jill's arm around her. Nurse Jill went into instant shock, positively slack jawed. What she witnessed, couldn't be explained away.

KIDS TODAY

Nobody was giving much thought into my role in all that had just transpired except the class, and the boy in the front row. Standing in front of the class with the source of power the boy had wielded over them in my hand instead of his, empowered the class to come to life all at once. Sooner or later somebody would ask how I knew about it all. I could lie, I could keep my mouth firmly shut, or I could change my vocation immediately, but the truth was not an option.

William Homer Sumerlin was the only child of Karen and Yared Sumerlin. Mr. and Mrs. Sumerlin were sweet, hard working people. Their son William was nicknamed affectionately by his parents, Billy. He preferred William, having no understanding at all for nicknames, nor could he grasp the need for affection. William would have seemed to be from any outsider anywhere to be a perfect candidate for glasses with tape on the bridge, a pocket protector, and pants short enough to see almost all of his socks to the shoe. The truth of it is that he was a very good looking boy, with no need for corrective lenses. If he needed glasses, he simply would have invented a cure for poor vision, and yes he was that smart. His lack of affection should not provoke the assumption that he was rude because he was not. William simply didn't possess the ability to be either rude, nasty, or affectionate. At home, he did chores without argument, and at just eight years old, was a help to his mom and dad above and beyond the expected. William, you see, was brilliant from the day he was born. Every day on earth since then, he'd gotten progressively smarter. The list of his accomplishments from zero to eight years old will just have to be accepted, even if not believed. The list is too long and are givens unfathomable, or imaginable by any stretch. At just eight years old, William had become so busy with the responsibilities he'd taken on for himself, he no longer had the comfort of time to do everything in the confines of a twenty four hour day, over twenty three of which, awake. Symptomatic changes were taking place, known to the parents but misunderstood. The day I escorted young William out of room 12 was a day that changed my life forever. An even bigger surprise was that it also changed the life of Ms. Farris. It started when I took William to the central office since I didn't have one. The busybody principal saw me trying to deal with the young child from where she sat at her desk. I was clearly out of my element, so she moved closer to the entertainment to grasp the plot of the story. She got herself within earshot to listen to me ask questions to a boy who could not get a handle on the purpose or meaning of any emotion. Right and wrong was something he knew about, but if he produced one of the two and it infringed on somebody else's rights, he was instantly confused.

"How could you use this contraption on anybody, let alone miss Haigonwrather?" I asked.

Ms. Farris had not yet put pieces of that puzzle together in that part of the story, so to get some clarification, she jumped in. "Wait a minute...what did he do to Ruth Haigonwrather?" She demanded clarification.

"William here, built some sort of device that froze his teacher in the middle of her lessons, so she was incapacitated!"

William spoke up with corrected facts. "No sir, that isn't quite correct. I call it a brain looper. She was NOT incapacitated! She was teaching the class with the thoughts she assembled before she spoke. In Miss Haigonwrather's case, she outlines all of the lessons she plans to teach in her head for the day. She is a very good teacher that way. Her brain loop kept that part of her lesson plan going on in her head for quite a while. Consider that if she was teaching math, for instance, the whole outline she had for math that day would play out in her head. I have her timed. She is predictable on just how long she will go on in a subject, so that when I let her continue, she wraps up where she left off. There aren't many people that do that. Most people wing it, thinking the same few sentences over and over and over when I loop them. If an hour lapsed, they would know they spent an hour saying one sentence. Thus, Miss Haigonwrather is in a minority that I can use the brain looper on effectively. I use it so I can budget my time to do other things."

Ms. Farris blustered, "See here young man! What you are saying is quite impossible, I..."

KIDS TODAY

"I have witnessed it first hand, Principal Farris. I recorded the class and I caught him using it. I have been concerned that Miss Haigonwrather has been stressed to the point of exhaustion, passing out in class. I have been trying to piece together who smuggled aspirin into school, as per your orders, and found out the device young William here uses, cause her to have extreme headaches."

"Well that's how you knew! I assure you, sir, she has been caused no harm." William said.

"To the contrary, sir." I replied. "She has been going through some terrible personal stress. Coupled with what you have been doing, hurts her quite badly. Not to mention that you have been stealing learning time away from the rest of the class!"

"That class?" He said incredulously. "That is what I have been working on up until recently. If their brains were self lighting matches, there isn't enough phosphorus on the tips to light one. I have been working to help bring a brain into sink so it can retain what it is that is taught. Everything poor Miss Haigonwrather teaches is a total waste of time on such brains. If I had the time, I could fix that!" William informed me. In his mind, he was rectifying an untenable situation.

"Is this what you meant this morning when you told me that you found out that none of the children brought the aspirin to school?" Ms Farris asked me.

"Yes ma'am, it was. I had no idea about young William here. I still don't, but I did know for sure that something was wrong. I knew that nobody would have believed me. But another student from Room 13 was headed for the boys room and saw Miss Haigonwrather passed out. He ran to get Nurse Jill. I overheard, knew what to do, and that brings us to this point."

"I am so very sorry Mr. Yatsworth." That was all the principal said.

"Mr. Sumerlin..." I hadn't known his full name until Ms. Farris addressed him as such. "...who made the device in Mr. Yatsworth's hand, may I ask?"

I did! All along I have been very interested in brain configuration. My mother and father both encourage me to learn new things, but I am not learning what they want me to. I have no idea what they want from me. This notion of theirs to sit with them to watch a good movie; laugh and cry over something they consider entertainment, escapes me. They went out and bought a video game to hook up to the television for me for my birthday. I attached it to the television, but the illogic of wasted time to use it to play games that have no challenge at all, bothers me, and pains them. Lately, we have battled each other over this. It has led to a developing problem. It occurred to me that I might have some kind of handicap, very similar to the handicaps the class in Miss Haigonwrather's class suffers. I feel my brain may be stealing portions earmarked for one thing, and using it in another. In the case of Miss Haigonwrather's class, there is no doubt of it at all."

"Interesting, Mr. Sumerlin. Then you see it as your responsibility to fix this inadequacy, in order to solve your own problem, am I getting this right?" Principal Farris inquired.

"Right now, I am fixing my own problem." he replied matter of factly.

"And may I ask how long you have been working on this project of yours?" she continued.

"Not long. This is a priority I took on fairly recently. My parents are very good people, and the pain they are going through when the see me, although I don't understand it, concerns me quite a bit. I have a larger problem I am working on just now."

"I understand, Mr Sumerlin. I commend you your accomplishments, sir, but you have to know that I can't allow you to go back to that class. Would you mind if I arrange to send you to an organization that tests all the different facets of your IQ? I feel strongly that you should be placed in classes with others of your kind and caliber, William."

"I don't know if I have the time." said the eight year old.

I listened as Principal Farris interrogated the boy thoughtfully and skillfully. It is the first time that I had ever been impressed with the woman. I must have appeared dumbfounded. Try as I might, trying to comprehend a mind such as William's with my security-minded thought process, baffled me. It also challenged me at the same time. I suddenly felt wasted here, even more than I had been. Disagreement with no tolerance policies were one thing. Being where I belonged to make a difference in the contribution to crime prevention was very much another. A quick thought passed through my head. With all the schools in Garretvivlle, maybe one of them could teach me to carry a real badge. "William," I asked, "do you think your parents have a learning handicap too?"

"No, I see my parents as average, but well rounded. They carry out day to day routines very well. Their hobbies and interests are varied, though I find them unchallenging, I can't fault them. They care for me in ways I can't understand so they can do something I can not. On the other hand, the students surrounding me here at Wickens, and particularly in Miss Haigonwrather's classroom, are childish, self absorbed, bullying at times. With great effort, I have them in control these days, but had to resort to silly threats to get them that way. Their minds wander, so they can't retain what is taught. The amount of their brains used to learn is negligible and will eventually lead to irresponsible behavioral problems."

My head reeled from his answers. Principal Farris seemed fascinated, both with William, and with me, as well. I think she found my question telling.

"Mr. Yatsworth...if you would be so kind as to keep Mr. Sumerlin company for a while, I would like to place some calls." She continued, "Mr. Sumerlin, might I be able to reach one or both of your parents at home just about now?"

"No ma'am, they both work during the day. You may be able to reach them there. I can provide you with numbers if you wish."

"I would appreciate that very much, Mr. Sumerlin." She said as she went to the counter separating the back of the office from the front to get a piece of paper and something to write with.

"There you go sir. If I get the okay from your parents, I would like to call a state agency I think may be able to help. Maybe we can have Mr. Yatsworth drive you there so you can talk to them—if that is okay with you Lyle?" It was the first time she ever called me Lyle, and I got instant pleasure from it.

"It would be my honor. William is the very first

exceptional kid I've ever met in my life. I would love to see him get to where he could utilize his full potential if there is such a place."

"As would I." she said with a wink and a smile at me."

"I think you are wasting my precious time." William told us both. This is what got me to this point to begin with!"

We were both guilty of not really listening to the boy just then, wrapping around what we thought was the correct course of action. Principal Farris disappeared into her office, closing a heavy wooden door behind her as she went in.

"William...how on earth did you get all the components you needed to fit into that flashlight?"

"Well, you see, all I....." I had tripped his interest button. He went on and on with technical jargon that went well over my head. I sat attentively anyway, nodding as though I absorbed and understood everything he said. I had no clue. This boy needed to work in some government agency somewhere, clearly established that he was on our side. After having met and talked to him, I could see good parenting, and I believed the Sumerlin household to have all good people in it.

"If you approve, Mr. Yatsworth, I would like to go with you both. I truly want to make sure that William here is taken seriously, and well attended to. I could help you find this place. It is not in town and a good forty miles away. If you want, you can drive my car to save gasoline?"

"I don't mind a bit. Am I going to get back to file my report at the office to get paid?"

"Why don't you get your paperwork, and we can stop by on the way back?"

"Okay then...but I don't mind driving my...."

"Oh be quiet now, I insist. We are taking my car, and I don't want to hear another thing about it. I managed to get a hold of William's parents. Both of them will meet us there at the institute in Morgantown. They are both leaving their jobs and will only be about an hour behind us. I gave them the address and instructions how to get there. They will have the opportunity to talk to these people to satisfy themselves that their son will be in good hands."

"Why don't you go ahead and bring him yourself?" I asked curiously.

"Well I would, but I hoped you would come with us, as a matter of fact. We could use the company, and William feels comfortable with you as do I."

I nodded with a raised eyebrow and a look of surprise on my face. "Alright then, good. I would love to see how this all plays out, but what WOULD happen to William if he ends up in good hands?"

"Nothing, yet. This is about setting up testing, and seeing that he is vouched for by the proper people. It isn't all that clear that Miss Haigonwrather was involved enough to know if William is extremely gifted or not. I took the initiative to pull his academic records. They show William to be an average student at best. I believe he may not have shown his true potential, and that he was bored out of his mind. It may be the reason William acted independently on his personal projects. Could this be true, Mr. Sumerlin?"

"It is not My teacher's fault. She has to work with a classroom full of students at all levels."

"It is precisely that reason that we have to find out what your true potential is William. After that, Lyle, William will need all the support he can get, especially from his parents. I am hoping to place him where he will be most challenged. I am not privy to all that information, but I would guess it could be anything from a magnet school, to some sort of university program. Where some of these resources are, remain to be seen. This much is certain—it is of prime importance that William be placed in the best of all places to deal with whatever his level of intelligence is. As I said, it may take our support, and the sacrifice of his parents to do what is best for William. Ideally, I feel the best place for him is to be with others of his own kind, if such a place exists. One thing is a given. We can not possibly deal with this young man's needs here. Even if accepted back into the school population, as William points out, his impatience to accept the aptitudes of his average classmates around him, have proven disruptive."

KIDS TODAY

"If it helps any, I have proof of how well his brain looper works. No average kid I know could come up with something like that." I offered.

"Yes, it certainly would be impressive to establish his credentials...still...William, can you tell me why your grades reflect so poorly?"

"Because every minute I waste my time here, is a minute I could be accomplishing something else, just like right now."

"Why did you put up with us then?" Asked principal Farris.

"Because my parents insisted."

"I understand, but why haven't you shown us what it is you CAN do?"

"I doubt you would believe me. I am only eight years old. I take care of an online business I established that I can't even own because I am too young. I do it under my parents names, and it helps my parents financially. I can't afford to spend time on school." So there it was. This was a boy trapped. His personal time WAS school, and even at school he was trying to solve things. Another piece of the big picture puzzle began to fit in.

"Young man, the jig is up. Your parents are right. Insisting that you complete school is exactly right. But we may be able to get you through all this so much faster, and in all likelihood you will be worth more to your parents in the end." Principal Farris informed him.

"No offense, principal, but you don't know what you are talking about."

"I disagree, because by getting qualified and getting help you will be free to do what you do best. Please, for the sake of your parents, just listen to the people I want you to talk to, and do your best. That's all anybody can ask."

"You don't understand. They are going to slow me down. I am wasting my time" he repeated.

I jumped in to add my two cents, knowing I was in over my head. "It's possible, but I don't think so. Do you want to know what I think? I think that if you get yourself in a situation that suits you, you're going to finally be happy. When I had you explain to me all about your brain looper, you should have seen yourself. You lit right up! If you get half that passionate, the people around you will be happy for you. That brings us to your concerns about your parents. If they didn't want this for you, they wouldn't be insistent that you go to school. I'll bet a million dollars I am right about this. It looks to me like you are the best son ever in the history of sons. Lighten up! You said it yourself...you're only eight. You have a long life ahead of you. Do you want to spend it running an Internet business?" Without touching foreheads together with Principal Farris, I knew that we needed to get this boy to a place where he could be handled. Garretville and Wickens Elementary were too small a place for a dangerous boy like William Homer Sumerlin. We were all in over our heads with this boy. A very interesting exercise was coming our way, as well. We haven't talked to his parents yet.

Principal Farris rode shotgun in her own car, directing me to drive through city traffic by following a printed out map. It eventually led us to a local chapter of the National Association of Gifted Children. When we finally arrived, this particular chapter of the NAGC turned out to be, of all things, a small office that seemed more administrative than resourceful. A matronly lady sat at a rather large heavy desk, a piece of furniture more at home holding paperweights collected by the CEO of a fortune 500 company. Scratches and wear hinted that it may have been donated.

"May I help you?" She issued the standard greeting.

"Yes, I am Principal Farris. I called you earlier in regards to William Sumerlin, one of the students in our third grade class at Wickens Elementary."

"Ah yes. Do have a seat so we can talk." There were only two office chairs in the office. A bench rested against a wall, that apparently had my name on it. Dressed in my guard uniform, I looked less the hall monitor, trading the job to personal security escort. When Mr. and Mrs. Sumerlin showed up, my chair would be the front seat of Principal Farris's car. Too many people in the small office would deplete breathable oxygen, not at all helping my nervous hyperventilating.

KIDS TODAY

"The purpose of our visit is to set up testing for young William as soon as possible. It is necessary to find out what is the best avenue to proceed with the boy. I believe...well, I'll reserve judgment until after testing, but what the boy has exhibited at Wickens can only be described as precocious to the extreme. We are not equipped to handle his kind of ability." Said Ms Farris.

"Are the parents coming?"

"Yes ma'am, they are. I can..."

"Please call me Ursula. Ursula Svensson."

"Mine is Harriet Farris. My young student here is William Sumerlin. My man friend over there is Lyle Yatsworth. Lyle is responsible for discovering the disruptive situation stemming from some of William's activities. Activities that need to be seen to be believed. William is quite talented."

"I see." She really didn't, but said so out of the obligation of the moment. That drives me nuts! She'd see when she was winked out to wake up later and not being able to account for her time! I was tempted to take William's device out of my pocket and demonstrate while we waited for William's parents. I resisted.

Principal Farris, I can not think of her as Harriet yet, wanted to move things along. She wanted to present the Sumerlins with options and choices when they showed up. It wasn't at all clear that it was possible. She included William in the conversation as much as she was able, not only to demonstrate his levels of ambition, but to stave off any boredom he might be experiencing. As the conversation got deeper, William easily revealed himself as somebody having the ambitions out of his age group. The determination that Ursula judged to be the best course to take was a university program. Testing could be done nearby, but programs suited to someone such as William could be pretty far away, and costly, as well.

"The kid—he has an online business..." I mumbled.

"What was that Lyle?" Ms. Farris asked, including me into the conversation for the first time.

"The kid runs an online business for goodness sake. He blows us all away!"

KIDS TODAY

William corrected, “It is in my parents names. I'm not old enough to own it. It was only necessary to...”

“Leave it up to your parents to help. You are always going to be their responsibility. Where are they, by the way?” Ursela asked.

“Would you like to call them to ask if they are having difficulty finding us, Lyle? They did say they could meet us a good twenty minutes ago.”

I called them on Principal Farris's cell phone.

I met the Sumerlins downstairs in front of the building, talking them through the last couple streets that I had trouble with myself. Had I not had the assistance of the principal, I would have ended up as lost as the parents. They showed up in the parking garage and responded to my wave. They parked in the first open spot they could find. I moved in their direction, catching up to them before they could even lock their doors. Shaking hands, and going through the motions of introducing each other, I must admit that they weren't what I expected. They were warm, friendly, and not at all the average hapless people their son portrayed them to be. It made me wonder how he viewed all of us.

“Can I ask you a question?” Asked the mother. I nodded for her to go ahead. “I see that you are a security guard. How is it that you got involved with our son?” It was a fair enough question.

“I'm supposed to keep the peace. It is something the school committee came up with. It was their solution to all the news these days of all the strange stuff happening in schools all over the country. I really don't know how I feel about it myself. In the course of patrolling the corridors, I happened to notice William's teacher passed out. I thought it was some sort of medical problem. She's been going through some personal stress, and I wanted to make the teacher aware of it. Her mother is terminally ill, and I thought her passing out was a symptom of her trying to cope with too much. But she didn't believe me, and I made myself look like a total fool in front of her, and our school nurse. I even began to think I might hallucinating the whole thing, but I know I saw what I saw. I backed off, but put a small monitoring device in the room before school opened, and turned it on for as long as I dared to. It was just a crappy little video thing. I ended up with about three hours of recording that I watched at night after work. That is when I caught William aiming this little doo dad at his teacher, which put her in a trance." I pulled it out of my pocket to show them the brain looper as William called it. "The teacher scared a little boy heading for the boys room, who just happened to catch the teacher passed out while the class paid no attention. I ran to the room, snatched this away from your son, and revived the teacher with it. Personally, I am afraid of your little boy!"

Both parents laughed pretty hard at that. Dad Sumerlin said, "You have no idea what it is like to have a son like this. If you think you're scared, try this; that device you have there is his latest gadget. He's already used it on both of us because we were disturbing him. We've had whole nights disappear. It is hard to say whether he is a unique gift from God, or a total nightmare. He has the intellect of all the finest brains you can think of. Yet he is only an eight year old. He is not only not equipped emotionally, he has no emotion at all. It came up in conversation one day. He wanted to know why we fussed so much about family time, and maybe enjoying recreational family time, like camping, swimming, or even video games. He told us all along that he does not understand the concept. What he does have is a fixation. He likes to work on a fool machine. He feels that by redirecting brain pathways, he might be able to send underutilized or handicapped sections of the brain, the impulses from parts that are healthy and unaffected. By helping others to be able to learn and retain what is learned, for example, he feels he may conquer retardation. But he is a boy and has a boy's concept of consideration. He has adult intellect and adult ambition. He is by no means adult."

"Well I came down to greet you before we go up to talk, because I wanted to tell you that I did my best to convince him that being around people just like himself, will help him to do the things he likes. The problem is that he might have to relocate to a campus that isn't in the area, and I felt I was stepping on toes. William said he didn't have time for all of this. I might be mistaken, but I think he is worried about his Internet business.

"I am a plumber, sir. My lovely wife here is a Registered Nurse. Nothing else needs to be said. William wanted money for equipment for some of his research. Our mistake was to tell him that we couldn't afford that kind of thing. The kid made it happen. Now we have a house that looks like a radio station."

"He told me that the whole thing is in your names because he is too young."

"ARE...YOU...SERIOUS?" said the incensed mom.

"Yes ma'am, that's what he said."

"We had the power the whole time, and he took it away from us!! Can you imagine, Mr. Yatsworth, what William will be like as he grows and gets older? He carries out the trash and helps with dishes, but he expects us to understand and support what he views as an important work. There isn't anything we can do about it...well in this case, there was, but we didn't know it. We had no idea he did all of that in our name. He is our son, and we love him. What would you do if you were in our shoes?"

"Let's see if we can get him to testing for one thing. From there, from what I overheard, he might have to move to one of the few facilities that take on young gifted children such as William. Come on, let's get upstairs to find out where they are at. I'm sure the lady from the NAGC is going to want to ask you questions. So far wondering where you are is all she's yapped about. You might need to vouch for his abilities and precociousness, or something. What ever else happens, Principal Farris and I are on your side. I think William is amazing. I don't think I can say as much for his teacher and his classmates though. His teacher just got a whiff in the wind that she got zapped by that brain looper of his, she didn't know. His classmates are terrified of him."

"No doubt!"

This is William's Principal, Harriett Farris. I believe you spoke with her on the phone. And this is Ursula Svenson. She is the director here at this local office of the National Association of Gifted Children. Ladies, this is William's parents, Karen and Yared

Sumerlin." They all shook hands, weak smiling at each other accompanied with other assorted nods and niceties. I went on." I was just telling them before we came in here that you would do your best to get help if it is at all possible for William, is that not so?"

"Possible is the key word there, Mr. and Mrs. Sumerlin. Funding for exceptional students of any variety is scant these days. Schools that tend to William's specific needs are even fewer and far between. Although William, if he qualifies as young as he, may put him in a select group. Only a handful of groups work with such individuals. Scholarships are scarce for these children though. Then it comes down to space."

"Can he be helped or not?" Asked his dad who wanted to get beyond all of the negatives.

"Well, yes, but it's going to take some sacrifices and some elbow grease to do it. First William is going to have to undergo some testing to determine just where he stands. Principal Farris suggests that he may well qualify for Mensa's standards. But that has to be proven to be accepted, especially in light of his scholastic records to date. What do you say, William? Will you allow for us to get you to fair, extensive testing? It would go a long way for us to get you taken seriously if you let us prove your full quotient."

"It seems that I have no choice." said William.

"That isn't correct! You hold all the cards here, young man. The more you prove your full potential, the more we can help you. Extreme talent does not always mean extreme intelligence, and vice versa. Possessing both attributes, as your principal is suggesting you do, is very rare indeed! But be aware, because it is so rare, the list of possible classes to place such young people shrinks with it's rarity. Although I am certain they would be glad to have one more in their ranks, it would certainly mean relocation, and absolute authentication of high testing scores. Shall I schedule you for testing Mr. Sumerlin?"

"I'm still wasting time, but like I said before, it is up to my parents. I have no legal rights to say yes or no at eight years old."

Karen Summerlin gave total permission quickly. "Billy, you know full well we want the best for you. We love you and think this is a marvelous chance for you to be your own person." Mary knew full well the nickname, and loving support would egg her son on to give the testing all the effort he could muster, and more. The term of endearment would cause his brain to go into it's own brain loop, and he would grab at anything to avoid more of it. William's logical mind didn't support any shows of affection, anger, or happiness for that matter. Even personal failures and successes were taken in stride. Emotions, accolades or reprimands short circuited an internal coping mechanism. He would shut down for a time like a computer that couldn't handle a processing job. He also wasn't capable of storing them in his organic ram for later. Recalling it would put him back in the useless loop, all focus lost. Knowing these idiosyncrasies is the reason his mom employed the strategy. He knew about the brain loops and avoided them. Putting others in a brain loop would seem unfair, except that William didn't comprehend fair, only necessity. His need to get a task done that he took on, superseded everybody and everything. Self centeredness and double standards weren't corrected by a sense of right and wrong.

William couldn't ignore what his Mother had just said. He heard her just like everybody else in the room. In a few seconds, his head laid sideways while still sitting tall in the chair he was at. His eyes were wide open, precisely the same as when I had seen happen with Miss Haigonwrather. This time though, no device was used. Shock was registered on all the faces in the room except his parents. His mom explained what happened.

"I felt that you all needed to know that this is William's handicap. It is something that just started recently. This is the reason he is working on his project. He's doing his damnedest to heal himself. You need to know that this happens to him and why. Oh don't worry." she explained, smiling at concern we all showed. "He will come out of it when his brain absorbs my endearment. I used his nickname, and told him we loved him. He can't comprehend such feelings. He will stay winked out for a minute or two until his brain can absorb what I said, and reset itself. He will come out of it soon and not remember a thing I said, but he WILL know he went into a loop. I'm hoping it will cause him to put everything he's got into the testing. He should throw himself into it obsessively. His father and I can certainly identify with him, and why it troubles him so to go into one of these loops. They are very troubling, disconcerting, and cause severe headaches. In the last three weeks or so, he has shut us down several times if we don't loop him first. As we told you downstairs, Mr Yatsworth, it has been a nightmare. It gives new meaning to being thrown for a loop!

William suddenly snapped to attention, turned to Miss Svenson, and asked, “Am I to be tested now?” He pressed two fingers to his temple and massaged.

“No, Mr. Sumerlin. I have to make arrangements for them. They aren't done here but at the university. I needed to get the permissions from all of you first. I DID take the liberty of calling them to find out if testing could be set up tomorrow, contingent on this interview. But I see no reason not to call them now to begin testing tomorrow sometime. Is that alright with you all?”

“If you send William to school in the morning like a regular day, Mr. Yatsworth and I will bring him to keep the appointment.” said Principal Farris “Does that meet with your approval?”

“Oh, yes indeed it does!!” exclaimed Yared Sumerlin, answering for both.

“Fine, I will call right now in front of you all.” said Ursula Svenson.

The appointment for testing was about a hundred miles from Garrettville on the State University campus. The time was set up for the test to be taken in the afternoon at one thirty sharp, but check in was after lunch at one. I guess it goes to show how critical I was to the ebb, flow, or security of the Wickens Elementary. I had street clothes on, and it felt good to start out my day looking like everybody else. We were out of the building at ten, and doing highway speeds at ten thirty.

Conversation was awkward in the car. It was due in large part to William's refusal to take part in trivial banter. This left the principal and I virtually alone. I'm ashamed to admit that she seemed more and more attractive every single time I've gotten close to her in the last two days. Her weird attitude to enforce no tolerance rules on babies seemed shaken. Two days ago William would have been a goner. More than that, taking a personal interest in his future was out of character. The only reason I could think of for the change would be the substitution of multi-grain toast instead of the horrible breakfast at the diner to go with her morning coffee.

“I think we should have some lunch before the initial meeting. We could be quite a while, and William will need optimum fuel to avoid a distraction from his successful testing. What is it that you usually eat, Mr. Sumerlin?” Asked the thoughtful principal that grew more unfamiliar to me with each passing minute.

“I have brought something my mother prepared, Ms. Farris. It should supply sufficient sustenance for me to get through the day. It contains a complete and balanced meal that I require of her daily.” William stated icily.

“Oh! Well then, the good Mr. Yatsworth and I did not think ahead, but there must be a cafeteria on campus where we all can eat before the testing begins.”

I told her, “Let's get a beverage for ourselves, Harriett. We can get something later to pass the time while William here is busy. It will be my treat. What do you say?”

“She smiled a most becoming smile, and said, “That sounds wonderful, Lyle.”

There was more than just the attitude shift. As I took side glance over to Harriett's side of the car to get her answer, I noticed that slim light pink skirt she had on had ridden up to show some shapely legs. She had slipped off the cream colored pumps she wore to be comfortable for the long drive. I couldn't help but take in her perfect feet, small, maybe six and a halves or so, with nicely painted little toes. I had already taken in the satin top she had on when we first met up. I kept my eyes off the vee that revealed cleavage I should not have been looking at in the first place. Greasy eggs and bad sausage had not spoiled her figure a bit. Her hair was different. I had not said so to her because it may have come off as some sort of line, but her usual coiffure of severe bun had been allowed to fall attractively around the shoulders. A security guard taking in the countenance of a principal that way seemed akin to beauty and the beast, except the beast would never turn into a prince. I felt tongue tied.

"I think I would like the company very much." She smiled at me with teeth that seemed to glisten like wet pearls between lightly painted lips. She smelled wonderful, not too strong, feminine to the extreme.

The university campus was laid out efficiently. Finding the well labeled building we needed to check in at was more than easy, parking was not. It was only a little after twelve o'clock. The plan to let William eat his lunch was the best course of action as there would be no one in the office just yet. There was a stainless steel lunch wagon parked by a grass covered treed mall. The mall had walkways lined with park benches. College students were enjoying the fresh air with books or notebooks cracked to study, most lying on the neatly trimmed lawn. Several picnic tables were stationed here and there under the trees. We chose out one, and I made sure that Miss Farris and William were comfortable. I asked them both what their preference of drink was. Again William needed no coddling. Miss Farris asked for a diet cola, and off I went to the truck. When I came back, William was in a trance.

"What happened?" I asked as I saddled up to the table. Miss Farris was standing over William looking close to tears.

"I don't know! I asked him if testing made him nervous. He told me that he doesn't get nervous. I remarked how amazing that was, and that he was quite a remarkable young man. That is the moment he winked out." She explained to me.

"Ahh, the compliment thing! He will come out of it soon, don't worry, and please, please don't cry! We simply have to remember that the boy doesn't get the compliment thing. His parents were serious I'm afraid. There was no harm done." Tears were flowing down Miss Farris's cheeks. I wrapped my left arm around her to comfort her with a hug. She settled into my shoulder, molding very nicely pressed against my body. There was a kind of chemistry, I think, because I swear I felt a pleasant electrical charge in my body. I let go because it was the proper thing to do. “Come on, he will wake up soon. Let's have a seat. I handed her one of the diet colas I had in my other hand.

As soon as we sat down, William came back to the world of the cognizant, and continued on eating his bagged lunch as if nothing had ever happened. Miss Farris turned her wrist to get the time from her wristwatch, a sniff or two still left over from her experience with William. To her credit, she made no mention of him dropping out of the land of the living at all. Instead, she said, “We have just a little less than thirty minutes before we have to check in. Such a beautiful campus! I just love it!” I sort of thought the boy would have looped out again with a statement like that. He must have used all his concentration for eating and not heard. Come to think of it, eating is a pleasure, his head could be preoccupied with the conflict whether or not to loop out, or deal with it as a necessity of life. William, I began to think, could be the one who lived in a nightmare. When William finished his sandwich and apple, he neatly folded the bags and threw them away in a heavy wire receptacle near the table, along with the apple core and an empty fruit juice box. Then he sat back down and addressed us both. “Principal Farris, Mr. Yatsworth, I need to ask you a question.” This seemed a landmark achievement to the both of us, and we straightened a little in preparation to what it was he felt the need to approach us with.

“Please, feel free William, by all means.” said the principal. I nodded in assent.

“I know that my parents would give anything to have a normal son and that they are very much wary of everything I do. But it is critical for me to continue my work, both for it's value to society, but more to myself. I must be allowed to continue. If testing does not provide me with the time and facilities to advance my research, and I think this is likely, I am asking that you sponsor me some time and space to finish what I started. I would not have imposed my will in class as I did if my parents could have seen the importance of my work, and forbid me to finish. I would not be a burden on you at all neither by shutting you down by brain looping, or financially. You are the first people to come along that are at least trying to look beyond the way I am. Please, I am begging for somebody to trust me that this is all worthwhile. I am very close, but the fight to finish is an all out war."

"What exactly do you mean by 'war'?" I asked.

"I can't really elaborate because neither of you would have the slightest inkling what I'm talking about. I am simply asking for trust."

"That's what we are doing William. We are trusting that you are more than what your scholastic record shows." added the principal.

"I know, but I also know that this will go nowhere, and I will be back at square one, battling my parents to continue what is so close to being done once and for all. I need a leap of faith that I can finish this."

I guess in my lack of understanding what it was he was driving at, I was guilty of appeasing the boy. "Sure William. I will be glad to help. But give this a chance. I believe in you. Principal Farris believes in you too, or we wouldn't be here. Take a breath. A couple more minutes to go and everything will be fine, I just know it."

"Yes, but will you help me out, trust me if it doesn't?"

"Sure, sure. Absolutely. I'm your guy."

"Yes, we will do what we can William." his principal added her support. We were both thinking everything would be okay anyway.

Miss Farris and I left the campus while the testing took place. We were told the tests would likely consume much of the afternoon, at least until about three o'clock, anyway. This gave us a chance to connect for a couple of hours, and to get some real food. We talked about a lot of things over the late lunch, early dinner. It all ended with a subject important to me lately. I told her that I suffered from a feeling of inferiority. It was an extension of how I really felt about my job, and where I really felt I might do the most good. It also contributed to how I interacted with the professional people that surrounded me in the work place. I felt as though I could never measure up.

KIDS TODAY

Harriet said that the staff had never given any indication they viewed me as inferior.

"Yes, but does anybody feel that I am making any kind of difference? Do you?" I asked.

"On that issue, I am not sure anymore, to be honest."

"There, you see?"

"But that isn't a reflection on you because I feel that some of my own priorities need to change. I think I have forgotten about education somewhere along the way, and more about enforcing the rules. If you didn't have this job, what is it that you would like to do?"

"I guess I would like to get myself into the police academy to join traditional law enforcement."

"You mean like a man in a blue uniform?" She said with a wry smile.

"Why not? I'm still young enough to pass anything physical thrown at me."

"I'll bet you can!" smile broadening.

"So you think my idea is a good one?"

"It is not up to me, but since you ask, I think it's an excellent idea."

"That settles it. I am going to ask questions as soon as I can. So do you really have a thing for men in blue uniforms?"

"I kind of have a thing for this man I know who wears a security uniform. I'm thinking blue would be even a better color."

It took about a week to get the results. Until they arrived, Principal Farris kept William isolated from his classmates. The boy kept himself busy in the school library all day long. When Principal Farris finally got a call with the results, she was disappointed. The principal and I were both wrong. After all the extensive testing, William came up short in all but math and science. In those subjects, he obviously excelled. Adult testing was used in those subjects, and his comprehension and problem solving skills were off the charts. However, language, reading, and communicative skills were average for his age. Social comprehension was not measurable. This led to SAT testing that when overall scoring was taken into account, he failed miserably. It was the recommendation of the administrator that tested him that day that he be kept at the elementary school level, where the opinion was he would benefit the most. It was felt that to recommend him to classes with extremely gifted children, would frustrate both him and his co-students. The students in the few classes that existed in the country were reading, writing, and comprehending on a collegiate level already. All of them could pass all of the college entry exams, and most, some of the exit exams. Only if some of the other areas that he was deficient in matched his math, science, and hand eye coordinations maybe it would be worth their while to admit William into any such classes. It wasn't their job to teach barely third grade reading, and grammar in these classes.

After giving the news to William, Miss Farris called me to join William and herself in her office at William's request. I did not know why. William took the news matter of factually, even expected. I would have felt sorry for him if he showed any emotion at all. He did not. But that is when he pressed me to keep the promise I made, one that I had all but forgotten. He talked to Principal Farris also. It was one thing to promise I would help, and quite another to know if I could help, once he told me what he needed of me. He asked me to talk to his parents to allow him to complete his research in a different place than at home.

"Where is it that you want to get the work done, William?"

"I was hoping you would allow me to come home with you until I finish. And as for you Ms. Farris, I am going to need help to get caught up with my class, especially after I finish my research."

"But..." started the principal.

"But you promised! With space, this work will not take much longer. After that, I will need all the help I can get. I can't count on my parents. Their interests are not the same as mine. We have a constant feud going on at home, which makes what I have to do quite impossible without shutting them down. Lately they have figured out a way to make me loop first, and nothing at all gets done. They have no idea of the importance of all that I am doing. Please trust me."

"What do you want me to ask of your parents then?" I consented with a sigh, no clue as to what I was getting into.

"I need to set up my equipment somewhere. A spare bedroom or something will be fine."

"Do you mean like spend the night? I can't cross your parents like that William."

"No, I need about a week, maybe a week and a half tops of afternoons, and I will be done. Ms. Farris will need to help me after that. She will know when."

"All of this sounds so mysterious...why?"

"Please don't take any offense, but neither of you could fathom what I am trying to do if I explained it. I will just say that with my understanding of the human brain after I am done, I will help millions. Please, I ask again, trust me. Someone must!"

"What do you think your parents will say if I ask them to allow me to take your equipment out of your house?"

"It is all I can do from keeping them from throwing it all away in the trash. They have no idea how bad that would be. Please!"

Perhaps it was the intensity of his devotion to what it is he wanted to accomplish, but I trusted him. But then again, I believed the boy was another Einstein when we first met, and testing proved he was not. "Okay William, tell me what to do, and we will work it out."

"Can I help?" asked Harriett.

"Sure. At this point, it appears I am going to need all the moral support I can get. William here sure isn't going to explain what is going on. This blind faith thing is pretty hard for me. I have a hunch though that he is legit. I'm a big bad security guy anyway, so I'll try to keep Homeland Security out of it. Could you call his parents for me? That kind of question might swing more weight coming from a sweet thing like you. If you don't want to, I'll understand."

"Oh no! It will be no trouble at all. If it is okay by them, we can go get the stuff together. Do you have space?"

"Sure do. I have a bedroom that has nothing in it, not even a bed. I don't know what he needs. I have a folding table that I use out in the backyard, but that's about it."

"You can take what I have it set up on now."

William said. “I will leave my computer where it is. I really don't need it for anything but the business. My parents impressed on me that they could not afford to buy the stuff I needed. So to keep them from stopping my work, I sort of earned my own way.”

“I could have sworn you said you were almost done.” I pointed out.

“I am. But now I don't want for you to stop me now either.”

“Drop it William, you have my support already. What else do you have to buy?”

“Nothing. It's all about calculations and circuitry now, I promise. I'm concerned about what comes after.” he slipped.

I picked up on that. “Why?”

“Nothing. I just can't wait to succeed, that's all. I will need help after that.” I detected something that waved a red flag, and I would be watching him like a hawk.

“Go back to the library now Mr. Sumerlin. I will call your parents again during the day. They're probably going to think that you caused more trouble. Don't give them any reason to think that. I will talk to you later in the day. I'll leave you to do your job.” As soon as William obediently went around the corner to the school library, Harriett said “Lyle. Come with me, I have something to tell you.”

“Uh oh.”

“Uh oh is right! I got a call this morning. It was a follow up phone call doing a background check from the police academy you apparently applied to.”

“I told you I would apply. I thought you would be happy.”

“I am! I'm totally pulling your leg. Bad boy...bad boy...when the hell are you...gonna go and wear for me some hunky blue!”

I chuckled. “Did you get a sense that I was accepted?”

“No, not really. They would be fools not taking you into the academy.”

“My goodness, are you biased or what?”

“No! Not me!.”

“Holy mackerel! I have to make my rounds now.

It's time for recess already."

"Before you go, what do you think is so important that William is grasping at any way he can finish it off?"

"I don't know. But I think we may get a clue if we get to see this equipment of his. I wonder if the reason he will need you later is because he needs to use whatever it is he's making on other people somehow. It worries me."

"I see your point. Without any emotions, his sense of right and wrong could mean anything. It could be what he is thinking. Between us, we should be able to keep him occupied enough to get those kinds of thoughts out of his head. I'm thinking of personally tutoring him so he can catch up to his class."

At the end of the afternoon, William found me after the final bell. I was filling out my report for the day, and William was just standing behind me. The kid spooked me, but I knew full well what he wanted when I turned around. "Come on, we should find out what your mom and dad said to Principal Farris." She was headed our way as we walked together toward the office. Her face was hard to read. If she got good news, a smile would be on it, but none was flashed. "Did they say no when you called?" I asked.

"No...no, they said it was okay by them."

"So why the long face?"

In front of William, she said to me, "Because they expressed their concerns to me. They have been frightened out of their minds by Williams project. They want it out of the house, and welcomed the plan for us to come get it out. They warned me to be very very careful that William could prove very dangerous." This news statement made William loop out right there in the hallway. This time his head went forward as if praying.

I looked at William. I said to Harriet, "You know...I think if there was anything sinister about what he wants, this would not have happened. Granted he seems not to be able to explain to us what is going on, but using the word dangerous knocked the kid for a loop. I say trust him."

"I wonder how long he will be out. Maybe we should move him into my office?"

"Good idea." But when I tried to scoop the kid up, but his body was as stiff as a mannequin. I stood him back up. It seemed we would wait the loop ride out where we were.

It took about two minutes for him to come back out of it, but when he did, he winced with a head throb. "Please," he said softly, "there isn't much time for me to do what I need to. Can we go get my equipment now?"

"I have to leave my report off at my home office, but sure, we can go after that. Do his parents know we are coming?" I directed the question at Harriett.

She told me, "Yes, but they are both still at work."

"This is the time I usually spend on my computer, updating my business results and making transfers into my dad's bank before they get home. But lately, it has become more necessary to finish off my project. I shut down the website a month ago so it doesn't generate activity. What I'm working on is more important than what my parents think. It's more important than you think." His urgency was plain.

His parents feared what was coming next, reading something sinister in what he was doing. But William wasn't capable of sinister. The fights were one way of controlling William, probably making William loop out more and more. I wished I knew what it was he was doing. I reasoned that my speculation evaluating William's equipment made a ton of sense.

"Harriett, we are going now. Give me a call in, say, an hour or so."

"There is not a chance of that! I am going with you. I will be with you all the way."

I chuckled in irony. The principal and I were bonding very heavily. I silently breathed a sigh of relief, as I did not want to do this alone. Was I afraid of William? Some. But it was more because of his lack of emotion that could cloud the boundaries of right and wrong. "All right then, let's get out of here."

"Let me lock up my office. I need my purse and keys." Moments later we headed out of the school after I locked the last of the doors in front of the building. The teachers inside could leave, but no one could reenter. It didn't take me long to leave off my report at Hanklin so we finally could put a face on William's project. Harriett took William in her own car, so I was to follow. The Sumerlin home was a tidy 1000 square foot bungalow, adorned with a self manicured landscape that contained an eclectic assortment of plant life. The whole compound was surrounded by a short galvanized chain link fence. There were no toys, no gym set, no 20 inch bicycle, pool, or any other thing that would give evidence that anybody other than adults lived there. A small drive ended at a side door to the house. There was no garage. Thank God William was with us because we looked like burglars.

William led us through a small but clean dated kitchen, through a small hall where William's room was about half way down. Inside was not what I expected. Instead of wires and hoards of electronic gadgetry, was an extended table off a computer desk. The room was only about 9 feet by 10 feet, most of it taken up by a twin bed neatly made up. The gear William referred to all this while, looked like what could roughly be described as a guitar amplifier. The back or front, it was unclear which, was faced forward so it could be worked on. Tiny potentiometers were mounted in ten colored organized blocks. Each block contained thousands of them, but only one bank of blocks could be seen, because it was hinged. More banks were behind that one, and behind that. There was no way of knowing how many banks there were altogether as the depth of the instrument was about twenty inches or so. The width was maybe two feet. The height, I would estimate to be around thirty inches, could have been more. It did have wires and odd instruments around it, but was by no means as intrusive as the parents described. Perhaps the fear of it alone is what magnified the description. However, there were small micro screwdrivers and mini tools scattered around the equipment. Then there were mounds of paperwork in the same notebooks I had seen him working on in room 12 of Miss Haigwrather's classroom. There were ten or eleven of them in all.

"This isn't all that bad William. What's the big deal?" I asked.

"It is simply not what my parents want me doing. I don't know. All I know is it is imperative that I finish, and they have been threatening to throw it all out."

"Did they have anything to say to you, Harri..ah...Miss Farris?"

"They just said all the more power to us, and to keep a close eye on him while he works."

"Did you do anything to them with it William?"

"No." he said flatly. "I looped them with my brain looper so I could work, but that stopped a few weeks ago."

"Why?"

"I have been looping out more and more. I need to get back to some critical adjustments that are close to being done. I need the time to bring adjustments into sync. They have to be. Synapse rerouting doesn't need just accuracy, it requires an exactness never before achieved. Voltages for separate neural pathways need matching on such a precise level that there is no room for error. I am running out of time, and I can't afford to waste a second of it having my parents haggling and arguing with me until we loop each other out. A lot is riding on this, and my parents are just not aware of it. I wish I could explain more to you and my parents, but I can't. I have had this conversation before."

As much as William was capable of, I detected his brand of frustration. He was racing for something that I didn't know what, and when it came down to it, I still didn't know why. All this eight year old was begging for was trust and a little bit of time. But for what ultimate agenda?

It didn't take long to pack his stuff to transfer it all to my house. The whole kit and caboodle fit in my car without using the trunk. The machine itself only weighed about twenty or twenty five pounds or so. In only a little more than an hour, William sat in a new workspace. He was working on some—well I couldn't tell you what kind of math. I asked if he needed help plugging stuff back in, and was told that it wasn't necessary just yet. Harriett and I got a first look at a dizzying maze of calculations in his notebooks. Literally thousands of meaningless numbers filled page after page, none of them even looked the least bit algebraic. He could see the confusion on our faces that went deeper than our faces showed when he said, "relatable tangentials." I met eyes with Harriett, who shook her head to mean 'beats me', without saying it..

"How long are you going to work tonight William?"

"I am going to do my calculations at home tonight. Then I need a night or two for adjustments. I am working on a few accidental errors that were made when my parents started looping me. I need to determine where and how much of that tangential flow has been caused to be out of sync. I have a clue because I know where I was working at the time. But I have forgotten the synced tangential numbers, which need to be found so I can bring them back into accuracy. Then I can continue with my final adjustments. If you would call my parents for me, I would like for you to tell them I will come home now if it is okay with you to drive me?"

"That's fine. Miss Farris and I have plans tonight. Set it up with your parents that you can go home with me after school tomorrow. Then I'll take you home around dinner to be with your family. What time do your folks get home usually?"

"They get home about six o'clock, depending on how their day goes and traffic."

"Then six thirty should work for you. I will bring you home then. Please tell your parents."

"Okay sir." William selected one of his notebooks. He took it with him. The kid had priorities.

When my day was in full swing, Harriett found me doing my rounds before recess. "William Sumerlin is absent today."

"Did you call his parents?"

"No...I didn't want to pester them any more than I already have. I think we have infringed on parental rights quite enough. They got what they wanted. The contentious equipment is out of their house, and they have their boy back without any influences. He could have gotten sick. He does seem to be pushing himself all out for some reason. All in all, any number of factors could be the cause here. Let's just wait and see how it all plays out. Maybe we could take advantage of it by going to get something to eat together after school? What do you think?"

"Great idea...and you're probably right. We may have played right into the parents hands and given them their child back. Although he isn't the most loving kid in the world."

The day proceeded in a normal fashion. I had heard no news from the police academy, but it was too soon for that anyway. No, without William in school, the day went by completely without incident. At the end of it all, Harriett and I left the building at days end, climbed into two cars, and finally left mine at my house in the driveway to go to a place we had talked about of interest to us both. Neither of us had ever been there before. Not only was it good, but we had the benefit of having early bird specials to choose from. Dinner conversation was intimate up until the subject of William came up.

"You think that we helped the parents out by having them win an argument for a change don't you?" I pressed her for her opinion.

"Frankly yes. I have to admit that winning doesn't exactly give them a warm family unit though. William is a strange boy. His obsession to that project of his is completely unexplainable; a total enigma. I wonder what his hurry is?" She asked.

"I don't know, but I love having you all to myself tonight. Let's forget about him for now."

Dinner done, we headed back to my house for a quiet evening together. It was nearly dark when we pulled up to my home. Lights were on, and I hadn't left them that way! "Stay here! If I don't come back out in two minutes, call the police." I commanded Harriett. I didn't want to put her in harms way should I surprise an intruder. I slipped into my house through the back door. The door was closed and still locked. I had to use my key to quietly, and stealthily let myself in. I went directly to the front door from the inside to find it locked, as well. There was no noise inside as I walked from room to room, but I found the intruder in the spare bedroom. It was William, sound asleep with his head on the table. I ran outside to catch Harriett before she called 911. "It's William....the kid broke in and was working on his calculations. He's dead tired, sleeping like a baby right where he was working. Such a headstrong kid! Come in, have a look." I had to keep up with her, she moved so fast. She was through the front entrance and into the room before you could say lickity-split.

"Lyle!" she said in a scolding manner. "There is a note. It's addressed to both of us."

A folded piece of paper read as follows: On the outside was written, "Instructions." On the inside:

Miss Farris and Mr. Yatsworth,

I did what I did because I had to. I unlocked a window last night when we brought my machine from my house. I really tried to warn everyone of the urgency to finish off my work. There has been an extreme malfunction in my brain that needed repair. At first, I was working on a way to fix retardation, and brain deficiencies. But one day about a month and a half ago, my parents found that I looped out. It just started happening one day, and there was nothing I could do to control it. They figured out a what it was that triggered it. So I adapted some of my work to build a makeshift tool to try to fix what it was that was going wrong with me. It did not work. It worked on others but not me. I found all of that out by using it on my mom and dad. I stepped up my efforts to complete my brain repair machine, but my parents fought back, looping me out so I could not work on it. I got the idea to bring my brain looper to school so I could work there. I found that Miss Haigonwrather had lessons thought up ahead of time so that she had no idea that it was happening to her. My parents and my classmates knew I used it right away because unexplainable time was lost. It caused disorientation in them because they only live from minute to minute. I threatened to use it to subdue them all.

My brain has been constantly awake. It began about the time I began looping. Concentration has gotten increasingly difficult. Eventually, without sleep, I'd die. This is some of what I could not explain. The other part is how my brain repair machine works, or the theory behind it. I didn't have the time to waste explaining it either.

Thank you for believing in me Mr. Yatsworth. The same to you Miss Farris. But I told you Miss Farris that you would know when I needed your help. I am

resting comfortably. I may be slow to rouse, and probably should sleep. Call my mom and dad after this, to tell them I am okay. When I do wake up, I am going to need your expertise. I may experience some temporary amnesia, but will come around quickly enough. There are some things that are going to have to be retaught to me. Other things, I never did know in the first place. You should find that I will be a quick learner. I will no longer be the William you knew. I will need retraining. I will need love and attention, and may have a tendency to be emotional. Please help me...you promised.
Yours truly,
William Sumerlim

We read the note together, and afterwards, checked William to see that he was breathing. When we did, I pried a strange microphone type device with a light on it from his hand. The other end was plugged into his completed machine. I then untethered the contraption from the power socket in the wall. Then I scooped up the boy to carry him into my own bed, took off his shoes, pulled up a sheet over him, and left him to sleep.

Harriett called the Sumerlins, gave them directions how to drive over, and hung up expecting the worst when they arrived.

When William's parents got to my house safely, I handed the note to William's mom, who read it, absorbing every word. She handed it to her husband. His mother was crying. “Can I see him?”

“Of course! He's right down the end of the hall in my bedroom.

She was very quiet but needn't have been. The boy was out like a boxer that had just been KO'd. She went to him and combed his hair with her fingers kissing his forehead sweetly.

Karen, Yared, Harriett, and I sat in my living room, doing our best to take in everything that had happened. None of us ever doubted for a moment that William had brought on some kind of repair to himself. The first of his predictions was dead on accurate. He slept until we all crashed exactly where we were. We didn't want to move. Every one of us felt a responsibility to the boy in a different way, and for various different reasons. The sun rose up over the horizon, and with it an eight year old confused boy standing in my living room staring at four adults sleeping upright on a couch and chairs. We all jolted out of slumber in surprise. The young man was crying!

"Wwwho are you people, and where am I?" he asked.

"I'm your mother, honey, and this is your dad."

Yyyou all look like people I should know, but I...just ...can't remember." He said as frightened as a little bird in somebody's hand.

All of a sudden he brightened and said, "Wait a minute...Mom?...Dad?...Sure!...I remember!...Miss Farris? Mr. Yatsworth?" He walked in our midst, straight over to his mom, and hugged her for all he was worth. His dad went behind him, burst into tears, and hugged them both at the same time. Shorty almost got suffocated in the middle. The poor kid was in a funny sandwich. The scene was heart warming at the same time. He was little Billy.

The problem was that we all had jobs. Harriet and I offered to take William to school with us since all three of us had to make an appearance at some point during the day. This would allow William's parents to make their living, and meet up with us later. We all agreed this to be a very good idea, provided we get together later to review how William really was. The time and place to meet was formed. It was to be at William's house, where he really belonged.

The relief that William was okay detracted from the facts. William had laid out a plan, reminded Miss Farris of her commitment in his note to rehabilitate, retrain, and teach him. It was for a very good reason. Remembering all of us, receiving love and returning it was the extent of his development. He was not responsive in Harriet's car as we rode together to get to school. He could not be engaged in conversation at all. Harriett escorted him to room 12, and left him there with the mindset that he would pick up where he left off. Later in the day, Harriett personally checked up on William with his teacher. It was Miss Haigonwrather's considered opinion that William was even more socially inept than he was before. He added nothing to the class experience, refused to answer the simplest of questions, was dull, and lifeless.

KIDS TODAY

After the school day, Harriett reported to me what was said on the way to collecting William to take him home. I reacted defensively, mentioning that it seemed laughable that she had no complaints with the boy when he was emotionless. But, as it turned out, Miss Haigonwrather had a point. In the car, Harriett quizzed him on his day, finding he had nothing to say at all.

Kids like this are generally lost in the school system. He acted like students that shut up, only to find they are illiterate, sailing along with the rest. I said this to Harriett, right there in front of the boy. He had no comeback, nothing indignant to say.

"I'm sorry that sounded so cruel, but this is what William meant in his note, Harriett. You did promise, and this is what he meant. You can't sell him short now. I can't tell you what it is he did to himself with that machine of his...by the way, what DID you do to yourself with that machine of yours, William?" I asked him, turning to direct the question over the backseat to the boy.

"Machine?"

"There, you see. He left himself with just the basics. He has to be reminded, taught, or retaught all the rest. It is just as he said it would be."

"This is where I live?" asked William when we pulled up into the Sumerlin driveway behind Karen and Yared's vehicle. They came flying out of the house to see their son. They may not have gone to work at all. William fumbled with the door handle. I reached over to pull the latch up for him so he could escape the automobile. "Mom! Dad!" he was picked up clean off the ground by his father. His mother was kissing him all over his face.

"Come in, come in!" Karen said. "I made something for us all to eat...." She was so excited and animated.

Over toasted garlic bread, spaghetti and meatballs, I began to remind the Sumerlins exactly what it was that William was trying to say in the note he left.

"Yes, he was very adamant that I promise to help him after Lyle here provided space for him to work on his machine. Now I think I understand why. We may have to homeschool him."

"...But we aren't qualified to do that!" stated Yared.

"In the United States, you would need a certified teacher anyway. William knew that when he asked. Ironic...saying that he knew it because I sincerely doubt he knows it now. I want to set up testing to find out his grade level. Can either of you spend time during the day with your son? He can't be left alone right now. I can't bring him to school every day, but I can come at night to make sure he is doing his lessons. I can take him tomorrow only so I can determine what it is we are working with. But after that, it is up to you people."

"I suppose I could ask for a shift change at the hospital if you think I must." said Karen.

"I do...I think you must. But I will be around to help. I DID promise."

In the days to come, a lot of changes came to the Sumerlin family, as well as to the lives of Harriett and I.

I was admitted to the police academy and had some serious decisions to make. Filling all the requisites for full time classes would take my entire savings. Part time could be accomplished at night, allowing me to keep my day job for benefits and such, but would take almost all of my time for nine months. I opted for the second choice, a commitment in of itself.

Harriet became very involved with the Sumerlins, working with Karen to provide lesson plans that maintained unusual growth. Initially, William tested out far behind his class. His reading skills couldn't compete with preschoolers. Inside of a few days, though, he was reading at the fourth grade level, and continued to advance exponentially. His aptitudes were not specialized. That is to say that he absorbed anything that was placed in front of him. His interests were all over the board. Even recreation became one of his many loves. In three months, William passed his high school equivalency and scored 2400 points in a sample SAT. An oral interview was scheduled, along with an entrance exam to the State University we had visited for help when the journey began. He posted the same score and was promptly admitted to regular classes to start in the fall. Karen and Yared got their loving child, but was still to lose him to a full time college curriculum. The heavy class load William planned on taking were without the benefit of scholarships. William planned to work his way through. He took no special treatments or classes adapted to young people such as himself, preferring instead to fit in with his typical counterparts.

If William's life wasn't odd enough, something strange showed itself in this brand new journey of his. He could not grasp the principals used to build his machine—or the brain looper for that matter. It was his driving goal to reestablish the knowledge to understand and use the technology used to repair himself. William told Miss Farris that it could take years to unravel his own computations. Some of the ciphering was just on the edge of his memory, but he could not, for the life of him, recall the meanings of what he had termed as *relatable tangentials*.

The Sumerlins wanted to put their house on the market. But their lives were so intertwined in the community, it was impossible if not foolish to detach from it. They needed to stay rooted, keeping themselves emotionally available to their son. William's room was put back together just as it was machine and all.

In the whole time I spent working at Wickens Elementary School, Principal Farris graduated from stage to stage. When I first worked with her, I thought of her as Ms. Farris. When we worked together at the beginning with William, she became Miss Farris. Then we worked closely with each other, spending time, working out what our places in William's life was. I began thinking of her as Principal Farris. We joined forces in the effort, becoming close. I started calling her Harriett. Soon her name will change again. This time it will be Mrs. Harriett Yatsworth.

Poor Miss Haigonwrather finally buried her mother. Then she buried herself in her work. Beyond the death of her mom, no one can feel bad for the woman. She is truly where she belongs, happy and content in her calling to mold young minds in the formative years, each and every one of them becoming one of her own. Every year she will add more to the list of young people that she has influenced, and all without birthing one of them! Personally, Harriett and I want to try for a William or Willamina of our own.

VOICES

VOICES

I was going to be late for work—again. It was doubtful anybody at the office would believe I was out of the house an hour earlier than normal for just a five mile drive. *Sure Dave...an hour...gotcha*, coworkers will say. My boss has shown signs of irritation around the edges. There are only so many times a person can pull off the fashionably late thing without being viewed instead as chronically tardy. But, I have to say this—big but—there isn't a blessed thing I can do about it, except to leave earlier. That is precisely what I did on this particular morning. The reason for it is that my street, 3rd Street, is the only way out of the neighborhood leading to the main drag, Homer Drive. There are other ways out, but you will find yourself sent in another direction, so it doesn't matter which way is taken to avoid traffic; side streets, whatever. There are no cutsies. The only way to get to the interstate on ramp south to downtown, is the 3rd Street light, left on Homer Drive, and a slight bear right to the on ramp. It's a take it or leave it thing. I can't really move because there is still time on my lease. In the mean time, one, sometimes up to three mornings out of five, that 3rd Street light makes me late for work because of the bottleneck choked with cars leaving at the same time. So yes, I find the whole thing irritating.

I was sitting at the aforementioned bottleneck, on an otherwise quite pleasant sunny morning. I had my windows down, soaking up the fresh morning air because there wasn't much else to do. Believe you, me, I was counting, it was coming up to the fifth red light cycle. Still, all I could see was cars in front of me. A good thing, though, is that the last time I was stuck the same way, I found myself one car ahead of a kid in a car with loud music. The pounding bass was so strong it vibrated enough to suck my ear drums out. Blood spurt out hitting the windows on both sides of the car. The high decibel range then bore a hole into my skull, causing cerebrospinal fluid to drip uncontrollably down my earlobes onto my neck. That is totally how it felt.

Thankful that same thing wasn't happening on this particular day was a consolation that put me in good spirits, in spite of the tardy situation. There was a woman selling newspapers wearing short shorts with lace trim, and high heeled sneakers. She used her assets to garnish attention for sales. She was holding the latest edition in the air, walking an imaginary runway past driver side windows, forcing all of the drivers she passed to feel guilty not ponying up a mere buck for entertainment. There was no other place to go anyway. We knew it, and she knew it. Of course, I bought the morning news. But the truth was I needed the morning news updates almost as much as the closeup of her fine pair of legs. I paid up, but for the life of me, I am embarrassed to say, I can't remember what she looked like. Her face could have shown the cumulative effects of a decade or two, 3 pack a day Pall Mall addiction for all I knew. That, my friends, is why one must always dress for power.

The other noteworthy observation I made as I perused the overnight local and state news developments was an old lady. She had rounded the corner from Homer Drive, just two or three light cycles away at that point. She may have been homeless, at least she appeared that way to my judgmental eye; dressed in a tattered dress, old crew socks, two different shoes on, an old dirty woolen coat, open-but worn on a 75 degree day, and a tube cap. She was talking to herself...loudly. “Oh no, you di-ent. You di-ent say dat! I can't believe you man! Just SHUT UP! Everybody thinks I'm crazy cause of you. You can't just say things like dat out loud you asshole!” Her outraged reprimands continued until she was out of earshot. Not only do people scare me to death with skitzo displays like that, but she was heading into the heart of my own neighborhood. A disconcerting thought crossed my mind that she was moving in close by before my lease was up. Or maybe she already lived there and lost her job being tardy because of the 3rd Street light onto Homer.

My captive audience entertainment finished about that time because the last fifteen cars ahead of me had quick drawn on gas pedals that got us all through, making the most of the light cycle. I was off and running, just fifteen minutes late for work turning the corner into Homer. With four and a half miles to go, I put the pedal to the medal. A quarter mile to the on ramp, an eighth of a mile for the on the ramp itself, and just one mile driven on the interstate gave me a grand total of three and one eighth miles left over to get to the office. A state trooper from nowhere, hooked a chain to my bumper, and I dragged him along for a portion of the ride. He was so close, I could see the self satisfied smirk on his face. He issued two short whoop whoops of his siren to draw my attention as if I had not already seen him. "Damn it all to hell!" I exclaimed to myself, suddenly feeling an affinity with the woman who talked to herself. Talking to yourself can be therapeutic. I used all the expletives I wanted before the trooper finished his slow-mo swagger over to my window. I issued quite a mouthful and even had the paperwork out of the glove box so we could speed things along in the time it took to traverse a car length from the door of his patrol to mine.

"Do you know why I stopped you?" the trooper asked when he made it to my window.

"Uh, because I was late for work?" I was given a $220. dollar speeding ticket because I couldn't contain my smart mouth.

For the rest of the trip in, I coolly formulated a plan to use the piece of paper from the clerk of courts for sympathy when I finally got to the office, even though the time of the issue was right on the face of it. It was a carbon copy though, and not really all that legible. I figured if I flashed it fast, it might draw the effect I wanted. The clearest part was the when and where to pay the thing. That part was sharp as a tack. I tumbled into the office, just a mere hour late overall. The work day was in full swing, and even the mail boy gave me a look of disgust as I sauntered toward my cubical. I passed in front of my boss's secretary on the way, who warned me that Mr Bigby, the city editor, wanted to see me immediately. There was not much use prolonging the agony, so I went right in to get it over with. I had my hand in my shirt pocket on my speeding ticket as I said, "I'm sorry I'm late boss..."

"Yeah, yeah, yeah...the 3rd Street light thing. I know all about it. Look, the reason I had you come in here is because of the story on page one. Did you see it?"

"Which one, the state budget impasse, or the one about the brutal homeless woman's murder downtown?"

VOICES

"Thaaaat's the one! Whadja do, pick up our rag on the way in?"

"I was just stuck there on 3rd. A pair of hot legs were pushin' our papers on the corner. I picked one up there to pass the time. I kinda' I figured to catch up at the same time."

"Good for you! Anyway—Dave—I need a human interest story about what's going on over there in the park. Part of the angle needs to shed some light on who might have done such a thing. I mean, I know they are homeless, but what kind of enemies could she have made to kill her like that? Doesn't seem like anybody too much cares either."

"She's probably on a slab somewhere with nobody to claim her; pretty damned sad." I commented.

"Agreed. See what you can do Dave. You know damned well any investigation is on the back of the stove with the burners off. I would appreciate it if you would get right on it. It doesn't sit right with me that there is such a thing as throw away people, although I don't have any answers on how to fix it."

I grabbed some things I needed off the desk in my cubicle, and headed out for the police station downtown to see what information I could glean in the first destination on my travel list. The car hadn't even cooled down yet when I started it back up, pulled back the gear shift lever, and pointed it into the heavy city day traffic. The drive gave me time to coordinate my thoughts on how to proceed with the story but one of my random thoughts on the subject brought to mind whether or not it was ethical to contact family of the victim that might not want to be contacted. On the other hand, sometimes it pays to have an obnoxious side. Budinski prying shakes out facts sometimes. I pulled into the station house parking lot on Tandy for my second encounter in one day with our uniformed finest. Inside the building after my parked my car got to hobnob with police cruisers, I approached a wall of glass in a kind of small reception hall. All sorts of unsavory characters sat on benches against two walls in the small entry, none of them moving. I could not determine if they were waiting their turn to speak into the little hole in the glass to officer Wizard of Oz, or simply waiting to be assigned somebody to deal with them later. I did not see a machine to take a number, so I marched up to the hole. A tiny unamplified voice asked, "Can I help you?" "Huh?" I asked back. The echo in the space I occupied jerked everybody's face to turn in my direction.

He then pulled a microphone on a flexible boom toward his face and said, "Sorry about that. Can I help you?"

"David Simpson...Daily Spectacle." I announced in the space of echoes.

"...And what can we do for the Daily Spectacle, Mr. Simpson."

"I'm looking for more information on that homeless woman who got herself killed last evening in Rollins Park downtown."

"Why would anybody, let alone the Spectacle, care about some dirty old Jane Doe that nobody wanted around in the first place?"

"So since you don't know who she really is, that means she isn't worth the time to find out?"

"We haven't closed her file, Mr. Simpson. If more information comes our way, it will be updated. But for now..."

"May I please speak to the officer in charge who wrote the report?"

"He's on duty right now. I will have him call at his earliest convenience."

"I appreciate that." I left my business card, my name and number on it with the Sargent beyond the hole in the glass.

At least to my mind, it seemed that where I had gone thus far on the story was a useless dead end street, except for the fact that she was a Jane Doe. My quandary over the tactfulness of talking to family was a mute point.

The next destination was over in Rollins Park, so I rejoined my car in the police parking lot for the drive over. In recent days, Rollins Park has become a problem as well as an eyesore in the city because of the homeless people loitering there. There were a number of establishments that fed the throw away people close by to the park, and it contributed to the problem of loitering for the next free meal. Another strange related problem, is that the homeless people were possessive of the new turf, and somewhat combatant in their demeanor due to alcoholism and drugs. That fact alone made it hard to tolerate, or even like them. The residents paying the bills found themselves afraid to use the park. Also, in a charming coastal city like Wickendon, the ugly scar of homeless people sitting out on dirty blankets in the picturesque park overlooking the water was both a visible and economic sore that was hemorrhaging, and nobody was coming forward with a remedy to fix it. It explained much of the attitude of the Sargent at the police station. Still, a percentage of these were people were clearly victims of some very bad circumstances. Which of them fit that criteria took detective work that nobody wanted to spend time on.

I came out of the police lot, drove a couple blocks to the northernmost part of Homer drive, the opposite end of the city I lived off of. But there was a similarity when I had come to the corner before I turned onto it. I sat at a light that had a man panhandling in an enterprising way. It was not even into the afternoon, and it was getting quite warm already. This man made use of the warm day, selling bottled water to the drivers sitting at the light. “One buck here for bottled water.” He yelled as he walked between three lanes of cars.

One lane turned left in its own lane, and two went straight or turned right. When all the cars were stopped at the same time, he made his run pushing water. He impressed me, so when he got close to my window, I handed him a dollar bill and took the bottle from him. The water was ice cold. There was a cooler sitting on the sidewalk, he was taking the waters out of it when he needed them. Apparently they were on ice. I took a good hold of it to open it up, when I realized it wasn't a standard labeled bottle, in fact, there was no label at all. It was a glass bottle, clean, the top had a cork stopper. It looked new and clean alright, but there was something unfamiliar about the bottle. I don't think it came from standard store stock, or any store rack I knew of. I took a small cursory swig of some surprisingly good agua. It seemed perfectly okay, so I took a good long hard slug of the thirst quenching H2O. Then I turned on the radio. It was 9:00, and the radio station was airing it's top of the hour weather and newscast. The news itself was the same old, same old national news, but when it got into the local stuff, there was a verbatim recount of the same story my paper had done overnight on the park killing.

Right there is when I jumped out of my skin. "WILL YOU SHUT THAT CRAP OFF?...IT'S THE SAME EXACT PIECE OF GARBAGE THAT YOUR PAPER PRINTED OUT LAST NIGHT. YOU WOULD THINK THESE ASSHOLES WOULD TAKE THE TIME AND EFFORT TO INVESTIGATE THEIR OWN ANGLE OF THE STORY INSTEAD OF COPYING WHAT YOUR PAPER DID. HOW LAZY CAN PEOPLE GET? AT LEAST YOU'RE GOING OUT TO FIND OUT A LITTLE MORE ON THE SUBJECT. FAT CHANCE THESE GUYS GIVE A GOOD RAT'S ASS ANYWAY." This came from a little gnome-like man sitting next to me on the passenger side front seat. He talked very loudly for a little man, and he had the open paper I had bought that morning on his lap. I instinctively slammed on my brakes, fortunately cutting my wheel sharply to the right or the man driving behind me would have hit me for sure. I did extract one very long push from the driver's horn as he drove on past me, cursing and gesturing at the same time. I jumped out of my car, got on the sidewalk where it was safe, and reached for my cell phone. The gnome man appeared next to me, magically, and said, "I wouldn't do that if I were you, not unless you want to look like some kind of nut case. The only person who can see and hear me is you right now, nobody else.

"WHY IS THAT?" I yelled hysterically.

"Calm down shithead. It's because I chose you. If I didn't want to be seen, I wouldn't have let you. I was in the water you drank which let you see me *if* I decided to choose you. Otherwise, I could have just kept to myself. Once I chose you, which I most certainly did, we are friends for life."

"WHAT?...You mean I can't get rid of you?"

"Now you got it doofus. You seemed like an alright guy, a little anal, but pretty smart. Now I'm having my doubts and it's too late. I am going to have to smack some sense into you if you don't get back into the car and act normal." I didn't believe the gnome until I yelled to a pedestrian to help me restrain the strange little dude. The man on the street gave me the eyeball that told me instantly that he was assessing my sanity. I tried again with somebody else and got the same results.

"Okay...okay," I said, "I give up." I opened the passenger door pretending I was going to usher him into my car, but pushed down the door lock, slammed the door, ran around the other side, and jumped in. I peeled out quickly. But the gnome-like little man was sitting right beside me with an indulgent smirk on his face. I did not dare resume my project until I dealt with the immediate problem, so I decided to indulge the little guy back. "So what's your name?" I asked as though I had resigned to the fact that he was my albatross forever."

"Traypid." He told me. "I used to be tight with Agatha Stromberg, but she died on me, the bitch. Let me rephrase that. She had her head beaten in with a brick or something, and left me alone."

"Who, may I ask, is Agatha Stromberg?"

"That would be the chick you are trying to find out about. She was my bud for years, going all the way back to when she had some loot. She walked away from it all though, like a damned fool. She said she couldn't handle me and the real world at the same time; walked away from her chain of apparel stores—gave them all up."

"Wait a minute! Are you telling me Agatha was this homeless person who got killed in the park last night?"

"Yup! Now you got it. Poor Agatha. I used to tell her I could help her get everything back, but she preferred to come off as loony tunes. I'm tellin' ya, I'm pretty smart, man, but she was as dumb as a stump to see it. Now it's you and me buddy!"

"Lucky me!" I said.

"What do you mean by a crack like that?"

...."So you are telling me that you belong to me up until the day I die, like Agatha?"

"Yesss, sssirrree, genius. If you use me right, I can be a real help. Agatha went the rest of her life putting me down; not using me at all. What a sad bitch!"

"Must you always be so crass? Can't you clean up your language a bit?"

"I am what I am. Nobody but you can hear me

anyway, so if you keep your big fat trap shut, nobody will have a clue what I am saying. I always tried to tell Agatha that. She never did believe me."

"So you say Agatha languished to the point of homelessness, and you could have helped her before she reached there?"

"Coooorect! Hey...you really ARE smart! So what are we going to do next?"

"We? Excuse me?"

"Not another one, jeez...how do I find them? Look, I'm telling you we are stuck with each other now. I can't undo that now that I chose you. I chose you for a couple of real good reasons. Number one is because I owed Agatha the life she deprived herself of because of me, and I thought you would be the perfect guy to handle that. Plus, I liked your style, and you seem like a smart guy and good people. Long story short, don't waste a good thing when it is right under your nose. I can help you get anything your heart desires, but I thought we could start off with Agatha's dignity first. Is that just too much for you to handle, man?"

I sighed, beginning to know what Agatha went through. "Tell me Traypid, are you the only one of your kind or are there others like you?"

"Hello? Is this thing on? Of course, there are others like me. The problem is, it's so damned hard to get you schmucks to accept that we can help you after one of us chooses you. You people can't seem to refrain from boring me and my colleagues. The likes of Agatha and the others have wasted our time and their own. Do you think you can at least listen?"

"All I can say is—I'll try, Traypid. You say colleagues; what do you mean by that?" I was in full reporter mode.

"We came here long, long ago, and we have been trapped here ever since. We have the ability to bond with your kind molecularly, as extensions of your minds. I was placed inside the water you drank. In better days, we used better methods, but essentially it adds up to the same thing. That is why nobody else can see us but the ones we bond with. But since it is a lifetime deal, we try to choose carefully. I considered not bonding this time around. I would have simply faded into oblivion. But when I scanned your thoughts. I saw an instant connection to you because of what you are trying to do for Agatha. I still feel there is a debt I owe her. She never functioned well after I bonded with her, not many do. But Agatha showed promise. She seemed so together when I first scanned her, just like you. I am coming to the conclusion that our will to survive as a symbiont to the host, is selfish and cruel. Agatha left me with a world of guilt after this last time I spent with her. She was not emotionally capable of sharing with me, even though I brought a lot to the table. I also took a chance to choose you because of your mental and emotional stability. You seem unusually strong, much stronger still than Agatha. I felt that we have something in common to start out this relationship with. I sensed you wanted to prove Agatha had a life before she wasted away and finally got herself killed. We really must try to get her dignity back, even if it is posthumously. In the process, I hope we can become friends. I can't help being crass—you people are idiots. In time, you will be able to see, and I hope talk to any another symbiont. It is just that most of the hosts will be useless to talk to, and making my friends weaker by the day. You are already coping twice as well as any I have ever been with. I'll try to be less crass, I promise."

"Well, thank you for that at least. If you want to be my friend as you say, I have to insist on civility. Otherwise, I'll cave in to being just as useless to you as Agatha was. I have a feeling there was a method to her madness. She probably figured to bore the heck out of you so you would stop this bonding process on your own. That would have been a noble sacrifice in my book, and I might do the same thing. Let's face it, you have no right invading any of us as you have. I still don't know if I can *cope*, to quote you. I mean, don't you and your colleagues have any sense of right and wrong? Good golly!"

"I'm sorry Dave, all right? I have to say that in all my years here, I've never had anybody make me feel so guilty. I thought Agatha was the coup de gras. What was your next on your plans anyway?"

"I was going to talk to people she might have hung around with at the park. But now I know her name, so I can't consider Agatha a Jane Doe anymore. I think I'll try to get somebody to confirm her identity. Did you see who killed her, and how come you didn't die with her, by the way?"

"I would have, but Ulsner and my friends rescued me before I slipped into oblivion. They produced the bottles with their hosts, then they placed my life force into some water. It was easy to get the host to do it and sell it on the street, he thought he would get enough money to buy beer—the dummy. The most important thing to him was beer. I had no way to protest what Ulsner and the rest were doing with me. I was, shall we say, indisposed at the time. The only time I had a choice to make is when you drank the water, and I had to choose whether or not to bond. But to answer your question, I never saw the man that killed Agatha, and I blacked out as soon as she lost consciousness."

"Do you know anything about her apparel businesses?"

"Not much. As soon as we bond with a person, we lose any ability we had to sift through thoughts. She refused to let me get involved with her past."

"It sounds to me that I would have liked Agatha. I think I need to do a search on this Agatha Stromberg. If you help me, you have to promise to point only. I can't be shushing you or answering questions, okay? I saw somebody talking to herself this morning at a light near my apartment, and I have to tell you, she looked pretty insane to me. She scared me a lot because she was headed toward where I live, and she looked like Agatha probably did just before she was killed."

"I see your point. What if I talk and you don't answer. Is that permissible?"

"I suppose, but under no circumstances, NO questions. Is that understood?"

"Okay, okay, alright already. But I have a question for now. Do you take baths? The people my comrades and I hang with suck. I'm surprised this big old nose of mine hasn't fallen clean off my face."

"Of course I take baths! But count on it, I'll stop if you can't follow some simple rules and guidelines. I'm not stupid, I totally got the idea that I am stuck with you. Now you have to come to grips with the reverse. Am I allowed relationships?"

VOICES

"You mean like getting laid?"

"HEY!"

"Sorry...you mean like getting it on with the opposite sex?"

"Preeee...cisely...to quote you."

"You know, I've never really left the room with anybody I have been with. I don't know if I can, but I'm willing to give it a try; you know, experiment a little."

"I would appreciate that very much. These are the things that will help us get along—not that I am forgiving you for bonding with me in the first place. That was just plain wrong. So what about this other thing you said; did I hear you can dream up stuff with your mind?"

"You heard that? I AM impressed!" Traypid said.

"I have to know these things if we are going to work out as a couple, Traypid. I also have to know this stuff if we want to find out who killed Agatha, why, and get a good story out of it. What else can you dream up with your mind?"

"Inanimate objects, nothing organic or alive. Beer is out. The schmucks we have been living with were always crabbing that they need the beer...Can't you give us beer?...Ooooh...whyyyy? What good are you guys anywaaaay?...wanh wanh wanh. Icksnay on food, drugs, or beer. You people are quite unbearable. I should have faded into oblivion."

"Can you do me a laptop computer, right here, right now?"

"Well—yeah, I can do that. Yyyou want a laptop—really?"

"Exactamundo, Traypid. Laptop—now!" To my ultimate surprise—srike that—shock, Traypid produced a laptop. Just like that—snap, it sat on his lap.

"Wow, Traypid, good stuff. I think I'm going to have to find a wi-fi spot to do us some searches on Agatha Stromberg. I could use some coffee and a donut anyway. By the way, do you eat?"

"No, doofus, I'm not really here guy, what's the matter with you?"

"Oh—I didn't know. How could I? Hey, wait a minute! You aren't really here—am I hearing that right?"

"If I was here dude, other people could see me too."

VOICES

"Oh—anyway, here we are." I said as I pulled into Harry's Donuts. Harry's is a sort of social hangout, where a person can buy any state lottery scratch ticket known to man. The floor probably has enough scratch off litter scraped off to poison well water in a two mile radius of the shop. I think the stuff is made out of lead. But the coffee is real good, the donuts are the best in the city, and, there is free wi-fi. I entered the shop with Traypid trailing me after I parked my car. I chose out a booth, put down the new laptop to mark my territory, and went to the counter to get some coffee and 3 glazed raspberry-filled crullers. I love those things. My waist doesn't, but my tongue adores them. The shop sports chocolate and plain glazed. I always get 2 plain and 1 chocolate. That day was not to be the exception. Company and potential heckler aside, there would be no problem at all sticking those big old sweet sticks of raspberry goodness down my throat. I adjusted myself for comfort at the booth, computer directly in front of me, goodies within easy reach. I pushed the power button on. The computer worked perfectly for a no name brand. Seriously—there was no name or logo at all on the device. In a few seconds, the screen flickered to life, the operating system was nothing I had ever seen. It went online automatically, no signing into the wireless network supplied at Harry's. The search window was prominent in the middle of the screen without clicking into a browser. The screen was filled with windows surrounding the search bar. Essentially the system was a browser. Sources for information were not plainly evident, only ready to view. New stories flashed in each window, keeping no more than four titled articles to view in each as stories were added. A window for every facet of culture, sports, science, finance, and weather was represented, but the news was represented best of all. One window was for local events, one for national, and finally one for international. Current updates superseded or enhanced stories that evolved in real time as you would expect in an economic readout window. It kept a pulse as it were, on everything going on in the world, all at once. When I clicked on one of the small windows, I was taken to a full screen of those specific subjects alone. I was able to get a synopsis of everything current in subjects going backward twenty four hours; extremely convenient. I figured to explore it all better when I as not as busy. “Nice.” I remarked to Travpid sitting next to me in the booth.

I went back to the home screen and entered Agatha Stromberg's name in the search bar. I was presented with information accessed by every search engine I knew of, and a few I did not. In the display, new pertinent information was divided again into blocked windows according to different aspects of the life, death, and accomplishments of anybody with the name of Agatha Stromberg; most relevant subjects or prominent people heading the list. One window caught my eye near the life and death section. The window was labeled, **Missing**. The article in it went back some five years or so. The computer proved to be very user friendly.

“Holy cow!” I said. I moved the cursor over the window to explore it further. Clicking it opened to a new page of windows, separate articles either printed or reported by various news agencies that covered the story at the time. One of the printed articles drew my interest. It was labeled, **Local female entrepreneur Agatha Stromberg vanishes without a trace**.

The article read; *Agatha Stromberg, principal owner and business mogul of Strom's Women's Apparel, vanished two days ago while expected for her regular work day. The company has kept hushed her disappearance until today, in order to keep business associates from panic. Police have disclosed that no notes or contact has been made. Many fear the worst for Ms. Stromberg. Ms. Stromberg is not married, nor has she any children. However, we have learned from undisclosed sources that her mother and father still live locally, and she has three sibling brothers. They have been protected from the public eye and scrutiny. Company officials we spoke to seemed very distraught. New details will be reported as they come to light.* The story was followed up articles that came out weeks and months later with nothing new to add. Family evidently had filed with the court to declare the woman legally dead. The intent was to lay claim her property and assets. Sufficient time had not elapsed so as to grant the family that wish.

"This reeks of foul play." I mused. My suspicious mind made me continue by entering a search for Strom's Womens Apparel. In this instance, the company had continued on without her presence. Associates working with her, and under her had maintained the status quo quite nicely. No family was involved. The care of Agatha's apartment wasn't stated, but held current with an existing address still belonging to her when I searched for it. I went on to search for Agatha's next of kin, finding her family, all three brothers, and where they resided.

My face showed anger, and Traypid made note of it. "What got your panties all in a bunch?"

"Because Agatha is lying on a slab, at least I hope she is. I need to get down to the morgue to find out what her status is. I might have to light a fire under somebody's butt area. I think that just because this woman was dirty and homeless, her identity is slipping through the cracks, or at least stalled until she is finally gotten around to. I wonder if they even fingerprinted her yet. I need to drop this bomb on them, so they take the case a little more seriously."

It seemed more and more that I was right about Agatha. I believed she disappeared from life so as not to give the entity that invaded her cerebrum any satisfaction of control, or possibly to bore it to death to stop future invasions. I kept these thoughts to myself. I was looking for ammunition to use against my own invasion. I did like the laptop Traypid produced for me.

"Come on, let's get out of here. I want to get to the morgue. I need to see if I can get the county coroner's ear before I call the city desk down at the paper."

"Okay boss." Traypid said amiably.

The ride over to the morgue was about five miles away as the crow flied from Harry's. It was already 10:30 and I wanted to make it there before lunch. A ton had happened to me since being stuck at the 3rd Street light onto Homer Drive. But I am not one to stand around and cry. I was in hot pursuit of a good story, courtesy of Traypid, and if I could multi task, maybe I could do something about him too.

I was driving a good clip, but not enough to draw another ticket in one morning. I thought it would be a good opportunity to pump Traypid for a little more ammunition—er—informaition. I began with casual conversation. "So...Traypid," I began, "I can plainly see you don't come from these parts. Where is it that you really come from anyway?"

"Don't freak out Dave, but the others and I have been here for several thousand years already. Out of that group, there is only one of us with any real power left. That would be me, but I am tired. We came here from another planet about 25 light years from here. It wasn't our intention to come here at all. What happened was that we were sent out on an exploratory mission to a nearby solar system on a carrier wave. There was no ship involved. Trajectory was missed by a minuscule amount that sent us soaring across the galaxy instead. When we were placed in this carrier wave, it put us in a sort of suspended animation, but conscious enough to think about it the whole time. The trip and everything we have been through up until now has been an eternity. When we got here, we placed ourselves in a similar carrier wave that resides in the imagination centers of your minds. We had no other alternative because we are no longer substantive the way we were when we left. Long story short, our planet is called Ranboes. As a species, we are called Lechichrons." Traypid summed up.

I started to smile to myself. Traypid noticed and called me out on it. "What gives—do you find that all funny?"

"No no, Traypid, actually I believe you. It makes total sense to me." I did not tip my hand to him, but more little bits of the puzzle began fitting into place. Being the good reporter I am, I continued my pumping. "So how did you think to place yourself in our imagination centers anyhow?"

"Simple. It was because we never lost consciousness for the whole trip. We all made the connection of consciousness to consciousness when we got here and began growing desperate. The process didn't really work at first, and some of us slipped into oblivion, but then there were the early successes. After a while, we learned that when we join with those of you that have good imaginations, we can then pool our resources to create things like that laptop you asked for.

It seems like eons since I experienced that kind of pleasure. For that, I owe you." Traypid said.

More bits were falling into place, but I got close to the morgue. I had to get back to the business of working the Agatha murder story. Going straight to the head honcho, the county coroner himself, I launched right into the meat and potatoes. "Doctor Haskell?"

"Yes? Can I help you?"

"Dave Simpson—Daily Spectacle. I'm here about the homeless woman found beaten to death in the park last evening. I have reason to believe that I know her identity, and I think you can help me prove it."

"You go boy! Tell him!" Traypid interrupted. It was all I could do to ignore the little gnome man. I would have lost all credibility right off the bat, so I kept my composure.

"I have to ask you Doctor. Why hasn't anybody discovered her identity already? Was she fingerprinted?"

"No, not yet."

"No? Why? What if I were to tell you that I think the body belongs to a missing person that went by the name of Agatha Stromberg, the missing mogul and owner of Strom's Women's Apparel. She went missing five years ago and hasn't been able to be found. I have a suspicion that you will easily prove this, and also be able to lift enough evidence off the body, and the murder weapon to find her killer. I think she was found accidentally, and brutally murdered for the obvious motive of the almighty buck. I can't tell you for certain, but that is your job. How about it Doctor, does that raise the priority a bit?"

"Thank you for reminding me that everybody is important. I failed miserably here, haven't I? I will assign somebody to do the autopsy tout de suite. Do you have a card so I can contact you upon completion—well—after the police are informed of course?" I pulled one out of my wallet, and asked him when I might expect a call."

"I don't think we should wait much longer. I would expect some kind of results by late afternoon, about three o'clock or so."

"I will look forward to your call Doctor."

On the way back to the car, I attacked Traypid, "I thought I told you to keep you mouth shut around people?"

"No---you specifically told me not to ask questions. I didn't ask you a thing."

"Oh, well, I guess you are right then." I said sarcastically. Do you think you can keep your trap shut while I call the city desk?"

I never got a call from the officer in charge that wrote the crime scene report, proving how high poor Agatha was on the list of police priorities. Getting a call from the coroner with important relevant updates should produce sufficient embarrassment. I wished I could be a fly on the wall when it happened. A reprimand would be coming from somewhere.

I reached Mr Bigby, my boss, on the cell phone back at my car to give him a run down of what I had uncovered on the story so far. I left him in a state of shock as to how I unearthed so much so soon. He wanted to know the chances of getting copy by the end of the day. "The coroner may not give me a call back until after three, but I should have something ready for the morning edition, sure."

"Good work, son." Mr Bigby hung up. I hoped to talk to him later that afternoon anyway.

I gave some thought on what I learned about Traypid as I drove away from the morgue. I engaged him again, but this time more gingerly. I probed, "Look, Traypid, I'm a little short for cash. You couldn't possibly produce me a pot of gold or something?"

"Oh my God! That is something I haven't heard in...I can't even remember how many years! I can't have something as big and heavy as that in the front seat here. Where would you like it?"

"How about back there in the trunk of my car?"

"Sure, can do boss!" He told me excitedly. He seemed genuinely happy to be asked for something he could do for a change. "Okay boss...done."

For the second time in a day, I screeched to a stop by the side of the road, reaching near the side of my seat for the trunk release. I got out of the car, walked to the back, and lifted the trunk lid, slowly, not really believing something would be there. There was! A big cast iron pot with a brick oven handle on it. Inside was filled with gold coins, unstamped round disks without a denomination of any kind to mar them. My knees almost buckled, but I looked over at Traypid, smiled, and praised him for helping me out. I shut the trunk lid again and got back into the driver's seat. My next questions for Traypid dealt with facts he supplied to me on his not being real, that is, lodged in the imagination portion of my brain. I plucked his brain as much as I could on the subject, trying to get a grasp on how to deal with him. A plan slowly gelled as I pumped him dry. Before I stopped for lunch, I made a detour to a herbal shop I knew of on Jasper. The establishment sold incense, jarred herbs by the ounce, tinctures, teas of all kinds, and talismans. I parked in front of the store front when I got there, and entered. Without asking for help, I went directly to the teas. I knew exactly what kind I wanted. I constructed a charade by picking up a box of dieters tea laced with senna, acting as though it was a choice I had made many times before. Traypid watched, but did not seem to be suspicious; something I hoped I could pull off. I paid for the tea, making no unnecessary conversation with the young lady at the cash register, who had other customers she was advising anyway. I then stopped at a book store so I could relax, order a cup of hot water, and write my story.

Traypid grew more enamored with me with each passing moment. It was after lunch time, about 1:15 or so. The day was progressing nicely. I set up the laptop Traypid produced for me on a coffee table. It was in front of a couch intended for use of the patrons to sit and read, perhaps have a bite to eat at the same time; a living room atmosphere if you will.

"So boss, what are you going to do now.?"

"Well you're going to be quiet unless I ask you a question while I sit and write this story for the paper. I can tweak it with any added facts from the coroner after he calls if I don't guess most of what he is going to say beforehand. I feel like a cup of tea. Excuse me while I go get a cup of hot water."

I came back moments later, noting Traypid did not follow me to the counter. It was of no consequence if my plan worked. Traypid was on his best behavior even if he was only fifteen feet away at any given time. I fired up the laptop, fumbling around the window system for an office program, but found none. I didn't complain though; instead, I searched for, and then signed into my personal email box. I opened compose, and began writing while two of my new tea bags steeped in the cup of hot water. Five minutes or so later, I took the bags out of the water, placed them on a napkin, and sipped the vile brew while I wrote. I gave the impression that I relished every sip. After writing the story to the best of my ability, I managed to consume the whole cup of tea. I sent the email off to my office email so I could retrieve it when or if I got back to my cubicle at the office, then shut off power to the laptop. I noticed just before shutting it down that none of the battery power was used at all. It was still at full strength, 100 percent. In fact, there was no way to charge the contraption. Traypid and I then left the book store.

The next destination was Rollins Park. I acted as though the visit was part of the Agatha Stromberg story, but the real reason was to see if I could spot more Lechichrons. The ride there provided me with the same information, but with clearer insight. Traypid kept telling me that he alone possessed any power. Over the years, the other Lechichrons had weakened considerably by joining with hosts that had low levels of imagination. That is why his friends were desperate to preserve Traypid's remaining life force. There was not much they could do without him, and it was a stroke of luck that Agatha was killed nearby, or nothing at all could have been salvaged of Traypid. But Traypid told me earlier that he considered fading into oblivion, evidence that Agatha's non participation was somewhat of a success. Traypid's friends probably had no idea that he considered ending it all. Just before we got to the park, I asked him if it was a waste of time to talk to any of the hosts, or any of his friends, for that matter.

"All I can tell you is to try. They may or may not have seen who killed Agatha. If they did, all we can do is hope they give us a description. That would help, wouldn't it? But you may find them obnoxious in their present state. Just warning you is all. Please don't yell at me, okay? My friends have been living with folks who aren't all there, so the imaginations they've been sharing, haven't been too good. The Lechicrons have no power, no life, nothing to think about. All of them would be better off in oblivion. They didn't even know it anymore. Agatha was dragging me to that place too. This little bit of time I have spent with you has given me hope; rejuvenated me."

All the while he was chattering away, my stomach was rolling. Nothing was in emergency mode yet, but a chemical reaction was definitely taking place down there in my bowel area.

"There they are! Do you see them?" Traypid bubbled excitedly at the sight of seeing familiar faces. It was the first time in a while he had seen them, and they were family to him, such as they were.

I looked in the direction he pointed, to a motley looking group of wasted humanity sitting, lying down, roaming aimlessly in a section of the park that was over run with the lowest levels of humanity. As Traypid and I moved closer, the Lechichrons could be heard nagging and complaining at the hosts who were stuck in their own private hell, most of it by their own hand. I looked over at Traypid and asked, "How did your friends produce the bottles that they placed your life force in?"

"It was a group effort, believe me. Oh wait a minute. Did I say produce? I misspoke I am afraid. About the only thing they are capable of now is convincing a couple of their hosts to find suitable bottles, wash them out, and fill them up with tap water in the rest room sinks over there."

My stomach started to retch more than the chemical herbal reactions already taking place down there. It's funny how the mind works. The mental picture Traypid planted to flash in my head caused instant nausea. It added an air of realism to what I was trying to accomplish.

We got into the mix of the group, the Lechichrons were raving like lunatics. Traypid tried his best to get the attention out of any one of them, not one even looked his way. I could not confirm this theory, but my best guess is that the time Traypid spent out of the proximity of his friends, had made them grow even weaker. Traypid was asking where this person and that person was. He was ignored. I surmised that some of the hosts had wandered off, explaining the woman I saw in my own neighborhood on 3rd Street about a mile and a half away. I did not bring the subject up. Traypid seemed to have enough problems of his own to deal with.

One of the nagging Lechicrons was yelling irrationally. "OH I KNOW WHAT'S HAPPENED HERE! IT'S ALL THESE CIGARETTE BUTTS TOSSED ON THE GROUND. THEY ARE CONCENTRATING THE NICOTINE AND OTHER CHEMICALS, AND ALL OF IT IS LEACHING INTO THE GROUND WATER FROM THE RAIN. WE'RE ALL GOING INSANE AND IT'S ALL OF YOUR FAULTS, YOU FOOLS!"

Another had the ear of his host, was on a soapbox. "DO ME A FAVOR. DON'T TAKE ANY MORE BATHS IN THE FOUNTAIN POND. THAT CHLORINE RASH OF YOURS IS SPREADING ALL OVER YOUR BODY, AND NOW YOU ARE DEVELOPING TURRETS SYNDROME! BATHING IN THERE CAN'T BE GOOD YOU KNOW. EVEN THE GEESE THAT SWIM IN THERE DON'T KNOW ENOUGH TO FLY SOUTH IN THE WINTER. THEY JUST STAY THERE TILL THEIR LITTLE PADDLE FEET GET FROZEN IN THE ICE!"

Another Lechichron was giving his host an earful. "I DON'T SEE WHY WE HAVE TO LISTEN TO YOU BITCHING AND BITCHING ABOUT ALL THE YOUNGSTERS *DOING THEM DRUGS* AS YOU ALWAYS SAY. YOU WENT CRAZY THE OTHER DAY ON THE HOT DOG VENDOR. THE POOR GUY WATCHED YOU TAKE OUT ALL HIS BUNS WITH A BIG STICK. YOUR ATTITUDE CAME OUT OF NOWHERE YOU NUT CASE! I DON'T SEE ANY OF THEM YOUNGSTERS YOU COMPLAIN ABOUT DOING THAT KIND OF THING! WHAT KIND OF DRUGS DO YOU TAKE ANYWAY? DO YOU EVEN KNOW? THAT AIN'T ASPIRIN YOU'RE TAKING YOU KNOW." The guy he was preaching at stopped a stranger to ask him if he smoked so he could bum a cigarette off him. When he didn't have any, he asked him for a quarter instead.

Everywhere I looked it was the same thing. "Traypid, let's get the hell out of here. This is all too whacked out for me to handle. No wonder Agatha was put in a cooler for later on. The humans are too hard for me to watch, and the Lechichrons are giving me a headache. I want to go back to my apartment to wait on the coroner's report. There isn't too much we can do here."

VOICES

The truth was that I wanted to go to the office, but I didn't dare. Too much was at stake, and I was feeling the effects of the overdose of senna. If I was right, when my colon erupted, the beginnings of a complete body cleanse would start to commence. I needed Traypid where I could see and observe any effects my body would have on his consciousness. I also needed to be as close to a toilet as I could get, and very soon.

"Let's go—now." I told him again.

"But my friends, they're so pathetic! Maybe between us we can imagine something to help them." He pleaded.

It was kind of funny to watch, he needed me more and more as the day went on. "Come on, live to fight another day." I lied. But the next part of my story was the truth. "We need to vindicate Agatha's life. Her sacrifice to give everything up that she worked so hard to build, begs for you and I to find a way to give it a little meaning. You owe her that. The son of a bitch that took her life needs to pay too.

It wasn't two minutes inside the door of my apartment that I had one hand on my belt buckle, the other on my zipper. I made a mad dash to the bathroom. It was the first of several purgings. In between, I steeped another cup of hot water with two more bags of the senna. It was going to be moving day for Traypid if it killed me, both literally, or laced with pun if preferred.

Traypid still trailed me like a puppy, even after five flushings. It didn't matter, I had the advantage of time and something to do. I chose Traypid's laptop gift over my own desktop in the apartment. I had grown fond of the laptop's no nonsense search capability and information retrieval. I got exactly what I searched for time after time without reentering. Using it gave me the names and addresses of Agatha's three brothers, one older, two younger than herself. It was just as easy to find where they worked, how much they made, and their current addresses, all of them out of state. I didn't need any special people finder apps to do it. When it came down to it, the laptop was more useful, with three times the ease, than the computers at the newspaper hooked up to a huge database. How the laptop accomplished this was an enigma.

With the information I garnished on the three siblings, I was presented with the most logical likely suspect. The oldest brother turned out to be the one who petitioned the court unsuccessfully to declare Agatha dead so it could initiate probate proceedings. He was also in the most need of money, with the least amount of education. Essentially, he was looking for something for nothing. The two younger brothers were doing well for themselves, and probably cared less except for the loss of their sister. I determined to monitor what the authorities did. More than likely the evidence would point to him anyway. If it did not, I could always point the police in the right direction, directly, or through the story I was writing. I preferred letting the law follow it's natural course, and they probably would do just fine without my interference. I could be ready with facts on follow up stories if I stayed on top of it all though.

At three twenty three, the coroner called me as promised. Luckily for me, I had just finished my latest body purging just before the call, the toll of it all taking a large payload out of my body. Still, I had Traypid following me to my phone when I answered the call.

"Dave Simpson?"

"Yuh? I snapped into the mouthpiece, getting crabby because of what my body was enduring.

"Doctor Haskell here, getting back to you with the results of the autopsy, and the findings of the victim's identity. I enlisted the help of one my colleagues. I sent her with a photograph of the woman to the police, so they could contact Agatha's parents for help with a positive ID. They voluntarily brought us the most recent picture they had of the deceased, and came in to inspect the remains first hand. Hair, DNA, and fingerprints were sent out to the state police, who ultimately contacted and enlisted the help of the FBI. The FBI sent one their own to assist us with the autopsy so as not to destroy or waste any forensic evidence, including the murder weapon that could lead us to the killer. We had some success in that area, but, unfortunately, need to withhold that information from you to protect, believe it or not, the rights of the suspect. You can rest assured, however that the apprehension of the killer is probable.

VOICES

Thank you once again, Mr. Simpson, for bringing this to my attention. The parents may get some peace from the discovery, but being a homicide, might take some time, poor people!"

I thanked the good doctor for holding up his end of the bargain. I hung up, but was faced with a dilemma of my being able to drag myself into the office to complete the story, getting it to the city desk in time for the morning edition. I called Mr. Bigby, and told him of my physical complications, but that I could finish off the story, and forward it to him at his desk within a half hour.

My boss reassured me. "Thank you son, that will work just fine—good work. I expect to see you tomorrow morning. Do you think you could try not to be late?" He added that last shot just before the line was cut off.

Traypid was sitting down in my easy chair, not looking too healthy. Good thing too, as I wasn't feeling too good myself. "Anything wrong Traypid? You seem to have something bothering you."

"I have this strange headache that came over me, and I don't even have the strength to bitch about it."

"I would offer you some aspirin, but since you aren't really real, they wouldn't work anyway, right?" I asked helpfully.

"No, but maybe my friends are draining me somehow. I'll just sit here for a spell."

Just then, a new wave of rolling hit me square in my intestines, and I ran to the bathroom as fast as I could go, fearing a total loss of control on my living room carpet. Traypid sat just where he was for a change, a deviation from his usual trailing me like a puppy tethered with a leash. It was the first time since Traypid joined me that I had some privacy, and he was at least 20 feet away.

This time it felt as though a section of my lower intestine came out of my body. I have heard some of my coworkers complain that preparing for a Colonoscopy felt similar to my experience, but I was encouraged to bear the pain, already noting changes in Traypid's behavior. I also had new empathy for my older coworkers, and the words to an old song came to mind; *I hope I die before I get old*. It took longer in the bathroom for every visit, and I wondered if all the times I showed up late for work and I came up with excuses why, that being told I was *full of shit* might actually have some validity. Thirty minutes later, I came out of the head to find an unresponsive, cursing, vulgar version of Traypid. He was still sitting in the same spot I left him. The condition he was in helped me imagine how his friends managed to install him in tap water in the first place. He had no substance anymore because I could see right through him. If I was capable of picking him up to carry him to a sink, I could have dissolved what was left of him myself. But my hands would go right through him. Another Lechichron might have had that skill, and they probably did when they all still had the acumen and their faculties. Now all the Lechichrons I saw were only capable of nagging thoughtlessly as they faded away.

Traypid's mouth had not been diminished one bit, and the vulgarities spewing out of his mouth needed the assistance of a priest bearing holy water to bring it under control. If the remnants of once strong Lechichrons were reduced and still joined with the hosts, it was plain to see what somebody passing by would see. Coupled with substance abuse, alcohol, and poor diet, the resulting mixture would be quite vile. I had no remedies I could put my finger on to make what hosts that were still joined, any better by ridding them of the mental parasites clinging to what life force they all still had together.

My stomach retched one more time, this time I felt more like heaving than expectorating out my anus, and I did just that. When it leveled off to dry heaves, I finally had the strength to leave the porcelain throne that had done so much duty for almost four hours straight.

Staggering back into the living room, I got to share the last moments with Traypid as he faded away, presumably into oblivion. Even oblivion had to claim him cussing and bitching into the new realm. "MAN THESE HUMANS SUCK! NOT ONE OF THEM IS GOOD COMPANY! I HATE EVERY LAST ONE OF THEM! I THINK THERE'S SOMETHING IN THE FOUNTAIN DRINKS OVER AT THE 24 HOUR MART. WHO KNOWS WHAT'S IN THOSE ELECTROLYTE DRINKS, ANYHOW? FURTHERMORE, THOSE DAMNED PACKAGES OF DONUTS SMELL OF CHEMICALS! POLLUTION, POLLUTION, POLLUTION! I THINK IT'S THAT

ANYWAY; COULD BE THOSE CRAZY MICROWAVABLE CUP OF SOUPS, WHY if I ever ge....."

Traypid was gone, I think forever. I was still so sick from the senna concoction, I had a problem moving, but I dragged my empty, newly freed carcass out to the parking lot with keys in my hand to check the trunk of my car. I just had to see if the gold made an exit with my personal gnome friend. Walking like a cowboy with bowed legs, I popped the trunk for a look see. There it was, the same as before. I was in no condition to lift something that heavy just yet, but relief sent me back indoors before I confronted my next toilet emergency. Back inside, the laptop given to me by Traypid was still on the coffee table where I left it. I sat down in front of it, to check it out as I had with the gold in the trunk. All was as it was before. Power was still at 100 per cent. It still searched just as it had while Traypid was still around. It provided proof if only just to me that any of it happened at all.

I suppose there is an argument to be made that I took advantage of the Lechichrons, to which I would answer that it was the other way around. How many lives had they ruined, including potentially mine, just to survive at all costs? I say good for me that I was able to steal some lucky charms away from the Lechichron at the end of his journey from Ranboes. It seems even more fascinating to me that through the years, some of the slurred speech from some of the witless hosts was taken to mean that if you catch a leprechaun at the end of a rainbow, you will be rewarded with a pot of gold!

CHURCH OF THE MODERN APOSTLES

CHURCH OF THE MODERN APOSTLES

It all started when the great State of California took on what they thought was an essential discussion about the perceived travesty of having the lives of certain endangered species of dogs and cats dangling precariously over an extinction pit. The primary underlying reason was revenue. The ensuing debate clarified that certain animals falling into ridged guidelines could be protected, spelling out these guidelines to the letter so that there could be no misunderstanding. These and only these totally domesticated animals; trusted members of a certified and qualified household, could apply for licensing. The state postulated the idea to the public since it did not want to exceed it's pervue or authority to enact legislation that the entire voting public might not want. It was their desire not to commit political suicide, so a decision was made to place the referendum on the voting block in what, from that point, would be the next state voting session.

The referendum attached the issue, which read as follows; The following shall be written into state statutes, to wit, parties owning or possessing pairs of male and female dogs or cats that can be demonstrated to be on the close to extinction list, and are willing to assume full responsibility caring for said animals, shall be able to have said animals be bound. That is to say that with proper verification, the trustees of any such animals fitting the criteria set by the State, can apply for licensing for marriage institution of the male and female, and trustees to be held liable for the health and welfare of the animals until death, unless expressly released by legal divorce in the State of California. Thus, animals bound by this agreement shall be recognized, and duly registered by the official state licensing department.

The state passed the referendum in overwhelming fashion, and the law was promptly signed into law by the Governor. The public misconstrued the idea somewhat, taking the words, 'marriage institution' to mean Holy Matrimony. The authors of the bill, in their lack of infinitesimal wisdom, failed to address the exact meaning of their intent. Now too late to spell out more clearly, there was a wave of nausea coming from most of the established denominations, a lot of them drawing lines that could not be crossed. This inevitably led to the disillusionment of large percentages of the various denomination's parishioners, ultimately showing marked reductions of memberships. At about that time, a large contingent of hierarchy from most of the wide assortment of Christian faiths plus Rabbis representing a few Jewish community tabernacles, got together to attend a consortium to iron out how the situation might be handled. A general consensus could not be reached, however.

Public relation discussions were held by Cardinals from all over the world in all the main medias, dispatched and briefed directly by the Vatican. They attempted to spell out just what the world could expect of the Church's policy. Conversely, an endless list of church affiliations, Episcopalians, Presbyterians, and most of the evangelical family of Protestants quickly distanced themselves from the fray. To the average layman, it appeared as though the issue took these groups by surprise, with all of them hiding out in individual boardrooms to figure out how they actually felt about it. This led to even more disillusionment.

To the credit of the Jewish community, it was clear from the starting gate that no such nonsense would be considered 'kosher', so to speak, and no participation would ever be entertained, past, present, or future. However, as to the remaining faith groups, seeds of doubt were introduced, just by virtue of the fact that the public was being appeased to some degree.

The good people in the Muslim and Islamic communities kept to themselves, but fringe radicals had a natural feeding frenzy, and rightfully so, pointing to the lack of western moral ideals. It became distressing to be held accountable by the same fringe groups that we were at odds, all because of a single push of a highly visible nonsensical idea. This was an unnecessary fallout and need never have happened at all.

Naturally politicians had to become involved because the issue of national security entered into the mix, because of the fringe group hoopla. Addresses came from every corner of our huge bevy of elected officials, including the President, the Secretary of State, Speaker of the House, the Senate Pro Tempore, as well as some grandstanding by the highest ranking members of both parties. From something simple, government was forced to consider reactionary policies. Many of the proposed fixes were worse than jam that the country found itself in, but all of them judiciously expressed and explained, so that the rest of the world not view us with any less esteem than it already did.

Who could have imagined that from a basic idea to protect some endangered species, and a state's scheme to collect fees on the licensing, that it would result in so much turmoil? The average, run of the mill Joe could have cared less, and the portion of Joes that did not read or watch the news did not know anything of it at all. The percentage of those people in relation to the ones who took the issue seriously, was quite high indeed, sort of both ends of lunacy.

But a group of disgruntled ordained ministers who had found themselves running against the grain of their own church affiliations, came out of the woodwork, promising to comply with the people's wishes, and for all intents and purposes, all systems seemed a go. A bunch of extremely strange weddings were planned, and heavily reported.

Fortunately, the Federal Government stepped in by filing appeals, with the end zone goal of getting a hearing into the Supreme Court. Six months later, the court agreed, and the law was overturned, on the merits that it was against Federal marriage mandates under the Constitution of The United States.

As a consequence of all the drama, the confederacy of The New Order Of Churches was born, spearheaded by a highly charismatic preacher named Rev. Rupert Moroni. It was he who eventually became a Pope of sorts to the fledgling religious order and secular movement.

It became clear to a small minority that of all of the churches were established and united to the new order by discordant preachers. Some were women who couldn't establish leadership roles within male dominated traditional theological sects. Others were outspoken, with ideas that were too incongruous for their superiors to swallow. But Rev. Rupert Moroni had none of these problems, and it was easy for him to unite all of these individuals under one umbrella of similar values. Rupert was a successful televangelist in his own right. His ideas sounded Godly enough, but had carnal undertones that came out subtly enough to be overlooked; most made in funny quips in weekly televised sermons. But backed by the churches that were rapidly adding up and joining The New Order Of Churches, he and the rest of his new minions became a tad more brazen; emboldened by their unity. But the sickening truth was a broad swath of the public was buying the whole package.

Rupert used his television ministry to build the tenets of the new church affiliation, letting it evolve in plain sight using social media from the cyberworld and the airwaves. It created an air of grassroots involvement that the public believed they had a stake in. None of the churches displayed any of the gaudy trappings of their traditional counterparts. Before the very eyes of the growing numbers of followers of the television audience, the church became known as Church Of The Modern Apostles.

Rupert's own church was a broadcast studio, no live audiences to bolster his charm with applause, or to fill the camera with gazes of awe, love, or respect. It was just him and a camera, dressed in suits supplied to him by his sponsors, who he gave full credit to. He filled those suits better than a male model, with a wide face that held dark eyes under a hooded brow, cleanly shaved but still left with a shadow of black stubble, and dark brown hair that neither drew your attention or detracted from his rugged good looks. He stood an imposing six foot five inches, body chiseled out of two hundred thirty pounds of hunky flesh. His voice was perfectly pitched, somewhere just above a baritone, having a natural full effect. The timber of his speech brooked no boredom, his words tumbling out of his mouth were never in the range of monotones, or too much animation.

The focus of his ministry seriously much included all of the new satellite churches, pounding concepts into the heads of hungry seekers willing to listen. Very simple, actually, The Church Of The New Apostles taught that accepting the Lord into ones life brought prosperity. To be saved meant forsaking all the old notions that anything was impossible. All things were possible. More than that, all things were acceptable. Absolution came because Christ was the one who died for your sins. He took them on his back and carried them into the depths of hell, lifting the burden that you needed to worry about them any longer, no need to confess continually because it was a given, all men are sinners and come short of the glory of God. Simply stated, when we shed these earthy bodies, the rewards we get at the other end are directly commensurate with what we put into the support of others that we fellowship with. All of us can go it alone, yes, but leaning on one another would reward us both here and in the afterlife, with all the benefits of not worrying what will happen to us should we stumble here and there in this life along the way. But the choice, as in all choices, are up to the individual, just as long as he or she accepts that Christ is his personal savior; But 'Leaning on the everlasting arms', as the song implies, would gain us so much more. Even the interpretation of a song twisted to mean what he wanted to convey.

Why 'Modern Apostles' was chosen as part of the name for the new church was explained by pointing out biblical fact. The Apostle Paul went out the preach to everyone he came in contact with, not constraining himself to a certain cross section of people. He preached to the hated Romans, as well as many others. Paul devoted his life to the demonstration that his message needed to be delivered to all men. It ushered in a new era at the time, sanctioned by God himself. Church Of The Modern Apostles would continue on that avenue as it should be.

It was further pointed out that the holy matrimony of two important parts of God's creation was a perfect example of how churches clearly think that they are holier, and cuts above the rest of us. Should these creatures that God himself created be allowed to extinguish from the earth forever, just because we are too selfish to commit to the care of creatures that are not men? It was up to the New Church Of The Apostles to teach as much as they had to, combating that kind of condescension.

These kinds of messages resonated with scores of people who willingly made commitments to the new church. It didn't help that the vehicles of those commitments weren't self serving just to the church, but benefited both church, and it's membership, or clientèle as it were. It made it hard for other denominations to criticize. Thousands of home based internet businesses were set up for all types of goods and services. A giant base of web servers were owned and maintained by the church, and this was how they made some of their money. The fact that the church helped to create jobs, keeping people employed, sweetened the sour taste that all the money the church made, was not taxed, but all the money made by those working people and businesses were. Sponsors supplying goods or services were provided with free advertising, like the sponsor who supplied the suits. The church had huge investments in satellite communications, and a robust, thriving religious network, helpful in keeping the message on cable. But popularity brought invitations to be televised on mainstream networks hoping to gain some of the viewership lost to the other network. This eventually led to a regular spot on Sunday mornings.

The gains in popularity were exponential. But it also made the New Churches more brazen than ever to express ideals of self indulgence. Nothing so obtuse that these self indulgences would do harm to others or break laws, but the point was made that it is okay to be happy. It's okay to enjoy your life, good food, make money, enjoy spending it, and to make occasional indiscretions. All of these things are what makes us human, and if it made God crazy that we continually embraced them, it was the reason he came up with the plan of sending his son down here to die on the cross in the first place.

Every single modern apostle in every New Church were saying the same things, in different places. Being human is an affliction for which there is no cure until the day we enter the Kingdom of God and the slate is wiped clean. It is silly to think we can fully rise above the wages of sin while we are in the flesh. All any of us can be and do is the best we can with what we got. God would not want us to waste our lives, wasting the best of what life has to offer, and he would want us to fight to enjoy everything he designed our bodies to do.

The next part of this chronicle of one is the most

historical events that the human race has yet to live through. It is a transcription of a televised sermon delivered by the Rev. Rupert Moroni, two years after the church was established, at the zenith of his influence. An official record needs to be kept because it is critical to be remembered and should never be forgotten. It is only a side fact is that it was televised in California where the movement began because there were many all over the world that let Rupert feed them his pablum from the scriptures without checking it out for themselves.

Sunday morning, 6:00-6:30 Meditations with Rev. Rupert Moroni:

"Good morning my good people. I want you to pour yourself a cup of coffee, sit down, and spend some time with me. I won't keep you long. Giving a little of your time back to think about spiritual things and consider what the Lord plans for all of us is the very least you can do for all the gifts that he lets us have here while we are alive, with the promise of so much more when we end our days here on earth. Make no mistake, it will happen soon enough. I won't stand here and debate which day is or is not the actual Sabbath, but I will say that it doesn't matter because it won't kill us to set aside some time to acknowledge his existence, and to heap some praise on him because he deserves it. But this morning I ask you to learn.

I feel blessed to be chosen to bring some of his words to you, and I hope, that through me, you can see some of the truths about your short lives. The first thing I want to touch upon this morning is; Faith. Faith in this instance is an important aspect of our spirituality because it is based on a promise. A promise that even though every one of us is, deep down, a piece of scum, with flaws none of us wants anybody else around us to know about. But God does. He has watched all of us from the first day he created us, and every single time we let him down. God is a sinaphobe. A sinaphobe is like a germaphobe only much worse. He is a holy being that can't be in the same place with sin. So what is he to do with all of us that he went to the trouble to create, in his own image I might add? He sent his son. The purpose of sending his son was to experience first hand what it was we have to wrestle with, and why it's so extremely hard to shake these tendencies. Now his son, no doubt, was a lot better at handling that sort of thing than us, but he got some insight, a taste of what it is that gives us pleasure in this life experience of ours. But the plan all along was to take the punishment for us, because God would have to destroy us all rather than be in the same room as us. So Christ had to heap it all on his back, die for it, and give us a chance to be able to be in the same place with God when it is our turn to die. All we need to have now is faith. Faith... It's still a big hurdle for us because it's for something we can't see. Some of us will, some of us won't... take on this faith process that is. But it's pretty much all he is asking from us. He's saying in essence, accept that I went through the time, bother, and trouble to die for your sins, and you will be saved. The Apostle Paul said it best in his letter to the Romans chapter 6, verse 23: 'The wages of sin is death, but the gift of God is eternal life through Jesus Christ, our Lord.' He goes on to say in chapter 14 verse 23: 'And he that doubt this condemned if he eat, because he eateth not of faith; for whatever is not of faith is sin.' Summing it up, all we have to do is have faith after that acceptance, and we get to join him at the end.

The next thing I want you to consider this morning is; Spirit. When there is transformation of flesh to spirit, it transforms us, ridding us of things that are natural to the flesh, unavoidable I might add. Jesus himself points this out after he rose from the dead, choosing not to come back as a ghost. Luke chapter 24 verse 37 speaks to this: 'But they were terrified and frightened, and supposed that they had seen a spirit.' So he went ahead and proved it to his disciples in verse 39: Behold my hands and my feet, that it is I myself; handle me, and see; for a spirit hath not flesh and bones, as ye see me have.'

He then succumbs to the universe of flesh in verse 41, 42, and 43: 'And while they yet believed not for joy, and wondered, he said to them, Have ye here anything to eat? And they gave him a piece of broiled fish, and an honeycomb. And he took it and did eat before them.' He demonstrated completely unavoidable desires of the flesh. Only in the spirit world can we not have these things pester us anymore.

Another thing I must point out is that the enjoyment of material things gained at the hands of prosperity is not to be shunned. Again, these are pleasures of the flesh, and can not be avoided until God himself takes us into his fold and none of it is needed anymore. I take you back to the book of Psalms, written by King David himself, in chapter 35 verse 27 he says: 'Let them shout for joy, and be glad, who favor my righteous cause. Yea, let them say continually, Let the Lord be magnified, who hath pleasure in the prosperity of his servant.'

Choose your pleasure, and any one of them are pleasures of the flesh. If you repress pleasures of the flesh that are permissible because others say they aren't, then worse manifestations can and will take root that aren't permissible at all, like anger, deceit, murder, rape, theft, and a host of other things that are clearly against the laws of man. Isn't it better to succumb to what isn't against the laws of man and are permissible except for the pious among us? Consider the famous passage in Ecclesiastes chapter 8 verse 15: Then I commended mirth, because a man hath no better thing under the sun, than to eat, and to drink, and to be merry; for that shall abide with him of his labor the days of his life, which God giveth him under the sun."

This is when the calm, usually soothing demeanor of Rev, Rupert Moroni got a little too passionate. He ran his mouth to incite that went over the top.

"My good people, I say to you, if God doesn't want you to enjoy all the wonderful gifts of the flesh that he designed for us while we are here, then he should turn every one of us over to Satan's domain immediately, because it was a foolish mistake from the beginning!"

It happened at precisely ten minutes into Rupert's message, at exactly ten minutes after the hour in four different time zones. Every accountable male and female adult apostle and their followers disappeared;

CHURCH OF THE MODERN APOSTLES

vanished. It was a catastrophe of biblical proportion, leaving uncountable numbers of instant orphans, unattended properties, transportation and business infrastructures, machinery of all sorts left running with anybody to keep control.

It has taken two years to clean up the mess, leaving a nervous population to do the job. Not one man or woman felt the need to take the Lord's name in vain, wail or complain while they did it.

All the many churches left to carry on have walked on egg shells since that day, carefully making study of every policy, adopting a softening of absolutes. There has been a considerable amount of hand holding, temperance, and tolerance.

What happened that morning was quite obviously the opposite of a rapture, claiming the souls of seemingly good people, or at least good enough to bring on examination of the rest of us that remain. The goodwill that sprung up as a result of the event is a refreshing reaction to the bloodletting. The majority of us that are left in this country, and the world for that matter suffered an experience that brought on a greater good. But human nature being what it is, there are signs that the effects are temporary, and that is the reason for this documentation. Evidence points to the fact that memories are short.

www.ingramcontent.com/pod-product-compliance
Lightning Source LLC
Chambersburg PA
CBHW062009170626
46813CB00001B/83